Praise for *Soil*

"Let us stand, brothers and sisters, to applaud the arrival of an exquisitely deranged new voice to American fiction. Dig your hands into this *Soil* to find gutty and peppery writing, an almost recklessly bold imagination, audacious empathy, and a story so twisty and volatile that nearly every turn feels electrifyingly unexpected. This rough-and-tumble model of Southern literature—the vehicle of choice for the late greats Barry Hannah, Larry Brown, Harry Crews, and William Gay—has felt stalled on the roadside for several years now; but Jamie Kornegay has just pulled up with some big-ass jumper cables."

—Jonathan Miles, author of *Want Not*
and *Dear American Airlines*

"Jamie Kornegay's novel *Soil* heralds the arrival of an exciting new voice. This book is atmospheric 'as all get-out,' as my grandmother might have said, and it crackles with intensity. It's everything I want a novel to be, a fine story well told, with characters I won't forget, set in a world so real you can smell it and taste it. Kornegay's something special."

—Steve Yarbrough, author of *The Realm of Last Chances*

"Mississippi has done it again, given us yet another brilliant writer. Welcome, Jamie Kornegay, to a long line of kick-ass storytellers. *Soil* is one of the most memorable novels I've read in years, with a killer story told in killer language. Highly, highly recommended."

—Tom Franklin, author of *Crooked Letter, Crooked Letter*

"Jamie Kornegay's prose is as rich and fertile as the Mississippi Delta landscape that spreads across the pages of *Soil*. It is poetic, both in its language and in the soulful complexity of its characters, all of them fallen and trudging along the hard-worn path of redemption on dirty hands and knees."

—Michael F. Smith, author of *Rivers*

"Marked by wry humor, unforgettable characters, and riveting suspense, Jamie Kornegay's *Soil* is a spellbinding Greek tragedy played out against the backdrop of the choked river bottoms, sprawling fields, and dusty roads of the Mississippi Delta . . . a brilliant, haunting portrait of the havoc one desperate man's decisions and dreams can wreak upon himself and those around him. This remarkable novel springs from rich earth indeed, and the end result is a book that will leave readers reeling."

—Skip Horack, author of *The Eden Hunter*
and *The Southern Cross*

"A darkly droll, epic novel told in a style I'd have to call a deceptively swift amble through a most vividly rendered, watery Delta world. Anyone from Coleridge to Twain to Faulkner to William Gay would have loved reading this book, and you will, too."

—Brad Watson, author of *The Heaven of Mercury*
and *Aliens in the Prime of Their Lives*

"Jamie Kornegay's powerful debut novel, *Soil*, is just as rich, dark and primal as the title suggests and it is hard not to discuss the various characters' plights without slipping into metaphor as they both literally and figuratively dig and tunnel and turn up all that is buried. This novel is brimming with suspense while continuously locating the fine line separating good from evil. Just as the soil delivers all that is decomposed and lost, it also brings promise of future growth and in this case, it is in the form of the protagonist's son. Kornegay's rendering of hope and innocence against the backdrop of depravity and darkness is admirable and moving."

—Jill McCorkle, *New York Times* bestselling
author of *Life After Life*

"Kornegay's skillful writing keeps the story gripping and the atmosphere haunting."

—*Kirkus Reviews*

"Kornegay imbues his characters with depth and his story with suspense, but the real star of the book is the pungent and foreboding Mississippi earth itself. A promising debut from an assured new voice in Southern fiction."

—*Library Journal*

"This marvelous book resembles the Southern Gothic novels of the past, such as the classic *Eternal Fire* by Calder Willingham."

—*Smoky Mountain News*

"Clearly, Kornegay is working here in the Southern-noir tradition of Faulkner and Flannery O'Connor. Cormac McCarthy, too, would understand Kornegay's bloody family feuds, dark humor, and the remote, harsh landscape that shapes its independent-minded, often-violent residents much more than they shape it. For my money, *Soil* is contemporary fiction of the first order, written straight from the heart in highly imagistic, often poetic prose, by a gifted storyteller who's as wild and fearless and true at heart as they come. This is a hilarious, horrifying, and, just beneath the surface, heartbreaking novel."

—Howard Frank Mosher, author of
A Stranger in the Kingdom

"Mississippi independent bookstore owner Jamie Kornegay has penned a debut novel that will establish him as a major force in the pantheon of elite Southern writers. I spent most of the time wondering why he didn't write a book sooner. It's not fair to keep something so wonderful away from readers. Would it be weird if I read it again?"

—Emily Gatlin, *Book Riot*

"First, with his debut novel, *Soil*, Jamie Kornegay has delivered a rip-roaring sucker punch of a tale, a page-turning lightning bolt of prose that crackles with keen insight, bold storytelling, pathos, and humor. There's more to it than that, however: if tragedy and comedy are the same object, only viewed through different lenses, Kornegay has minted a turbulent world where nothing is quite as it seems. The wretched is often hilarious, the gruesome elicits an uncomfortable chuckle of recognition, the well-meaning are revealed as self-serving—and finally, digging through these layers, we see the humbling and deeply touching struggle for love, for understanding, in a world that offers small hope for either."

—Jeffrey Lent

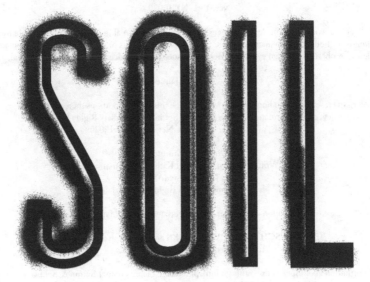

JAMIE KORNEGAY

Simon & Schuster Paperbacks

New York   London   Toronto   Sydney   New Delhi

Simon & Schuster Paperbacks
An Imprint of Simon & Schuster, Inc.
1230 Avenue of the Americas
New York, NY 10020

"Dirt in the Ground"
Written by Tom Waits and Kathleen Brennan
© 1992 Jalma Music (ASCAP)
Used by Permission. All Rights Reserved.

First Simon & Schuster trade paperback edition March 2016

SIMON & SCHUSTER PAPERBACKS and colophon are registered trademarks of Simon & Schuster, Inc.

For information about special discounts for bulk purchases, please contact Simon & Schuster Special Sales at 1-866-506-1949 or business@simonandschuster.com.

The Simon & Schuster Speakers Bureau can bring authors to your live event. For more information or to book an event contact the Simon & Schuster Speakers Bureau at 1-866-248-3049 or visit our website at www.simonspeakers.com.

Interior design by Robert E. Ettlin

Manufactured in the United States of America

1   3   5   7   9   10   8   6   4   2

The Library of Congress has cataloged the hardcover edition as follows:
Kornegay, Jamie, date.
  Soil : a novel / Jamie Kornegay. — First Simon & Schuster hardcover edition.
    pages   cm
  1. Organic farmers—Fiction. 2. Murder—Investigation—Fiction. I. Title.
PS3611.O7433S86 2014
813'.6—dc23

2014011468

ISBN 978-1-4767-5081-1
ISBN 978-1-4767-5087-3 (pbk)
ISBN 978-1-4767-5090-3 (ebook)

To Kelly

What does it matter, a dream of love
Or a dream of lies
We're all gonna be the same place
When we die . . .
We're all gonna be
Just dirt in the ground.

—Tom Waits

PART
I

PART

1

The drought began in May and lasted three months. It turned the earth to stone and the vegetation to yellow wisps. Then it rained all of August. The ground couldn't drink fast enough. Ditches ran over and then the creeks and then the rivers. Water collected in every furrow, making marshes of yards and farmland. Crops disappeared, fields became lakes.

By September the water had crested, lying stagnant in the valleys and heavy in the atmosphere. Cut down in its prime, the heat returned to settle a score. It took weeks but the water slowly retreated. Heaps of mire and bracken puddles festered, causing the dead grasses and shrubs to sprout anew in the untimely swelter. Wildlife gradually returned. And things were uncovered that might have been, for the betterment of all, left hidden.

One afternoon in this supposed fall, in the bottoms near the Tockawah River, a slovenly woodsman tottered through the underbrush, using an old pool cue to keep himself upright. He seemed put together from two separate men—the upper one plump, decisive, and keenly observant; the lower one lost and withered, flailing along in a pained shuffle. His way was fraught with a thousand irritations, and he addressed each one with a sigh or a groan or a fit of whispered curses. He might have been a troll trampling through the forest, so miserably did he announce himself.

Behind the woodsman came his companion, an old half-coyote who looked deranged with her one eye and mangy fur and arthritic lope. She seemed equally dismayed as they passed through the lattice of twisted limbs and dangling vines, stepping over fallen trunks and around leaf-strewn mud-holes. They had trespassed over a pasture and down into the hollows, search-ing for a swampy patch where the woodsman enjoyed poaching game birds. A series of afternoon cocktails had distracted him from his whereabouts, and now he had gotten turned around in the thicket.

The woodsman was a ways yet from being elderly but hastened his decline through bad luck and careless bachelor living. Drunken haphazard rambles and forays into evident danger were all within his casual realm. He'd earned his bowlegged scramble several years earlier while working at a local oil mill. He was slacking off, standing against a steam pipe when it ruptured. The rush of steam swept the blue jeans off his backside and broiled his flesh from hip to ham. He was drenched in hexane coolant from the pipes, and the chemical seeped into his tissue and made him crazy for a short while. First responders found him writhing on the factory floor, laughing hysterically, emphatic that giant lizards were eating his legs.

Months of skin grafts and years of rehabilitation followed. He still walked like someone who had taken a picnic in a bed of poison ivy. A cash settlement bought him early retirement and kept him in pain pills and cold beer. He spent his days exploring the shaded contours of society. It was common to spot his garish pickup truck lurking along the back roads, him there sitting high in the driver's seat atop an inflatable donut. He had a perverse interest in simple murder and had come to the river for something to shoot.

His dog hadn't eaten all day and was nosing through the leaves when she caught a scent and scampered off. The woodsman grumbled and limped after her into a clearing where the ground was spongy and white from river mud that had dried in the sun, appearing on the leaves like a bed of ashes over the earth.

"What is it, girl?" he called.

She'd discovered a jumble of bones at the base of a young oak. Seven feet up, in the crook of its branches, a skull and antlers were wedged. The skull was blanched white, fully scoured by blowflies, and the collapsed pile below was picked similarly clean, only a few swatches of fur among the leaves. The woodsman puzzled over the scene, trying to reconstruct the circumstances that had created the buck's misfortune. The strange had become common under the upheaval of nature.

He reached up into the tree to collect the antlers but his head went light and he wavered. He pulled a bandanna from his trousers, wiped his flaming pink face, and consulted his hip flask. He looked up at the midafternoon sun and hobbled south until his legs were dazed and he felt no sensation of walking at all.

Finally he arrived at the riverbank, where a foundered picnic table sat legs up in the shallows. He leaned on it, heaving with exhaustion and pain. The dog tumbled in first, splashing and lapping up water in aggravated snaps. He rested his weapon against a tree and stepped gingerly out of his jeans, unsnapped and peeled off his shirt. He doffed his straw hat and then slowly waded into the pool, clutching branches and bolstering his descent with the cue. Water rose to his waist, the coolness cutting under his wounded flesh like a reversed burn. He tensed as it covered his bulging stomach and climbed onto his chest and took his breath away. He imagined steam coming off him, the hiss of an open valve. The shock of cold drew the piss right out of him and away on the current.

The dog made her spastic climb ashore, and he reached for her, ran his hand over her slick fur as she scrambled up the bank and shook off. She took a shady place beneath the scrub and rubbed at the ever-festering scab around her swollen-shut dead eye. Years ago he'd made the mistake of reaching for a pork rib he'd dropped in front of her and had to stab her there with a screwdriver to break her bite. It was the only time they'd ever harmed one another, which was more than he could say for some couples.

He crouched and closed his eyes and felt the water tingle against his chin, listened to the dog's peaceful snores, and then he began to enter a shallow trance himself. Something thrashed downriver. He felt sure there were no gators this far north, not in a cool, flood-swollen river like this one, no matter what the old coffee guys were saying. Nevertheless, something clawed at him, some premonition that told him not to linger here.

A far-off engine whined, an upriver boat or jet ski. It grew louder and by the time he opened his eyes and craned his neck, it was upon them.

A man astride a four-wheeler had come barreling out of the woods and slid to a halt just beside the bank, not twenty yards upriver. A beagle pup ran up behind him, excited and breathless to the water's edge. The young dog spotted the woodsman and seemed prepared to dive in after him, but the stranger snarled and the pup heeled on the bank. The woodsman caught himself even as he opened his mouth. The stranger had not seen him there in the water, obscured behind a clutch of branches. There was something disturbed about this character, something familiar too. He was gangling and mud-encrusted, gasping in the heat and nervous, chiding himself or the dog or some absent third party. The woodsman could have been looking at a spry version of himself.

The stranger scanned the bank and the river and all around but still did not detect the woodsman or his dog there. A busy beard and wide-brimmed hat obscured most of his features. He unhooked a large cooler from the four-wheeler's rear rack and lugged it down to the water in spastic jerks. He knelt beside the cooler, opened it cautiously, and peered inside.

The woodsman's eyes darted to his mutt. Most folks took one look at her long feral muzzle and high ears and would not believe she was tame. She stood there, a little discombobulated, until the young beagle scampered up stupidly and jumped her in rough play. She stopped the pup with her bared yellow teeth and a gurgling snarl. The young dog retreated with a whimper, and the nervous stranger rose to attention. He slammed the cooler shut and marched around to find the commotion, stopping short when he saw the ragged bitch with her arched fur and cold cycloptic glare.

"Hello!" the man called out.

The woodsman didn't reply. A call from the water and a word of explanation would diffuse the situation, but he didn't want help climbing out of the river, like some old invalid, pathetic in soggy underwear.

The stranger called out again and waited with nervous suspicion. "This somebody's dog?" he hollered.

The man looked around, took a few anxious steps. There was still the stink of guilt or madness about him, and the woodsman watched for several minutes as the stranger walked back to retrieve a plastic bucket from inside the cooler. He returned and uncapped the container and set it down in front of the old girl. She sniffed and retreated, came back and sniffed again with a submissive bow. The pup moved in to sniff, but its master chased it back. "Go on and eat," said the stranger to the woodsman's dog. She sidled up and began to devour whatever mix was inside. Every now and again she hacked and sputtered, looked around, once back at the woodsman, who slipped beneath the water and took up hiding under broken limbs.

The woodsman surfaced silently and there was just enough headroom under the branches for him to see the stranger crouched there, waiting for the dog to finish eating, studying her with perplexity. Finally the man asked if she was done. She licked her lips and leaned in for a scent of him. The stranger patted her head, and she licked his hand. He held her beneath the jaw and appraised her, as the woodsman gnashed his teeth and craved her attack.

Instead the stranger stood up and removed his hat and pulled off his T-shirt as if he might take a dip. He bent down and used the shirt to wipe the dog's mouth, twirling it around her muzzle like a game of tug. She let her guard down, her tail wagging, and in the next instant he'd pulled a pistol from the back of his shorts and pressed it into the balled-up shirt and fired. She let out a short whimper and collapsed, the report no louder than a cracking branch.

The woodsman sank. He tried to push up from the bottom and hurl himself toward the shotgun propped against the tree, but he'd gone numb from his chest down. He saw the stranger, like some spinning discus hurler, toss her by all four paws into the middle of the river. He heard the muffled kerplunk, felt the reverberations from her deadweight entry. He lay low until his lungs began to burn and teased his lips over the surface to steal a shallow breath.

The woodsman watched the stranger's silhouette move along the bank. On level ground he'd have a fighting chance, but not here in this vulnerable blind. Somehow, beyond the woodsman's capacity for luck, the stranger still had not seen him under the brush or the weapon propped against the tree or the pool cue or the blue jeans and shirt laid across the bank, all of it out of place at the water's edge.

The man returned to his cooler and bent beside the shore. He washed his hands in the river and then doused his face and hair and neck; he crouched still for a moment and listened, took several long, deep breaths, and then returned his attention to the contents of the cooler by his side. With a sudden steadiness he reached in and pulled out a fish, which he slowly passed into the water. It floated stiffly on its side out into the current, followed fast by another and then another.

The woodsman watched in terrified wonder from the dross as the current carried them one by one toward the middle of the river, each frozen stiff as firewood, a wisp of steam rising up from their scales, going their own passive ways. The man fed nearly a dozen fish back to the river before he sealed the cooler and stood to watch them pass downstream, oddly bereft of purpose, as if drifting toward some new demise.

– 1 –

Before the flood, a stouthearted young couple was putting down roots in the nearby town of Madrid, where they'd settled after college—a man, his wife, and their young son. They painstakingly refurbished a house and planted an attractive garden in the back, where the father let the toddler dig and explore and pluck green tomatoes too soon from the vine. Smiles were never absent from their thankful faces, and if there were troubles then no one bothered to recall them. But a young man, especially one so clever, will grow restless and sometimes throw away everything when he turns elsewhere to affirm his life's purpose.

The trouble started with compost. He first began making and experimenting with it for his job in soil management at the local Farm Service Agency. He started small, a few wooden bins in the backyard of the home on Nutt Street. He collected kitchen scraps and coffee grounds, raked leaves and grass clippings. He spread one ingredient over the next in lasagna layers, sprayed them down with the water hose, and turned the piles regularly with a garden fork. If properly maintained, the compost would actually become hot to the touch and would belch plumes of steam when stirred on cold mornings. He loved the earthy smell that rose from the mounds, the whiff of rot and fiber, the way the soil broke and fluffed a little more each day. Here was nature at work, made more efficient by man's guiding hand.

He began to judge everything for its recyclability. All matter was either carbon or nitrogen. Soon he was collecting bags of lawn debris from neighborhood curbs and canvassing farms for straw bales and manure. He sorted leaves by species, made flowcharts of dung potency. Bins and mounds multiplied as he tinkered with ratios and tested fertility. He tilled up every square inch of backyard and planted vegetables and herbs, lined the front walk and driveway with big terra-cotta pots, each plot a test patch for some specially formulated recipe.

When he submitted a sample to a USDA-sanctioned exhibition, earning the highest marks in soil friability, nutrient retention, and water solubility, the local newspaper caught wind of it and dubbed him Compost Man. This gave his colleagues a good laugh. Even his wife joked to their friends about his growing "mudballs" out back and said she'd prefer him sneaking off with her lingerie catalogs than ogling the seed brochures the way he did.

One morning he walked out back to turn the piles and found that someone had laid a cruel turd atop one of his prize mounds. It was definitely human. The stench was complex and he found a fast-food napkin with brown streaks nearby. He couldn't believe the audacity. They'd just hopped up on the bin, draped themselves over the corner, and let one rip.

He paced the back porch and spent hours at the window, profiling every neighbor who walked by with a pet. Every jogger, every biker, every long-haired mischievous teen. What was this compulsion to foul something so pure and constructive? Who was deranged enough to do such a thing? He walked out back with his hammer and studded the rims of each bin with nails. Next time someone came snooping pants-down in the dark, they'd pay with blood.

His colleagues thought it was a hilarious prank. Even his wife suggested gently that he was taking it too hard. "We eat out of that soil, for God's sake!" he replied. "You want to end up in the hospital with a bacterial infection? Can you see our little son, dead from E. coli poisoning?"

She was skeptical of this, but he scoured the internet to prove the causes and insufficient cures of various bacteria and infections, moving on from there to viruses, superbugs, pandemics, extinction events. The deeper he dug, the more perils he uncovered.

Likewise the prank grew epic in his imagination. It was a pointed statement—"I shit on your life"—made by a lone creep and endorsed by a society that deemed him irrelevant. Somehow the smallest things can break a man, and the hairline fracture deep within the young scientist spread over the next several months. It did not depress him or slow his obsession but rather excited his research, leading to more compost mounds and more outlandish experiments. He upset the whole neighborhood when he planted a late-season crop of corn right there in the front yard. His wife was horrified by bean and cucumber vines planted in the rain gutters, cascading down like gaudy Christmas decorations. "You're turning our beautiful home into a feedlot," she accused him.

He read incessantly and became an expert on diverse farming techniques from ancient to modern civilizations. His interpretation of historical patterns convinced him that poor soil management had led to the downfall of societies throughout time. He relayed all of these findings to his farmer clients and expounded on the hazards of modern farming. They were hidebound men who planted cotton, soybeans, and corn as their families had for generations, trying to eke out modest livings against increasingly volatile world markets. Times were tough enough. They had no use for antiquarian farming theories promoted by some arrogant, pencil-pushing upshot. Nor did they appreciate his accusations that they were squandering the soil by leaching it with chemical fertilizers and pesticides, casting a blight upon the land and rivers and seas with their shortsighted and unsustainable methods, virtually ensuring that their grandchildren, along with everyone else's, would wander the famished countryside like starving refugees in a desert of poisoned dust. All they wanted from him was help filling out subsidy applications and disaster relief forms.

The soil scientist grew bitter and withdrawn. He felt rather like a young suburban Moses, entrusted with critical information from on high that the general rabble was too distracted to glean. The agency confirmed this by requesting his resignation.

Their idyllic life threatened, his wife went back to school to get her teaching degree while he stayed home with the boy. But he did not mope and feel sorry for himself. Just before his forced retirement, the young farmer had attended a regional ag conference where he heard a lecture on advances in hydro- and aeroponic technology delivered by a famous environmental scientist who made the stunning admission "Plants don't actually need soil to grow. Just a fissure for their roots to spread and soak up moisture and nourishment."

It was an offhanded remark, on the way to a larger point, but to the soil scientist it felt like an atom bomb. The statement was so simple and staggering, so obvious. *Soil-free farming.* Why had he never seen it? Look at the bonsais and cacti in their rock gardens, the weeds growing up from cracks in the sidewalk.

His imagination vaulted years ahead to farms that operated indoors, fields stacked one atop the next in glass high-rises, each floor its own crop grown in recycled water and mineral baths. He saw farmers in white lab coats appraising the beautiful plants, no bugs or blemishes, no sweat or sunburn, not a speck of dirt in sight. *The future will be spotless!* Hoes and plows became droppers and beakers. Computers monitored optimal growing conditions. All of the equipment was powered by the sun and the wind, a perfect organic machine. The greatest pitfalls of agriculture—pestilence and disease, the unpredictability of weather, poisonous pollutants and industrial runoff—could be solved by making the whole process simpler, cleaner, and more efficient. He could build it and lead the innovation. He could make the world healthier and more peaceful. There was no time to waste. To proceed authentically, he would have to start from the ground up.

He searched for a piece of land, spent two months sorting through overpriced and unsuitable plots until he found a house with seventeen acres twenty miles south of town. It had been a rental property for years, but the owners had come on hard times and were looking to unload it quickly. The house was a charmless pile of bricks compared to their town cottage, and the backyard was full of castaway equipment and scrap. The fields were grown over, all scrub and marsh and raw potential. Beyond the house was pastureland and forest, even a river, the wild and portentous Tockawah River, which ran along the southwestern edge of the property and would serve as a constant source of irrigation. It was the perfect site for his experiment. All of it could be his for a song.

He composed his pitch and approached his wife. She listened to him describe the experiments and the laboratory and the farm tower he would erect, how he intended to produce enough fresh food to supply the local population—"Not a farm so much as a growing system, indifferent to the whims of markets and nature." The way he described it and the completeness of his vision revealed a surprising logic born from his craze, and she became seduced a little.

She wondered about the home they'd made, the comforts they'd earned. Couldn't they live in town and start a farming business on the side?

The start-up capital to make this dream a reality required both the proceeds from the Nutt Street house and the inheritance she'd recently received from her stepmother, an unexpected gift which might have been wisely spent paying off student loans or starting a college fund for the boy.

"What better way to prepare a boy than to raise him in the country?" he asked. Teach a boy to hunt, fish, and farm, and you've paved the way for an honest, salt-of-the-earth man to live free come hell or high water.

She got a far-off look in her eye. Could she see it all before her, just as he had? Or was she scared to say no, knowing that if she kept her husband and his ambition shackled here she risked losing the very things she loved?

She had faith in him and his passion. He was asking her to double down on their young fortune. They took the leap together and spent some of the best days of their marriage in this shared endeavor.

A year later they were ruined.

– 2 –

He looked like a scarecrow propped up in a johnboat with his floppy hat and weather-beaten cabana shirt, his sagging cargo shorts and big rubber trash-can boots. Clutching a limp cane pole, he fished idly, occasionally shoving himself into the shade with an old tennis racket he used for an oar. He looked twenty years older than a year ago, all gaunt and strung out now, sporting a wiry beard, hair dripping to his shoulders, sunken eyes hidden behind truck-stop sunglasses.

His name was James Mize. Those who still knew him called him Jay. He was out on the pond photographing the devastation for his insurance adjuster, and there was plenty to document.

The leased tractor, parked under its protective lean-to, was up to its axle in sludge, its engine clogged with mud and soon to be rusted shut. Thousands of dollars of tiered and raised garden beds, hoes and picks and shovels, acres of sprawling PVC irrigation lines—all of it lay submerged and useless beneath the waterline. The steel framework of his uncompleted greenhouse laboratory rose from the swamp like the upturned rib cage of some extinct prehistoric beast. He'd run shy of funds before installing the glass panes and solar panels, so those at least wouldn't have to be replaced.

He was completely out of money, not a dollar to his name. The lights and water had been shut off, along with the phone, internet, satellite TV. A preppy goateed lawyer from town had come snooping around, knocking on windows, jimmying business cards in the door. The bank had grown skeptical of its stake in all of this. Bankruptcy was imminent.

He was near starvation, all the crops destroyed and the last of his non-perishables consumed. The only sustenance at hand was what he could pull from this miserable fishing hole beneath him. Even if hunger hadn't weakened his will, he had no means to escape this disaster. The gas tank was nearly dry in the sad hand-me-down Bronco given to him by his father, who'd died unexpectedly last winter.

Worse than all of this was being alone. No one to lend a word of encouragement, not even a critique. He reached inside his knapsack for the disposable camera to fire off a few shots for the insurance man, but he found himself fondling instead the little snub-nosed .38 Special he'd brought along to shoot snakes. The thought occurred to him—maybe he should make like his old man, just get it over with. This wasn't the first time he'd sat in the boat and considered it. Every time he guessed he'd hit rock bottom, it was just slow sinking mud underfoot, and there was no telling how low he might get, how long it might take to disappear completely.

Tockawah Bottom was a lump of yellow valley below the petered-out hill country, some of the last shrugs of Appalachia before the countryside pancaked down into the old Mississippi floodplain. It was a thankless hole that gave forth a reliably dull harvest of beans and corn and, if growers were so inclined to cast their lot in with the flagging cotton markets, that white gold for which the state's agriculture was latently famous. These lowlands were the basin for two minor conjoining rivers, the Tockawah and the Bogue Hoka, which dumped out in the Mississippi and then on to the Gulf of Mexico. At their confluence, these two rivers were apt to spill over.

Local naysayers warned him it was fool's play to farm these bottomlands. The river flooded every twenty years or so, and it was due for another. Besides, the market didn't pay out. It was cheaper to feed yourself from the grocery store than to till and plant and hoe and gather alone. You're gambling with your life, they said. If you don't starve, you'll work yourself to an early grave. There's good reason farming went out of fashion, they told him—it's too damn much trouble.

Of course, Jay was aiming to change all of that, and by then he was too deeply invested to take their caution seriously. He'd spent that first autumn engaged in heroic work—clearing brush, digging trenches, building and transferring soil, fashioning rain catches, erecting supports, staking out field plots. He'd cobbled together coops and pens for livestock, hired builders to pour the concrete footing and raise the framing for his lab. He imagined that in a matter of years, students and proselytes from all over the world would travel here to study the latest, most efficient growing methods, and they would adapt his techniques for use in their own cities and villages.

But neither could he completely reject his skeptics. Their warnings played into a concern which had been lurking in the back of his mind, and which had begun to take rapid shape now that he was caught up in real labor and had recognized the fickle tolerance nature held for man.

What the naysayers didn't understand was that it wasn't some quaint old notion or a naïve fondness for yesteryear, not even an entrepreneurial move toward trendy organic farming that made him come out here, all the way to nowhere, to invest the family savings in this house and the soggy field and all the tools and equipment required to make a proper start. He'd read the books on climate change, energy crises, and colony collapse. He'd read *The Road*. He'd studied the ancient prophecies, the newer ones too, noting all the harbingers of environmental and economic ruin. A comeuppance was due, and he didn't want to be stuck in town among the bleating mobs when it all went down. He aimed to be prepared, to protect his family from it when it came, whatever it was and however awful, this thing he'd begun to believe like a religion.

He tried explaining it to his wife, Sandy, but she was a pragmatist who held little patience for his dark projections. He didn't push the issue with her because he knew that when the time came she would be able to adapt to anything, whatever calamities the world might bring them.

And that's why it was such a blow to him when, some ten months after they'd started on this dream together, she came to him out of the blue and surrendered. She was taking their six-year-old son, Jacob, with her back to town, where the burdens were more civilized and could be blotted out with television and pills.

She told him he was losing his mind, that he was putting the family in jeopardy, all for some paranoid assumption that civilization was sliding into a new dark age. He saw the opposite—society had lost *its* mind and he was only protecting his loved ones from the ramifications—and he couldn't believe they'd become so diametrically opposed over something so obvious to him. He tried to convince her to leave the boy, who had taken a shine to country living and had adopted a puppy and had only just begun to explore the wilderness, but she wouldn't hear of it.

Perhaps his greatest mistake was letting them go, but at the time he was too encumbered to chase them. Bills were pouring in, the summer harvest had to be gathered and sold. Before he ate them all, there were chickens to tend. The orchard had to be planted by fall. The cold frames and greenhouse for next winter's crops wouldn't build themselves. He knew his wife and child would be safe in town with her father, a retired professor with a large house to himself, and that they'd return once the hard foundation work was complete.

As the season wore on, the sky refused to rain; insects seized the crops. He overcompensated with heavy irrigation, which invited mold and rot and disease into his beds. What didn't die, the deer and squirrels and other woodland menaces devoured.

Many days he struggled to remember why he'd started any of this in the first place, and then other days he managed to pump himself up, feeling rather like some tobacco-road Job who would be redeemed only through suffering and whose rewards would be congruent to that which he could bear.

Then came the August rains, which were surely nature's ploy to finish him. The Tockawah overran its banks and engulfed his property, bringing with it all the leaves and limbs and fallen trees from the nearby woods, loads of detritus from upriver too. A turd in the compost was a speck compared to what the Tockawah shat out over his crops, making a lake of his field and a mockery of his attempts to do good by the blessed earth.

And so, finally, this is where ambition had wrung him out—a lonesome little man in a toy boat, bobbing around his mud puddle. It was all in the world he still possessed, and even this, a brief illusion of lakefront property, was retreating daily by the foot, leaving only a stretch of black goop and a band of rotten grass and cane and brush that grew wider every day, hemming him in like razor wire.

He glided along the shrinking margins of his field and snapped photos. He rowed in and out of the rusted armatures of his watermelon forest, under the monkey-bar trellis for his stalled pea vines. It was difficult to imagine what had attracted him to this work in the first place. It seemed nothing would ever grow here again.

But then, in the lump of collapsed mud that was once his ziggurat herb garden, he noticed basil sprouts and remembered that life stubbornly returns every time. Maybe he was no Job after all but instead Noah, the tormented visionary who'd ridden out the flood while the scourge of history was washed away. What if the river had not destroyed his land but wiped clean the old mistakes and deposited a whale-load of rich, free fertilizer—all the river soil and fish meal and rotting plants that make a nice compost—for next season's cultivation?

As he knew so well from his science, civilizations throughout time—in fact, every form of life on the planet—were perpetuated by this cycle of decay and regrowth. It was only his impatience, the tempo of society and not nature, that had prevented him from seeing it before. And as he felt the white numbing warmth of the sun on him and enjoyed a new cleansing breath of pure air, he believed that he could still win his wife and son back, that he could still coax his fields to fertility, and that his setbacks, the ruination of his farm and the disintegration of his family, would one day be charted as necessary bumps in the road over which all great achievement must pass.

Out of this reverie Jay heard an idling engine and then saw it there on the road behind him, a pickup truck with camouflage detailing pulled over to the shoulder. The passenger window was down and the driver leaned out the window, braying, "Hey, buddy. Anythang bitin?"

Jay stared back, trying to recognize this person. He thought it might be an old friend having a laugh, but after a moment he realized it was only an interloper making small talk. Who wanted simply to know how things were biting? The guy was probably angling for money or permission to fish, some preface to a scam.

"This is private land!" Jay shouted back.

He snatched his racket and gave the boat a bitter shove away from the road, back toward the house.

Privacy, he believed, was the fastest vanishing civility among men. He'd already posted a No Trespassing sign by the road, a futile gesture to defend his field from the carloads of illiterate country tramps who showed up with their poles and tackle, fishing the ditches, sometimes casting right from the front seats of their old beat-down cars. Who but a common thief would just walk up and take food from a man's crop? He'd recently caught a pair of shirt-less teenagers whipping around his field in their daddy's high-powered Bass Tracker like a couple of Panamanian drug smugglers—as if the spilled river had negated all property division!

Just then a vile stench rambled down his throat and turned his stomach. Something dead, too potent to be beached fish or rotting timber. This was something sweet and worse.

Up ahead some fifty yards, a turkey buzzard balanced itself with awk-ward wings, betraying the carcass in a clutch of tall mud-tangled grass. Was it truly something or just a wet, gnarled log poking out of the murk? He rowed closer, burying his nose in his shirt. It was hideous, all contorted and half-submerged, reared back and eaten with lesions. He thought it could be a deer or a heifer.

The bird's head bobbed and wrenched, tearing off wet mouthfuls. It stopped midchew to give Jay a daring glance. It made no distinction about its prey. Dead is dead. Something in the bird's savage possession told what it had and the lengths to which it might go to keep it. He turned back toward the road and squinted to see if the camouflage truck was still there, but the road was empty.

He looked again at the buzzard, slurping and gagging, its neck contorting as it choked down scraps of brown meat. Jay took a swing at the bird with the racket. It hissed at him and then rose aloft with much clumsy effort, making a few passes overhead before lighting on a tree branch some twenty yards away.

"Holy God," said Jay, studying the remains. He leaned over the bow of the boat and looked into the face of it, into scraps of flesh that once gave expression. There were horrible festering holes from which eyes had been plucked and the hollow nasal cavity where a detached bulb of cartilage flapped. Receding lips exposed its teeth so that it looked like a whinnying horse. Some green congealment had bubbled up from a jagged divot in the skull. The face reminded him of the alleged alien autopsy photos from the UFO crash at Roswell, all bloated and fabricated. Against all doubt, he noticed clearly a hand, just under the water's surface, in a rigid palsied gesture. Five fingers grasping for some last mercy.

A car sped past on the road. Jay righted himself and whipped around, his eyes darting nervously over the field. A six-foot wall of tangled scrub and young trees barely shielded him from prying eyes. Any nosy passerby with a pair of binoculars and a pestering, fool-sighted curiosity could observe and jump to conclusions. Next thing you know, the entire sheriff's department would be on the scene by nightfall. It was not outside his own rational line of thought that he might spend the night in county lockup.

Jay thrust his racket under the water and shoved himself furiously toward cover. He wasn't getting anywhere fast enough, so he tumbled out and waded through the sucking mud with the sensation of running away in dreamlike suspension. At last, towing the boat behind him, he made it to the safety of low-hanging willow tree branches on the far side of the field, up near the gravel driveway. He tied the boat to the tree and climbed back inside. He dumped his boots and sat with wet socks for a long time, watching the heap at the far end of the lake.

Finally he began to wonder who the corpse might be. He chased his memory for clues—strangers he'd seen, fishermen from the bridge, clumsy hitchhikers who might have tumbled into the flooded field or fallen out of

Jamie Kornegay

boats on the river. But this was all pretense, for he knew who it surely must be. He did not know him exactly, but it was someone he could imagine.

He craned his neck to the road, wondering what the idiot in the camo truck had seen. Meanwhile the buzzard had returned to poke at the body. Jay opened his knapsack and gripped the .38. He considered firing on the bird, but a gunshot might create a memory for anyone within earshot, a memory that might turn up later as a courtroom distortion.

Jay recalled isolated incidents from the past few weeks that now seemed to coalesce in light of this discovery. The composite was unflattering to him. It might not hold up in a court of law. He ran scenarios in his head and defended himself as his own character witness, as if to convince someone, possibly himself, that he was not responsible for this death. He wanted to row out and view the corpse and its broken skull again, just for clarification, but not as long as there was a glimmer of daylight in the air. Instead he sat in the boat, hidden beneath the willow, stunned until dusk.

The falling light made lavender waves of the clouds. Imagined traffic rose and died in his head, replaced by the menace of crickets and bullfrogs. The buzzard had flown away engorged.

Finally Jay climbed out of the boat, scrambled through the brush and over the levee, up the gravel driveway to the house. He turned back to the road, fearful of passersby, and then to the lake, where the dead man was just another dark ripple on fallen limbs.

— 3 —

The house was still when night passed into the mudroom, making only the slightest creak through the storm door, brushing curtains in the kitchen and snuffing out the candle on the counter. Even the banjo and fiddle on the crank radio had wound down to nothing, giving stage to insects singing their strange unison.

Jay jerked awake on the couch, opening his eyes to a darkness greater than sleep. He took in short fish gulps of air and listened through the liquid black stillness. Night had beaten him here.

He jumped off the sofa, cursed himself for falling asleep and missing his twilight ritual of locking down the house. Out here in the wilderness, meeting the night required preparation. After weeks without electricity, he understood how the mind functioned differently in prolonged darkness, how it intensified and overreached. Lights and air-conditioning afforded comfort where it didn't belong, and comfort was a luxury, good for sleep but not for survival.

Most nights, lying in the dark, he ran through a list of hypothetical dangers and resolved how to confront them—burglars and scavengers coming through the front door, the back, the bedroom window; a tree crashing through the roof in a thunderstorm; a wild animal rooting under the carport or entering from the basement; fires, floods, earthquakes, tornadoes. The list grew exponentially more dangerous. But never this. This was an unexplored contingency.

Jay felt his way through the blind house, bumping into walls, knocking over books and papers stacked all along the baseboards. He found the kitchen and relit the candle. It took a moment to recall what had happened, what was day and what was night. He paced the room, his pond socks leaving crisscrossed footprints on the muddy linoleum.

There were dozens of explanations for what he'd seen, but he could conjure none of them for the sheer fact of dwelling on it—grotesque and demoralized, all blistered and septic in the middle of his peaceful lake. And to think, it was out there right now—a dead man dumped in a mudhole!—a whole life just used up and tossed away, left for him to decide how to dispose of it.

His first instinct was to hide it. He'd rather be rid of it and back in his malaise. If he left it in the field, the buzzard would finish it. There would be more of them tomorrow, making their high beckoning whirls, alerting anyone within view of the county road, all the houses and camps for miles around. The law would be called. Questions would be asked, answers would be presumed. They'd all seen him hanging out on the lake in his boat. There was no denying that he knew what was out there in the mud. Why had he not reported it unless he hoped it wouldn't be found?

Jay held the candle and rifled through kitchen drawers until he found the cell phone. He punched it on, but the battery was dead. In the unlikely event that it worked and the account was active and a signal could be found in this remote outreach, who would he call who might believe him? It was too convenient to think he had done this. Never mind logic. The world was ruled by convenience and stupidity, after all. That's the way of it, generally, before everything goes to hell.

If not him, then who else had killed this man, this stranger trespassing on the Mize property? Suppose someone had murdered this man and done it right there in the field. The killer could be down there now, hiding in the brush or just outside the window.

Jay snatched up the candle and took it to the foyer and looked out the window through the front of the house and into the field, but he saw only his own reflection staring back. He blew out the flame and tried again, cupping his hands against the glass. Nothing could be seen through the impenetrable black.

The only sensible recourse was reporting the body to the deputy. He didn't have enough gas to make it in to Madrid, and so he'd have to hitchhike into town or else walk across the road and tell Hatcher. Maybe his neighbor would make the call for him. Hatcher would love nothing more than to be the grumbling father savior to Jay's distraught child. He unbolted the front door and stepped out onto the porch, looking both ways to make sure no one was crouched there, and then squinted to find a flicker of light through the trees, some confirmation that Hatcher was still awake. There was nothing tonight, no moon or stars, not a ripple of heat lightning or even a firefly's neon blink. He sniffed the air for a sign of the body, but there was only a fecund heat. Invisible trees loomed in the darkness, pulsing with the screams of insects. Their screeching felt like a whetstone falling over and over him.

He retreated indoors, secured the front entryway, and made his way through the darkness to his bedroom at the back of the house. He took a flashlight from the night table and switched it on and searched the drawer until he found the deputy's card.

Shoals. He'd been here just two weeks earlier in search of a missing person. Jay had promised to notify him if he came upon any clues. He'd be charged with obstruction of justice if they found the body before he reported it. Even if he called them right now, the chances of sliding by without suspicion were slim. Too much water under that bridge. Jay knew that once he entered their system, the gears would turn too fast against him to mount a fair defense.

He took a change of clothes, dark pants and a black turtleneck, and made his way to the front of the house, waving the flashlight down the cluttered hallway. He nudged his way past a mound of fly-swarmed garbage bags in the mudroom. The room stunk of rot and mildew and fertilizer, a little soap powder and peat moss. He cast light into corners and bins filled with cobwebs and dirt clods, across surfaces filled with sketches and scribblings and dog-eared books crammed with notes. He found a pair of old sneakers. Wadded up beneath the utility sink were his brown rubber wading pants. All the while his mind raced—was there a way to float it out of there, to send it back toward the river and let it wash up on someone else? Could he shift the blame to the bridge fishers, the man in the camouflage truck, the speedboat teens?

He opened the back door and went outside to search for answers among the piles of junk under the carport—paper bags with screws and nails spilling out, milk crates filled with dusty parts, a disemboweled engine. There was Jacob's bicycle, the batting tee and baseball and ruined mitt, the unused rod and reel hanging overhead on nails, all the birthday and Christmas gifts he'd never taken the time to show his son how to use. He imagined Jacob in town, blue street light streaming through his bedroom window, curled up inside his sleeping bag over the bedspread, fast asleep with a dead man's gaping mouth. And Sandy alone, glistening eyes awake, waiting on the sun.

Surely they would believe Sandy, a fine upstanding citizen without a blemish on her record, her character above reproach. He couldn't explain why he had not bothered to get in touch with them. What sort of stubborn point was he trying to make? Simply put, he was a fool to have cut them loose and probably deserved this.

He switched off the flashlight and lay back against the concrete and listened to the insects in the trees and felt others light on his face, scrambling over his skin and through his hair, thinking, *This is what it feels like to be left for dead.*

– 4 –

The greatest inconvenience the flood exacted was washing out the old Bogue Hoka bridge, the only covered bridge in the county, down the levee road that ran in front of the Mize place. The road wound south out of Bayard County, crossed U.S. 7, and ran straight into downtown Flintlock in the neighboring county. A section of the levee road itself had been flooded for two weeks, and when the water receded, it left behind a mud-caked surface littered with tree limbs, black brush mounds, the carcasses of fish and birds and rodents. The county supervisors came out and shook their heads at the mess. They'd get to work on the bridge, but no one could say when. Many in the bottoms were dismayed that a generic concrete bridge might be rebuilt in its place instead of the rare old-fashioned covered bridge, which had become a point of pride in this rural community and the only thing worth photographing aside from tumbledown shacks or the odd frenzy of mating cranes.

There were other, smaller disasters, no less consequential to those who were affected. Past the bridge and up the road a ways toward Flintlock, water flooded the rectory of the Lord's Spiteful Loving Grace Church, ruining the new carpet it had taken three years of collections to afford. A few mobile homes capsized into a gulley with the half-buried dwellings from previous floods. Near the county line, mud and water got into the ground wells of the Pump 'n' Dump service station, spoiling the fuel and unleashing a tsunami of household garbage from the adjacent landfill.

Out on U.S. 7, uphill from the flood, after the rains had stopped and in the wee hours of the second Tuesday in September, an eighteen-wheeler from a Delta catfish processor plowed into four walking horses that had escaped their waterlogged paddock. The rig was bent up pretty good and the trailer overturned, dumping fish into the road. The horses had exploded all over the highway, scraps of meat on the asphalt, in the grass and in the grille, hanging from the trees. It was a scene of carnage that witnesses struggled to describe. The photo on the front page of *The Flintlock Repositor*, depicting a close-up fish head casting one baleful eye on the soft-focus devastation behind it, would hang on local refrigerators for months as a reminder that God was watching.

Danny Shoals, the sheriff's nephew and most privileged deputy, arrived late to the scene, the cleanup well under way. The state highway department had taken control, instructing the county's road crews and trusties to sweep up fish heads and horse hooves with giant push brooms. Firefighters followed behind, hosing down the pink blacktop.

Shoals inspected the scene, cool but good-natured. A one-man special unit with an ear to the ground and a bulge for keeping the peace, he had the air of a professional observer, just smart enough to keep his mouth shut. Everyone thought he knew the score, and he was careful not to prove them wrong, offering only gracious one-liners, off-color banter, a furrow of easy concern. He had classic quarterback good looks, muddy whirlpool eyes, and a crooked upper lip that made him smile even in rare anger. Nothing about him spoke protocol, from the tanned suede vest over the tight black security T-shirt to the cowboy boots and Western-style leg holster. The patch of fuzz under his bottom lip was a special touch. He was the only deputy out of uniform, an unspoken perk reserved for sheriff's kin.

He naturally sought out the highest in command, in this instance a highway patrol lieutenant named Keesler. They shook hands, and Shoals exchanged nods with another pair of patrollers standing around. The lieutenant described the accident. He hadn't seen such gore since 'Nam. The trucker was shaken up pretty good but not seriously injured. The owner of the horses,

Rakestraw, was an enormous, boisterous man making plenty of demands and complaining about the government. He was highly pissed, not just about his horses but that he might be held accountable somehow.

Shoals propped his foot up on the bumper of a cruiser and gazed over the debris-strewn roadway. "I don't know, Lieutenant," he puffed. "Something seems fishy about this to me."

The officers laughed obligingly, though the joke had been made several times already. Such was the deputy's devil-may-give-a-shit appeal, even among superiors.

"You ask me, those horses saw their chance and took it," Shoals said. "I wouldn't be surprised if that big boy Rakestraw was raising them for meat."

Before they could laugh, one trooper called him out. "Hey, that's my wife's cousin!"

Shoals cut him a side grin. "Relax, F-Troop, he's a buddy of mine too. I'm just messing."

Keesler reassured Shoals that it was all paperwork now, which satisfied the deputy. He volunteered to sink back into the county. Disasters like this had a tendency to ripple in strange directions.

While the human costs of this incident were minimal, the accident had caused major traffic snares. Since the Bogue Hoka bridge was down, the most sensible detour around the collision was cut off. Traffic had been rerouted way the hell out—back west and then north along the reservoir highway, east over several hill roads, at least one of them a gravel private road straddling counties, down through Silage Town, and over several more winding county roads back to the highway, some twenty miles total distance. There weren't even enough Detour signs in the district to mount an informed route. Most drivers gave up and returned from whence they came.

Shoals had some business down the levee road and was vexed that his route had been cut off by the washed-out bridge. He yearned to give someone hell over this inconvenience and found one of the county road foremen sitting on the back of a pickup eating a sandwich and watching the scene.

"Look out now, is that a fish-head po'boy?" Shoals asked the foreman. "You better have paid for that."

"Finders keepers," the man mumbled.

"Y'all gonna start repairing that bridge after your dinner there?"

The man chewed awhile, wiped his mouth, and replied, "Naw."

"What's the holdup?"

"Waiting for state emergency funds. Could be spring before we even get started."

"Spring!" the deputy cried. "Well shit, can I get across?"

"Not unless you got a boat."

"You got a ladder I can use?"

"Tell you what, Danny," the foreman replied, "I'll have some of my guys bring a load of dirt down there and you can try and jump it in that pretty car of yours."

"Hell, don't bother," said Shoals. "It would probably be Christmas before you could get a requisition for shovels."

The deputy sauntered back to his vehicle. Due to a lack of squad cars, Shoals had convinced his uncle to let him drive his unmarked 1970 Mustang Boss 302, a real conversation piece in its original Grabber Blue. It was known all over the county by its novelty tag, which read SUGAR. Wherever he pulled up in that sweet-ass ride he earned instant respect and authority. A lap around the block with a reluctant witness always loosened the tongue. It teased the hotheads out into the open, made ne'er-do-wells confess if only for a front-seat ride to the station. And with its horse team under the hood and his dashboard beacon, no one in the county dared outrun him.

Yearning now for a long, winding detour, Shoals quickened his pace until he passed something shiny in the tall grass. He doubled back and crouched on the roadside. "Be damn," he said, plucking up a heavy iron piece in the weeds. One of the smashed horses must have thrown a shoe. He wiped a speck of blood off and tucked it in his back pocket, a bit of superfluous luck, and then carried forth toward his own waiting steed.

The Mustang roared to life like a beast lying long dormant, hibernating in its own musk. It never failed to charge him like a squirt of gasoline in the heart. He grabbed the stick and threw it down, left a few marks for the county stripes to clean. No detour too far for a little plainclothes mischief.

Shoals made the most of his journey around the reservoir and down the back slope into Tockawah Bottom, gliding through curves and throttling the stretches, whipping around slow-moving vehicles and honking at penned-up cows grazing close to the road. By the time he came to the Mize place, he was a little giddy. He loved working the sticks and had been looking forward to making this particular civilian squirm.

He stopped at the foot of the driveway. Water from the nearby river had flooded the adjacent field and come up nearly even with the road. The last thing he wanted was to slide the Boss ass-down in a stagnant lake, at the mercy of an angry landowner and potential adversary. He eased his ride up the gravel drive, noting the house on the hill and the little yard with its high weeds and sticky mane of shrubs, the useless implements scattered along the side yard.

As he crested the drive, Shoals was startled by a long and unkempt piece of white trash lurching out from beneath the carport. The subject wore a gas mask, baggy shorts, and a Bermuda shirt. He looked like a tourist on some toxic adventure vacation package. Shoals stopped and let the Mustang rumble in the driveway. They each stared the other down, one waiting for the next to make his move. The subject lowered his mask to reveal a man in his thirties, possibly forties, with a scruffy beard and hard jittery eyes.

Shoals cut the engine. He didn't want to make a show of whipping his piece out from the glove box, but something told him to get strapped. Out here in the bottoms, any country boy in a gas mask was likely cooking meth and possibly high on it. He tucked a canister of pepper spray into his rear waistband and stepped out of the Boss.

"What's the emergency, buddy?" cried Shoals, drumming up swagger and friendly bombast.

"What emergency?" the man stammered.

"That's what *I'm* asking," Shoals replied. He sniffed the air for the tang of certain chemicals, scanned the yard for a shed or trailer that might serve as a cookhouse. There was an aluminum shed set thirty yards back from the house, but it was crammed full of junk, no apparent ventilation. "I saw you in that gas mask there and thought we might have a toxic event on our hands."

"Who are you?"

Shoals flashed his shield. "Deputy Danny Shoals. Detective for the county, sir. And you?"

The subject stopped to consider. Shoals used the opportunity to walk wide of him, trying to steal a view into the backyard.

"I didn't report anything," the subject said.

"Well that's fine," said Shoals, making a note of the dozen or more blue barrels scattered in the backyard. "Just a friendly visit. What's your name, friend?"

"Jay Mize," he replied. He was adamant and possessive, sober all of a sudden. "Did someone call me in or something?"

"Naw," Shoals said. "What for?"

"I don't know. Just not accustomed to cops coming around." He pulled the mask from around his neck and tossed it into a nearby cardboard box filled with bottles of water and boxes of ammunition. "Thought my car tag might be out of date or something."

Shoals laughed good-naturedly while he surveyed. "Mize, you say? I know that name."

Mize shrugged and shifted uncomfortably.

The deputy asked of his origins, and Mize said he came from Memphis, that he'd married after school and recently moved to the country.

"Where's the wife?"

"Temporarily separated."

The deputy chewed on this a moment.

"You any kin to Mitchell, by chance?"

Mize went cold and tense. "Does this have something to do with him?"

Shoals smirked. "Naw, I was just curious if you knew him."

"Yeah. He was my granddad."

"Really?" The deputy was impressed.

"He's dead," said Mize.

"Well, yeah, of course. I know Mitchell Mize."

"That's funny, because I never did."

"Well, not personally."

"A lot of folks *think* they know about Mitchell Mize," the subject replied, glowering, but the deputy didn't flinch.

"I guess then you know he was a pretty famous fella," said Shoals.

"Is there something I can help you with, Officer?"

"Deputy," the deputy assured him. "Sure, sure. I don't want to take up too much of your time, but I *am* on official business. You'll have to forgive me for getting a tad starstruck."

Mize betrayed nothing, but Shoals knew he'd gotten under his skin. "What is it you do, if you don't mind me asking?" the deputy asked.

"Organic farming," Mize replied.

"Organic farming. Now what's that exactly?" Shoals was messing with him a bit. You always wanted the subject to believe he had the upper hand, an old trick he'd learned from Andy Griffith.

"It's farming without pesticides or chemical fertilizer."

"So what's in them barrels back there?"

Mize turned to look. "Rain. I'm collecting it."

"I can see that. All out front too."

Mize snickered, a little condescending snort. "Yep, whole crop's lost this year. I'm pretty well pissed about it."

The deputy nodded and gave a half-nod back to the fields. "I imagine so. You didn't bargain for this, I'm sure."

"What do you need, Deputy?"

"Well, you'll be interested to know, I'm hunting a man who disappeared around here two, three weeks ago. You seen anybody fishy around here?"

Mize must have misheard. He became excited. "Hell yeah, everybody out here. They fish off these bridges every evening, all day on the weekends.

I liked to have hit one last week. He ran out in front of my truck. They're all the time just standing out in the road."

Shoals nodded, considered the complaint. "Blacks?"

"Pardon?"

"Are they blacks? Whites?" the deputy clarified. He couldn't decide if the guy was slow. Probably just stoned. He seemed put off by the question.

"They're both," Mize replied with a touch of righteous indignation.

"Reason I ask," the deputy said, "is this one that wandered off is a black dude from Ohio. His family's looking for him. They're worried he might have run up on some trouble down this way. Some folks still think it's a death sentence to send a Yankee black man down South. Ignorant people mostly."

Mize had a pained, quizzical stare on him. "There's been several parked on the roadside there, fishing out of my field," he said finally. "I spoke to a few, just to run them off. I didn't detect any accents or see anything that led me to believe they were an Ohio sort. They all sounded like local fools and lurkers."

The deputy imagined fishing in a bean field and laughed. He exaggerated a bit, hoping it would relieve the tension, but Mize bristled as if he were the subject of ridicule. Shoals studied him. He searched for common ground but felt no kinship, which made that between them all the more exotic.

He wanted to know more. "What all were you growing?" he asked, turning to survey the field.

"A little bit of everything," Mize said.

"What's all that metalwork?"

"A trellis for watermelons."

"I'm no farmer, but I know watermelons don't grow up."

"It was a watermelon tree. I was experimenting with different growing techniques for small-space cultivation." Mize began describing his alternative methods and biointensive ecologies. It all sounded fairly new-age to Shoals, who believed he was dealing with a recreational drug user. If not a tweeker, then possibly a late acid freak with pickled senses, but most likely just a stoner. Probably if he tromped around a bit on the property he'd turn up a few plants out among all the scrub, maybe back in the pasture behind the house. He wouldn't go snooping as long as the guy remained civil.

Mize had loosened up a bit talking about his farm, and Shoals thought it safe to pry. "You raising all this just to eat yourself?"

"Yeah, mostly. Some to sell."

Shoals looked him over, then back at the field. "Looks like you might go hungry this winter."

"You never know," Mize replied. "We might all go hungry."

"Not me. Hell, I got Mickey D's in town. And a freezer full of deer meat at home."

"Maybe not, if gas prices keep rising. The trucks may decide it's not worth hauling that junk food all the way down to Mississippi. The dominoes fall in elaborate patterns. Next thing you know, the power company can't supply your electricity and your freezer dies. What will you do then, Deputy?"

"Sounds pretty far-fetched."

"Actually, that's the simplest of scenarios. This little rainy season was a trial run." The subject's gaze became more focused and intense. Shoals had pushed the right button. "We're just getting warmed up here with all that's about to go down."

The deputy plucked his chin. "What's about to go down, friend?"

Mize cocked his head, as if sensing the deputy's disbelief. Maybe he never believed that a simple servant of the county had the capacity to imagine large-scale environmental devastation. He gave a halfhearted response, describing the litany of natural cataclysms forming in the atmosphere and oceans. Mankind's demise was closer than anyone believed, he said.

"You sound like one of those global warming conspiracy theorists," Shoals replied.

"Damn right," Mize said. "But it's nature's conspiracy, not mine. She's had her fill of us. Look around you, man."

Shoals gave a smart-ass nod to his left and right and then shrugged. "You never seen a flood? You think just cause it's hot in September? This is Mississippi, man. Surely you know, we specialize in this shit!"

Mize shook his head. "Whether or not you believe it, the earth is warming, the ice caps are melting, the seas are dying. And all the while, mankind is like a child kicking the legs on the table where this house of cards sits. Not that it matters, really, because the sun is growing restless too, of its own accord. One day it will be obvious even to the most fervent deniers. All I can say is, hold on for the ride."

Shoals was wearing his best grin. "I don't mean to punch holes in your boat, Mr. Mize, but I think you're seeing things through your own troubles. Your situation here probably seems worse than it is. Just cause it's your first time to get flooded don't mean it's the first time there's ever been a flood. Your number just came up is all."

Some folks couldn't see the forest for the trees. Shoals could tell by Mize's empty glare that he wasn't buying it.

"You ever listen to Hotdog and T-Bone in the morning?" the deputy asked. He guessed from Mize's stubborn silence that he had not. "Well, they had a scientist on just the other morning, fella said there's no more hurricanes on average now than there was a hundred years ago. Said the ocean temperature might've gone up a degree or two overall in the last hundred years. It's all part of a normal pattern, or how'd he put it? 'Abnormal is normal.' People are just freaking out over the same things people have been freaking out over for thousands of years."

Mize looked down and shook his head, a big knowing smile like everybody else in the world was such a fool.

"Some'll tell you this whole global warming thing is just a means to promote worldwide government," Shoals continued. "You think you got trouble with the ice caps, buddy, wait till you got some ayatollah or some damn prime minister from Russia calling all the shots, telling you you can't burn leaves in your backyard or can't flush but every other shit."

"Look, sir," said Mize in a superior huff, "you can take your cues from Hotdog, and I'll take mine from nature and the world around me. It's telling me all I need to know, and with all due respect, I don't have time to worry what anyone else thinks about it. Now, I think I should get back to my work. I wish I could help you today, but I sure can't."

The deputy shook his head, unruffled. "T-Bone," he said finally. "He's the smart one. Hotdog is there for comic relief."

"Sounds just goddamn hilarious. I'll be sure and give them a listen," said Mize with snide deference. "Now if you'll excuse me, I have to get back to something. I'll give you a ring if I run into anyone from Ohio."

Shoals had hoped he could delve a little deeper, but the conversation was obviously going no further. He had a fair sense of the man's disgrace.

"Will you do that?" he said, handing him a business card. "And, hey, sorry to hear about your marriage. And your crops, of course."

"Thanks," said Mize with a queer glare.

"Don't mention it," Shoals said. He stood there a minute, nodding, searching for the final word. "Be damn, I sure didn't expect to run into Mitchell Mize's grandson today."

With that, he climbed into the Boss and cranked the engine, gave it a few good carbon-spewing revs before retreating down the gravel driveway, screeching out onto the county road, and letting the engine unwind along the highway back to town, wide open to his next curiosity.

– 5 –

Some two weeks later and long past midnight, Jay emerged rigid and encumbered from the aluminum toolshed like something out of a science-fiction movie, all clad in dark rubber waist boots, black turtleneck, and gas mask, haloed in a dim red glow. In the grip of his heavy chemical gloves he held a musty brown tarp, which he dragged into the yard and unfurled, shaking out the pits of water and thumping off the slugs. He folded it into a tight square and wedged it down the front of his waders.

Inside the shed, the four-wheeler sat parked in silent collusion. If the deputy returned to investigate, it wouldn't take long to figure out the vehicle did not belong to him. "Where did you get it?" he would ask, and Jay would be forced to confess the ridiculous truth—"It just showed up here, don't know whose it is."

He'd discovered it in his driveway back in August, before the flood. It was in good shape—a couple of years old, empty rifle mount, a few bungee cords wrapped around the rear rack. The key was in the ignition. He left it overnight to give the rider time to return, and when it hadn't moved the next day, he cranked the vehicle and rode it to the end of the driveway and up and down the road, trying to flush out the owner. Days and weeks passed. No one showed up to claim the vehicle, so he assumed it for himself, his distrust over its presence slowly giving way to his joy in possessing it.

In hindsight, Jay wondered how he'd ever justified keeping the vehicle, or how he would have explained it to Jacob, who would have been out of his mind to ride it. Finders keepers didn't cut it. Putting all the pieces together, it seemed unlikely that the machine and the body were unrelated. The question was, had it been left by the man in the field, or by the person who killed him?

A new theory surfaced regarding the deputy. Originally Jay had dismissed him as a complete rube, assuming the lawman had been operating on a misguided hunch, or else wanted a piece of the Mize family legacy. But as the picture came clearer into focus, it occurred to him that the deputy's visit might have been a setup. This corpse could just as easily be the deputy's handiwork. Maybe he had not been investigating a missing-person case at all but instead trolling for someone to pin this on. Who better than an outsider with murder in his blood? Once he'd found his mark, all the deputy had to do was dump the body in the owner's field, wait to get the call, or else just wander out when the water got low and make the discovery on his own.

Enlightened by this new wrinkle, Jay convinced himself he had to move the body immediately, this very night. It couldn't wait until morning if he hoped to avoid scrutiny—from traffic on the road, clever Hatcher across the way, rangers in the woods, or helicopters and crop dusters in the sky. Even satellites and unmanned drones observing the earthlings from above. Nothing could be left to chance.

He set off down the gravel driveway against the thrum of crickets and frogs and miserable birds. The red-lens flashlight allowed him to see only a few steps ahead. He'd purchased the light in town at the Army Surplus and Survival, where he made regular supply trips. The proprietor, who had humped up and down Vietnam on recon missions, told him the red beam was shorter than standard white. It didn't affect night vision and made it difficult for enemies to spot in the bush.

Jay used the light to find his way back to the willow, where he climbed inside the boat and untied the rigging. He switched off the light and pushed off into water so black and devoid of reflected light that he could only trust it was there and not some dream substance over which to row. He dipped the racket with delicate strokes, careful to make the tiniest of trickles, a sound impenetrable against the din of midnight. The boat nudged against something in the dark, and he shone his red light to reveal a scaly body floating facedown. His eyes adjusted. It was only drifting timber. A few strokes later something brushed his arm, a figure looming port side in the water, and he nearly tumbled out of the boat with fright. It was only his drowned tomato vines, planted in high dirt mounds and rising up like gray wraiths crucified on crossed stakes.

Halfway across the flooded field, he pulled down the gas mask and let the scent snag him like a towrope. He waved the red light over the water. There it was, just as he'd left it—half-submerged, broken and putrid in the terrible summer lake. A dozen or more frogs, feasting in a cloud of flies, bounded from the corpse's head as he approached. He pulled up his mask and sat there for a time watching it through the mud-smeared plastic visor, trying to win familiarity, wondering how he would accomplish what he had come to do.

The longer he sat and imagined it, the closer he came to talking himself out of it. He might be inviting more scrutiny, possibly even arrest, by moving the body. If indeed the deputy had planted the corpse here, would he, upon discovering it had disappeared, simply move on, relieved to find his deeds vanished? Or, once convinced of Jay's complicity, would he hone in and press for an investigation? Jay felt hemmed in, outfoxed by this cunning redneck. He'd been so distracted by his own misfortune and abandonment that he failed to see the trap that had been laid for him.

As he sat there appalled, with insects devouring him cell by cell and the rotten stench penetrating his mask, he settled on the only unassailable fact amid the tangle of bitter prospects—no body, no crime.

Jay stepped out into knee-high water, reached deep into his rubber pants, and produced the tarp. He unfolded it with deliberate care, wincing at every deafening crinkle, and spread it full inside the boat. He turned to the corpse, tried to study it with forensic interest. It could have been the black man from Ohio. Something in the remaining shape of the melted wax face. The skin was brown, but so was everything out here in the muck. He abhorred its lip-less, skeletal grin. All dignity had been erased from this person and hence from all humanity.

He was unsure what gesture to make toward it, unsure even how to make his body move in its direction. It was so grotesquely decomposed that he imagined it would fall to pieces in his arms like a slow-cooked stew bird. He tugged at its arm halfheartedly, but it wouldn't budge. He reached deeper for a grip on the torso, but it was snagged on something underneath and wouldn't yank free. He shoved and pried until the corpse wriggled as if it had woken up. A belch of obscene rot surfaced and slithered up under a broken seal beneath the mask. Jay turned and lifted the headgear and puked up his starving insides.

He walked away several steps and removed his gloves, dipped his hands into the water and brought the cool liquid to his face. His throbbing heart stole breath from his lungs. He heaved and thought he'd puke, but instead he burst into tears, a reflexive sobbing beyond his control, just the body performing a necessary function. It wasn't sadness for the dead man. He was too amped on fear and dread to summon the slightest empathy. Perhaps it was only emotional exhaustion or a tragic loneliness and bewilderment. What was he doing here? Would he have taken this same recourse had Sandy still been around? She'd always brought a calm sense of reason to his manic fixations.

And what about Jacob? What example was this for a boy? Would he be down here stowing a rotten corpse into their fishing boat if his son was up the hill, asleep in his bed?

He could find a million reasons not to do this, but then he noticed the subtlest shift of royal blue light on the horizon, the sudden vague outline of trees in the distance, and he was back on task. Night was escaping. Neighbors and scavengers would soon be on the move. One pair of eyes was as good as a thousand. The sun would rise and continue slurping up the lake, exposing the perception of a crime. Someone else had done this, but it belonged undoubtedly now to him.

– 6 –

The deputy barreled into Madrid on the old Silage Town Road at twice the speed limit, slowing only when he hit the curves by the college apartments. He craned his neck and waved to the sunbathers and power walkers. The prettiest young women in the entire South flocked here to attend the university and to gain popularity, maybe even find their first husbands. He'd known several of them intimately and was always a little love struck.

The sheriff had told his nephew, when he deputized him and turned him loose on the populace, "Keep one thing in mind. We're not policing citizens. We're policing friends, neighbors, and voters."

Headquarters was in town, but their jurisdiction was the county, and these two were distinct entities. Madrid—pronounced with a short "a," like the famous New Madrid fault line to the west—had filled up in recent years with spoiled college kids, liberal professors, weirdo strangers, and carpetbaggers trying to make a quick dime off local quaintness.

Change came slow beyond the city limits. The folks were sparse and scattered, still living by the old ways, still a bit wild and tribal. They didn't think much of strangers and were quick to scuffle, the women as much as the men. As neighbors, they'd either give you the shirt off their back or burn your house down. They were a great big dysfunctional family, and with family you gave special consideration:

Don't screw their wives.

Drive them home instead of giving them a DUI.

If they're underage, dump their booze and call their parents.

If they're high, confiscate their drugs, but make sure they're not trafficking. If they're selling drugs, then they'll need to sit awhile in Parchman.

If they're speeding, let them off with a warning, unless they're wasted, then see above.

If the plates are out of town, write your tickets and make your arrests.

Otherwise, unless they're making real trouble, let it slide. But always keep your eyes open.

As the eyes and ears of the Bayard County Sheriff's Department, Shoals found that the job came easy to him. He wore the badge like a backstage pass, using it for access and leverage and always knowing just how to play it. He had good ole boy charm and society skills, having done a couple of years at the university cultivating his fraternity airs. He mixed well with the country club set and the boys at the feed store. He wasn't policing so much as scouting opportunities, obtaining information, accepting gratuities—things like free rodeo tickets and comped dinners, use of a time-share in Orange Beach, the occasional canned ham or Cohiba cigar.

Cruising the back roads and currying innocent favors was all well and good, but lately Shoals was looking for more. His talent for extraction and manipulation, he believed, would serve him well as a detective. Driving back from Tockawah Bottom that day in early September, Shoals figured that Jay Mize had mistaken their brief exchange in his driveway for a ridiculous imposition. He probably thought the deputy was just out and about, scratching his ass, looking for a brush with mild local fame. He'd laid a fine cover, but he'd meant to confirm certain lingering suspicions and had indeed left with a better understanding of this man and this type of man in general. In the event their paths crossed again, Shoals might regard Mize as a humiliated grandson and a failed farmer and thus walk tall past his fussy intellect.

He detoured through campus on his way back to the office and tooted the horn at a crowd of young ladies bending into yoga poses on the front lawn of their sorority house. He never minded stopping at the lights and four-ways because he loved to hear the rumbling engine, to smile and shoot the citizens a grin or a thumbs-up, and every now and then he'd impress them with a little smoke and screech coming out of the intersection. He made a loop downtown, turned in to the city baseball field parking lot, and then coursed the side streets toward the municipal district, where the courthouse, fire station, and various police outfits made their headquarters.

He whipped into the department lot, claimed his reserved space up front, and cut the ignition. He liked to sit for a minute and listen to the Boss pant. The fire station across the street reared up in his hind view with the crude statue of his dad, Big Jack Shoals, looking over his shoulder. The Jackhammer, they called him, a true legacy. Few folks intimidated Danny, but that statue did it every time. A concrete god immortalized in helmet and suspenders, ax slung over his shoulder, boot propped up on a hydrant. No county servant was more revered than his pop, at least by old Madrid. Most any native over the age of forty-five could tell his own version of the day Big Jack and two of his men were killed by a collapsed mountain of burning cotton modules during the Cabbage Hill Gin fire of 1979. The whole town must have turned out to witness. If only those modules hadn't been aflame, Big Jack would have punched his way clear out of there, the old-timers told it. But there was no way to escape them lit ablaze, like a river of gasoline tumbling over him.

Shoals sighed and climbed out, strode into the station like a hero in the making. The dispatcher at the front desk—a wild, curt-tongued, and busty black gal by the name of Desdimona—buzzed him in, hollering, "Come on, wit'cha."

He passed through reception and stopped at her desk, leaned over to admire her cleavage. He reached in his back pocket and dropped the horseshoe on her paperwork. "Today's your lucky day," he said. "If you aint doing nothing after work, I can take you over to the Skyline Motel and tie your legs back, tap that in for you."

Desdimona cut her eyes up and waved her scimitar lashes. "I don't rope easy, Sugar, you know that," she said. "You wanna tie me up, you gonna have to wrestle my ass."

"What about can I lure you with an apple?" he said, stroking his belt buckle.

She smiled devilish and shook her head. "I can take that in one swallow. Then what you got?"

"Woman, I gotta whole mess of tricks for you," he said, locking eyes and pursing lips. "Whenever you decide to give me half a chance." He gave her a wink and an air kiss. He liked to play with that one, but she was all talk, strictly devoted to her man, Rocket, who had a car stereo place across town.

Shoals strolled the hallway, past closed doors and holding cells, around the bend to an office with a large plate-glass window. The sheriff was visible within, hunched over the keyboard of his ancient computer, pecking out some report or memorandum. He seemed out of place in an office and he was too gentle to be out running the field. He and Aunt Gil had been like second parents, helping raise young Danny after the Jackhammer's tragic end, always taking their turns on weekends, giving little Danny's poor grieving widow mother a break. He might have been a better preacher than a sheriff, but they were a family of public servants anyhow and aspired to answer their call with decency and fairness.

Shoals rapped on the jamb. "What say, Sheriff?"

The sheriff turned, defeated from his concentration. "Hey, Danny," he sighed.

"I went out to check on that horse wreck for you," he said, walking in and dropping into a chair. "Those Tennessee walkers made quite a splash on Highway Seven."

The sheriff frowned. "Well, it's a miracle no one got hurt."

"Yessir," said Danny. "I got another interview on our Ohio boy while I was out that way. This fella Mize near Silage Town. Mitchell Mize's grandson. Know him?"

The sheriff frowned. "Grandson of Mitchell Mize? No, I guess I don't."

"Real strange dude. Said he was from Memphis originally. Went to school here, lived in Madrid for a while, and just moved out to the bottoms."

"Did he know anything?"

"Naw."

"Hmm. Did Robbie put you onto that?"

"No sir. I found him myself."

The sheriff rubbed his eyes and tapped his fingers. "Well, you better give him what you have. I think he received some updates this morning on that missing person."

Shoals grimaced. It was Chief Deputy Robbie Bynum's investigation. Bynum was older, in his fifties, had come from the St. Louis city force several years back and talked himself right into the sheriff's good graces.

"So what's next?" Danny asked, hopeful. "You got anything for me?"

The sheriff looked away, half back at the screen, considering it a moment. He reached for an envelope on his desk. "Larry Reynolds wants you to come give your drug assembly in two weeks. The twenty-fifth."

School kids loved to hear Shoals tell stories of deadbeat drug pushers and the dangers of crossing the law. If it stopped one kid from going to jail, then it was a success, and it laid the way for favors later. "My calendar's wide open," he said. "Anything else?"

"I don't reckon, Danny. Just keep your eyes open."

It was his simple chief assignment, always the same. No more, no less, and he executed it well. That was fine. He'd have some lunch downtown and then head out to the state park, see if that pretty lifeguard was still closing down the swimming pool for winter, maybe finish up at the gym with some dips and lunges. Sometimes you had to make your own work.

Shoals got up and thanked his uncle, told him to just holler if he needed anything. On the way out, he stopped at his desk in the station room, where the deputies sat and filled out reports and took phone calls. Bynum was already there, king of the station. He'd pulled two desks together in the middle of the room and sat amid stacks of papers and files. His red hair had retreated to the sides, leaving a glowing dome on top, and he leaned to portly a little more every day.

"Got anything new on our Ohio BOLO?" Shoals asked, rolling in beside Bynum.

"Yes," said the chief deputy, putting up both hands. He seemed put out today and always a touch on the fruity side. "He is no more our problem. Our man's truck turned up in Rayburn County over the weekend, burned out in a field somewhere."

"He in it?"

Bynum cut his eyes up. "Who cares? He's out of our hair."

"Well, what if somebody stole his truck? You think he might still be hanging around?"

Bynum sighed. "Danny, I have no idea. But if Rayburn County wants to suck that teat for a while, they can be my guest. I've had my fill of it."

"I reckon the state takes it from here."

"Whatever," Bynum said, dismissive, focused on his computer screen.

Danny felt no need to reward him with the info on Mize. He'd keep that in his back pocket.

"You got anything for me?" Danny asked.

"Nope."

"Well, all right, I'm outta here," he said, clapping Bynum on the shoulder. "I've got some stakeout work to do. Maybe get a steak while I'm out."

"Why don't you go to the shooting range and brush up?" Bynum gibed as Danny was leaving. They never let him forget that he was the only deputy on the force not certified. Technically it was required within two years of joining the department, and he'd been on about six. No one checked up on it, and the sheriff must have believed he met all the major criteria—driving, self-defense, shooting—even though he'd never fired a shot on duty, just at some beer cans in the river. Hell, maybe he'd just look into taking the test, give the bastards one less reason to feel superior.

He ignored Bynum and leapt over the Dutch door into the hallway, blew Desdimona a kiss good-bye. "Don't be talking dirty to me over the radio this afternoon, Des," he called, pointing her out. "I'm liable to have something in custody that might get jealous."

– 7 –

Jay awoke to sirens in the driveway. He reached under the bed for the loaded twelve-gauge and lay there paralyzed for a time, flicking the safety off and on, waiting for them to burst in on him. But the house remained undisturbed. The benevolent white of day burned through the windows and a breeze fluttered the curtain. Birds conversed cheerily beside the window. It was only the Wednesday noon tornado drill howling over the county.

He exhaled and his pulse slowed to a cruise. For a moment he felt the relief of waking up from a bad dream, the subsiding fear and urgency like cold water over him. Then he looked down at his mud-streaked arms and legs, all the filth that had wiped off on the bedsheets, and everything came back. Surreal though it was, last night was no simple nightmare.

He had to will himself out of bed. Surges of adrenaline had scorched his muscles. He peered through the curtains to confirm that he was alone and flinched when he caught sight of himself in the mirror. Who was this madman, hair in shock and dipped in shit? Wild bloodshot eyes confessed a guilt more telling than words. Also there was an unconscionable stink emanating from him and his nest. Wet clothes moldered by the bed. In the reasoned light of day, he felt like a drunkard waking up in shame to the consequences of an impossible bender.

He fumbled through the house for a trash bag and filled it with clothes, boots, bedsheets, towels—everything that had come into contact with the body and the pond, everything he'd touched subsequently. It was all tainted. He filled the bathtub with tepid water from a rain cistern he'd rigged in the backyard, lathered up, and rinsed several times. From a jug of preboiled water he brushed his teeth repeatedly and then gargled and spat with the dregs of stale mouthwash.

With a soapy rag, he wiped down every surface he might have touched or left a streak of invisible evidence on—doorknobs, countertops, bedposts, chairs. He swept and mopped every floor in the house, working around waist-high piles of books and papers lined along the walls of the cramped hall-way and spilling off the shelves in every room, all hallmarks of an obsessive hoarder. The titles—on conspiracies, prophecies, speculative science, arcane and forbidden wisdom—suggested a dangerous, paranoid mind. He would burn them later, anything to return the house to a state of normalcy. Since Sandy had left and the rains had numbed him into inertia, the house had fallen to chaos, filthy and uncollected, every webby angle a catch for dust and death. That would have to change. This was the inner sanctum and must reflect the clear, tranquil mind of its owner.

He brought the trash bag outside and scanned the property, trying to see it through a detective's eyes. It looked like a weed-choked landfill, strewn with garbage, decaying furniture, tire piles, rusted farm implements, mounds of rotting compost, the blue plastic chemical drums that had raised even the deputy's witless suspicion. It only needed loose goats and chickens, maybe a few mangy, gimped-up dogs. He was living in a junkyard, like any common inbred bumpkin for whom death was an acceptable punishment for trespass-ing.

And thus the more pressing matter, rancid on the breeze, called his atten-tion. If anyone came within fifty yards of the toolshed, they would smell it. Hell, if the right wind came up, keen old Hatcher across the way might even get nosy and come to check things out. Tracks from the stolen four-wheeler, etched over the yard like fingerprints, drove right to the shed, and the buz-zards were bound to roost by afternoon.

In need of an upwind perch to consider his options, Jay scrambled up the hill and into the waist-high pasture behind the house. He sat on a clay outcrop and contemplated his predicament. He was unable to escape the notion that he'd conspired in a heinous crime. By the letter of the law, yes, it probably could be construed as criminal—tampering with an investigation and that whole bit. But there was nothing to be done about that fellow being dead. It was not as if he, Jay Mize, had killed the guy. Of that he felt quite certain. But it didn't matter that he'd done nothing morally wrong by moving the body from the field. No one would understand why he had done it, and that would be as good as wrong.

In any native culture, he reasoned, moving human remains from a flooded field to a swift burial site would surely be considered respectful. Of course, there were rites and rituals to enact. Here was the thin line between burying a man and hiding his body, and it was where the law would start their case against him.

But then again, he wondered, did the public really care about a stranger from Ohio, dead in a toolshed? Perhaps not. A brief shame, but then on to other concerns.

But if it was murder—and that would be the default assumption, right?—then the culprit must be caught before he struck again. This sort of violence was too much for the society to bear. But worse, an anonymous northern black man found dead in the county, harkening back to the old days. The old embers of shame rekindled. Better to close this case quietly without the old recriminations, best that someone should be imprisoned immediately and that no one should be required to second-guess the truth of his guilt.

Who fit the bill? Perhaps someone living on the fringes, someone who did not contribute to the system—a self-sustaining man, a loner living for his own benefit, who had rejected all the ways of society, including his wife and child. If they convinced themselves that Jay had committed this crime—and honestly, who made a better scapegoat?—and if they came for him with the strength of their combined convictions, then he did not stand a chance. Without friends to rally behind him, who would speak for his peaceful nature?

And once they realized the notorious Mize lineage, the story would be too perfect to deny. Hatred come full circle. Probably the news trucks would be here to give the whole world an opportunity to throw stones. Like some redneck Christ, he would pay for all the sins of Mississippi.

He didn't deserve to take the fall for this. He had too much good work still to perform. He suffered from personal shortcomings, certainly, but they were correctable, and his family—

A rustling nearby rousted Jay from his nervous rationale. He sensed something half-obscured and straining in the tall grass. The buzzard had returned. It was crouched in the grass before him, taking a shit right there as would any other flightless creature, vulnerable, slightly abashed. He took another step toward the bird. It gave a demented squawk, raised its gangly arms in defense, and scampered away. Jay walked over and studied the pile. The bird's grievous digestion had made an unseemly paste out of the dead man. This was someone once loved, now splattered in the dust like old gravy. If only Jay could find a method so efficient to dispose of the rest of him.

The possibilities intrigued him. He paced the field, trying to determine the necessary tack here. What would he do with any other dead animal? Bury it under lime? No, takes too long and leaves too much evidence. With today's high-tech crime-solving techniques, every molecule of it must be swept clear of the property. Every instrument at the county's disposal would be employed to catch him in a lie.

He sidestepped a hill of fire ants and considered them momentarily. He was certain they could strip a corpse bare, but he couldn't wait even two weeks for it to happen. Twenty-four hours was too long for comfort. Burning seemed obvious, but burning made smoke and smoke made stench. Boiling seemed unwieldy, improbable. He'd need a cauldron or tank of some sort, and what to do with the stew afterward? There was hydrochloric acid. That was how it was done in the movies. But where might one procure so much without raising suspicions? He was sure the stuff didn't come cheap.

Burning made the most sense. If anyone showed up, he could say he was burning all the fallen trees and limbs and washed-up river brush. But what about the smell? Fire would broadcast this damnable stink for scattershot miles. He could burn cedar or pine with it. It still wouldn't be enough to cover such a heinous aroma. He could build a filter to cull both smoke and scent. Maybe sand or gravel or charcoal briquettes.

And that's when it hit him—charcoal.

The ancient rain forest tribes of Amazonia had dug trenches and filled them with tree limbs, bones, and crop wastes. They set the whole thing on fire and buried it, letting the fire smolder underground. The resulting charcoal acted as a potent fertilizer, retaining the carbon in the soil for the life of the field, so long that modern archaeologists had uncovered strata of ancient crops still rich with fertile black soil.

It would require way too much effort to do it the native way, but with modern science, the process could be simplified. He'd read extensively about making charcoal, had seen the process performed at a bioengineering conference, and had even collected some materials with the idea of creating his own char as a natural fertilizer. There sat the fifty-gallon oil drum he'd bought at a junkyard for that precise intent, spilling over with trash out by the shed. It would require some outfitting, but he felt certain he had all the raw materials needed to build a backyard crematorium.

Jay scurried around the junk-strewn yard, a clearheaded eagerness about him now as he switched on his scientific mind. If he could render the body to charcoal, he reasoned, it could be pulverized easily, dust unto dust and so forth. It was more than achievable. It was brilliant. He might have failed at farming, along with so many other things, but he was still Compost Man. Perhaps now he'd found a way, however terrible, to earn back his true potential.

— 8 —

In town the next morning, Sandy Mize arrived late to her first-period English class. She swept in with the tardy bell and was startled, even a bit flattered, when her students met her with whistles and catcalls. She'd made herself late trying to look her best for a lunch appointment later that day. Her hair was in glamour curls, and she wore a new white tie-neck blouse and blue skirt with dramatic folds, a playful zigzag hem. She'd even put on heels and adorned herself with dangly earrings and scented lotion.

Passing before her thirty-odd seventh graders, she detected the tingle of their urchin eyes on her body, a hint of ridicule in their applause. She set an armload of newspapers on her desk and turned to stare into their primate ranks. Hormones and expectations filled the room like noxious gas. Snickers and whispers rebounded off the cinder-block walls. A desk leg screeched and someone snorted up a throatful of mucus.

Today is a new day, she reminded herself. Last night, rock-bottom in a vanquished tub of powdered donuts, she vowed to correct all the miscalculations that had brought her here, so many blind corners gone from where she needed to be. No longer would she simply let life happen to her. She would struggle back to normal and then advance toward the excellence she'd forsaken somewhere during the past year.

The spell was broken by a kid in the corner scooting his hand across the desktop, drawing a farting squelch from the laminate. The noise earned an equal clamor of praise and rebuke from his classmates.

"That's enough now, everyone settle down," she demanded.

"Miz Mize, why you look so nice today?" cried a girl up front, Balivia.

"I said *everyone* quiet!" She actually shouted at them and rapped the desk with the flat of her hand, surprising even herself. "Now take out your journals, please."

There followed a general murmur of disapproval. They probably thought she was a bitch for refusing the compliment, but Balivia's loud graceless pleasantries were insidious and had to be routed straightaway. To apologize or confess gratitude would show weakness. They were animals who would just as easily turn on her as seek favor.

The intercom crackled to life with morning announcements. A rotating cast of students and faculty read dispassionately of club meetings, upcoming sports events, birthday listings, and a prayer disguised as "daily reflection." The students listened halfheartedly, their restlessness creating a kind of vibration in the room.

Last year had been effortless. She'd shared a profound rapport with her students. Some of them still stopped by to visit and called out to her in the hallway. She'd been recognized as Most Outstanding First-Year Educator at awards day last spring, and some predicted she would achieve Teacher of the Year in three to five. But now, six weeks into the new year, she hadn't synced with these kids. They were still battling for trust that should have been won weeks ago. She knew it was her fault. When life was good, you were happy to share inspiration, but after the sudden disintegration of her marriage and the new squalid conditions she'd made for her young son, she simply hadn't been able to muster the will. It was like climbing a mountain each day with no prospect of reaching the summit.

But she'd revised her outlook. According to her father, it wasn't the peak she needed to appreciate but the climb.

By order of the intercom, the students rose and directed their attention to a limp dusty flag propped in the corner. She observed them, hands on hearts, awkward and fidgety as they droned through the Pledge of Allegiance, and then collapsed back into their seats, looking around to each other for validation or else down at their desks, striving for anonymity. She'd devised an assignment that might engage them, get them talking to each other and thinking for themselves. She gathered the armful of newspapers and walked up and down the rows passing out pages from the Sunday *New York Times*.

"There's a big world outside of Madrid, and I want to know what you think of it," she told them. "Just pick a story from your section and write about it in your journal. Whatever comes into your head."

Balivia rattled her paper, staring bewildered. "What's this word, Miz Mize?"

Sandy peered over her shoulder and recoiled.

"Drought?" she replied.

"Drought?"

"Yes." She worried Balivia wouldn't be able to comprehend the article if she couldn't read the headline. How did these kids pass from grade to grade without such rudimentary knowledge? She looked around and noticed similar confusion on the faces of other students.

"Just do your best here, push yourself," she said. "The only way to fail is by not participating."

The district discouraged teachers from touching students, so Sandy patted Balivia's desk. The wiry unkempt girl looked up, one eye bulgier than the other, and bared a baffled, candy-stained smile. Sandy winked in return. She thought the girl didn't mean to make trouble, only yearned for some validation that no one else in her life had cared to offer.

Sandy took a seat at her desk and watched them trying to make sense of the words. One of the girls in the back resembled Lila Jenkins, her best friend in junior high. She thought back to all those weekends she'd stayed over at the Jenkins house. Lila's divorced mother, Sissy, would come in from work like a hurricane, always on her way somewhere else. She'd have Lila mix her a drink while she ran from closet to clothes pile, cursing at someone on the cordless phone, burning their frozen pizza in the oven. Later, as the girls pretended to sleep, came the laughter and strange male whispers, followed by horribly adult moaning and creaking, gasps and slaps, the shouting and sobbing and slamming of doors—things a child shouldn't hear. They'd only wanted to play dress-up and be left alone with their sleeping bags and corn chips and R-rated horror movies, but Sissy kept exposing them to this futility of adulthood.

Now, twenty years later, Sandy had recently squirmed through one date herself. She'd wanted to prove that she could make it on her own without Jay. It was nothing more than a brief, awkward dinner, but it felt like a betrayal— against her estranged husband, sure, but mostly against her son, Jacob. If she was going to truly be single and wanted more than simple conversation with an adult, how could she ever bring a man like that back to their cramped apartment? What if Jacob were sitting up at night, listening to their groping and fleeting lust behind the bedroom wall? What kind of hatred would she be sowing inside of him? Already, at the age of six, he was facing life at a deficit. She shuddered to think what kind of man he might turn into, having witnessed his father unraveling.

Just then, out of the corner of her eye, Sandy caught her mentor and savior, Mrs. Puckett, walking past in the hallway. She jumped up to catch her and told her students, "Everyone quiet, let's pretend we have manners."

She scampered into the hall on precarious heels. "Mrs. Puckett!" Sandy called.

Mrs. Puckett turned and smiled. The tall, elder teacher was dressed in bland attire, an embroidered sweater and long denim skirt. They met halfway between their rooms. "My, don't you look stylish today," Mrs. Puckett said, brushing a hand against the fabric of Sandy's blouse. She detected something else in Mrs. Puckett's remark, just under the surface—*It's a bit much for school, don't you think?*

"Thanks," said Sandy. "I like your sweater."

Mrs. Puckett accepted the fib politely.

"Can I ask a favor?" said Sandy.

"What is it, hon?"

"I have to make a delivery at lunch today, during my open fourth period. I was wondering if you would mind looking in on my fifth-period class in case I'm a few minutes late?"

Mrs. Puckett tightened her lips and considered the request. "You know, Principal Reynolds is on the warpath about leaving kids unattended."

Sandy hadn't expected resistance. "I suppose you're right," she replied. "I just didn't want to go through the ordeal of calling in a substitute for five minutes."

"You know I wouldn't mind. I just don't want it to reflect poorly on *you* if something goes wrong. Turn your back for a minute and these kids will be at each other's throats."

That was a rather pessimistic generalization for Mrs. Puckett. Sandy smiled in the awkward silence and considered her options. She had to take her father to the doctor at 3:30, otherwise she could have run her errand after school. Regardless, this was an appointment she couldn't put off any longer. It was the first order of her new action campaign.

"Oh, but aren't you lucky?" Mrs. Puckett said at last. "I nearly forgot, there's an assembly after lunch. Tell you what, I'll keep my eyes on your bunch in the auditorium. You'll still need to get back as quick as you can, before the program ends. I'd hate for anybody to worry something has happened to you."

"Without a doubt," said Sandy, relieved. "Thank you, Mrs. Puckett."

"You're welcome, my dear."

There was an edge to her voice, a growing distrust. Last year Mrs. Puckett had been Sandy's greatest advocate, but there was no denying she'd cooled toward her this semester. And she wasn't the only one. Maybe this was how some women were treated after leaving a husband. Another teacher had warned her, after Sandy won first-year honors, "They'll be gunning for you now."

She returned to her classroom, and sure enough there was a commotion in progress. Sitting in the front row, red-faced and humiliated, Myla Robbins straightened her white blouse while Scotty Dawson behind her gave himself away with a sneer.

"What's going on?" she demanded. "Scotty? Myla?"

The girl tucked her head. "He was trying to turn my shirt around backwards."

"You did what, Scotty?" Sandy marched over to confront him.

"Ms. Mize, that wasn't none of me!"

"It was too! That boy done lied!" cried Balivia.

"Ms. Mize!" Scotty pleaded.

"Scotty, out of my room!" The class drew in a breath.

He feigned shock. "Ms. Mize, what'd I do?"

"I don't accept that."

A knock at the door drew everyone's attention. The gaunt rat face of Principal Reynolds hung there.

"Just the man we wanted to see!" cried Sandy.

The principal's beady gray eyes betrayed no emotion. He dodged his authority by stating flatly, "Ms. Mize, this police officer is here to see you."

Her first thought, always, was for Jacob. A montage of tragedies cycled through her imagination. The classroom broke out in scandalized whispers.

She swished into the hallway, where she was surprised and then relieved and finally mortified to see, leaning cool against a row of lockers, the deputy Danny Shoals. He wore a tight blue T-shirt with the words "Clean Living" rippling across his hard chest and abdomen. He shot a glance back at Reynolds's hunched silhouette slinking away and then straightened to attention. "My Lord, girl, you look pretty today. Didn't nobody tell you smoking aint allowed in school?"

She felt his eyes moving hungrily over her. He was the aggressively friendly deputy with whom she had shared the awkward dinner date some two weeks prior. Since then he'd turned up so frequently she feared he might be stalking her.

"What are you doing here?" she demanded in a whisper.

"I was invited to give an assembly about the dangers of drugs." He laughed like it was a joke between them. "Anyway, I thought I'd stop by and give you and your class a free preview."

"I don't think so, Danny, I'm—"

"Oh, come on, I want you to see how these kids react to me. You'll love this."

He walked around her and entered the classroom, clapped his boisterous hands and launched straight into his spiel. "All right, listen up! I'm Deputy Dan. You can call me County Dan, Doctor Shoals, whatever. I've been asked to give you this warning—there's a killer on the loose, in this very school. He's roaming the halls looking for his next victim."

Sandy cringed in the doorway, watching her students as their eyes went wide with terror. Some clutched their book bags, ready to run. They'd all been dreading the day when one of their peers brought Daddy's gun to school and made everyone pay for his teenage humiliation.

"All of y'all have heard about this killer. His name . . . is drugs."

The class breathed a sigh of relief, all murmurs and smiles. The deputy had them, and there was nothing Sandy could say to derail this.

"I know your friends will tell you it's cool, but believe me, I've seen plenty of dope pushers laid up in the jailhouse, and every one of em are exactly the same. Ugly, stupid, teeth falling out. Drugs make you do terrible things, like hurt people and steal stuff. And that's when guys like me step in. And let me tell you, buddy, I spare no punishment for drug pushers."

The deputy made tiger strides back and forth in front of the kids. They were all a little frightened of him and plenty interested too.

"I remember one old butter-toothed junkie, took a mess of drugs and beat up his own mama. We threw him in the holding cell and later that evening I caught him drinking out of the toilet like a dog! Look here, you don't understand . . . we don't hardly ever clean them bowls. Can you imagine doing something like that? Drugs will make you do it. Even things ten times worse."

The kids rocked in their seats and whispered to each other, their mouths open in wonder. This was real life, not some incomprehensible newspaper.

"We found him dead the next morning," Shoals said soberly. "Pooped his pants and drowned in his own throw-up."

He paused amid cautious laughter to let that image linger. Sandy wanted to escort him from the room, but then he might direct his wayward commentary on her.

"The killer had struck again."

The kids were all suitably impressed and shocked into silence, all but

Balivia, who cried out, "Deputy Dan, you need to arrest that boy right there." She stood up and pointed to Scotty in the corner. "He been acting mannish. Stretched that little girl's shirt right there."

Shoals wandered over. He gave Myla a tender look and then turned a scowl on the culprit sitting behind her.

"Ma'am, is that true? Did this boy stretch your shirt?"

The girl nodded and clutched the neck of her blouse.

Shoals stepped forward and loomed over the head-sunk Dawson boy. "That's no way to treat a lady, son. Didn't your daddy teach you that?"

The boy cowered in disgrace for his tribe.

"You wanna wind up like that old junkie, useless to the world? You gotta respect women so you can respect yourself. Think of every woman like your own mama and love her accordingly. Now what do you say to this sweet girl?"

The boy shrugged.

"Come on, now!"

Scotty leaned forward and issued a dribbling apology.

"Say it like a man who means what he says."

"I'm sorry for twisting your shirt, Myla," Scotty said with vigorous shame.

"That's more like it." Shoals shook the boy's hand and patted the girl on the shoulder, crouched down to whisper his own tender condolence. He stood and stepped again before the class.

"Y'all think about what I said about using drugs, now. There's a lot more where that came from. I'll tell you the rest later at the assembly, a'ight?"

The kids babbled affirmatively and set the room abuzz with anticipation for the full session. Shoals turned to Sandy, who had come into the classroom and stood by her desk. She could feel his eyes under her shirt.

"Boy, them two." He chuckled and nodded back to Myla and Scotty. "Wait till they discover what a powerful drug love can be."

Sandy flushed pink and crossed her arms over her chest. She'd gone mute and felt as though she'd left her body and was pinned to the ceiling by spitballs.

"Speaking of which," said Shoals. "I ran into your husband down around Silage Town. He didn't seem real put together. What's his poison?"

"Jay, you mean?" she stammered. "I don't know. What are you saying?"

"He seemed pretty reeled out on something. It's a good thing you took off when you did. Hard to watch a junkie take down his loved ones when he goes bad. An awful thing."

Surely he was mistaken. Jay indulged in a little pot once in a while, drank a beer or two in the evening, a couple of bourbons for a special occasion. But he was no abuser. She opened her mouth to defend her husband.

"Well, gotta get ready for my show," Shoals said and gripped her shoulder, gave her a few firm thumb strokes. "I'll drop by and see you sometime."

The deputy turned and waved to the kids, rallying good-byes and basking in their excitement as he strutted toward the door.

His retreat sucked all the audacity from the room, releasing Sandy from her dumb trance. She gripped her desk and took a seat. She neither understood nor trusted the sway the deputy held over her. Also she was skeptical of his assessment of Jay. He wouldn't turn to hard drugs, would he? She'd spent the past two months angry at her husband, but what if there was something truly wrong with him? He'd lost his wife and child after all, not to speak of his father. He was so eager to make his stand against a cruel, dying world, yet he'd let it beat him before it even placed a square blow. As she tried to imagine what was happening to him out there all by himself, a flood of shame and regret washed through her. Her eyes welled, her chest pooled with a numbing coolness.

The children, meanwhile, were still reeling over the deputy's performance. Their appraisal crescendoed, and out of the clamor came Balivia's proud wail—

"Ooo, Miz Mize. That man *like* you!"

— 9 —

The night conspired without flaw or remorse. A waxing moon tucked itself away into clouds that had jammed in late that afternoon, and the overblown chatter of frogs and insects put up a wall of protective ambience. Even a swarm of early blackbirds had descended across the road and over the next neighboring hill, shrieking their late-day diversion.

Out behind the Mize house, over the hillside and down into the pasture, a modest campfire burned in a little hollow at the edge of the woods. A glowing dome tent had been erected a few yards away. There appeared nothing amiss at the campsite but a devilish stench, followed soon by erratic shadows lunging forward and back across the nylon wall of the tent. Faint whispers and curses from within, an occasional grunt and crackling of plastic. A silhouette advanced in violent, aggravated rhythm.

Finally Jay exploded from the tent, breathless, as if shot up from the sea, yanking his gas mask aside and gasping for air. He stumbled out dribbling yellow bile down his chin and onto his gore-streaked apron. The hatchet fell from his hand, and he peeled away pink rubber kitchen gloves.

He went toward the high grass on the bluff in search of better air, but there was no escaping the fetor that cinched the hollow. He took up the thermos of clean water and drank deeply. His flesh crawled with imagined infestation, flies and larvae that were nothing more than sweat. He shed his clothing and doused himself with water to chase the smell and taste away.

His first impression of something remotely close to this had occurred about the age of six or seven—men squatting around a fallen deer brought down by his father or maybe an uncle or cousin; the men casually ripping into its belly with a knife, fetching up the sack of dark organs, disentangling the greasy handfuls from the sheath that contained them like plastic wrap; the shock of seeing this creature, which he'd only just admired for its fleet and agile body as it scrambled and flew from the wail of their guns, now without a flinch of life left in it, being dragged, jerked, hoisted, and bled, and the molten puddles of blood, brilliant red to black, swirling in the dirt as if his dad was changing oil under the truck. He'd known the mystery of this sudden gulf between the living and the dead, and when he asked his dad later *where did the deer go?*, his dad's answer, and all the church school stories that followed, could not adequately explain what he'd seen in those woods.

So who'd cleaned up the mess on the patio, he wondered, his father's skull and brains? Did the coroner do that, or was it hired out, some firm who specialized in suicide cleanups? He'd never truly grieved for his father, maybe because he couldn't stop visualizing the act itself—his father's half-blown-off face, his mother's horrible surprise, the hot tub's roiling pink water. The shock wasn't that it was unimaginable but that it was too imaginable. As if it had happened to him as well.

He stood and walked back, the smell of it under his skin, permanent in his head. Something like ripe garbage or rancid fat or burnt coffee. He stopped at the tent flap to muster the will, reapplied the gas mask and pulled on the gloves, found the hatchet in the grass, and ducked inside.

He reemerged from the tent some while later, calmer and more workmanlike, back and forth carrying plastic buckets. He placed them near the campfire, the wet contents shimmering. From one bucket a bone jutted up like a stick of gnawed wood.

He walked to the bluff and bathed his arms and face, scrubbed the gloves and hatchet, put on a fresh T-shirt and shorts, and tied a bandanna around his nose and mouth.

Pulling the man from the muddy field and hacking him to bits were just the beginning. Now he had to reduce the body to its finest elements and disperse them back into the world. To properly incinerate the remains, he'd have to generate as much heat inside the metal drum as possible. He'd punched draft holes around the top and bottom of the barrel, ensuring a nice flow of oxygen. To retain every degree of hot energy, he'd pulled duct insulation out of the attic and wound it around the inside of the drum, screwing it into place with pliable sheet metal.

If the drum was the oven, then his roasting pan was a five-gallon beer keg he'd found in the woods, probably discarded years ago by renters. He sawed off the head and filed the rim down to make a smooth open-top receptacle. He'd spent the evening shearing the bones from their stubborn cinches of ligaments and muscles, all fastened together with a sticky collagen that enveloped him like a spider's web, and now he crouched over the campfire in Neanderthal mode, throwing them on one and two at a time, turning them with grilling tongs. The smoke smelled like burning dung. He seared the bones quickly, his eyes watering even behind goggles, and the bandanna plastered across his face did little to buffer the stink. When they were ready, he took a boning knife and pared off the blackened muscle and cracklins into a bucket. At last he pitched the scorched bones into the keg. He managed to fit them all—the humeri and ulnae and radii; femurs sawed into quarters; severed spine, collapsed rib cage; detached cranium and mandible; two feet but only one hand, the other one gone missing, whether lost in the field or left in the boat, perhaps a preexisting condition. This troubled him faintly, but he moved on to the old crawfish-boil rig—a propane tank, burner, and forty-two-quart stockpot, tall enough to accommodate all the brown lumps, fatty sacks, and stinking ropes he'd spent the night unraveling. There was about half a tank of propane left to keep a fire burning under the slop. Enough, he hoped, to cook them down and render them unrecognizable as human remains.

The trick was getting the open-mouth beer keg full of bones upside down in the bottom of the drum without spilling. It took a few tries, but he managed it at last. He set the drum upright on bricks to get some air flowing underneath, and then he poured in bags of pre-collected kindling—twigs, wood chips, hacked-up branches, shredded books and boxes—packed all the way

Jamie Kornegay

to the top, forming a dense combustible layer around the keg. He pulled up a few shovelfuls of embers from the campfire and sprinkled them over the kindling and waited for a blaze to take hold. The twigs smoldered awhile and finally came alight. When the fire could stand on its own, he fastened the lid down and secured it with the bolt ring. He'd prepared a hole in the center of the lid and now placed a flue pipe over it and stood back skeptically as white smoke chugged from the top. It resembled a moonshine still or some backwoods meth cooker, certainly nothing lawful.

The hope was to achieve pyrolysis, whereby the insulated barrel fire cooked off all the water and hydrocarbons and leftover flesh from the bones in the keg. When the noxious gases escaped into the drum, they should combust and burn off clean as carbon dioxide and water vapor. It took a few nervous minutes with the contraption blowing a tall narrow plume of dirty smoke before it settled into an even burn, and only a wavy vapor and a wisp of steam every now and then emerged from the vessel. Even though he'd seen it performed, he couldn't believe it was actually working.

He sat in a lawn chair and admired his homemade stove, which did its work in relative silence, just quietly thrumming and pinging, popping now and then. A dark ring moved down the cylinder as the fire burned within. This and the occasional puff of dark smoke were the only evidence of the mysterious alchemy taking place within.

Hypnotized by the slow process, he dozed for a while, only to be awakened by the chattering cook pot. A cloud of vomitous steam erupted when he lifted the lid to stir and adjust the heat. He put in several handfuls of onion, rosemary, sage, and thyme to cover the stink, but the herbs did nothing to erase the sinful aroma, only identified it as something unfit for consumption.

At this point, his guilt was unquestionable. If someone wandered into camp with a common phone camera, it would be the sensation of the year. "Redneck Cannibal Massacre Caught on Video." He would be cast in the national lore along with school shooters, child abductors, and serial killers, the most reviled symptoms of a society gone amuck.

The horrible exertion of his chore had taken its toll on his body, and he could barely will himself to move. He just sat there in his lawn chair with this crude metamorphosis all around him, holding a murderer's remorse. If he could last until morning, he knew that, as with any successful experiment, the moral ambiguities of night would give way to the scientific certainty of day.

– 10 –

The rattling Maxima shot out of the school parking lot, across the highway and down through the residential neighborhoods, around the ball field to the little shitbox rental where Sandy and Jacob had spent the past month and a half. Sandy left the car running while she ran inside to get the dog and briefly considered changing clothes, something a bit more modest, but there wasn't time. She clipped the dog on the leash, led him into the backseat of the car, and aimed south of town.

They made jarring stop-and-go progress through the shortcuts and back-streets and stoplights and four-ways of Madrid, which had become a city crammed into a village. Ever since the university's football team started winning games and the rich alumni returned, the town could hardly accommodate all the traffic. The new coffee shops and bars and boutiques downtown were great, but the outskirts had become nearly impenetrable with strip malls, condos, big-box stores, quik-stops. It was increasingly difficult these days for Sandy to find her place in the ever-shifting landscape of her hometown.

Near the middle of town she passed the old Nutt Street sign, a little tilted among the otherwise straight-arrow neighborhoods. She glanced down the way but couldn't make out their old house. The new owners had overhauled the garden and taken out much of the landscaping and painted over the brick. Selling it was surely the worst mistake they'd ever made. Jacob barely remembered living there, even though they had photos and videos of Jay twisting them up in the hammock, chasing them around the baby pool with a rubber crocodile, launching sparkly firecracker disks all along the sidewalk. She missed their bohemian friends and the back-porch acoustic jams, cooking for writers and architects and professors. Such a perfect little life. They'd probably still be together if they'd never moved.

By the time she hit the city limits, she'd already lost fifteen minutes. The traffic cleared, and she flicked on her hazards and plunged over the foothills, taking the curves too fast. She'd driven each mile a thousand times and could run them all blind by now.

The first time she'd come out here with Jay to see the farm, she thought she'd seen the rest of her life. Sure, the house had no charm. It stunk of mildew and twenty years of tenant sweat. Repairs had been made hastily, quick fixes already undone, and the outside looked like a junkyard filled with the unhaulable waste of decades. But she embraced the potential. She imagined the glassed-in farm tower, the solar panels and windmills, the row of dogtrot barracks where students and colleagues would stay while they learned Jay's science and helped shape his vision. She never told her husband because it seemed so fanciful, but she harbored her own idea about developing a new township around his farm. Maybe they'd section off some of the property or acquire more and encourage friends to build. She saw a little commissary or fish house with a stage for live music. A pond, nature trails, corn mazes for the kids. Start from scratch and bring the city life they loved to the wide sensible country. Maybe one day she'd even be mayor of this place. Mizeville, or something more poetic.

As she came out of the hills and into the straightaway, the dog panted and simpered in the backseat. She invited him up front and let down the window a couple of inches to give him a snootful of breeze. The smell of water and woodsmoke spilled in, a whiff of clean mud from rutted pastures. The dead crops were fallen together in the fields, some of it blanched in heaps of sunlight like rotten gold. She passed familiar old shacks and brick homes and yards of old cars, silver propane tanks and trampolines and spray-painted tire planters. She used to make this drive twice a day and didn't realize how much she missed it.

She'd begun teaching last year just to bring in a steady check while the farm was getting up. Each day she would come barreling home like this to see what progress had been made. Often there were people there working with Jay. Builders raising the greenhouse or their neighbor Hatcher helping lay the irrigation pipes. Their contributions lent the project a sense of legitimacy and progression.

In the late afternoons and on weekends, she worked with them. She enjoyed being with her husband and sharing in the labor. He taught her to build compost and the importance of double-digging the beds. They raised seedlings under grow lamps set up in the dining room. They concocted liquid fertilizers by steeping compost in water like tea, studying a dropper's worth under the microscope and charting each potion's effect on the tender young plants. She began to see the value in this meticulous effort, and for a while it seemed they were growing something significant together.

When the shocking rift opened between them, it was like an earthquake that upends a village in a matter of seconds. Nothing could be taken for granted, she knew that now. There had been tremors, which she'd mostly ignored, but then Jay's father died that winter. Jay didn't want Jacob to attend the funeral, and so she stayed behind with him. Why hadn't she asked her dad to watch Jacob while she went to stand by her husband? She'd lost a parent and knew that devastation herself. It was nothing to suffer alone.

After the funeral Jay was a different person. At first, she found him brooding and withdrawn. He labored in his field without joy, as if it were penance. At night he holed up in his mudroom office, reading books on end-time prophecies, mass extinctions, and societal breakdown. She noticed him becoming more manic and tortured. She'd come home in the afternoon to find him sitting in front of the TV watching paranoid news shows, taking furious notes, and shouting back at the hosts. Once she stole a glance at his papers and found schematics for a network of underground bunkers behind the house and under the pasture. It looked like an ant farm drafted out in floor plans, little caverns connected by crawl spaces, each family member assigned a burrow. Had he moved them out here to set up a sanctuary for some vague doomsday notion, or was he building tunnels and hatches to stash arms for the inevitable uprising he'd been studying? Suddenly all of his obsessions, which she'd laughingly dismissed as quirks of his personality, had taken a serious turn.

She thought, *He no longer sees our life for what it is. Because his heart is broken, and he can't see through the darkness.* She gently encouraged him to visit a psychiatrist, an offer he bitterly dismissed. But there was something else, a sprawling new hubris, that diminished her sympathy for him and enraged her as he relegated her to the role of pioneer wife, just someone to cook and to clean and to be there with open legs when he came home sweaty and lustful from the fields. Here he was—mad artist, rough-hewn settler, and know-it-all prophet rolled into one—sliding off his rocker.

She could have stood a battle of wills, but she despaired for what it was doing to Jacob. A separation seemed unavoidable. Just temporary, a break from their overstressed life. She believed that a couple of weeks apart, an absence among fond hearts, would bring everything back into proper perspective.

But the relief of that absence nudged her toward greater independence. Two weeks became two months, and how was it that she'd only just made the decision to see him? And why was it all on her? He hadn't tried to reconcile their damaged marriage, hadn't even called to see where they were or how they were doing. The longer he remained silent, the more resolute she became. It was a clean break, or a standoff. She used their new routine in town as a buffer against the fact that her life had come unraveled, that she didn't know how to help her mentally unstable husband.

She'd watched his bank account drain, the utility and phone cutoffs, and waited in vain for him to respond. It shamed her to suppress her mounting dread. The past three days, she'd been sick worrying what had gone wrong, what had become of him. It was almost a relief to hear Danny's preposterous accusation. At least he'd been seen alive. Could it be true? Given all that he'd been through in the past several months, it wasn't a stretch to imagine Jay's self-destruction, or even a legitimate accident. He'd been killing himself with work the whole spring and summer anyway.

At the Grinder's Switch turnoff to Tockawah Bottom, Sandy was stopped by an ominous orange road sign set up in the turn. ROAD CLOSED TO THRU TRAFFIC. She idled in the intersection. Could he be reached?

She checked the dash clock. Thirty minutes had elapsed, and the assembly would start in thirty more. How could she have allowed herself so little time to confront the colossal mess of her life? Even if she found Jay, she would have to turn right around and come back. Just enough time to make things worse.

As she grew nearer to their former home, the realization struck—that she might arrive to find not her husband but his decomposing remains. It was in his genetic makeup—as it was in her son's now too—this potential to take his own life. It was nothing she understood or had ever considered. But when the world falls suddenly all around us, she wondered, can we truly be blamed for lacking the strength to keep from snapping in two?

– 11 –

Morning reeked of barbecue and damnation. Pyre smoke hung like haunted fog in the trees, and below, scattered across the pasture floor, lay evidence of his midnight science. Jay shot up from sleep and flopped out of the lawn chair. He found the water jug and turned it up, drinking past the taste of tepid death.

The char barrel was quiet nearby, its surface tarnished by oxidation. When he reached to touch it, it hissed and nipped at his fingers, and he drew back with a curse. He put on the giant gloves and removed the flue stack and pried the lid off. The packed kindling had burned down to ash in the bottom of the can. Little wisps of smoke escaped, and a roasty tang shot up his nose. He turned the barrel on its side, shimmied the scorched keg onto the ground, and sat it upright. The pieces were wedged in there just as he'd put them, and when he set the keg up they fell together in a chalk-stick clatter. Black powder rose and lingered like dust motes in the light. It was definitely charcoal.

He selected the cranium on top of the pile. It was lighter now and solid black. He pulled it close and sniffed, a burnt smell with still a whiff of the flesh. Shades of green and lavender were etched finely across its crystallized surface. The structure was intact, even the teeth, preserved perfectly in their upper sockets, and he plucked a molar and crushed it between his fingers, as brittle as a dried mud clod. He placed the cranium on the tarp, folded the sheet over, stomped it once, and then unfolded the plastic to find the skull in a dozen shards or more. He reached down for a broken piece, placed it on the end of a sitting log, and pounded it with the flat head of a hatchet. It went to grit in a few strokes.

He sighed in relief. He laughed. This was it, he'd done it. Cremated the body. Cooked it to its base elements. With just a bit of grinding, the man would soon be dust scattered in a thousand innocent directions.

He came to the cook pot, which had gone quiet too. The flame had expired in the night, and now the pot was barely warm. He lifted the lid and ladled up some of the black clabber. There arose from the fly-swarmed soup a fermented glandular funk, which made him crawl straight for the leaves and let his digestive tract wring itself out, all those recent sips of water and some old resident slime. He hadn't eaten in two days at least, and the hunger was having an effect on his stamina and balance. His organs were stealing nutrients from each other.

He stood up, pale white and shambling, emptied the contents of the keg into the open tarp, and sorted through the bones, breaking some with the hatchet and culling certain others that hadn't cooked completely. These would need a second run through the fire pit. He hacked the finished pieces into manageable shards and stored them in a dry plastic bucket, which he carried out of the hollow and over the pastured ridge and back down to the house. He cleared a wide surface under the carport and began smashing the pieces with a mallet. They broke easy but not fine, and each blow sent little shards skittering over the concrete. Anything less than powder was still evidence. He tried whacking them under plastic, rubbing them under sandpaper, clapping them under bricks and concrete blocks, but every friction made a greater mess. Dust blew back in his face, watering his eyes, filling his nostrils with black goo. He wished he'd bought that leaf and bark mulcher last fall. A hand grinder at least. He had to remind himself constantly what he was doing and why—rendering unto dust, playing God with a dead stranger, eliminating sin.

After nearly two hours he looked like a cartoon character caught holding an exploded bomb, all fried hair and soot face and glowing red eyes. His muscles were locking up, his mind going dim. He fell asleep right there in the grit and awoke from a brief dream in which wild dogs were tearing at his limbs. He slapped himself with a smeared hand and struggled to his feet, knees buckling. A sophisticated new hunger had beset him with irrational cravings. He went for a rope of onions drying on a porch post, pulled one free, and bit straight into it, spitting out the dusty paper coating and devouring the flesh like an apple. Its spice ran across his tongue and revolted in his belly. He stumbled into the yard for water and collapsed beside the cistern.

He lay on his side, slurping slow and long from the cool stream. He might have lightly dozed under the stream, a wet dream in the center of a waterfall, splashing in his ears. He felt himself sinking into a lake, becoming entangled at the soft slurry bottom, lungs engorged. There was a burning sensation, a bird feasting inside his nose, and he sat up suddenly choking, banged his head on the cistern. Dripping and hacking, he caught his breath and remembered where he'd been all along. It was this same inconclusive life. Heartbeat in his ears. A low crunch, a mechanical whirring. The unmistakable sound of tires on gravel. He turned off the spigot and stopped to listen. A vehicle climbed the driveway. They were coming for him.

He reached for the missing pistol in his waistband and then scurried to the tarp, folded its edges hastily, and shoved it beneath the Bronco. He made a break for the house just as the vehicle pulled into view.

The pistol was on the kitchen counter. He had just six shots, the spare bullets in his other pants. How many would there be? He craned his neck to peek through the window but saw only taillights. He heard a car door slam and ducked down behind the cabinets.

It wouldn't take them long to find everything they'd need to haul him away. But he wouldn't be going with them. No, he would prefer being slain in the front yard, maybe even take a few of them with him if that's how they'd like to do it. He refused to waste away in a cell for their mistaken presumptions. If it was punishment they sought, then they could take it all at once.

If it was guilt they required, then he was prepared to give it honestly.

- 12 -

Sandy coasted over the levee road. The world had come to ruin here—great lakes on either side of the road, even the field below their house. Just as Jay had envisioned it. She pulled into the driveway, stopped at the foot of their property, and stared at Jay's field, just a big puddle. There was a large brush-stroke where the water had swept in and the burnt edges where it was retreating. The river had always been just an idea to her, silently looming out there on the periphery, but now it had claimed almost everything—the greenhouse, the tractor, all the canted fencing and crooked stakes and naked framework.

She thought of last fall when Hatcher had brought them the iron fencing, a piece he'd found at the landfill up the road. It was the missing trellis for their cucumber and melon wall. The neighbor helped them stake and raise it. Afterward they sat in the dirt with cold beers in their hands, the first timid bite of winter on the air. She recalled the peculiar pink grapefruit quality of the light in afternoon, Jacob tumbling over the blank rows in boots and flannel. As a joke, Jay had planted a bed of broccoli in the shape of Mississippi with a magnolia-shaped cluster of cauliflower in the middle, and he basked in Hatcher's approval. *Call me when you need a hand, I'm all yours*, Hatcher had promised. *And by yours, I mean Sandy's.* They'd smiled and watched the sun set on everything.

How could they have gone so long without talking? Her stomach pooled with dread as she put the car in gear and lurched up the driveway. The place looked unattended, possibly abandoned. She thought she wouldn't find him here, at least not alive.

She pulled up to the carport. The Bronco was still parked there, so he hadn't gotten far. A shadow darted out from behind it. She cut the engine and opened the door to get out, but something was not right. There was an eerie burnt stillness. She closed the door and rolled down the window. "Jay!" She called him again.

He emerged gradually from the shadows a moment later, barefoot and shirtless into the light of day, this wild-haired, sunken-eyed grisly specter of death.

When she saw and believed it was him, she felt a blush of relief that he was alive, if barely. Was he sick? Was he insane? Certainly malnourished. It occurred to her that Shoals might be right, that her husband was strung out. She thought she might have to leash him and get him into the car and back to town for rehab.

He walked over nervously and ducked to peer through the window, first at her and then at the dog whimpering in her lap, lunging to get out. He had the halting, brittle posture of someone just sprung from solitary confinement.

"Sandy?" he said with dumb uncertainty, as if they hadn't seen each other in twenty years. He smelled terribly of onions.

"Who did you think it was?"

"Well, what— What are you doing here?"

He seemed terrified. Was he shacked up with another woman, some peroxide-blond meth skank? That was all she needed to move ahead with a divorce.

He stood upright and ran a hand through his clumped mess of hair, trying his best to recover. "I wasn't expecting you. It's been . . ." He fumbled with the car door handle but it was locked. "Where's Jacob?"

He stepped back, and she wrenched open the door, which squealed for grease. She got out and straightened herself, stood awkwardly for inspection. His eyes scurried over her, trying to discern his friend and lover. She softened toward him, despite his dreadful appearance.

"You look like hell," she said with frustrated concern.

He inspected himself, torn and stained shorts, crust and grime etched all down his skin. His hair and beard practically declared him insane. He gave an exasperated snort. "I do?"

"Jay! I can see your skeleton!"

He looked back at the carport. "What? What are you saying?"

"I'm saying, you're skin and bones! Are you not eating?"

She wanted to take him home and clean him up, feed him, phone in sick the rest of the day to care for her child of a husband. But there was something wrong here. "It smells weird," she said.

"I know," he replied. "I burned a deer in the pasture."

"What?"

"It died, I had it in the shed back here and it smelled horrible so I took it out there."

She withdrew unconsciously against the car.

"It must have died in the flood. I don't know if it just wandered up or somebody hit it with a car. It was the strangest thing, Sandy, you wouldn't believe me if I told you . . ."

"Relax," she said. "I believe you."

"Okay."

She asked him about the flooded field. "Did it reach the house?"

He told her that it had not flooded near the house, though she wouldn't have guessed it with all the trash flung about, the dead grass and the mud-slide face of the hill out back.

"Where's Jacob? How come you didn't bring him?" he asked.

"Jay, I— He's at school."

"School? Already?"

"Yes, we both are! For like over a month now!" He had a drugged vacancy that annoyed and worried her. She dared not mention the deputy's allegation.

"How's he doing?"

"Jacob?" she asked.

"Yes!"

"He's fine . . . considering."

"Considering what? What's wrong?"

She sighed. Now that the shock had worn off, and she was relieved to find him alive, she could vent her anger. "Considering that he's moved into a shitty rental and hasn't seen his father for almost two months, and his father hasn't cared to visit or even call or to write and ask about him. That's been a little confusing for him, Jay!"

"I—" He stammered, trying to lob something back. "I didn't leave!" he cried. "I didn't walk out on our life here! *You* walked out! You took him and you left me here to deal with this alone! *You!*" He wagged a dirty finger at her.

"We had an agreement, Sandy. We were supposed to do this together. You left me holding the bag, and now you send a . . . a . . . a fucking *divorce lawyer* out here . . . without a word of warning?"

"What lawyer? Get real! I've sent no lawyer. I can't afford a lawyer. When would I have time to arrange that? I've had to make a new life for me and Jacob!"

He squinted in disbelief.

Here was the Jay she'd fled, bound up inside a withered husk. "And what have *you* been doing?" she demanded.

His eyes went wild and rolling. He spun around, speechless, unstable. "Ha! What have I been doing? Well, let's see . . . Do you really want to know?"

"No, I don't think I want to know," she said, seething now. He wouldn't be let off the hook, no matter how poorly he seemed. "You've let this place slide all the more to hell, and then look at you. You can't even take care of yourself."

Her words had twisted him appropriately, and he'd gone all twitchy trying to form a rebuttal. This wasn't how it was supposed to go. This was to be a reconciliation, the beginning of the mend.

She opened the car door and released the beagle, which jumped out and drilled Jay in the crotch with his snout.

"I just came to make a delivery," she said.

Jay pushed the dog aside and watched him dart around the yard, taking in all the exotic and old familiar scents.

"I need you to keep Chipper," she said. "Jacob needs you to keep him."

"Why?"

"My landlord won't let us have him."

"Your landlord?"

Sandy sighed. It was as if he'd woken up from a coma, never imagining that any time had passed since they were last together.

They stood in awkward silence, watching the dog scramble around the yard, nose down, lifting his leg now and then to squirt his claim, and finally disappearing over the hillside into the pasture. Jay watched him with a pained grimace, as if terrified at the prospect of keeping something alive besides himself. She popped the trunk, retrieved a giant sack of dog food, and heaved it into the yellow grass next to the driveway.

"You don't seem well," she said. "Can I get you some help?"

He stared into the yard with a lost gaze, nibbling his lip, scratching violently at his head and body. Was he even listening?

"Are you on something, Jay? You seem high or strung out."

He shook his head. "How would I get drugs? I can't even afford to drive into town."

"Yeah, the electric company has been calling to collect the bill here. I can barely scrape mine together, I can't support you too."

It was a bit of a fib. Sandy's father had been helping them. She could have paid enough maybe to get the lights turned on, the water up and running.

"When are you going to get a job and start acting like a grown-up again?" she wanted to know.

"Do you really want to help, or did you just come here to further humiliate me?"

She'd come here to save him, hoping that he'd come to his senses. Hoping they could put their life back together because this wasn't good for any of them. Obviously they were only capable of functioning as a unit.

"I told you," she replied. "I came to drop off the dog."

His eyes glistened and swelled. "I'd still like to see him, Sandy. I just . . . if you knew what I've been dealing with." He rubbed his face, which appeared red and ready to slide right off his skull.

"I should really explain something. What I'm dealing with here, what this flood has brought . . . I'm not sure I can even . . ." He gestured wildly with his hands. "Look, before when you left, that was one thing, but this is . . . it's entirely different. There are things that will never be fixed. I've done—"

"It's all just *stuff*, Jay. And besides, I don't think you need to worry about fixing this right now. You need to get your hands in something structured and earn some money until you get back on your feet."

He inspected his hands. "I don't think you—"

"Why not ask Hatcher if he has any work? Or better yet, go back to the agency and ask Burt Petit for your old job back."

His eyes cut into her, slashing up and down until it made her uncomfortable. "God almighty," he said, "you look so good to me right now."

She couldn't help but laugh and had a compulsion then to embrace him, to let him know that she hadn't given up on him completely. But he was so grimy, and then she imagined the bell at school ringing and knew the kids would be crowding into the auditorium, and she'd bought all the time she could with this. He was fine, he would survive.

She apologized for having to leave so soon. They shared a fraught silent moment in which anything could have happened. A quiet tension shuddered between them.

Finally she climbed back into the car. He crouched down beside the open window and stared at her, reached out and pulled down her sunglasses.

"Sandy, you *can* help me."

He worked up the nerve to say something. She thought he was going to ask if he could come with her.

"Give me ten dollars for gas. I really want to see you and Jacob."

Unflinching in the face of his crypt breath and jittery eyes, she judged his sincerity, considered telling him to get in the car and come now to see him. Instead she sighed and dug into her purse for a twenty. He took the bill and inspected it. "Thank you."

"Just come see Jacob."

"I will, I promise."

"And take a bath, for God's sake."

He sniffed himself and frowned.

"A shave wouldn't hurt. You look like a festival groupie."

She gave the car several wheezing attempts to crank.

He sat back on his haunches and smiled. "You're right, I'm gonna be okay," he said. "I'm just tired, worn out. You're right, as always. I've been working too hard. It's gonna take a lot to get everything back in shape, but you'll see."

She dipped her brow skeptically.

"You wouldn't know it now, but at one time during all of this, it was really beautiful out there," he said, nodding down the hill. "The entire front field shimmered. Like the lake house, remember?"

Many years ago, before Jacob, a friend had let them spend two weeks at his lake cottage in Michigan, two of the most relaxing and enjoyable weeks of their entire relationship. Since then it had served as a touchstone for when times were tough. A better life was only a two-week vacation away.

She nodded up the hill. "What's he into?" The dog bolted over the bluff, carrying a large blackened stick, possibly a bone. "What on earth is that?"

"No," he hissed and ran after the dog, shouting and waving his arms, chasing him back over the hillside and into the pasture.

She waited a moment for Jay to return. They'd been on the verge of acknowledging something, but in typical fashion, he'd run off into his field. She gave the car another crank and it sputtered to life. She maneuvered a turn and was headed back down the hill when she heard him shouting. He came running into the rearview.

He ran up beside her, breathless, keeled over and barely able to stand. "That's funny, Chipper had a deer bone."

"Jay." She smiled. "I gotta go."

"Okay," he huffed. "I'll see you . . . in a day or two."

"I hope so."

She drove away and then stopped short, put her head out and looked back. "By the way, you remember we used to laugh at that teal house sticking out like a sore thumb on Waller, across from the baseball field?"

"The shitbox?"

"Yeah, that's the one. We live there now."

He winced.

"I know, right," she said, pulling away. "Nowhere to go but up."

— 13 —

Jay waited until she was out of earshot and then drew trembling aim on the dog as he dragged the tarp by his teeth around the yard in proud loops. The dog had almost blown his cover. Having him here was a needless risk and complication. He could just run him out into the pasture and shoot and burn him. Would he be able to look his son in the eye and tell that lie? There were many ways, after all, for a country dog to meet an untimely end.

Jay lowered the pistol, released the hammer, and tucked it down the back of his shorts. He loved his son too much to shoot this dog, even if he'd become a man who would contemplate murder for nothing less than irrational fear.

He whistled and Chipper came taunting ten feet away. Jay poised and clucked his tongue, drawing the dog a few feet closer, and then he threw himself on the tarp and ripped it from the pup's mouth. He snatched the dog by the leg and Chipper yipped and tried to pull free, but Jay had him. He was still small enough to cradle like a baby. The pup surrendered, tucking his ears back, smacking his wide mouth, a confused look of love or terror in his black eyes. "Why does that boy love you so?" Jay asked Chipper, who answered with a tentative wag of his tail.

He put the dog in the mudroom with bowls of water and kibble and came outside, where he sat in a lawn chair and closed his eyes and listened to the dog yelp. It wasn't Chipper that troubled him, though he created a distraction and new potential for mistakes. After all, there was a smoldering pit over the hill waiting to earn him a life sentence.

Seeing her again had shaken him awake from this ridiculous dream he'd been living. Their paths had diverged, and he couldn't even recall where or why. He'd wanted to tell her everything and might have spilled his guts except he couldn't risk losing her again.

He wondered, had she fixed up her hair in those wild curls just for him, or was there someone else now? The whole time she was standing there—hiding behind sunglasses and a forced scowl, her sharp nose and those randy disapproving lips—he'd wanted to throw his arms around her, almost in anger, an impassioned anger. He imagined she would smell different, like a musty rental, or perhaps a new perfume. He wanted to sniff out her true scent, buried deep in that styled hair and soft neck. She seemed fleshier to him, like town living had filled her out. He imagined the unfamiliar doughiness of her arms, the press of strange fabric. The blue pilot light flaring inside them both, reigniting with a whoosh. Prickly legs from a two-day stubble. Inhaling without permission her bare pooch, dusted with fragrance, like warm bread to a starving man. It was a simple peace, this image of a last-ditch carnal frolic across the hood of a dusty Maxima, but could everything have really been saved in just that instant, slipping back into their old impassioned ways?

Blood rushed from his head to his lap and he stood up dizzy and shook off this fantasy. Her visit had also confirmed his fear that anyone could drive up out of the blue and catch him in the act. There wasn't a moment to waste. He had to strike the campsite, get rid of the drum and keg. There was so much left to burn—the tarp, the half-baked bones and sacks of soiled clothing, both his and the corpse's. The boat tied to the willow tree, the missing hand. All the tools and machinery, which he'd have to either clean or destroy. The shards of bone in the bucket and in the tarp, waiting to be broken, just sitting under the carport where any joe looking to borrow putty could find them.

He stomped over the hill and into the pasture and back down to the scorched, foggy hollow with his neck hairs on end, as if he'd encroached on the scene of some ritualistic killing. He gathered up the scattered leg quarters that the dog had pulled from the ashes. Maybe Chipper wouldn't mind refining these cold organs if he was so hungry. Jay held his breath as he poured the chum into a bucket. Some of it splattered on the ground. He'd have to come back with a shovel and collect this ground. There was plenty to get. The whole site was a crime scene.

He lugged the bucket over the hill and down to the house. Under the carport he pulled a pie tin out from beneath a pot of mint leaves and poured up a dish and then released Chipper from the mudroom. The dog ran around, sniffed the pan, and then lay down at the far end of the carport, panting, tipping his brow up now and again. "Must be nice to be so full of chow, you little satisfied bastard," said Jay, dumping the gruel back into the bucket.

The hunger was on him again. He opened the door to the exterior utility room and checked the deep freezer for leftover game. He'd rigged this freezer up to a solar power grid on the roof that generated just enough wattage to keep his supply of venison and fish and vegetables frozen. But the freezer's motor had been dying for a week or more, rattling like a golf ball in a tin cup, and now he heard nothing. He raised the lid and peered inside. The frost barnacles were shrinking like the polar ice caps. A memory of deer steaks drew a squall deep in his empty belly. It would have been nice to grill up those few last fish, but they were all caught from the spontaneous pond, and the thought of eating them now pained him more than his own hunger. He opened a freezer bag and pulled one out, still frozen. Judging by the little fish-lip divots on his dead man, schools of these river fish had feasted on the corpse. He shivered at the thought of how many he'd eaten fresh. And what about the bridge fishers who'd camped out on the margin of his field and cast their lines into his pond and stolen his fish? How many of them had eaten scraps of the dead man? An entire cast of county deadbeats were complicit in this man's disappearance, carrying the evidence in their cells.

He found an ice chest and pitched in every bag of fish from the freezer. He placed the bucket of stew inside and closed the lid and retraced his steps from late yesterday afternoon until Sandy's arrival, performing a cursory sweep of the property to find any evidence in need of elimination.

He fetched a shovel and bucket and scooped out the dirt floor at the back of the shed where the body had sat for an entire day, and then he went out and dug the pasture ground where he'd trampled and dripped and spilled.

He filled buckets of dirt and even the hot coals and ash from the fire. The gut buckets, the tools, anything in need of scrubbing. He had to get it all to the river for washing and disposal.

Jay pushed the four-wheeler from the shed to the driveway, up close to the Bronco. Now that he had a little cash, he could afford to share the last of the fuel. With a hatchet, he lopped a length of garden hose right off the dry spigot and began siphoning gas from the truck to the four-wheeler. He dipped the hose into the ATV tank and let it drain for a minute, tried to crank it with no luck, then fiddled a bit with the choke, gave it some more juice, cranked it finally, and let it rumble. He loaded the cooler and several buckets onto the rear rack, fastened them with the bungee cords, then climbed astride and set off for the river with Chipper in pursuit.

Jay traveled a series of paths through the woods and came to a spot along the river with a shallow bank that would be easy to maneuver. He switched off the ATV and stared at the water. It ran high and fast and full of debris, not only tree limbs and logs but buckets, tires, paint cans, plastic soda bottles, a half-inflated pool raft. He saw a tube fluorescent lightbulb slide by, miraculously intact. How much had been swept away by the retreating flood and how much had been simply tossed in by the criminally stupid and lazy?

Aggravated by the state of the land, he climbed off the cycle and began to unstrap the buckets and cooler. He hissed at Chipper, who was tromping through a mudhole. The current would whisk him away if he ventured too far. Jay gathered the buckets and was preparing to dump them at the water's edge when he heard a scuffle in the leaves behind him. He found Chipper tangled up with another dog, a larger, savage-looking animal. If not for the collar, he would have assumed it was feral.

Jay looked around for an owner. He called out. Maybe someone was nearby relieving himself or slow to catch up. He strained to hear a response from someone in the brush. There was only the frantic flow of the river and birds chirping in the forest. Maybe the dog had wandered away from a neighbor's, or someone had dropped it off on one of the country roads, too old to care for anymore. He called out again.

Surely the dog belonged to someone. It stared at him with wild suspicion but also the look of an expectant pet. It was hungry. Jay waited an anxious moment and then fetched the gut bucket and pie plate and poured a dish for the strange dog. It showed no restraint, going straight for the gruel.

Jay knelt down in the leaves and watched the animal gobble up the cold mush. It reminded him of Daisy Duke, his childhood dog. A German shepherd with big gnawed ears, a silly old sad-looking mutt. Daisy Duke had come home from the woods one day stinking of skunk spray, her leg injured with teeth and claw marks. The wound never healed, and the dog got sicker and sicker, couldn't keep food down. Her uncomfortable eyes went rheumy and possessed, and her behavior turned strange and volatile. Jay's dad told him it was rabies and that the dog wouldn't live long. He took Daisy Duke out for a long walk one day and came back alone.

Chipper became interested in the stew and stuck his snout in to inspect. The strange dog snarled and bared its fangs, running Chipper back to cower and pout. Something about the dog's aggressive satisfaction with the meal, the exaggerated lip licking and grunting and burping, disgusted Jay. The rotten teeth, the patchy mottled fur, the one red weepy eye swollen shut. He poured the dog a second plate, which it devoured and then came sniffing around again, even licking the rim of the bucket. The organs were gone.

Would the dog follow them home now, expecting a warm place to sleep and dinner too? Or would it wander home and raise the suspicion of its owner when it sprayed heinous diarrhea all over the patio or the living room rug? The dog licked its chops and belched. Jay wondered if DNA could be extracted after running through a dog's digestive system.

He reached out to pet the dog's head and let it sniff him. He rubbed it under the muzzle and felt the jaw tighten. Maybe the dog was still hungry and had developed a new taste for man, he considered. If the dog became aggressive, he wouldn't have the strength to fight it off.

Jay pulled off his T-shirt and wrapped it thick around the dog's crown and reached back to his waistband. The balled-up shirt muffled the pop of the .38. It was like someone else had done it.

He watched the animal collapse and shiver in its last spasms. Blood chugged from the wound and into the leaves like spilled milk. Chipper sniffed and whimpered with confusion. Jay booted his pup back and grabbed the dead animal by all four paws, twirled, and tossed it into the river.

He stood at the water's edge and watched the animal sink below the water. He thought, *This is how it soon will be.*

After society's collapse, men will be forced to do things that their civilized minds would never have imagined. Decency and decorum, the lives of others—all will be expendable in light of your own survival and that of your family.

PART
II

PART

II

The woodsman, whose name was Leavenger, wrenched his ankle climbing out of the river. Streaked head to toe with mud, he left his pants and hat on the bank and limped through the woods with only his shirt and pool cue. Dusk beat him to the pasture where he'd parked his camouflage truck. He was hobbling around and punching the panic button on his key set, unable to locate the vehicle in the high grass. Then he stepped in a divot and finished off the ankle. Writhing on the ground, with no one at home to worry over his whereabouts and his only love, Virginia, now sunk at the bottom of the river, Leavenger regretted that he'd left his gun behind or else he might have ended it all right there in the weeds. But then he heard the far-off truck horn and slithered like a beast out of Eden toward the blinking headlights. He groped his way into the passenger seat, situated himself atop the inflatable donut, and drove out cross-legged, half-drunk and heartbroken, to the emergency room in Madrid.

At the hospital they wrapped his ankle and assigned him a pair of crutches. The doctor assured him it was just a sprain but might take longer than normal to heal due to his wilted legs and reprehensible diet of drive-thru fare and cigarettes and cheap canned beer. They gave him a sedative and a bed for the night, and after they discharged him the next morning, he stopped to have a smoke with some of the other patients milling around the concrete patio by the front entrance.

As such conversation is struck up outside a hospital, he began relating the details of his injury. The other patients, in their threadbare robes and grimy tracksuits, sporting week-old beards and terminal bed-head, pulled close and listened to Leavenger's exaggerated account, first of the ruptured steam pipe at the oil mill and later the mysterious man and the killing of his dog, and, strangest of all, the release of frozen fish back into the river. It was a fine story, refreshingly different from the litany of complaints against doctors and nurses and insurance providers. While many ignored him, some pumped him for more details and offered their condolences for the dog at least. The consensus suggested that he find that SOB and make him pay. The more often Leavenger told his story, the more outraged and persecuted he felt.

And so, over the next several days, he made the hospital courtyard a regular stop on his route through town and country. It was a good place to gossip and rant, and he came to know some of the same tired sufferers who dragged themselves out to get a breath of fresh air or to smoke or make a phone call or to smuggle in decent food from delivery cars.

On the first day of October, Leavenger made one such customary visit to the hospital courtyard. He took a seat on the stone bench and waited to bend someone's ear. A pruned woman in a flimsy nightgown, scooting around with a wheeled IV and a bored nurse in tow, was too concentrated on walking to speak to him, and he became annoyed by a young black man who strutted up and down the courtyard, gesticulating and speaking loudly, presumably into the hands-free phone wedged in his ear. Leavenger moved over to a familiar gray fellow in a wheelchair, Emphysema Ollie, who bummed a cigarette and complained about the oxygen tank strapped behind his chair. His insurance had lapsed after he was laid off at the pallet factory. He'd been in ROTC in high school ages ago and hoped he could pick up some latent benefits.

Leavenger snorted. "I hope you don't expect the government to pay for it, cause they aint." He leaned in, conspiratorially, and stated loud enough, "You're the wrong color. Now if you were black, I bet they'd just write it off. That's how they do, you know."

"Hold up, hold up," the young black man said. He leaned over to Leavenger. "Hey, you got something to say about something?"

"Hell no, I'm not talking to you!" Leavenger cried, indignant. "Don't you see me talking to this man here?"

"Naw, man, just some old white dude talking shit about some shit. It aint nothing." The young man walked away, back into his own chatter.

"Shit *I'm* talking?" Leavenger cried. He leaned in to Ollie. "Hell, I don't even know what language he's speaking."

The young man kept cutting his eyes over to Leavenger, which made him nervous, so he pulled himself up and lunged away on his sticks. He'd gotten as far as the hospital entrance when he crossed paths with Shoals, the deputy sheriff, carrying a big bouquet of flowers and a balloon.

"What's happened to you now?" the deputy asked with a grin, as if the woodsman's misfortune were a frequent and hilarious occurrence.

Leavenger was not amused. He motioned down to his bandaged leg. "Broke my goddamn ankle."

"Were you drinking?"

"No," Leavenger lied. "I fell trying to climb out of the river down in Tockawah Bottom."

The deputy became interested. "What were you doing down there?"

"I'll tell ya," Leavenger said. He shuffled away from the automatic doors, which opened and closed like a defensive bird flapping its wings. He leaned against a garbage can and pulled a cigarette, lit it and puffed, catching his breath.

"I was down there walking my dog, checking things out. You know it flooded that whole bottom."

"I'm aware," the deputy replied.

"Okay, I was tramping around down there, scoping it out before bird season starts up, and I got overheated. So I walked down into the river to cool off when this fella comes riding up on a four-wheeler. Crazy damn look in his eyes. He's got his rack loaded up with all kinda stuff, he's shuffling around at the river's edge all wild and suspicious. Then outta nowhere, the son of a bitch up and shoots my dog."

"Shoots your dog?" the deputy asked, more in disbelief than dumbfoundment.

"Shoots her a few times and kicks and spits on her, then pitches her off into the river like a sack of trash."

"What'd you do?"

"Nothing, hell, I was hiding in the water under some limbs. I thought he might shoot me next."

"What'd he look like?"

Leavenger shrugged and winced, trying to climb out of his own embellishment to recall the man's features. "I didn't see him all that clear, but I know he had a big hat. A thin rascal. I probably could've taken him if I'd had pants on."

The deputy raised an eyebrow. "Whereabouts was this exactly?"

Leavenger's eyes got wide and stymied. "I don't know exactly. Off behind Mel Fellows's place. Way off prob'ly. Just down on the river there back of his."

"Mel aint nowhere near the river."

"Shit, I don't have the goddamn GPS code," Leavenger replied, frustrated. "It was off on the river, somewhere between Kitter Road and Tockawah."

"Hmm," the deputy replied. He turned to study a young lovely prancing by in pink scrubs.

"I'm just pissed the asshole shot my dog," Leavenger said. "For no reason at all. Just to kill something, I suppose."

"He didn't see you?"

"Nope. He dumped some junk in the river and rode off. Had a dog with him."

"His dog?"

"Hell, I reckon. He didn't shoot it, so it must've been his."

"What kind of junk was it?"

"Fish."

"Fish?"

"Yeah. Looked like it was some frozen fish. Whole fish, head and all."

The deputy shook his head for a while, either thinking or daydreaming. "Well, man, I'm sorry to hear about your dog," Shoals replied finally. "And your ankle. You might file a report with the sheriff. We could look into it."

"I just did file my report . . . with you," Leavenger said. "So you ought to look into it. There's something not right about that dude."

"Sounds like he's got an issue with trespassers."

"Good thing he didn't see me down in that water."

"A good thing indeed," said the deputy. "All right, I better get moving."

"You got somebody sick?" asked Leavenger, nodding to the deputy's bouquet.

"Not really. Kinda."

"Hope you aint paying for it."

Shoals smiled, clapped him on the shoulder, and hurried away. Leavenger pegged off toward his truck. He doubted the deputy would give his predicament another thought. Justice, he knew, if sought in a mild instance such as this, would have to be got by the victim all on his own.

– 14 –

Shoals had never once pulled over a female for personal gain, or flagrantly abused his position in any way. But that's not to say his assistance had never been requested, or that he'd never engaged in a little mock interrogation with willing young ladies, a few of which resulted in backseat tussles, containment by handcuffs, and ultimately his brandishing "the full arm of the law."

The deputy's prowess in the sack had earned him quiet esteem among the county's single moms and the recently divorced, disaffected housewives and feisty widows, coeds, even the occasional homely teenager. His standards ran the gamut. Playing the long game and sampling the widest array of local beauties required practiced discretion. His playboy reputation was known, but few could name names, for he was never one to hunch and tell. His lust was insatiable, his capacity to give pleasure unlimited. Secrecy was part of the allure for him, and he took great pains to cover his tracks. He'd learned how to make love comfortably in the Boss's cramped backseat. He also loved to rut outdoors and conceived elaborate rendezvous on back roads, in wooded picnic areas and open fields, where the tall grass obscured his animalistic thrashings. He knew every secret cove on the lake, had blankets stashed near every scenic hill. He'd perfected the art of three-minute ecstasy, and none left him disappointed.

Then came Sandy Mize, and all bets were off.

They met at a high school football game in late August. She was pulling teacher duty, standing position at the bottom of the bleachers, watching and waiting for unchaperoned kids to make trouble. He saw her from the press box, where he sat as guest color commentator for the local radio coverage. At commercial, he pointed her out to the assistant principal who called the games and learned she was the most recent junior high English teacher. He scampered down after the halftime review to talk her up.

At first he thought she was dismissive, but she was simply focused on the crowd, scanning for troublemakers, not letting her guard down. This got him hot. Giving it her all, even for a sad gig like teacher duty. She was a cool duck and pretty as all get-out. She kept her effortless sex appeal hidden by casual attire, but her full mouth and well-conditioned hair gave her away. He commented on her eyes and she blushed a little. They had at least one serious connection, but she wasn't jumping right into his arms. This fish would need more than a nibble to land. He watched her from the booth the rest of the game and then got distracted by the thrilling finish, a last-minute, game-winning two-point conversion. He lost her in the stands, in all the hoopla and excitement for the first win of the season.

The next week he made a point to casually run into her. He spent a couple of afternoons at the public library, the downtown coffee shop, the grocery store produce section—wherever he'd fantasized about meeting a knockout English teacher. But she never turned up in these places, so he sat in the school parking lot, waited for her to come out, and tailed her home. He staked out the house, a rental by the ballpark, and monitored her comings and goings. He found out where she shopped for groceries, when she took her son to school and picked him up, where she filled her car and got her oil changed. Even from a distance he detected her sadness, a longing for something more than her simple, frugal routine. The more he watched and followed, the more he wanted her. It killed him that such a pretty girl should be left wanting. She needed a man to make a fuss over her, to do her heavy lifting and calm her worry. And he was a man of simple pleasures himself. If he could just get her out of that blouse and enjoy a gander at those cantaloupes, he believed they could find lasting happiness together.

Finally he orchestrated a chance encounter at the gas station, small talk in front of the refrigerated soft drinks. He bought extra potato logs and a pack of gum for her and the boy. She flashed him a smile of pleasant surprise. She was a keeper, worth the hunt, so he went in for the kill. "This may sound crazy," he said, "but have dinner with me. I'd love to talk with someone my age about serious life stuff."

"How old *are* you?" she asked with a mischievous grin.

"Twenty-seven," he said. "You don't mind hanging out with an elder, do you?"

She smiled, flattered, since she was thirty-two. She told him she was busy. Life was too complicated at the moment.

"The best way to deal with life's difficulties is to share and talk about these things. Don't you get sick of just watching TV, keeping it bottled up?"

"I like TV," she said.

"How about this Saturday?"

She nervously considered it. He bit his lip, tried to keep himself from begging. He could tell she wasn't one to jump into a stranger's car, not even one as bitching as his. He would have to employ great skill and patience to whisper this skittish filly into submission if he ever hoped to ride her.

"Look, I realize you don't know me, but I'm an easygoing guy," he said. "We can meet somewhere if you like. Neutral ground."

He worked out at the gym for three days straight. He shaved, trimmed hairs and nails, even contrived his own scent with a mix of aftershaves. He made sure he had a few skins and a wad of dough in his wallet, put on his crispest, tightest T-shirt and firmest jeans.

Except for the country club, where he was not a member but enjoyed honorary dining privileges, he supposed one of the classiest restaurants in town was Hungry Dragon. At night they rolled the buffet off to the side, put out white tablecloths, and piped flaccid jazz through the sound system. The dining room was low-lit by table candles and aquariums built into the wall. They offered chopsticks or forks. Indeed there was an aphrodisiacal quality to the scene, and when she arrived in her fitted jeans and taut cashmere, he knew he'd have to sit on his hands to keep from touching her.

Things got off to a rocky start. When they sat down to study the menu, he playfully referred to the restaurant as Hung Dragon, which she struggled to ignore. Then the nervous waiter spilled water that nearly soaked her leg, but Shoals reacted fast and caught it all in the tablecloth. They moved to another table, one next to a wall aquarium, and Shoals explained how their waiter, who seemed nervous and sleep-deprived, had probably just gotten off the boat. "You know, they ship them over in cargo containers. He probably stowed away in a shipment of fortune cookies or cell phones."

She reacted strangely to everything he said, and he couldn't tell if she was sensitive or nervous or what. He finally shut up and let her talk. He listened patiently to her troubles. Their new rental was not suitable. The baseball games would go late some nights, and often they'd hear home-run balls landing on their roof or whapping against the back door. Kids roamed around at all hours, filching small things from the back porch—a cooler, a garden hose, a water pistol. She'd witnessed conspicuous dealings in the parking lot, whether drugs or sex or both. All hours of the day people found it a suitable spot to come and carry on loud phone conversations or just sit while their cars thrummed with bad music. Then there was the landlord, who didn't care for the dog. Naturally, Shoals offered to keep it at his house, but she was too polite, didn't want to put him out.

In fact it had been Shoals, posing as a neighbor, who'd called the landlord to complain about the barking. He needed to be rid of it after he'd slipped up the back alley a few nights earlier, hoping to peep in and catch her lounging in a sexy way, maybe spy her walking into the bedroom, her uncupped breasts cavorting beneath a thin nightshirt, a sliver of soft butt cheek peeking out from below the hem, but the dog went berserk. He'd never get close enough. Wouldn't it be grand, though, to have a private perch and a sliver of raised window shade to see her from behind, freshly showered, dropping her wet towel and bending down to pull on some plain white undies. His heart swelled at the prospect, and these were the torrents he lived for. He could snap his fingers and have some dizzy tease bobbing his apple out in the parking lot, but he wanted something more precious, something forbidden. He was a man of few subtleties except where this was concerned.

She seemed to grow more at ease talking, helped by the fact that he was actually listening and perhaps that she'd already ordered a second glass of wine. She was taking it down pretty good, he thought, and if things proceeded in this vein, he might have to claim his room on hold at the Skyline Motel.

Her tongue loosened, Sandy tried to coax him out of his silent attentiveness. "I noticed your license plate," she said, sampling the crab Rangoon appetizer. "What does 'sugar' mean?"

"It means I'm sweet."

He could tell she wasn't buying it. "Naw, it's just an old nickname."

"How'd you come by it?"

He paused, reaching for a fib. "Just something my mama used to call me. I guess you could say it stuck." He shot her his prized grin. Maybe later, he said with a gaze, the true origin of the nickname would be revealed.

"What's your favorite sweet?" she asked.

His mind went south, but luckily he caught himself, stopped, and tried to summon a reasonable answer. It was too early yet for dirty talk. Instead he confessed his addiction for homemade cobbler with ice cream.

"I love half-frozen strawberries in syrup," she said. "Preferably with whipped cream." Was she trying to stir him up? He smiled, stowed that away for later. He was game for food play whenever she felt comfortable and ready.

They batted desserts back and forth good-naturedly as she became more at ease. Comfortable small talk, he imagined, was the cornerstone of a healthy relationship. He'd always made a show of clamming up and pouting whenever he wanted to be rid of a woman, so it was nice to see his silence work in reverse.

When the waiter appeared, she opted for the Thai noodle special and he went for the spicy General Tsao. She giggled when he pronounced the "T," and he took it for flirting. He winked, dipping two fingers in the red sweet and sour gel, and made a show of licking it off. She excused herself and hurried off to the restroom.

She returned with a sense of decorum that, to his disappointment, took them back to square one. They each inquired politely about the other's work, then wondered why they'd never crossed paths. Shoals had gone to Bayard County, while Sandy attended Madrid Central, separated by city limits and school districts like star-crossed lovers. He noticed she had switched to drinking water. By the time the entrée arrived, he was less confident in his chances and chided the waiter for being stingy with the beers.

At some point during the meal, she dropped the bomb—she was married. Separated but married. It didn't deter Shoals, of course, who already knew this. His investigation had revealed a name and address in the county, where he'd sent his lawyer buddy Fussell to gather intel, posing as a divorce attorney. But Danny could tell that it bothered her. Perhaps she had only recognized in the midst of their evening, bathed in sparkling aquatic reflections, that she was on a date, a romantic excursion, and she'd started to feel guilty. He decided the only way to make her feel comfortable about it was to bring it out in the open, so he inquired about her husband. She told him who it was, asked if he knew him.

"Mize," he said. "I wonder, is he one of *the* Mizes, as in Mitchell Mize?"

"Yes, I believe so," she said. "That's Jay's grandfather."

He set his fork down in wide-eyed disbelief. "No! Mitchell Mize is your grandfather-in-law?"

She said she'd never heard it put quite that way and looked around nervously, hoping the connection had not been made for any other diners. "It's really . . . I don't know much about it. It's not a fond topic in the family. My husband didn't even know his grandfather. I certainly didn't either. He was dead many years before we married. Before we even met."

"Have they told you the stories?"

"No," she said, defensive. "I told you, his name is never brought up. My husband only ever mentioned him a couple of times."

Shoals took a breath and gave her a little room, not much. He proceeded cautiously in this line of difficult questioning, hoping to fan the ember of shame between husband and wife so that he could sweep in and hose her down.

"That's so interesting," he said. "What do you know in general about old Mitchell?"

She told him she knew only that the elder Mize and some others had been convicted of a heinous race crime in south Mississippi during the 1960s. He'd been sentenced to life in prison, which he served out in Parchman until his death some twenty years later.

"That's true," Shoals assured her, "but there's more to it than that."

Shoals had always been a collector of Mississippi crime stories, and most proud old-timers demurred at perpetuating the state's checkered lore. In order to get the scoop, he had to pal around with other types of men, who regarded Mize and his ilk as outlaw folk heroes.

The way it had always been described to him, Mitchell Mize was not some kind of sadistic murderer or staunch racist. Mize had always maintained it was a joke gone bad. He and the victim, a man named Harvell Bussey, had been friendly, in fact. But Bussey was kind of a dope, prone to get drunk and uppity. They called him Shitty Boy because he sold manure. He was famous in this particular little Mississippi hamlet for his manure cart, which he hitched up to a mule and drove all over the back roads, tossing out manure for his customers. Even the Mizes bought it. They loved Shitty Boy.

One night Mitchell and some buddies were tooling around the countryside when they came upon Shitty Boy's place. They were a bit high in the head and thought it would be funny to scare Shitty Boy, so they crept onto his place and spied his manure cart parked under a lean-to just up the hill from the house. Supposedly Mize lit the pile on fire and pushed the cart down the hill into the front yard. They might never have guessed the pile would be so combustible, for when the cart hit the front porch and tipped over, the fire exploded and engulfed the house in a matter of minutes. Shitty Boy had been inside sleeping, along with his wife and two kids. No one escaped.

"That's horrible," Sandy replied, setting her napkin on the table.

Shoals may have told the story with a shade more mirth than it deserved.

"A lot of folks thought so. It was one thing killing Shitty Boy, I guess, and another thing killing his wife and kids. The FBI swooped in and threw Mitchell's ass under the jail."

"Don't call him that, please," Sandy said.

"What?"

"That . . . the man who was killed."

"Shitty Boy? That's what they called him!"

Any ground he'd gained during the meal was lost by the time the dessert cart rolled around. Sandy passed on another course and excused herself again. Shoals gave the waiter his credit card and scarfed down a powdery beignet-type pastry while he planned his next move. If he could just get her in the Boss, he'd have her. Something about having a woman's derriere in his bucket seat drove him wild. Like sitting in the palm of God, he'd tell them, and they melted every time.

She came back, all polite smiles and false reserved cheer. She said that she needed to fetch her son, who was staying at her father's house. He tried to get her talking about her son and her father, but she threw up roadblocks at every turn. Evidently he'd been too tactless with his conversation.

"Well, can I call you sometime? I'd love to take you for a ride. I could show you parts of the county you probably never knew existed."

"I bet you could, Danny, but honestly, I'm incredibly busy and just in a difficult place right now," she said.

"I understand," he replied with tender reservation. "I probably shot off my mouth trying to impress you, and I'm sorry for that. I was just trying to make you laugh, make you forget about your troubles. I've been trying to imagine what you're going through. I know how hard it is to be alone. Sometimes it seems like the rest of the world has forgotten about you. It has to be twice as hard with a kid."

She smiled, and he detected a softening in her gaze. His final volley may have scored a hit.

"If you ever feel that way, like everyone has forgotten about you, give me a call and we can do this again," he said.

He stood up like a gentleman and began to walk out with her when the waiter hollered across the restaurant. "Sir, sir, you forgot your card." Shoals frowned at his overeagerness and waved him off. He wanted to escort her to the car. There was always a chance, when faced with the prospect of returning home to her sadness, that she would change her mind. But she simply shook his hand, thanked him for dinner, and flittered off in a rush.

The slugger Shoals had struck out. But as he watched her drive away in her sad lttle Maxima, he remembered a lesson his uncle taught him. The best gains come from a hard day's work. And while he considered himself a romantic, he knew there was no magic formula. Familiarity built trust and comfort and ultimately love. He believed if he just showed up and did the work, convincing Sandy of his loyalty, then her desire would eventually tilt his way.

– 15 –

Autumn drove a lance up summer's ass that last weekend in September. The sky spewed rain and hail. Violent winds and lightning lashed the already broken land. A big twister cut a swath just north and west of the Mize place, ripping up what the flood had spared. In the storm's wake, a new chill descended. All manner of nature would now take its cue to start dying.

Jay awoke from a deep hibernation, sobbing in the overcast dawn. He was unsure where he was or on which side of reality. The last thing he recalled was being in a house he could not place, some combination of houses from his youth, and his lumbering ape of a father walking in with a .22 rifle, gesturing for him to come and see something. Jay assumed he'd killed the dog and followed his father reluctantly to a side porch, where they viewed not a dog but Jacob, shirtless in a small pair of khaki shorts, lying on his side, a neat little tear above his heart, his eyes open and lifeless. As Jay crouched down to gather the boy, whose body was slick like a fish and resisted his embrace, his father stood by with silent idiotic pride. Next Sandy appeared, and when she recognized her son's body, she attacked Jay first with a book and then with her fists.

And that was it. Short and precise, distinctly lucid and undreamlike. Almost farcical, but there was nothing funny about the way he felt when he woke up. He'd succumbed to a true emotion, one with the weight of premonition. It felt like he'd touched an alternate reality at the dead end of slumber.

He writhed in bed awhile, trying to come back to life. Much of the ache inside him was physical hunger. He'd not eaten since the porch onion—days ago, he guessed—and he still tasted smoke and blood in his throat, raw from all the dust and fumes. Chipper smiled lazily, lying next to him in bed. The house reeked of shit.

He got up finally and stumbled through his barren home, looking for something clean to ingest. The rooms were cool, the hall and kitchen. A pitcher of water went down him like a blessing.

In the pantry he found the same old carton of baking soda and tub of shortening, a sack of beetle-infested flour, the odd birthday candle and plastic fork. On the floor lay the gnawed-open sack of dog food to which Chipper had helped himself. Jay went down on all fours to inhale the grainy stench of the empty bag and was enticed by all the powdered fats and rendered essences of bygone animals.

Against his better judgment, he went to his emergency rations, bound up in a box with several layers of packing tape and a scrawled warning—"Don't eat except in emergency! Women and children only!" Even if this was an emergency, and he was beginning to think that it might be, he still didn't qualify. Nevertheless he bore into the cinched box like a campground bear and plucked out a can each of ravioli and black beans, stabbed them open with a butcher knife, and choked down the contents. In the stash was an unopened bottle of good tequila. A drink would do him right, but he opted instead to place it above the cabinets, a prize to accept when Sandy and Jacob returned.

He also found a pill bottle containing a few hard buds of marijuana. He sniffed and remembered it, a potent batch. He put it away lest he be tempted. To smoke it would only amplify his misgivings.

In the living room he scooped up the dried turds in a dustpan. By the door he found his mud boots, so shiny they were like new. He stepped into them and walked outside to greet the cool new season. It felt good to breathe again. There was a cleansing wet as opposed to a rotting wet in the air. A few leaves shuffled about, trying to start a movement. He tossed the turds under an azalea bush, and when he came back to the carport, he found Chipper sniffing under the brown tarp at the bucket of charred bone fragments. He knelt down and opened the bucket, sifted his hands through the black grit and splinters. It wasn't a dream after all. Here was hard proof, just lying out in the open for anyone to walk up and find. *Proof of what?* he wondered.

He decided he needed to untangle his mind, to bring himself back to a balanced temperament more in tune with the earth and its natural cycles, so he went inside and crumbled and smoked a bit of the marijuana. It clawed at his throat going down and didn't take long to grab hold of him. He felt every sensation more acutely. A light came on inside him and he could feel his body's points of entropy.

He took the .22 from behind the mudroom door and walked outside. The wind had picked up and the dancing branches created flickering shadows along the ground. He stood and stared, his mind creating narratives for all the furious shadows. He could not discount that this arbitrary play of light and darkness might hold the answer. Anything was possible and everything was ripe with significance in his current disposition.

He whistled at Chipper and together they headed for the woods to scare up a rabbit or squirrel. They started over the hill and into the pasture, down near the hollow. Gauzy light through the dying foliage conjured a fog, perhaps smoke still lingering from the burn, or old ghosts wound through the trees like cotton candy. They retreated and set out for the woods along the river instead.

Occasionally during their hike he was seized with a surfeit of thoughts or waves of crackling energy inside his abdomen. He stopped and listened to the woods—a lone mosquito chasing him, complaining in his ear; the pulse of the river ahead and the flitting of birds from bough to bough; the scratch of tiptoes over damp undergrowth, walking Indian-style. He heard a distant shotgun, probably a hunter priming his weapon for dove season. Or maybe someone sitting out back on his patio, taking his life out of his own hands.

Jay's mother insisted it was an accident, but who cleaned his shotgun in the hot tub? He could understand her denial, but not his sister's. Their father had never been a happy man. How long could you carry around shame like that? The insurance company alone would admit the truth, if only to nullify the life policy.

He'd gone to the funeral by himself, refusing to expose Jacob to it. Few showed up for the service or burial. What pity that ever existed for Mizes must have all been used up by previous generations. He stayed a few days to sort out odds and ends. They found a few dumb-luck investments that might allow his mother to carry on with the bills for a while, after all the penalties and fees that accompany death. Jay couldn't wrap his head around it and expressed his frustration as outrage. He gave the family lawyer a royal cussing for no good reason and embarrassed his mother, who was looped on barbiturates. His sister finally asked him to leave. Months had gone by and he hadn't spoken to either of them.

Mourning his father had not been what he imagined. Instead of crying over his casket, Jay had wanted to open it. He had a sadistic need to see his father, to judge the hole in his head where he'd blown out all knowledge of his careless ancestors.

Jay had learned about his grandfather in eleventh-grade social studies, during a unit on civil rights atrocities in Mississippi. The teacher was a young man from the north who taught this lesson with self-righteous vitriol. He wasn't teaching so much as berating them, as if to say, *How could all of you unborn have let this happen?*

They sat ashamed in the dark, whites and blacks alike, and watched the parade of evil projected against the classroom wall while the teacher delivered his scathing indictment of civil rights assassins—the Rays and De La Beckwiths, Milams and Bryants, and all the anonymous lynch mobs from the hills to the Delta to the piney woods and coast, villains and citizens who accepted murder for the preservation of a dominant white society. When the teacher mentioned Mitchell Mize, classmates turned to stare. It all came together— his father's hostile ambivalence when asked about his old man; vague rumblings of some family member in prison and sympathies for a long-suffering grandmother he never knew; the morning after Halloween when he was ten or eleven, waking up to find a white-robed and hooded effigy swinging in their front yard. *Just a ghost, a silly prank,* his mother had assured him.

He went home after class in an adolescent rage, demanding answers. It earned him a smack across the face, the first and only time his father struck him. That blow told it all. If we were all meant to pay for our daddies' mistakes, then who would be left innocent?

Jay never mentioned it again, only satisfied his curiosity by reading every account he could find of Jim Crow injustice. In all of his delving, he did not find atonement, only a darker shame than he could sufficiently bury, unlike his father, who'd finally reached bedrock.

Jay was startled just then by a fit of barking. Chipper had flushed out a scent in the brush and charged a live oak. He stood against the trunk on hind paws and bayed. Jay raised the rifle and peered under the leaves. There appeared indistinctly a naked black man on a high heavy branch, stone-still, staring down at them.

"Who's that?" Jay called up. "Who's in this tree?"

The perched man did not respond.

"What do you call yourself doing up there?"

Jay walked ten or twenty feet away and then turned around to check again. The world around him was real enough—the smell of rotting leaves, the spongy ridges of tree bark beneath his fingers, the tendrils of light spilling through the trees, and the sound of a large truck distant on the road. The prospect that his mind was projecting two sides of reality, toggling back and forth at its own demented pleasure, worried him.

He went back to confirm that the man was still there. "You'll have to come down from there this instant!" he cried and crouched low.

No, it was the buzzard. Had it been there all along? He took up the .22 and popped off several shots, scurrying around the base of the tree, angling for a clearer shot. The bird stood and raised its wings, reached up and disappeared into the greenery.

He sat down on the splayed trunk, overcome, short of breath. He grabbed Chipper in a needful embrace, but the dog was intent on his flown quarry and wouldn't even stand to be loved. Jay wound up clutching himself but was repulsed by his own stench and wanted a bath, maybe a dip in the river. A cold shock to reset his brain like electricity.

He stood and made slow, stammering progress through the woods as Chipper trailed along behind him, finding interest under every hollow stump and in every turned burrow. Soon he came to a glen and froze when he saw two deer twenty yards distant. They were both too distracted to notice him. He raised the .22 and sighted the buck, his rack a wide twelve points. It would be a difficult kill with this small caliber, only a clean shot to the brain would do the job. His hands were shaking, and he leaned against a tree, rested the barrel on a flimsy branch, and took slow, deep breaths. He watched the buck nose up behind the female, his tongue flickering over her backside. He made a clumsy attempt to mount her, and she pulled away, ran a few steps ahead, stopped, and raised her tail to taunt him. He swung his antlers and came back around, climbed atop her a second time. She stood still, ears back and eyes terrified as he rose over her in a supplicating hunch, tugging her close with his legs, licking her neck and stabbing her underside with his engorged red prick. His hips pulsed as he found purchase, and they locked in a moment's synchronous ritual. Jay's finger rubbed the trigger. He could take either one of them in their ecstasy.

Then came Chipper howling down the glade. The stag scrambled over the doe, kicking free of her, each bounding in a different direction. They were gone by the time Chipper arrived, sniffing and pissing and rolling in the leaves near their lovemaking. Jay lowered the rifle, surprised to find himself aroused by these animals and their unabashed, difficult partnering.

He walked on toward the river, where he stopped to watch the waters roil and tumble. A few trees on the opposite shore had collapsed and were kneeling head-down in the current. Chunks of earth were ripped away by floodwaters. Jay imagined this was how the land defended itself from the onslaught of water, a sacrifice of trees and banks of mud, damming up and fortifying, forcing the water to dredge deep instead of wide. He inspected his own side of the river to find similar features and encountered a washed-out cleft where part of the shore had come away. Holding on to a vine, he climbed down for a closer look. The mud snatched his foot and yanked, sucking him into the heart of it. He flailed in a panic, worried he'd stumbled into quicksand, but it was only a knee-high bowl of cold mud and clay that tingled against his skin and left sweet stains on his lips.

Along the edge of the pit, the mud was as smooth and supple as flesh. He wallowed around, enjoying the sensation, like a million fingers on him. He closed his eyes and imagined human touch, the musk of the earth ripe and familiar. He tilted his head back and let the slough take him. Behind the flickering pink light of his closed lids he saw his wife caressing the vine, poised in her careful descent, her naked white body overcome by gooseflesh from the wind off the river. She'd made herself up for him, the curls and red lips. She balanced herself, arms out daintily at her sides as she moved through the ooze toward him. Her shadow enveloped him and then lowered and straddled him. He crawled out of his pants and flopped onto his stomach. He nuzzled his face down into her pristine pale skin and then entered her body, which was succumbing to the dark mud until she had disappeared. The slop worked him like a generous hand. He lifted himself over it slow, gaining rhythm, thrusting again and again, the wet suction completing his fantasy quickly in a fit of twitches and airy whimpers.

He lay spent on his back for a moment, breathing in the mist falling from the trees, listening to the river's patient hustle close by. The mire covered him head to toe and it felt cleansing. The smell poured into his nostrils like fresh air. He sat upright and began rubbing mud deep into his skin. In his desperate repetition, scouring away the stench and all of its incrimination, plying the craft of creation to himself, he attempted to make a clean new man from old scum.

– 16 –

It was about 9:30 in the growing cool of evening, and the cicadas rustled like coins in the dark. Shoals was sitting stakeout in the parking lot of Li'l Nine's Skate 'n' Skeet. He held a flask between his legs and watched the teenagers come and go in their mating struts. He had the windows down, a quiet trebly blues issuing from the car radio. He loved to hear the guitar notes bending just out of tune and played police protocol the same way, enough to be daring without breaking groove.

Take this stakeout, for instance. It was just over the line in Tuckalofa County, out past Flintlock. Technically he had no jurisdiction here, but the rink owner, Daw Robison, was a friend of the family. A bad element had turned up at his place and was running off the respectable customers, kids from well-to-do parents who'd never before worried about dropping their twelve- and thirteen-year-olds off with a pocketful of money. But word had gotten out that disenfranchised teens and junior college dropouts were hanging around. One kid, presumed to be on bad ecstasy, freaked out to the strobe lights during the slow skate to "Stairway to Heaven" and crashed into a child's birthday party. These were good, impressionable church kids, and Robison didn't want to compromise their innocence by allowing a few meth heads and would-be dealers to hang around. He also didn't want to involve the local sheriff's department and risk drawing the newspaper's attention, so Shoals agreed to sit and watch and send a message that unlawfulness would not be tolerated. In return for this sit, Shoals knew he could count on a freezer full of deer meat all winter. And no telling what else. Favors fell in his lap all the time.

Shoals had been sitting in the parking lot for nearly an hour, waiting for the clouds to pass so he could get a few bars of coverage and maybe give Sandy a call. A mysterious night chat to expand the relationship a millimeter or two further. After the mixed reviews on their first date, he'd kept close tabs on her movements and found her and the boy on the playground one Sunday afternoon.

He wheeled in and waved hello.

"I thought that was you," he called, making cool strides from the parking lot. "This must be the boy. Jake?"

"Jacob," she said.

"You're a handsome fella," he said, offering his hand to the kid. "I'm Deputy Dan." He threw back his suede vest where he had cleverly pinned his badge inside. The kid loved it.

"Hey, I've got something in the trunk you might enjoy," he said and took off for the Boss. He'd planted a Wiffle ball set there, still in the packaging.

"You ride around with children's toys in your sports car?" Sandy asked. She was suspicious, a sign of real intelligence.

"Aw, it's just something I had for a kids' charity auction. I'll just pick up another one, no big deal."

"Hmm," she said. "You sure you're not some predator?" She was feisty today with her sly grin and dangerous accusations. It made him want her all the more.

"Honey, I'm the antipredator. I take pleasure in putting creeps away."

While she pretended to read a book, he willfully ignored her and taught Jacob how to grip the bat and keep his eye on the pitch. The kid had no coordination whatsoever. Obviously the father couldn't be bothered to show his son the basic thrills of boyhood. Every now and then he'd cut his eyes back at Sandy, shoot her an all-pro grin. The less said the better, he'd determined.

After about forty-five minutes of play with the boy and a few random, playful barbs back and forth across the playground with the mother, Shoals's

CB radio squawked and he jogged over to answer. It was just one of the deputies assing around, but he thought it would be smooth if he played it like an emergency.

He hustled over and gave little Jacob a high five, told him he had to run off and catch some bad guys. "Practice your swing, little dude," he said, giving Sandy a cool wave. She smiled and waved back, told him to take care.

"I'll give you a ring sometime," he yelled, since she wasn't offering. He laid smoke and rubber all over the lot screeching out to the street.

A distant shriek brought Shoals back to the skating rink. A redhead in white pants emerged from the shadowy side of the building and clopped across the lot. Her hand was clutching the neck of her shimmery tank top, and she was weaving distraught through the cars, shaking her head and sobbing. She approached the vehicle across from him, a thirdhand SUV, and rummaged through her purse. She shook like she was being chased, kept looking back at the dark corner and finally threw her face in her hands. He watched her for a moment and contemplated getting out. Probably her boyfriend's hands had gotten a little too fast, or else he'd made a careless remark in the heat of foreplay.

She inspected her face in the side mirror, and that's when she noticed Shoals. She shuffled over and leaned down to look through his open passenger window. "Can you help me?" she asked.

"What's a matter, girl?"

"This guy I'm with, he has my keys." She was breathless and slurry.

"What happened?"

"He's got a knife," she said, nodding toward the rink. "I think he wants to rape me."

Shoals squinted into the dark but couldn't see the young punk. Pulling a gun here outside of jurisdiction would be foolhardy, so he focused instead on getting her calm.

"Did he hurt you?"

"He stretched my shirt," she said. Sure enough, the tank was all yanked around and the neckline plunged, giving him a box-seat view of her tender ladies. She stood up suddenly, realizing she was showing her goods, and wobbled a bit. She was tight and trim. All he could see was her red hair and decisive bust. Definitely of age. He guessed twenty-three or twenty-four.

"You need a ride?" he asked. He reached over and opened the door.

She covered her cleavage and looked in.

"Go on, sit down if you want. I'm Danny," he said. "Now don't you worry about him. He won't get his hands on you with me here, I can promise you that."

She sat down in the bucket seat noncommittally, left the door open, one leg draped outside the vehicle. He extended his handkerchief, and she dabbed her face and caught her breath. Her face was puffy with drink and shame. Her makeup was smudged too, but that could be straightened out. There was definitely something there. Was she of age? Big dumb green eyes and her nose and mouth were slightly disproportionate, like they still might be trying to declare themselves. Maybe more like nineteen or twenty. Surely no younger than eighteen.

She looked back at the dark corner to see if he'd emerged, maybe weighing her options. Who was she better off with?

Shoals sensed her unease. "You want me to go get your keys?" he said. "I'll put his lights out for him, if that's what needs to happen."

"No, it's his car. I was just the designated driver."

"That's commendable."

"What a dick!" she said, her face turned away. "I should have known better."

"Hey, you didn't do anything wrong," he assured her, placing his hand gently on her forearm. "You assumed he'd act like a gentleman instead of an animal, and that's a perfectly reasonable expectation."

She considered her options. "You a cop, aint you?"

"Off duty," he replied.

"Does that mean you can't take me?" She cut her eyes up at him, all tipsy innocent. Something had changed between them. She'd shifted up, he could tell, even if she didn't know it yet. Often it happened so easy, as if preordained.

"Not at all. Get in."

She craned her neck toward the lot once more, whether hoping to see him or hoping he saw her. She tucked herself in the passenger seat and shut the door.

She winced when he cranked the engine. *She must really be a little flower*, Shoals thought. Off in the tall grass with the rough pups. Or maybe this was all a game and she had it planned this way. He gave the engine some gas and let it rumble her seat. He sunk back, became one with the car. His skin was the leather upholstery caressing her. "Wow, I bet this thing goes fast," she said, a touch of nerves in her voice.

"As fast as you want," he replied, easing out of the lot with caution, taking his time to look both directions as they pulled onto the dark county road. He was winning her confidence inch by inch.

"Which way you live?" he asked.

"Madrid," she replied.

"You're a long way from home tonight."

"You can drop me off at a friend's near Flintlock if you want."

She was proud of her little body, had her chest all thrust out. The ridge of her bosom, where it swelled and dimpled down, was as pure and smooth as any heaven. Her foamed-out bra didn't fool him with its angles and indentations. It created a false expectation, which may have had something to do with that unseemly business behind Li'l Nine's. But he, being a man of experience and a deep admirer of the subtleties of the female body, didn't hold such illusions.

"I don't mind taking you all the way," he insisted. "If that's what you want."

She considered how far she wanted to go and said Flintlock would be fine. She said if she changed her mind she'd tell before they got too far along.

They sat in silence for a while, just the engine thrumming. Finally he asked, "Why get involved with a guy like that?"

"He said he had some reefer."

He nodded, let it slide. As an agent of the law, he was obliged to warn her off drugs. But he was off duty tonight, and she was testing him. "Well, you're too pretty for a redneck like that," he said.

She said her name was Kerri and made silly chat for a while. She told him she was a sophomore at the university.

"You grow up around here?"

She said yes but wouldn't say exactly where. She could put on all the college airs she liked, but Shoals could hear the twang in her voice and knew it by her taste in men, she was country all the way. He enjoyed watching her nervous tic of rubbing her hands up and down her thighs slowly. He took it for an unconscious cue.

"You can't be too careful," he said. "There's some cold customers hanging out around that rink. You gotta be smarter than that."

"I'm smart enough, aint I? I found you."

"Hell, you don't even know me," he said and looked over at her. Their eyes met, and he pushed back against her vixen tricks. "For all you know, you might still get raped."

She sat there quiet for a moment, working her thighs again, her chest heaving slowly. "You don't have to rape me, Danny," she said. Her hand found its way into his lap.

"You trying to shift the gear while I'm driving?" he asked. "You might jump the transmission, girl." She giggled nervously and apologized.

He kept going a ways, plunging through the hills and whipping around blind curves, letting her see what a powerful beast she had leapt astride. He loved teasing them, making them wait. Holding back drove them wild.

Finally he pulled off onto a gravel road, then down into a dry turnrow where he cut the engine. He kept the radio on, rolled down the window a few inches. "Will you reach in that glove box and hand me my kit?" Shoals asked with gentlemanly ease.

She opened the compartment and retrieved a brown shaving bag. "What's in here?" she asked playfully, unzipping the bag and sorting through the contents. There was a baggie of white powder and several small foil packages. "Is it dope?"

He smiled. "Let me show you."

Apprehensive, she handed him the pouch and watched carefully as he turned on the overhead light and pulled out one of the little foiled whipples. He removed the back tab and showed her the contents—a spit of buttery vegetable spread such as one finds beside a plate of diner biscuits. He opened his pants and out he flopped like a quick draw. She gave a slight gasp of admiration.

"You ever buttered a hot ear of corn?" he asked.

She nodded.

He placed the spread in her fingers and invited her to grease him up. She was graceful, rhythmic, and when he was ready, he pulled her hand gently away and told her to lick her fingers clean. She obliged slowly, taunting him with her rehearsed harlotry.

He reached back into the kit for the bag of white powder, which he held up. "It aint dope," he said, raising himself in the seat. He dipped his shimmering appendage into the sack, clasped it tight, and gave himself a solid dusting. He pulled out, refastened the bag, and stashed the kit.

"Think of it more as a late-night, sugary snack," he said, reaching over, urging her in with an embrace, then pulling her willing head down ever so gently to sample his sweet ghost-white manhood.

– 17 –

Jay stopped midscoop. *There are more microorganisms squirming through this shovelful of dirt than there are humans inhabiting the planet.*

He wheezed through clouded lungs and a swollen red nose, sweat beads clinging to his skull, quivering, mud-sliding down his body. His hands, scored red with oozing cracks, gathered a handful of earth. He held it to his ear and listened to the sounds of labored breathing. *This is what the earth sounds like from the heavens,* he decided.

Had it been weeks or days? This work of digging out civilizations and tossing them aside formed a span of hours unjoined from the rest of time. Now he stood at the bottom of a massive pit, surrounded by a ten-foot wall of soil. He would have done anything to keep from pacing the rooms and hallways of the house, where the books read themselves aloud to him from the shelves, or the carport, where the blackened bones resisted his feeble attempts to break them. One of his buckets had taken on rain, and he discovered that the bones sitting in water turned to paste when he ground them, so he soaked the rest and crushed them under brick like an old abuela making cornmeal. But he couldn't take the smell of it any longer. It was a scent no mask could erase. No proximity could halt its advance into his nasal passages. In a foolish, tormented moment, he tried to break his nose by slamming the shovel into his face. He lacked the power or conviction to break it, and so, after the blood and the stinging metallic taste, the smell was still there. It was not in his nose, he decided. It was in his brain. This malignant stench that would live there and spread like advancing societies.

That's when he started to dig.

He dug at first without knowing why and then slowly began to ascribe reason. Reason, with its many spreading tendrils like a root system or colony maze, had always existed. It was not something buried but something that needed not to be found.

He'd read somewhere that scientists were concerned by seismic activity and magma collecting in the basin of the Yellowstone Caldera, which suggested the massive underground volcano below the national park out west was ramping up to blow. Whether it went in two years or two thousand, who could know? The only certainty was the total decimation of America. A blanket of ash would block out the sun for ten to twenty years, killing all agriculture, most wildlife, anything that couldn't burrow underground and sustain itself for a generation. Never mind the bed of decaying uranium under the volcano. It was the loaded gun on the bedside table if the earth ever decided to off herself. No doubt the jihadists were studying how to drop bombs down a geyser and set the whole thing off, if only some dumb-ass Washington politician didn't get there first, lobbying to tap the damn thing and risk a holocaust all for a little oil.

It didn't really matter who did it. Everyone knew it was coming. The collective psychic will of humanity cried out for mercy and in anticipation of it. The story had to end, or at least begin a new chapter. Few would survive, but he was determined to be ready and would protect his family from the horrible fates that awaited all the others with their heads up their machines, killing their instincts, fattening their bodies for the mass sacrifice to the gods.

He'd seen a television documentary about the subterranean colonies of naked mole rats, the only mammals that lived entirely beneath the earth. They resembled human fingers with tiny legs and arms, eyeless in dark caves, which they'd gnawed out with their enormous protruding buckteeth, living like ants in a highly organized system of tunnels and chambers. His plan was similar—to dig three or four large pits and connect them with tunnels. It would be like a house, each burrow its own bedroom, trussed up with heavy timbers, maybe some amenities from their man-made past, like fake windows with photos of nature to make them feel at home.

For eating and breathing, he'd conceived a kaleidoscope garden, which would allow them to grow food underground. It was a series of stackable food plots encased in a cabinet of mirrors that were arranged to refract sunlight down from a skylight. He was eager to build a prototype to see if it was possible to grow food underground this way. Water would be scarce unless he built over an aquifer or filtered and recycled urine. Sunlight would be weak from the ash cloud unless he could enhance it with magnifying glass. Maybe a system of crank lights, everyone taking a turn on the stationary bike to charge the lamps. The plants would provide the oxygen needed for living under the earth, and the Mizes would provide the subsequent carbon dioxide and fertilizer to keep the plants alive. Symbiotic bliss within the earth's crust. Perhaps he could build a whole city under the pasture, caves and catacombs for a worthy new race of humans who recognized the privilege of survival and weren't bent on killing everything.

Jay and Sandy would be the new Adam and Eve. He imagined their squinting babies crawling through the burrows, waiting on the light to reach them, waiting for nuclear winter to end. Perhaps they could teach each other how to communicate by sign language or brain waves and repopulate a silent world.

He missed her at this time more than ever, when night was a distinct possibility. She knew how to be happy and settled in this world, and he needed her as an expression of this knowledge. She didn't know it to say it, but she embodied it, and getting a glimpse of himself without this, he didn't think it was possible to be happy without her. His smarts were all tricks, ideas borrowed from books, but her knowing was real and sacred. He'd failed to protect her, failed in his role. The husband was only for seed and for guarding against the night, but he and millions like him thwarted duty by collecting wealth and building monuments to themselves.

He put the shovel down and climbed out of the pit, which he'd dug in a wedge to keep from having to hoist himself up and down. He would build her a palace underground if that's what she desired. It wasn't too late to lure her back, only he had to make this place pure again. He had much to bury and burn, ashes to haul, a severed hand to find.

Jay fetched the retort barrel with the keg inside it and rolled them into the pit and went to clanging on each with a ball-peen hammer, flattening the rims until the sides collapsed and they lay at the bottom of the hole like crushed beer cans, and next he took the cook pot and flattened it similarly, and he threw over top several bucketsful of dirt and stamped it down to conceal it all well, and then he ran back and forth to the house and brought the old wheelbarrow into the field with its multiple dumploads of shiny pieces, which he carried down bit by bit, careful not to spill—first the steering and pedals and rack engine, the gas tank and suspension, the brakes and exhaust and ignition and transmission, the gun mount and rear rack, and then all of the tiniest components—the screws, washers, valves, seals, gaskets, bearings, and chains—and after all the metal was disassembled and laid to rest, too far down for detectors to make, there were the sliced tires and guards and cables, the seat covers and handles, a layer of dirt tamped down meticulously over each so that little would be left, and when it was complete and there were a couple of wheelbarrow loads of dirt to take down to the compost bins, he covered the long rectangle of freshly turned earth with plant debris, blended it well, and believed that within two weeks it would look like it had never been disturbed, and after that another century or more before the sense of its contents could be made.

And if anyone was lucky enough to be around to find this, maybe they would be reminded that we've only ever been here, scurrying across or just beneath the Mother's skin at her own gracious mercy, a self-propagating food stock for her deep crumbling hunger.

He slept well that night and much of the next day, and when evening came he crawled again into the pasture, toting a cumbersome garbage sack. He composed a fire for the boat, which he'd splintered with an ax that afternoon. Paperbacks provided the kindling, just a few old classics of paranoia, read and remembered. When the flames shot erect, he dipped the shovel into the sack, pulled up the corpse's jeans, and handed them to the fire. The garment muffled the inferno just a bit and drove into the clear night a tall plume of smoke, which the wind took straight and mercifully away. The flames adjusted, welcomed the fabric, and fanned out. The jeans appeared to be melting in the heat. After a few moments, he reached in with the shovel and lifted them, and they fell apart like burning paper.

He kept building the fire in layers, first the brambles and leaves, followed by a filthy bedsheet or blood-coated tennis shoe, then more branches. He burned it slow, a clue at a time, and then he'd sit back and stare off into the glow for a while, imagining that he'd always been destroying these things and that he would spend the rest of his life destroying them too, tending this sulfurous hell pit till kingdom come.

When it seemed well enough past dinnertime he unwrapped some rations he'd tucked up in a bandanna. A little cake with a special filling he had recently discovered. It had started innocently with that first taste of honeyed mud at the washout by the river and then later the taste of dust and sweat across his lips. He'd licked the wall of the pit, a yellow-brown strata of clay, and enjoyed the seductive taste, pulled a nugget and eaten furtively. It tasted of rich vinegary mustard greens. The salt and the sugar were present with the sharp bitters. He heated a pan's worth over the fire, fried it up with onions, just a little heat to kill any hookworms. He made flatbread with the old beetle flour and rainwater and ate them together, a dirty taco. A little gritty but uncommonly delicious. This could pass in finer restaurants, he believed. What more were your truffles and mushrooms but ambitious mud?

Chipper, meanwhile, was roving the bountiful acres of unsniffed pasture when he stopped at the top of the hill and set to howling and barking. Jay crept up, flattened himself against the earth, and peered over the ridge. The moon spotlighted a trespasser under the carport. The shadow passed behind the Bronco and lingered before the dark window, peering into the house.

Jay instinctively pulled the pistol from his waistband and cocked it, waiting to see if he recognized the figure. He heard a ripple of plastic. Someone was nosing under the char tarp. He popped off a warning shot, which brought a dose of adrenaline.

The trespasser stopped and moved toward the gunshot. Jay stood, cocked, and fired again into the air. "Don't shoot," called a deep, familiar voice. The long broad figure moved out of the light and into the shadows of the pasture, the orange glow from his cigarette creating an orb of light around his face. It was Hatcher, his neighbor across the way.

Chipper recognized him and darted down the hill. Jay ran to cut him off. Hatcher was extremely clever and would make him answer for everything that was amiss at the campsite. They met awkwardly in the middle of the slope. "What're you shooting at?" the neighbor inquired.

"You," Jay replied.

"Well, you got shit for aim," the neighbor croaked. Not given to expression, he was almost impossible to read, all eyebrows, spectacles, and mustache. He wore a broad trucker hat over gray hair pulled back and tied in a ponytail. "Is that raincoats you're burning back there?"

"How'd you guess?" said Jay.

"Smells like somebody baking tennis shoes."

Jay froze, grasping for a lie. "It's some of Sandy's old clothes." It was an idiotic response he regretted instantly, nearly as bad as the truth.

Hatcher took it without a flinch. "I saw her car over here the other day. Y'all get your mess sorted out?"

"Not exactly."

"Didn't think so, you burning her clothes and all," Hatcher replied. "She aint in em, is she?"

Of everyone, Hatcher would be the hardest to fool. His instincts were unequaled, almost paranormal. He could smell bullshit a mile away.

"She's not," Jay replied, managing a smile.

Hatcher craned his neck up the hill. Men like him were drawn to flames. He looked back and eyed Jay suspiciously. "What happened to your nose, she slam a door in your face?"

Jay fingered the scab of his misguided self-mutilation. "Tree branch whacked me in the face."

Hatcher looked down at Chipper as if seeking confirmation. The dog was staring up with a dumb smile, wagging his tail.

"Look, I'm sorry," said Jay, impatient. "I'm all out of weed."

Hatcher was an old hippie, lost between worlds. A toke now and then would put him right, as it did for Jay. A year or so back he'd lost his son, a military hero in Iraq. Since then Hatcher's wife had found religion and couldn't abide him having grass at their house.

"Well, I sure hate that for you," Hatcher said. "But some crossed my path the other day. I come to share."

There was something ominous in Hatcher's flat, expressionless tone. Jay urged him inside, where he had some rolling papers, anything to lure him away from the fire over the hill. The neighbor might go berserk if he found Jay burning a perfectly good boat.

"What's all this?" Hatcher asked, swatting the tarp as they passed through the carport.

"Just some compost experiments," Jay said, moving fast inside.

Hatcher blew a snort of derision. Like many old hippies, he'd lost his optimism and pretended to disapprove of Jay's sustainable farming experiment.

"How'd that compost work out for you this year?" the neighbor taunted.

"Not too well, Hatch," said Jay. "But it wouldn't, considering the circumstances, don't you imagine?"

"Should've grown rice this first year," said Hatcher, handing over a folded-up paper towel. "Like I told you. Rice don't mind a flood."

Had he, in fact, predicted the flood? Jay seemed to remember something about it months earlier. Hatcher was nothing if not a harbinger of misfortune.

"Something you could eat at least," Hatcher said. "Aint you got no food? You look to be wasting away."

Jay unfolded the wadded paper and broke the dusty green nugget apart with his fingers. He reached into his pocket for papers and rolled a bittersweet beauty, which he passed for Hatcher to fire off.

"The deep freezer quit on me, spoiled all my fish and venison," Jay said. "The solar panels worked great. It was the goddamn battery. One too many cloudy days, it kept tripping the inverter off and on. The old motor couldn't take it."

Jay tried to get in there and speak the old guy's language, but Hatcher was having none of it. He just shook his head. "You know, it'd be a hell of a lot easier if you just pay your light bill."

Jay bristled at the continuing assault. Hatcher sucked up the joint, held it for several seconds, and exhaled like a steam drill. White billows swirled around him, and smoke seeped out of him when he spoke. "You strapped for cash or something? Need a job?"

"You got work?" Jay asked, accepting the joint and taking in a breath that expanded him to twice his normal size.

"Always got work. And more than enough knuckleheads on the payroll who I wouldn't mind shitcanning."

Hatcher ran a small plumbing outfit out of the shop behind his house, mostly small domestic chores. He once told Jay that he'd grown so depressed by the all-around shoddy construction he found on his jobs that it ruined the work for him. He hired out these little chores to a bunch of young trainees and just fielded calls and managed the workload. He put on a good act over the phone, sounding like a preacher with his assured bass. A roster of helpless old country widows kept him in business.

"I'll keep it in mind," Jay said.

"Sure," Hatcher replied, "but only if your farming operation doesn't pan out."

Jay couldn't decide if Hatcher was poking at him, or if he was simply paranoid, hyperaware and hypercritical. He studied the effects of the marijuana on Hatcher, who was staring at the wall. He rubbed his arm against it as if to measure it plumb. They'd gotten high together enough that Jay could detect the gears of Hatcher's mind switching in constant transformation. He seemed to possess the ability to hone in on some flyspeck in front of him, penetrate that point, and illuminate the broader implications, the reverberations spreading throughout all of time—past, present, future—always exposing something rotten and festering at the core of the universe.

Hatcher had his nose to the wall. "Something's dead," he said.

"Don't fuck with me!" Jay cried out. Hatcher was onto him, the tricky geezer. As the owl sees through darkness, he knew the fear in Jay's soul.

Hatcher looked back and wrinkled his brow. "It's probably just a squirrel or mouse or something, slipped down and got stuck in the crawl space. Not too old. You'll smell it tomorrow."

Jay moved against the accused wall and stood there inspecting it. He turned to watch through eyes engorged and red as plums as the neighbor floated around the room in scrutiny.

Hatcher noticed the gaps on the bookshelf. "What happened to all your books?"

"I got rid of them," Jay replied. "A man can't put too much emphasis on book learning these days."

"He can't?"

"No. There's too much real knowledge out there, the observable sort. I can't waste my time on fabrications."

Hatcher pulled down a dog-eared Dostoyevsky. "I kinda like the Russians. When I'm in the mood."

"Bored ruminations of men too frightened to wander out of doors. You like that?"

Hatcher paused and studied him. Was his behavior too erratic? Out of character?

"I noticed some activity over here the past week or so," Hatcher said finally. "Your hands look like they've been busy."

Jay looked at his hands, scraped up red and throbbing from the dig. He was gripped in a tingle brought on by the potent weed. His lungs felt full of concrete, his mind an engine that wouldn't turn over. A confession rose in his chest. "Yeah, I've been gathering up wood to make charcoal," he mustered. "For my cops. *Crops*. My crops."

"What crops? You gonna harvest them brown tomatoes?"

Jay offered a rambling, incoherent explanation of biochar theory, the whole notion of pyrolysis and carbon sequestration, the Amazonian fire mounds. Hatcher snorted and took another deep draw from the stub.

"You think some charcoal mixed up in your mud out there's gonna do the trick?" he wheezed, holding in the smoke, then blowing it all about the room. "Save the farm?"

"There's a research group in Australia that's done wonders with it."

"Australia?"

"Yeah. They've been taking the brunt of global wrath, you know? Floods and sandstorms, blizzards in the middle of summer. It's biblical, man. They'll try anything. That's where you see progress. It comes from desperation."

Hatcher glowered skeptically.

"I found a deer in my front field there," Jay confessed. He enjoyed the loosening in his chest as he began to unburden. "Drowned or killed somehow. I butchered him and made a batch of charcoal from his bones. Gonna see if it works."

"Let's see it then," said Hatcher. "Show me what you made."

"Well, it's . . ." Jay grasped for something. "It's not really done yet."

"Oh no?" Hatcher said. "Still just a theory? You must not be desperate yet."

This charade couldn't go on. He should just come clean. Of all the people he knew, who would judge him less than Hatcher?

Jay went outside and dug under the tarp to fetch the quart mason jar of black powder. He took it inside and handed it to Hatcher, who shook it, unscrewed the lid, and took a whiff. He sealed it back and tossed it to Jay and held him with a long suspicious gaze.

"What is wrong with you, Mize?" he said firmly. There was godlike authority in his query.

Jay wavered a little. He'd misjudged his neighbor. He thought they'd shared an allegiance to privacy and a respect for the cruelty of nature.

"I used to think you were a pretty sharp tack," Hatcher said. "Now I think maybe you're some kind of . . . forestalled man-child."

He took a step forward, pinched the roach out between wet fingers. Jay swallowed.

"You've got a beautiful wife. Smart, gorgeous. My God, if I had a woman like that."

Jay tensed, working his fists into furious balls.

"Your boy is polite, clever. Both of them, so far out of your league you're not even in the same sport. And here you are just playing in the dirt. Talking about how some jar of soot is gonna save your farm. Really? That's how you plan to get em back?"

Jay wondered what would happen if he reached out and grabbed the old guy's neck and wrestled him to the ground. What sort of wiry strength did either of them still possess?

"I'm sure it's none of my business, but I think you oughta stop sitting around your house smoking dope and find some real work. You aint scared to work, I seen you out in that field all spring, but I'm telling you, it'll never make you a dime. It's already set you back to zero."

"What, you think I'd be happier running toilet snakes for you? You think my wife would respect that?" Jay snapped. "Or do you just want me to come be your son?"

Hatcher stared into him with the entirety of his invincible pain and wisdom. "I oughta whip your ass for being such a trifling fool, you know that?" he said. "And believe me, you'd end up thanking me for it."

Hatcher placed the wet joint into Jay's palm and closed and held it shut. "You keep the rest, brother. I'm gonna let myself out to piss."

Jay stood there, an apology dissolving in his throat. There was no sound but for the muffled night and the quietly decomposing rodent behind the wall and the blood chugging through his head. He walked out behind him. "Hatcher," he called, but the night had sucked his neighbor up as if he'd never been there at all.

Jay sat down on a workbench. He just wanted to tear off all his clothes and steal into the night, naked as any animal, down to the river and the washout, into that cold judgeless maw of earth. But his body refused to concede, and he fell asleep there, clutching his jar of ash.

He awoke the next morning, shivering, Chipper's tongue all over him. A strange cooler sat beside his makeshift bed. Someone had left him a gift to go on—a generous hunk of smoked ham, some individually wrapped containers of beans and creamed potatoes, a half-dozen dinner rolls, and a sack of sweet corn. "Who left this?" he demanded of Chipper, who sat obediently licking his jowls in anticipation of ham. He tore into the meal, not even with pleasure but with a wolfish indulgence, sharing only the rind with the dog. He finished and had to lie down on the bench with a stitch in his gut. He thought it must have been Hatcher who'd left it, trying to keep him alive for some baseless reason.

He drank some water, managed to keep his food down, and studied the quart mason jar of dust. It amazed him how little was left of the unfortunate trespasser.

He took the jar and a shovel down to a corner of the field above the waterline, where he'd arranged a row of wooden bins, each containing a batch of compost in some various stage of decomposition. The bins ranged from coarse materials like straw and leaves and corncobs to husks of manure, procured from the horseman Rakestraw up the road, to coarse mixes and hot piles to fine rich silts, fully cooked and cured batches, black and rich, ready to spread.

Barring any more rain, the field should be ready in a couple of weeks for a nice winter garden. He'd put in some cold crops like collards and kale, spinach and garlic and onions. Maybe a few rows of overwinter parsnips and carrots. He'd plant winter wheat over the rest, good fodder for next season.

He removed the lid from the char jar, swirled the black grit. Little wisps rose like steam. He bowed his head, gave a thought to his mysterious friend who had sacrificed his life for the fields, then sprinkled the dust into a bin of his finest black compost. He worked them together with the shovel and wet the pile from a bucket of standing water, let it glisten in the midafternoon sun, thinking *There, I've buried you. Back where I found you.*

There was nothing to find. No one would be the wiser.

– 18 –

It began two weeks ago with Sandy's father complaining about a pain in his jaw. She convinced him to see the dentist, who prescribed an antibiotic for an abscessed tooth. The discomfort remained, so he saw his general practitioner several days later. Sandy thought it must have hurt him terribly, for her father, a former doctor himself, was stubborn and had always rejected medical attention. She could count on one hand the number of times he'd seen a doctor in twenty years, two of them last week.

The general practitioner diagnosed strep throat and prescribed more antibiotics. She visited her father several days later on a Saturday, only to find him in worse shape. He complained of dizziness, nausea, intense pain in his face, neck, and shoulders. Concerned to find him alone in such a weakened state, she insisted they go to the emergency room, and again she was shocked when he did not resist.

The ER doctor told them it was a serious bacterial infection and insisted he get more rest, sending them away with prescriptions for stronger antibiotics, pain pills, an antidepressant. Sandy sat with him over the weekend, and when she returned on Monday afternoon, he was severely disoriented. In between vomiting, he kept shouting nonsense—"Joggers are stealing my mail!" and "Did you take my tuxedo? I'm not paying the late fee!" She took him directly to the emergency room, pleading that the staff keep him and run tests, anything but send him home with more prescriptions.

And now here they were, her father off in a shallow coma. The latest in a battery of tests and diagnoses suggested encephalitis caused by West Nile virus. It was a rare infection linked to the virus, but all signs pointed to it. This was the hospital's first case, the doctor told her. Research was limited, but he thought they could get a handle on it.

She felt ill herself, not from any virus but from stress and lack of sleep. It reminded her of when her mom died of a stroke, impossibly young at forty-five. The life support machines helped her hang on for a few days at the hospital in Jackson where her dad practiced. It took several colleagues to convince him to let her go.

Months before the stroke, her mom had begun losing her mind. Little things at first, and then erratic mood swings, bizarre behavior way out of character. It annoyed them before they realized it was serious, but then it was too late. She hated for Jacob to experience this slippery slope toward death, his father losing his mind too. The boy just seemed bored. He watched mindless cartoons on the hospital TV while his little leg flopped off the side of the chair. To him this was probably just another gloomy detour. He didn't understand the severity of this, only yearned to watch giant robots shooting at each other. Seeing her son absorbed in the terrible cartoon with its outdated art and revolting dialogue created a displaced sadness that made her grieve for him too.

A nurse arrived, another one she hadn't seen before. Was it such a large staff or an inordinate turnover rate? This one was sullen and hefty and came awkwardly with her cart to check the patient's vitals. She seemed put out by their presence. Sandy didn't want Jacob to be here. Hanging out in hospitals could crush the boldest of spirits.

He had a four-day weekend next week. The school called it "Fall Break," though actually it was a two-day teacher training seminar that all instructors were required to attend. She would have to find something to do with Jacob. She'd just assumed her dad would watch him, but certainly not now. Even if he made a sudden miraculous recovery, he would be weak for a while. She couldn't afford a sitter right now. She'd begun to rekindle relationships with her old church friends, but Jacob hadn't connected with their kids and it was too soon to ask such a large favor. She was estranged from everyone, which she blamed on Jay. He'd plucked her up young, isolated her from everyone, tamed her instincts, and then released her back into the wild.

The job then would fall to Jay. He was the father after all. It certainly wasn't ideal. Based on her visit, he barely seemed capable of watching the dog, and the house appeared to be a less healthy environment than the hospital. Also, it bothered her that he had not made contact since their visit almost a week ago. She'd given him gas money, but still he had made no attempt to see Jacob. Maybe bringing the boy to his father would wake him up, make him realize what was at stake.

The boy barked out a raspy cough. "Jacob, honey, are you okay?" Sandy said. "Do you need something to drink?"

"Yes," the boy replied.

She caught the nurse's eye. "Is there juice available for him?" Sandy asked.

The nurse blinked and mumbled something that implied, *Yeah, but you know I'm a nurse, right? Not a waitress?*

"I can pay for it," said Sandy, who didn't wish to offend. "Thank you so much."

She pulled up alongside her father and grabbed his hand and clutched it dearly. When they left Jay, she went straight to him, and he took them in, cooked for them, cleaned up after them, gave her money, took Jacob to the park and the grocery store, picked him up from school. He gave her time and space to process her decision and to plan their life from here. He made them so comfortable that it began to unnerve her. She felt like a child running to Daddy for consolation. She loved and resented him all at the same time, even got snippy with him a few times, but he took it all in stride. Always the patient one.

Finally, she decided she would have to move out and tackle this on her own if she was to preserve any self-respect. "Stay here and save up some money," her father had insisted, but she demurred. It was his own self-reliance and determination that had rubbed off on her, and possibly Jay's stubborn independence she was trying to uphold. What kind of mother would she be if she just freeloaded off relatives? She didn't want Jacob to believe this was how to deal with trouble.

They'd been in the rental a little over a month before her father fell ill. It was such a shitty little hovel, the grime of previous owners etched into every stitch of the place. She'd killed dozens of cockroaches already, overcoming grave fear. And they had only one bed, a twin she bought for Jacob, while she slept on the couch. The refrigerator rattled and whined like an old propeller engine. The hot water took five minutes to heat and then grew tepid in five more. She'd made due with less than luxury before, but there was something especially depressing about having to submit Jacob to it, even though he probably didn't care. He was confused and sad, a bright light going dim. She was so pissed at Jay.

She accepted her share of the blame. It was her troubles that had stressed her dad and aggravated his sickness, made her less attentive and slow to respond to his symptoms. The doctor's confidence that he could rout this aggressive virus and that her father would make a full recovery had begun to diminish. Now he hinted about the possibility that her father's mind would not make it all the way back. Fevers and ailments often singed delicate parts of the brain, causing strange, unforeseen side effects. Strokes would be more likely, restriction of movement, blindness. "Your father is very sick," he'd said. She'd detected the slightest hint of uncertainty in his eyes, a waver in his voice, as if he were confessing, *I'm in over my head, help me.*

The nurse scuffed in with juice, dropped it on the rolling bedside tray, and slunk out.

"Thank you!" Sandy called, overzealous, borderline facetious.

"Mom," Jacob said, pointing to the juice without diverting his eyes from the robotic mayhem on television.

Sandy punctured the foil lid with a straw four times too deep for the shallow cup of liquid. She handed it to Jacob, who slurped it up instantly and asked for more. "In a bit," she replied.

"Mah-um," he whined.

What would they do if her father died? Move back into his house, she imagined. Worse yet, and she hated to admit it, what if he regained consciousness but had no faculties? Would she ever see him as a burden, his sagging, whiskered hobo face and adult diapers that needed frequent changing? How would she manage it, how would she afford it? Was she truly thinking so selfishly? Breath left her. She felt light and flaming inside. Her eyes welled, she gasped for air.

Just then someone knocked on the door. She stood up, hoping it was the doctor with good news. A balloon and bouquet appeared, followed by Danny Shoals, sporting a look of practiced concern. "Anybody home?" he inquired with a tender grimace.

Sandy flushed red. She looked at Jacob, who recognized the deputy and brightened instantly. His posture changed, becoming more erect and obedient.

"I'm so sorry," he said with longing. He leaned in and kissed her on the cheek, then set the balloon and flowers on the bedside credenza. He walked around the bed, opened the blinds a twist, and slapped five with Jacob. "What's up, big'un?" he said, squatting down to greet the boy. "You been working on that swing?"

Jacob wagged his head and grinned shyly.

"I brought something you might like," Shoals said, digging in his pocket. He retrieved a Swiss Army knife, not one of the little ones with five or six features, but a fat one with a host of flip-out devices.

"Maybe your mom will let you go down to the courtyard and cut something with this. There's plenty of cool features on this thing. Look, there's a screwdriver, wire cutter, toothpick. Flashlight!"

"Whoa!" said Jacob, wide-eyed. He looked up at the deputy with stunned gratitude. Shoals turned to Sandy and winked.

"That's too much," she said, still in shock at his arrival.

"Nah," said Shoals, waving her off.

"No, really. We can't accept that gift. It's too much."

Shoals walked over and leaned in conspiratorially. "It's nothing, really. We confiscate stuff like this all the time."

"Is this a drug dealer's knife, probably stolen in the first place?"

He chuckled, shook his head. He knelt down and demonstrated some of the knife's features to Jacob. "You can pick your way out of handcuffs with this," he said.

Sandy watched him intently, his gestures full of purpose. He believed with every fiber of his being that he belonged here, that he could bring comfort where no one else had.

"How did you find us?" she asked.

He came close, patted her arm. "I hear things, I act." She drew away unconsciously.

"What can I get you?" he asked.

"Nothing, I'm fine."

"You want me to sit with him while you go down and get some chicken strips or eggs or something?" He pulled out his wallet and turned to Jacob. "Hey, bud, you want a honey bun? Maybe some juice?"

The boy wagged his head. "Mom, can I have some candy?"

"What's a matter, you don't want a honey bun?" said Shoals. "Come on, I'll walk down with you." He turned to Sandy. "Is he old enough to go down by himself?"

Another nurse came in, nodded at Shoals, and smiled awkwardly. "Everything okay?" she asked, though it sounded to Sandy like *It's getting a little crowded in here.*

"We're all good, Belinda," Shoals called, jovial and loud. "What's Randall up to?"

"Oh, nothing. Just working," she said with a drawl and a grin.

"Y'all taking good care of the professor here?"

"We're keeping an eye on him," she said, a bit uncertain, a bit flirtatious.

"A'ight then, be good." He said it as a dismissal, which the nurse heeded.

"Hey, can I have a honey bun?" Jacob asked Sandy.

"You bet, little man, in just a second," Shoals replied. He looked at Sandy, who was horrified into silence. She had a disturbing vision that the three of them were a family. He misjudged her look and touched her shoulder, bent down to eye level.

"Hey, look, I know it's tough to see him like this, but everything's going to be just fine. I saw Dr. Pete down the hall and he said your dad's a fighter."

She felt aggravated by his simple assurance, yet part of her believed him too. "They don't even know what's wrong," she lied.

"Oh, they will, don't worry. Sometimes it takes a few days, but the tests match up and they nail it down. Then they'll shoot him up with the right juice and then problem solved."

He took her hand and stared at her father for a long moment.

"I've seen folks worse off than him turning cartwheels out of here in a week's time," he said, gripping her hand.

Disgusted by his presumptuous familiarity, she released his hand and walked to the other side of the room. She wanted to tell him to leave, but there was something in his positivity that she needed. And she didn't want Jacob to see her behave rudely in the face of kindness. There was also something inside of her, something that repulsed her, that made her want to throw her arms around him and bawl.

"Hey, bud, you wanna go for a ride in the squad car?" he asked Jacob.

Jacob whirled around toward Sandy. "Ooo, can I? Please."

"No, honey. We have to go home pretty soon."

"Come on, let him ride," Shoals insisted.

"I just don't think it's a good idea."

"Mah-um."

"Come on, little pecan Sandy."

That corny endearment put the nail in the coffin. She led him aside. "Danny, it's incredibly thoughtful of you to drop by, but we really need to deal with this privately. I just met you. You're sweet, but I really can't do this with you."

He grabbed her hand again, cocked his head, and spoke gravely. "Hey, I hear ya. I'm only sorry there's not someone more familiar to be here with you. You're a strong woman, but this aint easy. I've been here, wondering if my dad is going to make it back. Sometimes they don't. It's okay to need somebody to prop you up, even if it's just a quiet stone wall to lean against. I'm here, don't be shy to ask."

He patted her on the back like a pal and raised his trigger finger to Jacob. "Be good, big'un. I gotta run catch some bad guys. Rain check on that squad car ride. And you help your mama, now, you hear me?"

He winked at Sandy as he pulled the door closed behind him. Her relief at his easy departure was met by an inexplicable fondness for him, which must have been a result of his unfazed, doglike devotion.

She knew it was impossible, but Sandy thought it would be best if she never saw him again.

PART

III

PART

III

Leavenger climbed into Hilltop Grocery on his crutches. The tinkling bell announced his arrival. The woodsman made a point to stop by midafternoon two or three times a week to catch up with the retirees who sought habitual relief from their lives in this dank outpost. His skin was too thin today to sit with the old heels, but he took the risk knowingly, in need of human contact. The scars were making inroads, and he didn't know how to handle the emotions this exposed. The pills, which he took more frequently than ever, numbed only so deep. He was a creature of the external and needed simple cruelty, even if it was self-inflicted.

He gave Fletcher the shopkeeper a gruff hello, and the old clerk grunted and rattled his newspaper in reply.

"Lookee what crawled out of the shit ponds," one sipper cried in greeting as the embattled woodsman dragged himself to the table. "I thought I flushed you last week."

"Don't you mean scraped out of your Pampers?" countered another.

There were four of them, all looking like they'd just fallen out of beds or climbed out of graves. It had been ages since any of them had seen a comb or a bar of soap. One had a sick bucket at his feet. They were all blind to themselves, each guilty of his own prejudices.

"Don't you never bathe, Leavenger, or you scared to go near water anymore?"

The laughter was implicit, for they rarely cracked a smile. Anything clever heard here had been said countless times before.

Leavenger poured himself a cup and took a pained seat. The coffee, famously bad, tasted like it had been steeping all day in a rusty skillet.

"If I had as much money as Leavenger, I believe I'd be up in some sweet cooch instead of sitting around with these bums."

"Only way that's gonna happen is if you come back in the next life as a tampon."

"Sign me up."

"You got your government check this month?"

"They aint mailed em out yet, I don't reckon."

"Jim Boise got his disaster money. He said thanks but no thanks, now I gotta do this shit again next year. Sumbitch *wants* to go bankrupt."

"Leavenger, what do they pay you to limp around and drink beer? Shit, I'll pull my britches down right here and y'all can beat my ass with a hot iron for that deal."

"I guess his modeling career didn't take off."

"I might buy me a new shirt at least if I was on the government tit."

"He says the only tit he's on is your wife's," cried another, making up for Leavenger's silence.

"Be my guest," the target replied. "She's down at the nursing home shitting her bedsheets. I'll forward you the bills."

Leavenger sulked in his coffee, too aching and bitter to participate. There was no sympathy here, he knew not to come for that. They were miserable louts themselves, whose only comfort resided in their brief bull-market share of one-upmanship, or else the shame and suffering of those outside their coffee ring. He was no better than any one of them.

"What's a matter with you, Leavenger, you still got a bee up your dick over your dog getting killed?"

"You're lucky you didn't get your ass snatched by a gator. A boy up at the corps told me they were seeing two or three them scoundrels a day."

"Horseshit!"

"Go fuck yourself then!"

The door jingled and Leavenger glanced up. There he was. His hair had gone gray and he'd grown a ridiculous mustache, wore big sunglasses and a decent pair of pants, but those shitkicker boots and the limp hat placed him. Leavenger stood and strained to get a better look at the guy.

"What're you doing, shaking out a fart or what?"

Leavenger sat back down and leaned into the table. "That's him, y'all," he said in a whisper. "That's the son of a bitch who shot Virginia and threw her in the river. Then he dumped all them frozen fish back."

Silenced for once, the men turned to see the stranger for themselves. No one spoke. Their guns were in the trucks, and they didn't trust a man who shot dogs at random.

The stranger left as quick as he came and one called out to Fletcher, "Who was that fella?"

Fletcher ducked his head and glanced out the window, watched the man get in his truck and back away. "No idea," the proprietor replied and went back to his paper.

"He shot Leavenger's girlfriend!" one cried.

They turned their loathing back to the woodsman. "Why don't you go after him?"

"I think it's all bull. You ask me, I say Leavenger shot that dog himself after she come up pregnant with his own man-pups."

Leavenger stumbled to his feet and threw his seat back, then shambled away from the old goats, dropped a dollar at the counter on his way out.

"Uh-oh, he's gone to fetch his gun."

"You're too late! He'll be on the other side of the county fore you get to your truck."

They hollered after him as he left, the jingling of the door his only remark. They saw his shadow propped up there on the porch wondering what to do next.

– 19 –

The harvest sun drank up the rest of Mize's pond that first week of October, leaving behind a sheen of treacherous mud that reflected the light like chocolate glass. Eager to scamper out across it, Jay bided his time, spent his days readying plants, turning compost, and generally putting his house in order.

One of these windswept afternoons he sat in a rocking chair on the front porch, peering through binoculars at a flock of snow geese browsing the sticky terrain. On their way south, they'd landed in the field and were resting their wings, beaks down, sorting through the mud. He was pleased with their cleanup job. They were welcome to peck up every crumb of evidence.

He'd eaten everything from the ration box along with another charity plate left by Hatcher, but a nervous hunger had beset him again, and he had all but decided to fetch his gun and blast one of the geese for dinner when they erupted en masse. He whipped the binoculars down and ran into the yard to see them take to the sky, blowing over the roof and beyond the pasture.

From the road below came the sound of boiling engines and excited male voices. Jay focused the lenses and spied three young men standing by the side of the road, speaking feverishly, gesturing toward the field and up to the house.

Here they are at last, the sons of bitches. Either the killers in their mud trucks and ball caps or a posse of yokel vigilantes. Jay watched them climb back into their high cabs, wheeling and pivoting in the road. The first one began to climb the driveway.

His arsenal was never far from hand these days, and in a matter of seconds Jay was in position, fully loaded, safeties off. He watched them make their slow, deliberate uphill crawl, one truck royal blue and pasted over with decals, the other so caked in mud its color could not be discerned. There was something official in their ascent. There was no other good reason for them to show up here uninvited. He trousered the pistol and moved to the back door by the carport. He set the .22 against the wall by the door and held the twelve-gauge in the crook of one arm, arranging himself so that he could observe their approach and then charge out blasting if the situation required it.

When they reached the house, both trucks idled in the driveway. He wondered if the deputy had sent them, his armored truck division of backwater thugs. If Jay acted out of turn here, it would get back to the law in some twisted incarnation.

The first young buck leapt down from the cab of the hot blue mudder. He had a scrubby face, young and tough in his backward cap and muscle tee and big lavender shades. He moved with an affected, tottering swagger and rapped unnecessarily hard on the back door.

Jay whipped out from behind the window, and the young hot-rodder jumped back. "Shit, dude, you liked to scared the piss outta me!"

Jay wrenched the door open, leaving the storm door closed.

"Hey, man, what's up?" the kid shouted through the door and over the gurgling engines. Jay sized him up, all acne and wiener arms. He could easily take him if things went to the brink. He peered out at the other truck, containing two beefier boys, caps pulled low over their eyes.

Talking through the door had put this scrappy one at unease. He chewed his gum heartily and kept his hands in his pockets. Passive gestures both. After a moment of silence, the kid spoke up. "I just need to ask you something."

"Go ahead."

"I aint gonna bite ya," he said with greaser cheer.

Jay opened the storm door and stepped outside. The kid backed up, perhaps at Jay's crazed, disheveled appearance, accentuated by the gas mask pulled down around his neck and the shotgun dangling on a sling behind him.

"Hey, dude." He was all teeth and dark frames. "I'm from Old Indian Raceway, we got a mud course on the other side of the river up here about a mile. Our course got tore up by that tornado and we was wondering if we could use your field for our races on Friday night."

The kid had forgotten his manners, if he ever had any. No name, no handshake. Just, what can you do for me?

Jay made a point of scrutinizing his buddies. "You want to race through my field?" he said in disbelief.

"Yeah, mud racing. Save you from having to plow it up in the spring."

"How do you figure that?"

"Cause, we'll tear it up for you," he said.

Jay shook his head. "You must not know shit about plowing."

"Excuse me?" the kid said, his friendly demeanor gone in a flash. "My family's been farming here forever. I think *I* know a thing or two about plowing."

"Oh, and I guess I'm the whack-job with all the engineering and strange configurations. I couldn't know a damn thing about farming since I can't lay a straight row. God forbid we use the vertical plane!"

The kid froze solid at Jay's harangue.

"I'm just out making yard art, is that what you people think? Do you know about sustainability, friend? Do you have a clue about what's coming down the pike? If you did, you sure as hell wouldn't be out racing your buggies. You need to be putting by for a long-ass winter."

The kid smirked and turned to his buddies. He wagged his thumb at Jay and shook his head as if to say, *Get a load of this asshole.*

"Let me ask you, what good does it do me to have you tearing ass over my land? It makes more work for me in the spring, it ruins the soil, and then I'm liable if anybody gets hurt."

"Look, now, we aint like that," the kid said. "Aint nobody gonna sue anybody, and we'll cut you in on the winnings. Everybody ponies up for the jackpot. Sometimes it's upwards of three or four grand."

Jay didn't budge. The money tempted him to be sure, but inviting these morons onto his property was like throwing away all he'd worked for and then calling the law on himself.

"Hey, at the very least it's a good show," the kid added with a pothole smile. "Gonna be some pretty women there. Something about being out in the mud gets their sugar wet." He worked his eyebrows. "Let's just say come Saturday morning you might've had your own bumpy ride."

Something about the kid's presumptions got Jay riled up, sent a craze trembling through him. "Who are you?" he demanded.

"Hutch," the kid replied.

"You weren't running waves down here a few weeks back, you and another guy in a motorboat, were you?"

"Do what?"

"Who sent you here?"

"Look, dude, it's a simple yes or no. We aint trying to pull nothing over on you, we just need a strip to race is all."

Jay sighed and clenched his fist. He could raise the shotgun, walk the kid back to his truck. He could demand a thousand dollars up front.

"I'm married. What makes you think I'd cheat on my wife with some little redneck farm girl?"

The kid bowed up. "Listen now, my buddies out there in that truck sent me to do the talking cause I'm the friendly one."

Jay sucked in a breath to let forth a stream of hellfire. The words were at his teeth. But he knew it would snap the kid's simple dignity. A squabble would turn into a brawl when his buddies came flying down from their perch, and then a brawl would turn into manslaughter, twenty years for each boy, maybe life without parole.

"I don't believe I'll allow it," he said firmly, wielding the last grasp of his sanity. He retracted inside, closed and locked both doors, and crouched down in the mudroom, listening to the hollering hail of fuck-yous, the rumbling engines, wheels tearing ruts in his yard and slinging gravel as they maneuvered around and lumbered back down the road. He heard them squeal and rev once they hit pavement, the engines bellowing in rage, storming off to find some new country to rut.

He waited for their clamor to die and then paced the hallway and thought of a dozen comebacks. He went back outside and around the house, down to the field, where he stared at the muddy expanse. What better way to stir up and disperse any lingering traces of the corpse than to have a bunch of mudders running through the field, tearing and mixing and taking it away caked in their wheels and undercarriages and smeared up and down their truck bodies?

Maybe he'd blown an opportunity just then, or else closed the door on a far-fetched solution. Rebuffed another potential ally. It wasn't doing him any good to sit here and stew and hide, hoarding all the shame for himself. There was a great guilty world out there willing to share, willing to ride him mad or roughshod. He was bound now and nearly courageous enough to go out into it.

– 20 –

Sandy deposited Jacob at the Methodist Sunday school and told him she'd be back in an hour to attend church with him. First she planned to drop by the hospital. She believed her father took strength from her company, and in turn, she needed to borrow his courage to make her long-delayed return to Christian fellowship.

As she pulled out of the circular drive, Sandy's high school friend Tina Crump approached carrying a baby. Her slab of a husband, Dennis, waddled behind with two more children in hand.

Sandy rolled down the window to say hello.

"You doing a little drop and dash?" asked Tina, affecting a cute country lilt.

"You caught me."

"What's a matter, you too good for us?"

The accusation stung a little, even though it was meant as a joke. Sandy thought Tina's pious eyes and the high false register of her voice told the truth.

"I'm actually on my way to the hospital. My father's in a coma."

"Oh my goodness," said Tina, clutching her baby. She softened and reached out to stroke Sandy's arm. "Is he gonna be all right?"

"We don't know."

A look like genuine anguish came over Tina's face. The red-faced baby in her arms looked up, its bonnet-swathed head teetering on its shoulders. "You know I'm just messing with you about skipping church, Sandy."

"Of course. I was actually planning to come back for worship."

"Do, Sandy. You can sit with us, and we'll all pray for your daddy. I'll get Brother Wiles to say a prayer with the congregation."

Sandy thanked her and waved good-bye and then whipped out of the parking lot toward the hospital. She couldn't imagine going back to sit with Tina and her family and wait for the reverend to pray for the damaged Messlers and Mizes. She could see herself after the service, besieged by all manner of well-wishers with their questions and blessings and guilt-inducing blather. They weren't bad people, they just wanted her to be happy and exactly like them.

Why was it so awkward with Tina? Sandy still loved and felt indebted to her and all the other girls—Mamie, Hallie, Mary Laurel—but they'd lost everything they ever had in common. When she moved to Madrid after her dad married Miss Sue and uprooted her suddenly, so soon after her mother's passing, those girls had welcomed her right into the fold. Throughout high school the girls had all stayed active together in the youth ministry, the choir, and volunteer work. Sandy still had fond memories of supervised sleepovers with boys in the church rec center on weekends and trips to Memphis for bowling, skating, and Christian rock concerts. She'd made a pledge to Christ before the entire congregation at seventeen and believed the rest of her life was right here among them.

But during college she drifted, her priorities migrated toward new friends and different ideas, to road trips and hangovers and late-sleeping Sundays. Then came Jay, who'd been overchurched in his youth. To him it was all a country club scene. The Christians missed the point of a good history lesson and values system by dressing everything up in such ritual and hokum, he believed. He despised their blind faith. Salvation was something you had to work for, a personal struggle, not potluck dinners and musicals and fundraising for new church buildings.

"I can't believe you're dating an atheist," one of her friends told her, and aside from Miss Sue's funeral, that was the last time she'd attended church. Nevertheless, she believed a child should have a spiritual foundation, and she would risk being seen as a groveling sinner if it would help Jacob find peace.

Her father tried occasionally to entice her back to church, but she preferred talking matters of the spirit with him one-on-one. Every tragedy that befell him seemed to strengthen his faith. He believed there was a well of goodness in the universe, and our journey in life was to find it. It was hardest to find on earth but would get progressively easier, and the key was love. "It's not about who you are or how you were made, but what you do," he told her. "Help people, be kind, and peace will come, I swear it."

She believed he was a saint but doubted it was so simple. She was a nice enough person, and it had brought her no closer to peace. In fact, she seemed as far adrift from peace as she'd ever been in her life. And now the thought of losing him, even of seeing him cling to life in that sterile hospital room, was a prospect worse than walking into chapel and being deemed an apostate by all the faces from her former life.

Sandy made a detour to check on his house, located in a wooded neighborhood tucked away in a quiet, older part of town. She parked in the driveway and gathered the mail accumulating in the box by the front door. Inside the rooms were cold, but it smelled like home. The cat came up squalling for food and rubbing off hair on the hem of her black skirt. She fetched the bag of rust-colored chow from the pantry, poured a panful, and drew a bowl of water from the faucet. She dumped the litter box in a garbage bag with old food from the fridge and then took the trash to the curb and came back inside to tidy up.

She moved quickly from room to room, straightening and dusting as she went, becoming intimate again with her teenage home. Miss Sue had won it in a divorce settlement from her previous marriage. It was low and sprawling, surrounded by trees and fortified on all sides with patios and decks and lounge areas. Sandy had considered it very posh during her adolescence, her own bedroom set off in a separate wing where she lived until her sophomore year of college. The room still held mementos of her youth, her corkboard of photos with friends she never spoke to anymore, the shelf of devotional books and chaste romance novels, her framed academic honors and church citations.

She walked into the spacious den, swiping a dustrag across bookshelves laden with mystery novels and science texts and framed photographs charting their cobbled-together lives. It occurred to her that everyone was gone. Here was a photo of Sandy at six, sitting beside her mother, the quiet beauty. People told them they looked so much alike, but she couldn't discern the resemblance. There was a multiframe display from her father's wedding with Miss Sue, a casual backyard affair in autumn. Sandy was among the bridesmaids, a gawky girl of thirteen. Her mother would never have dressed her in that terrible paisley. Would she have been disappointed that her husband had remarried so soon? Sandy often wondered if he'd been cheating with Miss Sue even while her mother disappeared into the dementia that preceded her fatal stroke.

There was a lovely shot of Miss Sue, herself gone almost two years now following a quick and difficult bout with lung cancer. She had the hard look of a 1930s movie star and lived by a two-drink, two-pack philosophy, always quick-witted and edgy, easy with the off-color remarks. She hadn't a clue what to do for a girl except offer kindness and honest advice when solicited. Her previous husband still lived in Madrid, and together they had a son, Loren, a bachelor who had moved east. Miss Sue would always excuse her son, saying, "He just hasn't found the right woman," though now Sandy understood what that meant and why he rarely called or visited.

She gathered up some books and notepads on the coffee table and returned them to her father's study. There was a small book by a famous Buddhist and another on the Mississippi River flood of 1927. As professor emeritus at the university, he partook in casual reading these days. His office still contained heavy arcane medical texts, diplomas, a few token jars of strange objects in formaldehyde. He'd been a reputed surgeon at the university hospital in Jackson but resigned under foggy circumstances. After her mother's stroke, he started prescribing to himself and got reckless. Someone noticed, and the hospital invited him to leave. That's when, presumably, he met Miss Sue. Theirs was a whirlwind romance, six months and then married, house packed up, gone to Madrid, where her father began teaching biology at the university and became one of the campus's most beloved professors.

The doorbell sounded at the front of the house. Sandy's first inclination was to hide, but she felt protective of the house and went to investigate. An older lady wearing a velvety tracksuit and sunglasses stood at the door holding a foil-covered pan. Her hair was dyed jet-black and burst in a fashionable shock. She introduced herself as Mrs. Bender. They'd recently moved in next door and had already made friends with her father. She seemed to know all about Sandy and Jacob too and expressed sympathy for her situation without alluding directly to the separation.

"I saw you taking the trash and wanted to bring something over, just some dinner for you and the little one," she said, passing the meal to Sandy. Mrs. Bender patted her hand. "So sorry to hear about your father, we just think he's a splendid man."

"Thank you," Sandy replied with exaggerated kindness.

"And you are such a lovely woman."

"Oh, thank you, Mrs. Bender. You are so sweet."

"What are the doctors saying?"

"Well," said Sandy, bracing herself. "They're just watching him. Not a lot they can do, apparently. Just monitoring his fever, making sure his body is well equipped to fight the infection."

"Is it true that it's West Nile?" asked Mrs. Bender.

"Yes, they're fairly certain."

The neighbor clasped her hand to her mouth. "My husband Bill and I, we try not to go outside too much. The mosquitoes are terrible this year. We screened in our back porch. He thinks I'm crazy, but honey, you just never know. You hear these things on the news and you wonder if they're real. Imagine that, in our own neighborhood!"

"Well, don't get too worried, Mrs. Bender. He was just down in south Louisiana visiting friends."

"Oh my word."

"It's quite possible he was bitten there. It could've happened anywhere. And they tell me it's actually quite rare. This is only their first case."

"They say eating bananas will keep them away," Mrs. Bender advised, though Sandy wasn't sure if she meant doctors or mosquitoes. "I heard that on the television, and I eat four a day now."

The kindly neighbor didn't want to take up too much of Sandy's time. "I know this is so difficult for you, and I think you are just a brave and impressive young woman," she said, clutching Sandy's hand. "Don't feel like you can't call on us if the load gets too great to bear." They hugged briefly, and Sandy thanked her for everything, and then Mrs. Bender rushed back to the safety of indoors.

The stranger's kindness took Sandy by surprise, and she teared up, thankful for the unsought encouragement. She set the casserole pan on the kitchen island and removed the cover. It was a rigatoni dish, generous with cheese and Italian sausage, not even frozen. Had she thrown it together that quick or was there a batch waiting in the fridge for a random gesture of sympathy? Sandy grabbed a fork and sampled it cold. Not bad.

Sitting there at her father's dinner table—fretting over the past, something the Buddhist in her father would have discouraged—she couldn't help but recall the last time they'd all eaten together at this table. It must have been May? June? If the end of her marriage could be ascribed to a moment, then it took place right here.

In the adjacent living room, Jay had been relating to her father terrible news of the universe, new findings collected by satellites of how the entire galaxy was passing into an interstellar energy cloud, some patch of astral turbulence, and had begun to absorb dramatic amounts of energy. The earth was due for a prolonged holocaust of environmental cataclysms, all created by this excess energy and increased solar flares. The planet, Jay insisted, would be ripped slowly asunder for a thousand years.

As her husband spoke with alarm and authority, she'd noticed the growing sense of fear on Jacob's face. He was listening while pretending to watch

TV. She took Jay aside and asked him to tone it down. Of course he dismissed her and continued to rave. At dinner Jacob mentioned wanting some new video game for his birthday, which sent Jay into a tirade about electronic technology and how all of it would soon be rendered useless. He described the earth's magnetic field, which was generated from the active iron core and wrapped around the planet like a sheet. According to Jay, scientists believed the poles were shifting, tearing holes in the sheet, and allowing the sun's radiation to stream in unfiltered.

"Delightful dinner conversation," Sandy said. "I'm shocked I haven't heard any of this on the news."

"Sure, put it on the news and watch the world go insane. Looting, raping, pillaging. If the planet doesn't get us first, we'll do it to ourselves. Environmental extremes always lead to social breakdown."

He went off on a long discourse about how mass extinctions occur every 60 to 65 million years, and we were due for another just any time now.

"Okay, so if fleeing underground is the only hope we have for survival, then why on earth did you insist on buying the farm?" she demanded. "Isn't it pointless to grow our own food if the sun is going to burn it all up?"

Her father was smiling now. Perhaps he had mistaken this doomsday banter for spirited, tongue-in-cheek debate. Of course he quietly rooted for his daughter, but didn't he sense Jay's mania?

Jay shook his head. "Well, all that could take years to unfold. In the immediate future we're much more likely to see corrupt governments and crashing markets, leading to poverty, hunger, and civil unrest in the cities. Let's say a rebellion forms. Someone gets hold of a dirty bomb or unleashes a genetically modified virus that decimates the population. At least we could stay and farm and protect our land. That's the best-case scenario really. I mean, what if someone sets loose a fleet of self-replicating nanorobots?"

Sandy was astonished. In that moment she saw a new disturbance in Jay's eyes. He was someone else, someone not her husband. Someone to whom she would have never made the promises she did. At that moment her instinct was not to nurture him back but to attack the stranger.

"An army of nanorobots, really? Have you been watching cartoons with Jacob? You sound insane, do you know that?"

Her dad laughed and shook his head.

"The technology is real!" Jay insisted. "Do you deny that there are dictators and terrorists crazy enough to use it? What about our own government?"

"And a tree could fall on the house and kill us before dessert! A flock of chemically enraged flamingos could descend and peck us all to death."

Her father was laughing, for Jacob's sake, and the boy watched with excited eyes. But this squabble had lost all humor for Sandy.

"Jay, I cannot believe that I'm arguing with you about the end of the world. I cannot live this way, thinking like this. Every day that you harp on this gloom and doom is another day you miss the blessed life you have here, right now, this instant."

"Sandy, I agree with you completely. It sounds preposterous. But these are hypothetical examples. The point is—trouble is coming. I'm just reading the signs and trying to prepare so we can go on living."

She was near tears and made her point with violent jabs at the tabletop. "Who wants to go on living like this? Don't drag us down this road, Jay. Tragedy is self-fulfilling. I don't believe that you're thinking of us. I think that you believe your life will only have purpose if the world is falling down around you, so you're writing our life toward that end. If you want conflict so desperately, why don't you sign up for military service and go overseas? Let us have our peace and quiet."

Looking back, she realized that was the moment she decided to leave. She remembered the bitter rationalization—*I cannot wait for things to go back to normal, I cannot accept the direction my life has taken, I cannot stay with you even though I swore before my family and my friends and my God that I would.* And no matter how she justified it—she must protect the boy from poverty, from his father's emotional abandonment—in the end it was purely selfish. Because people can endure almost anything. But why do it when you don't have to? If a better life could be made, why not make it?

Now she despaired that she hadn't made a better life, that even the days of compost and paranoia were healthier for Jacob than this. She wondered if it was harder to leave someone you loved or to watch someone you love die.

A mandolin ringtone sounded from inside her purse and broke her concentration. Sandy thought it might be the hospital or the church. An emergency was always a strum away these days. She consulted the caller ID. It was Jay's mother, who had called the night before as they were preparing to leave the hospital. Sandy had put off returning her call. They hadn't spoken in months, since after the funeral, when Mrs. Mize called in a weepy daze to tell her how awfully Jay had behaved toward the lawyer and funeral director. Sandy had no idea if mother and son had been in communication but doubted it, since Jay's cell-phone account had been suspended, and so it would be left to her to dispense all the sad news. Either that or continue to reinforce the polite lies behind which the family maintained its constant façade.

"Hello," she answered before the final ring.

"Oh, Sandy!" Mrs. Mize greeted her with a familiar high-pitched, trumped-up excitement. "I was afraid I'd missed you again!"

They made small talk before Sandy asked, in a tone that expressed the unpleasantness that could be neither spoken nor ignored, "How are you doing?"

"It's been a trial since the accident, honey, I won't deny it. But Samson is helping me through. We had Miss Emma stay with us a couple of days. We tried to replicate Dotty Purifoy's pudding cake recipe, you know. Herbie's been here to fix the washer and get my medicine. We're staying busy."

Sandy had no idea who these people were, but Mrs. Mize went on this way for a while, reciting a litany of minutiae that made no sense out of context. "I'm sorry," Sandy interjected, "do I know Miss Emma?"

"Emma Paschall from Jackson, Tennessee. We were old friends separated over the years, but she heard about Murray passing and we've reconnected. She lost her husband, James, last year. I'm so thankful to have found my old friend again."

"Oh, that's wonderful to hear. And who's Herbie?"

"Herbie!" Mrs. Mize cried, as if everyone knew Herbie. "He's my young-est nephew. He's been away in the wars overseas and got hurt. He's a little slow now, but he's been such a dear help to me. It's funny who comes out of nowhere to help you in times of trouble."

Mrs. Mize was riding a medicated wave of enthusiasm, or maybe it was genuine gratitude. Whatever the case, it was reassuring to hear her so upbeat again.

"I couldn't reach Jay on his phone," said Mrs. Mize. "I hope everything is all right."

"He's fine," Sandy lied. "He just let his phone contract lapse."

"Is he available to speak?"

Sandy wanted to admit the truth but couldn't bring herself to disappoint his grief-stricken mother. "He and Jacob are at church."

"Oh, good!"

"I was just straightening up around the house."

"Well, I figured I'd hear from him after Herbie dropped off the bike," said Mrs. Mize. "Did he like it?"

"The bike?"

"The motor scooter or four-wheeler, whatever they call it. Murray left it to him in the will. He only bought it a few months before he passed."

"Oh yes, yes, of course," Sandy played along. She hadn't a clue what Mrs. Mize was talking about.

"Herbie said y'all weren't at home, so he left it in the driveway," she went on. "I hope he liked it, I really do."

"He did, yes, thank you."

"It's Murray, God rest his soul. You can thank Murray someday, dear. Someday we'll all be reunited."

Sandy assumed she meant they'd all be together in heaven. She thought of the old Sunday school lesson, how suicides don't make it to heaven, float-ing interminably in hell or limbo along with the Buddhists and gays and other non-Christians. It made her think of Jacob in a room full of strangers, where dubious answers were applied to life's most difficult questions.

She felt a catch in her chest. "Oh, my, I've let the time get away. Jay's truck is out of gas and I was supposed to pick them up from church."

"Okay, hon, please tell them I called. And how's your father?"

Sandy said he'd been a little under the weather and left it at that. The widow had heard enough about lost fathers and husbands. Any more bad news might break the poor woman's spirit.

Mrs. Mize began to plead for them to visit. She wanted to see Jacob. And Jay, of course. Family must cleave together in times of trouble and all of that. Sandy heard something disingenuous there, or else she'd lost herself to frustration, and before she realized what she was saying, she interrupted. "Mrs. Mize"—for in all the years they'd known each other, Jay's mother had never invited her to call her anything different—"can I ask you something?"

"Why, of course, dear."

"How did you do it? How did you work around that terrible family history that we've both married into? It's neither of our husbands' fault, but they carry it like their own burden."

Mrs. Mize paused for a long moment as if parsing the questions, separating accusation from advice and memory from fantasy. She replied, in a voice tightly bitter or possibly sad, "We just never speak to that. We lived through it, and it's nothing worth revisiting. It's the little bit we can do to leave it be."

"But I wonder if that's healthy. Why hide it and keep it for your own instead of getting it out in the open and accepting it?"

"Honey, the Lord is directing us. What need is there to understand everything that happens along the way?"

This was her usual stone-wall defense. Sandy felt the need to apologize. She didn't mean to dredge up bad feelings. Mrs. Mize returned easily to her script, and Sandy echoed her heightened good-byes and hung up. Something about the widow's sadness, her inability to share herself, and her insistence on projecting a simplistic and deluded understanding of the world broke Sandy's heart. She had to stuff her face with pasta to keep from going to pieces.

In a matter of bites she felt a crushing desire to see her son. She checked her watch: fifteen minutes until Sunday school let out. Maybe they'd skip chapel this morning, get donuts and chocolate milk instead.

When she stood up from the table, she was horrified to discover that she'd eaten the entire tray of pasta. A meal for a family of four, gone in ten minutes. She replaced the tinfoil covering on the dish and pushed the evidence to the dark bottom of the garbage can. Then she probed the kitchen for a piece of nice stationery and a pen, something upon which to transcribe her gratitude. All she found was a yellow legal pad and a red ballpoint pen. She took them to the table and sat down and composed her thoughts. The letter began:

Dear Jay . . .

— 21 —

Jay woke up Tuesday morning and walked out back, where he thought he saw a man bathing in the cistern. He wore a silver chain and a cavalry hat that resembled his father's. The man's back was turned, and he seemed to be slurping a cold bottle of soda until Jay recognized it was a shotgun barrel tilted up to his face. He ran into the yard and pushed the cistern over, and they tumbled together through the puddles. When he sat up at last, Jay saw the buzzard scampering off, flapping its wings dry.

The vision scared him, and he began seeking answers in unlikely places. He reached out to the unknown Creator, whom he'd always held in frustrated, one-sided reproach. But now it was time to bow down, to beg for answers and even forgiveness. He didn't trust himself alone anymore. It was one thing to reflect on his father's suicide, another to witness it replayed in his backyard. *Is this how it begins?* he wondered. *Does the mind trick the body into performing its bidding this way? Is this Your plan for me?* It only made sense that God would send someone, whether a buzzard or a dead man, to solicit his repentance. *Have I contributed to an act of evil by aiding its concealment? Can an otherwise decent man be damned unwittingly?*

In the face of these great inquiries, Jay was met with only silence.

He couldn't stand to hang around the house any longer, so he spent the rest of the morning walking the field, searching for the disembodied hand. The ground was still soft and glistening. Chipper dashed straight across, kicking up holes and slinging mud. Jay followed, slop-stepping right over to the spot where the corpse had lain. He found no sign of anything—no hand, no scraps of clothing, no indentations or footprints of any kind. The water had made its final authentication on this piece of damnable ground.

Chipper flitted from scent to scent, unearthing no clues, and after he'd walked the field twice over, Jay went and shuffled the compost with his yard fork. There were no visible signs of the charcoal when he inspected a handful, but when he put it to his nose or touched it to his tongue, he imbibed the smoky essence. Still a nip of man in there. It hadn't cured long enough. A good rain, another two weeks in the sun.

He couldn't imagine anything left to cover, only nature's quiet rendering to finish his deeds. But there was still the nagging sense of something undone. His mind retraced the events of the last two weeks, constantly accounting for what had set them in motion—*Who was this man? Why did he die? How did he end up here on my property?*

Suddenly Chipper bayed and shot up the hill and over the yard in a sustained howl. Jay jerked around and just noticed the car with flashing yellow lights pull to the top of the drive and disappear behind the house. He spread flat across the ground, his heart slamming against the wet earth. He heard two distinct car horn blasts, followed soon by three more, along with the continued yowling.

Jay stood and darted up the hill toward the house, coming around the far side with his pistol ready. He scaled the porch and peered around the corner. Whose battered maroon hatchback was this? It announced itself with another series of aggravated honks. Chipper had gone quiet, nowhere to be seen. Jay slipped up behind the driver's side with the pistol braced, but there was no one at the wheel.

"Where the hell have you been?" called someone from the passenger seat. It was Purnell, the rural mail carrier. "Yours aint the only certified letter I still got to deliver."

Jay tucked the gun away and leaned in the open driver's-side window. The portly mailman drove from the passenger seat, giving him convenient reach to the roadside mailboxes. In uniform shorts, his wide hairy leg was draped over the gearshift to operate the brakes and gas. A bucket of mail and catalogs rode in the driver's seat, and at his feet a box of fried chicken. Chipper was up on all fours, licking the mailman's slick fingers.

"Here," growled Purnell, a nub of cold cigar clenched in his teeth and a letter in his hand. "Need you to sign for that."

Jay took the grease-stained letter. It was from Sandy, postmarked yesterday. He scrawled an alias on Purnell's form and turned away.

"Hold on now, hold on," Purnell called. "Don't forget your chicken papers. Five-dollar liver and thigh dinner all week at Flash-in-the-Pans. Take your dog along."

Jay snatched a sheath of circulars and advertisements and watched Purnell perform a treacherous speeding reverse all the way down the driveway. He sat down on the Bronco bumper and opened the letter, scared of what he might find inside. It wasn't like Sandy to send something this official.

Dear Jay,

Sorry I couldn't call you or come to see you in person, but my dad is seriously ill. The doctors believe he's contracted West Nile, and they are not sure at all about his chances. He's in a coma. They're concerned about his mind if he comes back at all. Memory and vision, even speech, are vulnerable as the fever persists. He can't even get out of the bed to visit the bathroom.

It's a serious time, as you can imagine, and I need your help with Jacob. His fall break starts next Thursday, and he'll be out of school until the following Monday. I have to be in meetings, and I don't have anyone to watch him while I'm at work. I'll have to be with my dad the rest of the time. Will you pick him up from school Wednesday at 3:00 and keep him with you until the following Sunday afternoon? I can drop by to get him then.

*I know it's hard for you right now, but I have nowhere else to turn.
The unknown is so terrifying. I'm very scared and out of options.*

Sincerely,

Sandy

He read the letter again, folded the yellow paper, returned it to the envelope, and stuffed it in his pocket.

He was fairly stunned by this announcement. The professor in a coma? Was there a West Nile outbreak he hadn't heard about, an epidemic brought on by the flood? He'd need to score plenty of mosquito repellent in town if the stocks hadn't already been raided. And that was just the first of the provisions he'd have to buy. There was nothing to eat in the house, no heat. The nights were getting cooler. No lights or TV. And it would cost money to get Jacob's room set up. The bed was gone, no dresser or playthings.

Of course, his first instinct was to see Sandy's dad about the money, but obviously that was off the table. Jay had always found him a quiet supporter of their endeavors, gracious with advice, easy with charity. They'd gone to him a time or two for a financial boost, and he'd always given it gladly, explaining to them why he was giving it and how it should be spent without scolding and never checking up on his investment. In hindsight, he should have gone straight to Sandy's father during the summer to seek arbitration in their marital battle. He wouldn't have chosen sides, only sat them both down and sorted their differences, made them roll it back and forth themselves until they'd settled it. It would be a terrible blow to lose him, especially for Sandy.

But then, Jay considered, maybe this was his answered prayer. Sandy needed him. He was no longer a total waste and a burden. She'd want him back in the fold.

If only he'd received this letter last week, he could have worked a deal with the raceway guys. If only he hadn't dismantled the four-wheeler, he might have scored a few hundred bucks selling that. Now what?

He resolved not to ask Sandy for money. She was under too much stress to stop and consider a grant request. It was enough that she'd made this overture. He could go into town and sit with Jacob at their shitty little rental. They could come up with plenty of things to do. He would watch the boy as long as she needed and would come back to the farm every night if she'd float him some more gas money. But maybe she would need him to stay. A shoulder to cry on, a bedmate after sleeping alone for so long. People need each other for electricity in the night.

Perhaps these terrible circumstances were paving the way for a great reconciliation. Maybe the professor, in his usual selfless way, was giving Jay an opportunity to prove his readiness to be a husband and father again. He'd clean up and go to them, take a break from this country panic.

He went inside and studied himself in the bathroom mirror. Looking into his sunken eyes was like staring at a stranger, the sallow face with cheekbones jutting out, thin lips, the wiry and filthy beard and bird's-nest hair, sick and crazed. Would Jacob recognize him?

He toted in water from the rain barrels to bathe, brought a jug in for shaving, and decided how to fix his appearance. There was not only the boy to consider when going into town. There was also the legion of security cameras and nosy watchers. A culture of surveillance thrived in town, and he wasn't keen on playing into their hands. He snipped down his hair and beard, left himself a big mustache and chin scruff, and rummaged through cabinets to find a bottle of white novelty hair dye left over from Halloween. He sprayed it thick into his hair and goatee, aging himself thirty years.

He brushed his teeth and found a clean white collar shirt and a pair of ill-fitting khakis he hadn't worn in years, an old pair of wraparound aviator shades. He put on his hat and looked like a different fellow, someone clean and fresh if still not altogether sane.

At last he retrieved the twenty-dollar bill Sandy had given him, wedged between two books on the hallway shelf, and the shotgun and .22 rifle, which he stashed in the backseat of the Bronco. The little .38 found a comfortable home in the small of his back. He locked the house door and opened the truck to let Chipper ride.

The Bronco gave him a fit to start, but it finally came alive and bellowed. He eased out from the carport and pointed toward town for the first time in months. He said good-bye to the ghosts. He was going to his family now.

— 22 —

Shoals dropped by several times a week to visit his mama. Her house was nestled in the pines, the property butting up to state forestry land. It was an old county neighborhood that had been annexed and swallowed up by Madrid proper years ago. It was about as far removed and quiet as you could get and still pay city taxes.

Often he stopped in on his way home, a quick visit between work and evening pursuits. Sometimes he stayed and ate dinner with her or sat out back in the screened-in garden and had a drink while listening to her unbottled thoughts. She was a city girl gone country and didn't like to leave home except to the grocery and liquor stores, the beauty salon on Friday and church on Sunday.

The house was an expression of her personality, the walls and shelves covered in folk art and magazine clippings and old photos from a lost carefree world. She listened to obscure folk rock and country on the stereo, speakers wired and stretched throughout the house. She couldn't stand darkness. Candles burned in every room, so many he often feared she would burn the place down. They also helped to cover the aroma of exotic boas she kept in aquariums and lizards that were allowed to roam. It was nothing to have to move an iguana from an easy chair before sitting down.

She dressed in cutoff blue-jean shorts and paint-splattered T-shirts under sheer robes and kimonos, wore tinted glasses, and smoked long cigarettes. Her skin was pale as cream, her hair dirty blond and wild. She moved with casual grace. It was a great tragedy to the bachelors of Bayard County that the lovely widow Shoals didn't get out and mix with the populace. In a sense she had never reappeared from mourning, was closed for business except to her son, who enjoyed the special access he had to the strange and lovely recluse with her bevy of reptiles.

He'd come to her today with a simple request—would she make him one of her miraculous lemon pound cakes? He knew she would do anything for him, but it was not a quick process. The eggs would have to rise to room temperature and the butter would have to soften. Perfection was slow and earned.

They sat in the kitchen and drank iced tea and carried on easy banter while they waited. He learned about the goings-on of his cousins and aunts and uncles, information she gathered daily by phone. Then he related the more benign aspects of his work. He was careful to gloss over the seedier details. Even talk of a domestic disturbance or a bar fight made her throw up her hands and cringe. A little gossip was all she needed, just to feel like she wasn't missing anything being holed up in her house.

During their conversation, Shoals inquired about a rotten smell proclaiming itself through the dense perfume of candles.

"I fear one of the dragons crawled behind that bookcase in the den and expired, dear," she said in her smoky voice. "I would've moved it earlier but then I'd just end up toppling the whole thing."

It was an enormous shelf that filled most of the wall. Plenty of books with creased spines and framed photographs and trinkets and geegaws. Little glass and plastic reptiles, odd rocks, and mysterious mementos. Small potted cacti and a wild serpentine vine. He got low and canted the shelf away from the wall gingerly without knocking stuff off. But it was so top-heavy that some frames fell over and a delicate origami cat toppled from its perch. "Careful with Pickles!" his mother cried, scooping the paper creature off the floor and cradling it.

Sure enough, wedged between the shelf and floor molding, a stiff orange lizard lay upside down, mouth agape, emanating a ripe funk. His mama squinted and shivered, trying to hold back the tears. "Oh hell, Geronimo!" she wailed. "It had to be you, my bearded warrior. I began to worry when you didn't show up for dinner Monday night. I just assumed the owls got you." She plucked him up with a pair of kitchen tongs and set him in a tissue-paper-lined shoe box. "You always were a little adventurer. I should've known you could never be content in this tiny world of ours."

Shoals drove the shelf back into place, straightened the trinkets and frames. The photos were mostly of him as a boy. There was a staged prom photo of him and Mary Nell Ballas that always made him recall their midnight dalliance poolside at that hotel in Memphis. There was another, first year as a deputy in uniform, proud and sunburned, his arm around his uncle's shoulder. And there were plenty of his father too, with his prismatic glare and his famous sly half-twist of a smile. He seemed to be observing Danny, sizing him up from the afterlife. He was the same age now as his father was then, and yet Big Jack seemed made of so much more.

"How old was Daddy when he became chief?"

She would physically cave in a little when talk came around to Big Jack. She often had to sit down from the intoxication of his memory.

"Let me think," she said to explain away this flash of quiet grief. "He must've been a couple of years older than you."

Danny knew he was chief at thirty-two, dead by thirty-five. She stretched the truth to give him some leeway. There was still time for him to make something of himself. She probably believed he was floundering, or maybe she was just happy he was still alive.

"Quite a family of boys," she said. "Handsome and doomed."

There were three brothers in all, Big Jack and Uncle Bud, the youngest, and the eldest brother, Donald, a decorated soldier killed in Vietnam. No one spoke of him. There were no stories of him, only a few photos of a nondescript child, an occasional shot of a stern-looking teen. The parents, both gone before Danny could know them, smoked and drank themselves away. They were a family destined to die young, all but boring Uncle Bud, the passive lawman who tiptoed through life lest Death realize it had missed one.

"Not a one would be anything without their women," his mama said.

Danny wooed her back into the kitchen, where the afternoon light refracted wild through the jars of red jelly and green pickles on the windowsill. She deemed the ingredients temperate and enlisted his help creaming the butter and sugar. He tried to refuse, but she pushed him. "Just remember," she said, handing him the spatula. "It'll fall flat if you beat it too fast."

"You're telling me," he joked, but she was too innocent to acknowledge.

He took the spatula and beat it as she'd taught him many times before, the old-fashioned way, feeding sugar to the supple mixture a bit at a time, followed gingerly with vanilla, lemon juice and zest. He cracked an egg and whipped—another egg, another whip, over and over, working in the white powders with splashes of evaporated milk or a dollop or two of sour cream, steadily stirring and stirring, reaching and pouring and stirring.

"See there, you always could bake," she said. "You're just too stubborn and macho to admit it."

"Mine never turn out like yours," he said, placing the cake in the oven.

"Well, you oughta know my secret," she said.

She took him into the backyard, which she'd fenced in with fiberglass siding and turned into a greenhouse. It could get treacherously hot back there, but she had a huge fan at the far end and misters hanging from the ceiling, lots of wild tropical plants. They approached a spindly tree, the same height as him, yellow fruit hanging from the branches.

"Take some," she said. "Sour as you please." She bent down and ran her fingers through the soil. The tree was sitting in an enormous tub, roots escaping through the bottom. "Love from the ground up," she said. "That's the only way."

It was really the oddest, most fascinating little garden, tangled with alien plants and vines that seemed to grow before your eyes, always a ceramic gnome or top-hatted frog peeking out from under the leaves. She had grown all sorts of peculiar fruits he'd never seen as well as big spiny flowers and broad jungle brush. The thought of loose snakes sliding through the greenery kept him on guard.

They moved to the porch, where a pair of ceiling fans kept them cool.

The six o'clock mist rained down from the ceiling and tickled their cheeks and forearms.

"I love how you keep summer held hostage back here," he told her.

"Soon it will all go dormant," she said. "I'll miss them like friends, you know."

"You need to get out and meet some real friends, Mama," Danny said. He told her this all the time. "The world aint such a bad place when it's right in front of you."

She held a far-off stare, possibly recalling the handful of times when that simple assessment didn't bear true. Then she looked at him and sighed, smiled and patted his hand. They sat in the cool quiet and enjoyed the mist, followed by the late-season steam and the sweaty glasses.

He couldn't tell if she'd moved on from iced tea to rum, but she was taking it down in gulps. Often she'd get tight quick and start talking about the old man. One minute he was a saint, a giver, a poet. The next he was disloyal, a loudmouth, always criticizing or making fun of her. She talked as though he were still around. Danny rarely stayed late enough for her to turn aim on him.

A while later the timer buzzed and they returned inside to remove the cake. Only after it cooled on the wire rack did Danny tell her why he needed it. If she'd known she was baking for a stranger, she wouldn't have put her full love into it. She might have cut some corners on purpose if she'd known it was for another woman.

"Who is it you're seeing, Danny?" she asked.

He smiled at her shyly. "A lady I met in town, a teacher. She's having a rough time. I tried to think of the most special thing I knew to give her. Your cake, that's the thing."

"That's your cake now, baby doll."

"It'll always be yours."

She went quiet and absently removed a roll of wax paper from the drawer. "You don't have to bring her over here, you know. You'll probably just scare her away if you bring her over here."

"Mama, what are you talking about?"

"I'm serious. I forbid it."

"That's the craziest thing I've ever heard," he said. "Besides, we're not even that far along yet."

She was silent, intrigued. "Well, I hope you've found one. I would love to see you settle down, maybe find a nice job, a nice kitchen perhaps. Raise some kids."

It was odd hearing her talk this way. She'd always quietly sanctioned his philandering, never pined openly for grandkids or urged a conventional lifestyle, as if she imagined every marriage would only result in tragic death, single parenthood, doddering seclusion with reptiles.

"I've got the best job in the county right now," he said.

"Yeah, but for how long?"

"What do you mean?"

"Your uncle's not gonna be sheriff forever, hon. He always said he wouldn't stay in office past sixty. Next election he'll be sixty-one."

Danny shook his head, unable to fathom this. He'd rarely considered the next day, much less an election, retirement, any change whatsoever. "When did he tell you this?"

"He's said it for years," his mother replied, waving him off, tearing a sheet of wax paper to wrap the cake. "Wasn't there some big to-do about it at his over-the-hill party?"

Danny remembered the occasion last spring, a nice back porch get-together at his aunt and uncle's home on the lake. It was a rare outing for his mother, who even took a turn on the dance floor after a few drinks. A little bluegrass trio was set up, yodeling out the classics. He spent the party bird-dogging the fiddler's girlfriend, a round-eyed brunette in cutoffs and a flimsy checkered top. She'd left her brassiere at home, and Danny couldn't let it go. It was a rare dead end for him. Her eyes said yes, but she had a faithful country heart.

"You don't think I've got the stuff to be sheriff?"

His mother laughed and wiped sweat from her forehead, took a long flustered gulp.

"Well?"

"You can do whatever you put your mind to, Danny boy, but I sure would hate to see you take on a responsibility that size. It's not worth it in the end."

He felt embarrassed to have even mentioned it, just a knee-jerk reaction to news he hadn't anticipated. Of course the department would keep him on as deputy, but how would it go for him without his uncle's dutiful patronage? Would he have to put on the ranger suit, those horrible green slacks, and putt around in a county cruiser? That would be his tumbling fire bale, a fate worse than death.

Maybe, though, what stung was the undercurrent. She would never have come right out and said it, and her implications were tenderly concealed, but he knew it was there. She didn't have to say it. *I love you like no other, Son, but as a man, you can't hold a candle to him.*

He fixed his mama a fresh drink, kissed her on the head, and took his loaf with profuse thanks and love. He set out for home in the peaked evening, winding through the pine-swept neighborhood toward the highway, a high lonesome moan playing on a slow road.

– 23 –

There were two main routes into Madrid. The first was the old Silage Town Road. There was one rickety gas pump in Silage Town that sometimes worked, but Jay meant to steer clear of the village. Undoubtedly he would run into someone who would quiz him about his land, his wife, his white-dyed goatee. He decided to take the highway instead. Halfway to town there was a country store, Hilltop Grocery, where folks were less apt to know him.

Hilltop was an old clapboard house with four gas pumps in the gravel driveway. Big cigarette placards and rusty oil drums sat out front. A neon sign for a discontinued beer flickered in the barred window. Out by the road, a portable yellow marquee with its flashing arrow advertised, TRUCKERS TAN FREE. What looked like a scenic lake off in the distance behind the house was instead the sewage treatment plant, and often, especially in summer, the air got so sour it was hard to stay and pump a full tank.

Jay got out and uncapped the tank, removed the hose, and started filling. The pump hadn't been updated since the eighties, with its spinning number wheel and the switch lever you flipped to turn it on. The price was modern enough, almost $3.50 a gallon. He wouldn't be able to fill up, for damn sure. Barely enough to get to town and back.

The proprietor was a crusty geezer named Fletcher, who looked like a badger in a guayabera. He was always propped on a stool behind the counter. His family lived in the back. His wife prepared brittle sausage and crumbly biscuits in the morning, and a lot of the old kooks from the county met in the cramped sitting area to drink coffee and discuss fishing or what politics they'd picked up from raving TV jerks. Jay preferred leaving his meager bill here than at the corporate pump in town, with their automatic doors and security cameras, their wall of inscrutable beverages and Siamese-twin fried chicken addendum.

He stepped inside to pay for the fifteen dollars of gas he'd pumped. A harried lady stood ahead of him in line, and Fletcher yelled back at a teenage girl to get off the phone so he could use the line to run a credit card. Clutching his twenty, Jay chose a soda, a dusty bag of peanuts, and a mongrel sausage from a revolving display case. He noted the old-timers at the back of the room and obscured himself behind a display of music CDs when he felt them craning their necks for a nosy gander.

Fletcher rang his purchases, which came to twenty-one and change. Jay sheepishly asked to cancel the nuts.

Old Fletcher huffed. "Aww, just go on and take em," he said with a cigarette wheeze. He nodded to the back table of geezers. "I got more nuts already than I can stand."

Out of the corner of his eye, Jay noticed the men whispering and appraising him from their dark corner. He hurriedly scooped up his dinner and thanked Fletcher, vowing to bring the extra dollar next time.

"Whatever," the old man croaked from his perch.

Jay almost sprinted to the truck, jumped in and pushed Chipper out of his seat, threw it in reverse, and backed all the way out of the lot. He kept an eye on the front door. If they were so damn curious about him, then they could look all they liked, but he wouldn't give them the chance to memorize his license plate. He whipped around in the gravel, masking his plate in a cloud of dust, and hung a right on the highway toward town. He drove a quarter mile down the road with a nagging suspicion. Had they mistaken him for one of their elderly pals, or had they seen right through his disguise?

He pulled to the shoulder, made a U-turn headed back. He passed Hilltop and strained to see if anyone had come out to follow him. He saw no one but noticed, among the trucks parked off to the side, a pickup with camouflage detailing. "Son of a bitch!" He took the right toward Silage Town. The fool who'd stopped and asked him if any fish were biting! His heart skipped and dropped into his stomach. That was right before he rowed up on the body. Did this guy know anything? Had he seen it too? Why else make a big production about straining to see him and nudging his buddies?

Jay swung right into what looked like someone's driveway but was instead a little-known and rarely used third route into town. He urged the truck ahead, putting some distance between him and the grocery in case anyone had taken a notion to follow. If the guy suspected him or had some beef, he knew where Jay lived. Surely he would have sent the sheriff by now if he'd seen anything. It didn't matter, Jay tried to reassure himself. The evidence was gone.

The awkward encounter left Jay with plenty to obsess over as he disappeared into the back country. This remote gravel road cut through dense forest before turning to tattered, unlined pavement beset with shacks and mobile homes. The road ultimately dumped out in a fringe subdivision on the outskirts of Madrid and took twice as long to maneuver as the other preferred routes.

He had time to kill before Sandy was off work, so he decided to do some detective work. He navigated a series of backstreets to the public library, drove around the block a time or two to scope out the lot and look for any cars he recognized. He parked away on a side street, under a shade tree for Chipper. He took a moment to adjust his disguise. If he saw anyone familiar, he'd play dumb or speak with a northern accent. He adopted an elderly pace, affected a slight limp. Once inside he shuffled around the dollar book sale in the foyer, thumbed through an old *National Geographic* before slipping into the periodicals room, where he sifted through recent back issues of the local newspaper, *The Madrid Folk Standard*.

He found what he needed on the front page of the August 27 edition.

Bayard Sheriff Hunts Missing Ohio Man

SILAGE TOWN—The Bayard County Sheriff's Department is searching for a 43-year-old Ohio man believed to have disappeared while visiting relatives in the Silage Town community.

The missing person, Tovis Boyers of Dayton, Ohio, was last seen August 17 by his cousin, Eugene Weaver, 38. Boyers was staying at Weaver's residence in Silage Town. "He said he was going to the boats," Weaver said, referring to the canal-docked casinos ninety miles northwest in Tunica County. "Then we never seed [sic] him again."

Bayard County Sheriff Bud Shoals said his department is working closely with the Tunica County Sheriff to determine if Boyers made it to the casinos. Shoals said they are examining security camera footage and credit card receipts now to determine Boyers's movements on the days surrounding his disappearance, but so far they have no leads.

Meanwhile, Boyers's family in Dayton has made a heartfelt appeal to Bayard County authorities to find their beloved member. Boyers is the father of four children, grandfather of one. His wife, Monika Boyers, described her husband as "a responsible person with everything to live for."

Boyers serves as a foreman at Gimlet Alloy, a Dayton foundry that casts automotive parts and other industrial machine components, where he has worked for the past 13 years. His boss, Jerry Banghart, describes Boyers as "a class act and hard worker. We really need him back."

According to his wife, Boyers had built up two weeks' vacation time and decided to spend it visiting relatives in Mississippi. "We've been having stress at home and work, and he just wanted to relax awhile."

He enjoys fishing, dancing, and eating. His wife described him as "an especially good whistler."

Boyers drives a Dodge Dakota. He is five feet, nine inches tall and is missing half a finger on his left hand.

Sheriff Shoals asks anyone who knows Boyers's whereabouts,

or has seen him or had an encounter with him, to please report any information to the Bayard County Sheriff's Department, 226-4656.

Instantly Jay thought of the missing half-finger. Which hand of his corpse had gone missing? He tried to recall. Playing it back in his mind, he saw it either way and couldn't remember the truth. No missing fingers, he was certain. He remembered the charred bones, all five crispy digits. If Boyers had been murdered, the killer may have detached his hand to confuse identification.

As for the height description, he didn't remember the body being especially short or tall. Five-nine might have been about right. Jay studied the photo again, trying to remember the hair, the nose. None of it made a perfect match, but it was close enough to be possible.

He flipped the pages forward, hoping to find updates. Sure enough, a follow-up appeared two weeks later.

Vehicle of Missing Ohio Man Recovered

The Dodge Dakota belonging to an Ohio man who went missing while visiting relatives in Bayard County was discovered stripped and burned on a county road near Mullins in Rayburn County late last week.

The owner of the vehicle, Tovis Boyers, 43, of Dayton, Ohio, was reported missing on August 24 by members of his extended family with whom he was staying in Silage Town.

No mention of an ATV. And how did he end up in Rayburn County? Maybe this wasn't the same guy after all. Jay read on.

Rayburn County deputies conducted a search of the woods near the vehicle's location for the remains of Boyers. No clues were discovered, but the hunt goes on in the surrounding area.

Jay tried to remember when Shoals had stopped by to inquire about the missing person from Ohio. He checked the date of the issue, September 11. A memorable date, but he had no idea when the deputy had visited. He'd become a man without a calendar. Before the missing truck was found, right? Otherwise, why waste time searching near Silage Town? Unless Shoals knew something he wasn't telling.

Mullins was well south, nearly to Jackson. It stood to reason that the body would be found near there, but evidently it wasn't. And the fact that the vehicle was burned and stripped was odd. Boyers could have been killed and left near Silage Town, his car taken down to Mullins before being stripped and burned. Why go through all that trouble? Unless you were trying to cover something up. Jay was no detective, but it definitely sounded like foul play to him.

He flipped forward several more editions, hoping he would find an update that explained the whereabouts of the missing stranger, but there was nothing. He went back and combed each edition page by page and still found nothing.

He knew it was foolish, but he couldn't resist accessing one of the library computers to conduct an internet search on Boyers. He found the *Dayton Daily News* website, punched "Tovis Boyers" into the search engine, but came back with nothing. There was little about the man in the search engine, just listings on the Gimlet Alloy site and a church newsletter. The *Madrid Folk Standard* online articles weren't referenced. Jay searched the online phone directory and came up with a number, which he scribbled on a gum wrapper he found wedged into one of the hard-drive vents.

He looked at the phone number on the gum wrapper. Why had he written it down? Would he really call, or had he just created a piece of evidence? He memorized the number, then scratched it out, tore the wrapper in half. He cleared the browser history and cache, wiped prints off the keyboard with his shirt, and left calmly. He threw one half of the gum wrapper in the garbage on the way out and popped the other half in his mouth and swallowed.

Outside, he saw two kids standing by the Bronco on the street and got nervous. They were petting Chipper through the breach in the passenger window. "Hey, you kids, get away from him, he's dangerous!" he called, expecting them to flee.

"No he's not," said one, a pubescent boy. A younger girl echoed his sentiment.

"Well, he's got worms," Jay said.

The girl reached up on tiptoes. "I don't see any."

"They're microscopic. You can't see em, but they're on his tongue, and if he licks you, they'll grow in your stomach and you'll be crapping them out in a week. Big itchy worms, coming out of your butt."

The kids laughed.

"Where are your parents?"

"We're not supposed to talk to strangers," the boy said.

"Go home then!" said Jay, climbing in and cranking the truck and screeching off as the kids waved good-bye to Chipper.

It made him want to see Jacob. He knew his boy would be excited to see him, or Chipper at least. It would be good to hang out with his family again, start the process of reconciliation. If he timed it right, maybe they would feed him. He looked at the clock on the radio and thought it might be too early for them to be home. He could wait, maybe hide out in the park, the little wooded area behind the playground. No, someone might report him—a predator hanging out in the woods by the playground with restless hands in his pockets. Nor could he drive around wasting precious fuel.

The park near Waller wasn't far from the library. Jay had taken a roundabout way and approached from the rear. He saw the backside of the hideous teal house and then, out of the corner of his eye, caught sight of a familiar blue Mustang parked in the outfield lot to the left. He jogged his memory, trying to remember where he'd seen it. He came to the stop sign to turn onto Waller and saw the deputy standing in the driveway. Jay cut a calm right and cruised out of the neighborhood.

His heart raced ahead. He kept an eye on the rearview. What the hell was Shoals doing there? Was it a stakeout? Were they waiting for him? If the blue Mustang pulled out, would he have enough of a head start to lose the deputy through the maze of neighborhoods? He turned off Waller just in case, plunged downhill into a residential area, and took turn after turn until he'd lost his way in a new development and feared being trapped at the end of a cul-de-sac.

He wound back to the commercial district and pulled into the lot of Flash-in-the-Pan Chicken. He steered the Bronco around back behind a dumpster and switched off the engine to gather his thoughts.

One thing was certain, he wouldn't be staying in town to sit with Jacob. That would make a hell of a sight for the boy—his father spread out against a squad car, the flickering blue lights, the handcuffs and shouting and impounded Bronco. That image would define him for the rest of their lives.

A fantasy unfurled in Jay's mind, that the law had coerced Sandy into helping them lure him out with a fabricated story about Jacob's fall break. Once in town, Jay was on their turf and more prone to slip up and reveal something. It was a good thing he'd come to town, if only to uncover their plot. His paranoia had been justified. They were, in fact, waiting for him. They were onto him.

So where did he go from here? He wondered how much of Sandy's letter was true. To ignore her plea might invite suspicion. He'd play along, offer his help. But it would be on his terms and his property. They'd need a warrant to search. He'd make them work for it.

A rumble in the nearby dumpster gave him a start, and he slumped down in his seat. Chipper yipped, and Jay slapped him quiet with his hat. They waited a moment before Jay got out and peeked in the side hatch. Someone had deposited several bags of trash. He slipped into the otherwise empty bin and rummaged through the plastic bags. A lot of loose garbage, greasy napkins, half-eaten meals, empty drink cups. But one bag was filled with fried chicken. Whether it was scorched or too old to serve, it seemed like perfectly fine chicken. He took a bite of thigh. It was cold but still heavenly. He scooped up the bag and jumped in the truck to feast. He shared some with

Chipper, then pitched the bag of gnawed bones back into the garbage and sat in the truck worrying over how to proceed.

In the glove box he found an old pink carbon receipt from a long-ago car repair and crafted a note for Sandy, accepting responsibility for Jacob next weekend. Would he be playing right into their hands? Maybe so, but if this charade about fall break were true, he couldn't deny his son.

Jay cranked the engine and swung back around toward the park. He came in behind Waller again, but this time he pulled around by the dugouts and home plate, got out, and squinted to see if he could make the Mustang. It was gone. He closed in on the apartment with extreme caution, making a pass or two before he pulled up in front. He left the engine running as he ran to the house, stuck the note in the door, scrambled back, and hightailed it toward his country haunt.

PART
IV

PART

VI

Leavenger was scoping the back roads on a cool Saturday morning and believed he had it all figured out.

Earlier in the week he'd been at Fred Littlejohn's place and put the last piece of the puzzle together. Littlejohn farmed just west of Silage Town. He'd put in a full day and invited Leavenger to stay for a beer. They were sipping longnecks, sitting in rusty iron chairs on the chipped concrete patio, when Fred's son Hutch roared up in a noisy blue mud racer. The boy, all of nineteen, jumped down in a huff, and when Fred asked about his trouble, young Hutch let sail a stream of profanity—some so and so said such and such about this or that.

"Who're you talking about, boy?" Fred asked.

"That dude with the pyramid in his yard, down Silage Town Road."

Fred nodded. "Weird fella, younger? Tall and thin?"

Hutch stared dumbly in agreement. "Had a gas mask and a shotgun, run me off," the kid said, his face a red blotchy mess of embarrassment and anger.

Fred knew Jay Mize from the farm service, one of the field agents. Wound tight, he said, had strange ideas about things. "The guy would scoop a handful of dirt, then put it up to his ear and listen. He'd sniff it. Even put it in his mouth and taste it," said Fred. "He's crazy as hell."

It struck Leavenger like a fresh scalding. "That's gotta be the one," he said.

Somehow, through the haze of pain pills and drink and sorrow, he'd forgotten all about their awkward run-in by the flooded field. Probably a day or

Jamie Kornegay

two before Virginia was gunned down beside the river. Leavenger had been driving out the Tockawah levee road to see the bridge and noticed the man in his johnboat. He called to him for a bit of neighborly chatter, and the guy rowed off in a huff. The profile of an edgy, antisocial outcast and his peculiar farm on the river matched that of the dog-killing stranger with his cooler full of frozen fish.

Leavenger related this all to Fred Littlejohn as it coalesced in his mind, confirming Mize's physical description and offering his latest rendition of the riverside slaying, with all its gathering shades of menace. By the end, he was soundly convinced of the killer's identity.

"I wouldn't put it past him," Littlejohn offered in vague accord.

Now Leavenger had his name and address. All he needed was justice.

And that was why he'd driven out to Tockawah Bottom this morning, down the road from the dead-end bridge, right near where the culprit lived, guilty as the day is long. Was he ready to confront him, maybe pull a shotgun on him and give him a taste of his own medicine? Or perhaps Leavenger just needed to reassure himself, to look for signs, for further clues and confirmation.

He seemed to find all he needed as he approached Mize's place. Several vehicles were lined up on the shoulder in front of his property. He recognized a couple of the vehicles—Shoals's Sugarwagon, and there was Hutch Littlejohn's big blue mud machine. A county squad car, a couple of other unfamiliar trucks, and a rusty sedan were parked in a row.

"They got him!" Leavenger cried and slapped the dash, a little sorry that he'd not been present to lead the charge.

He pulled to a stop in front of Mize's driveway and watched several men walking to the road, stomping their boots and clutching their cups. Whatever had gone on here looked to be wrapping up.

Hutch, his spirits considerably higher since their last visit, was goofing with one of his pals when he walked by and slapped the hood of Leavenger's truck. "Hey, old man!" he shouted. Leavenger scowled.

The deputy Shoals followed, holding a leash with a pudgy blond Lab

200

panting behind him. Leavenger rolled down the window and called for his counsel. The deputy broke off from the pack, swaggering in his sunglasses and shitkickers, a big duffel bag thrown over his shoulder. He looked tired and grim.

"Hey, I already solved your case for you," Leavenger cried.

Shoals frowned. "Which case is that?"

"The case of who shot my dog Virginia."

"Oh, yeah? And who might that be?"

"You know who did it."

Shoals stared chilly through his shades. "I'm sorry, but I don't." The deputy seemed agitated, too busy for riddles and small talk.

"That son of a bitch right there," Leavenger said, nodding at the field. "Mize."

Shoals turned to look.

"Aint that why you're here?"

"No," said Shoals. "We don't usually assemble a whole team to catch a dog killer."

Leavenger huffed. "Well, what has he done now?"

"It's county business."

"Well, so's this. Let's go up there right now. I can identify his boots and his hat and his gun. The cooler and four-wheeler too. I'm telling you, that man right there, that Mize fella, he shot my dog. Now you gonna help me nail this son of a bitch or what?"

Shoals's face tightened. "Can we do this another time? Call me Monday morning and set up an appointment. You can sit down in my office, we'll go over all the details, and then, if need be, we'll come out here and question him." He spoke like he was trying to convince an old lady that no one was stealing her mail.

"Aint no time like the present," Leavenger said. "We're all here. May as well nip this in the bud."

"I've gotta get back to the office. There's a hundred fires waiting to be put out."

Leavenger refused to be put off so easily. "That was my dog, Deputy. I had her fourteen years. She went everywhere with me."

"I understand, Mr. Leavenger. And we're gonna make it right." The deputy had a false authority and careless condescension in his voice.

"Aint no right to be made, Deputy," Leavenger said. "But we can get square, sure as hell. Eye for an eye and such."

"You leave that up to us," the deputy offered as a cold warning. "Now let's talk Monday. Good day, sir."

Leavenger shook his head and cursed the deputy's ambivalence. "*Mister* Leavenger, my ass." No surprise that he wasn't willing to help. He hadn't cared a damn yet for this injustice. Leavenger decided that he'd come this far without the law's help. He could by god finish it himself too.

— 24 —

Shoals made the drop at three o'clock. The delivery was calculated to arrive about thirty minutes before Sandy got home. He knew her schedule, and she rarely deviated from it these days. He stood in her driveway, satisfied with this bait.

He'd left a cooler on the steps. Inside was a gallon freezer bag of fresh frozen strawberries in syrup and a tub of nondairy whipped topping, all packed in ice. On top, wrapped in wax paper and tucked in a brown paper sack, was his mother's homemade lemon pound cake. It was a frill, a little something extra if she so desired. He longed to spoil her.

He walked back to the Boss and sat under oak shade for a time, making sure no stray dogs or teenage punks came up and tried to steal his precious gesture. He began to visualize her eating the berries. She wouldn't put them in the freezer straightaway but would dig right in, handling the slushy fruit, maybe dipping it into the whipped topping, leaving a streak of red against the pure white. This wasn't your normal store-bought fare and should prove irresistible to her. She'd lick her fingers, a little dab of white in the corner of her mouth. He sat up ramrod straight. If only he could be there to watch the drama unfold.

He'd left his card in the paper sack, demure. If she needed him, she'd call. Maybe this gallant deed would be just the thing to break her ice. *Come over and help me eat this*, she'd text him. He'd come back by and find the door unlocked, the kid gone to play at a friend's house, and her lying down in the back bedroom wearing only a pair of tight gym shorts and the tub of whip slathered across her bare chest. He'd saunter over and relieve himself of his T-shirt, nuzzle down, and come up all pie-faced.

This was how things should go for him. He was expert at creating this sort of scenario. Why wasn't there a career in such things? If his life could somehow be devoted to designing these episodes and fulfilling them, then he would be a hero in his field. None better. There were plenty more frivolous vocations being practiced every day across this land.

But he had a real job, an important one, and certain people, he feared, had started taking the notion that he wasn't giving it the serious attention it deserved. He'd even begun to realize himself that maybe he was taking the job for granted. It was time to straighten up, if only for a short while, and start planning for tomorrow.

After his delivery, Shoals drove to the Pioneers Shooting Ranch, an indoor-outdoor range deep in the county. He'd been coming here lately, firing off several hundred rounds to practice his marksmanship. Some wise guy had made up life-size cardboard dummies of despised liberal politicians and encouraged members to blow them to strips at twenty yards or up to fifty. The lights were dim at the back of the indoor range so shooters could imagine scalawags lurking in the shadows. Shoals set up Al Gore at twenty-five and dinged him in the ear and grazed his elbow with the first two shots from his .44 Magnum, which had belonged to his daddy. He'd have to tighten up if he hoped to score high on the state accreditation test.

He'd found the opportunity earlier that day to prod his uncle about this proposed retirement his mother had mentioned the night before. The sheriff was standing around with some of the other deputies, who were griping about road conditions, when Danny offered, "You oughta lean on the mayor and make a big show for election season."

The sheriff disagreed. "The mayor knows. He drives these roads like we all do. He's working the state reps for more funding."

The sheriff was no rogue, for sure. His calmness and chivalry were probably what kept him in office.

"Besides," his uncle added, "I don't even plan to go again. One of you jokers will have to take my job."

They all laughed. No surprise on anyone's face. Was Danny the only one who hadn't heard? Were they all scheming for the job?

"Who you gonna pass the torch to, Sheriff?" Danny asked.

"Maybe we could make a game of hot potato out of it."

The men laughed again. After a moment Bynum, nibbling peanuts in the corner, said, "I'll take it."

Everyone got quiet, waiting for the sheriff to extend his opinion. "And you'd probably do a good job of it," he replied finally. "You won't get rich at it, so you better love the work."

It had left a bad taste in Shoals's mouth. He didn't really want the job, had never considered it until last night, but somehow he didn't think anyone else deserved it. His uncle's boots were too deep to fill. And if it had to be done, best to keep it in the family. He had six months or a year maybe to get close again with his uncle and to prove himself. Maybe at least he could convince the sheriff to stay on one more term, just another four years to teach him the ropes and make him an acceptable candidate.

Shoals switched to the lighter, standard-issue Colt .45 auto, tugged the cardboard dummy back another ten yards, and fired several rounds. He plugged the tree hugger in the groin and the kneecap, but everything else went wide.

On the way out he met Baby George Bundren, his old high school buddy and counterpart on the city police force. They didn't run into one another often enough, but when they did, they always swapped tales and talked a little filth, maintained an effortless camaraderie. Baby George said he was going over to the Delta that weekend. Duck season was starting early this year, and he and some of the boys on the force were going to bag the limit. He asked Shoals if he'd like to come along.

"That's mighty tempting," said Shoals. "I'd love to hang with y'all, but there's some races going on at Bobby Waterman's place in Tockawah Friday night. Those hot young things out there get wild when the mud starts flying. There's always at least one who crawls out of her britches. I'd hate to pass that up."

"Ha! You're a mess, Shug," said Baby George, a husband and new daddy. They all envied Shoals's bachelor pursuits. "You never change."

They laughed and slapped five and patted each other on the back, best to all and see you round. Shoals set out for home, an empty cabin on the lake, and he started to think about Baby George, who used to chase skirt with the best of them. He thought about how they'd gone their separate ways. He thought about responsibility, fidelity, stability. They aren't the things men normally crave, but Shoals wondered if maybe sometimes they were the things men need.

– 25 –

Sandy staggered in after four, her arms laden with groceries. She could barely get in the front door for all the gifts on the stoop. So much food, what would they do with it all? She tried to enlist Jacob to help her with the boxes and bags and foil-wrapped casserole dishes, but he was cantankerous this afternoon and shuffled off to watch television in the bedroom. The boy needed male companionship to relieve this aggression. He needed his father around.

After several trips she got all the packages inside and unfolded a pink note she'd found stuck in the door. A nervous hand had crafted a desperate plea:

> *Sandy*
>
> *Had an emergency back home sorry couldn't stay. Can get Jacob Weds but need $ for supplies!!! Any chance you can loan some?*
>
> *—J*

What a heartfelt surprise, the asshole! Not even a sentiment for her father, rotting away in a hospital. She wadded up the note and let out a few angry sobs and then washed her face at the sink before putting the groceries away.

What was the big emergency that he couldn't stick around and see his son? She'd already given him gas money for that purpose, and now he was asking for more. It was strange behavior, and it gave her a sense of foreboding about the arranged visit next week. She considered calling Tina to see if she'd like having Jacob around to entertain the babies. If it was too much, then maybe she could recommend a reputable day care at least.

Sandy was so aggravated by Jay's note that she caught herself slamming cabinets as she put away boxes and cans of food. Jacob came in and asked what was wrong.

"I'm sorry, dear, I had a hard day," she said. "I shouldn't be so mad. Look at all this food! How lucky are we?"

Jacob rifled through the covered dishes. "Beans stink!" he proclaimed. She'd already mentioned to him about going to stay with Jay. He'd packed a bag and would be crestfallen if she changed plans.

"Don't mix up the labels," she said. "I have to know where to send thank-you notes."

They sorted through the spoils, mostly sweets. There was a tin of cookies and a homemade blueberry trifle that appeared to have suffered outside for some time. A foil-wrapped smoked brisket and the previously sniffed container of cowboy beans.

Something smelled heavenly. It was the deep crockery filled with pot roast, carrots, and potatoes swimming in onions and gravy. She tugged a strip of roast, and the meat dissolved on her tongue, the taste sublime. She felt like she'd been sucked through a portal back in time to her grandmother's table. *God, how wonderful.* She felt it in her chest, a delicious yearning, like watching a sad movie.

"Who sent all this stuff?" Jacob asked.

"It must be friends of your grandfather," she said. "His church, I bet. They're so thoughtful."

"Whoa, what's in the cooler?" Jacob lifted the lid and howled. The boy retrieved a brown paper bag, followed by a tub of whipped topping and a freezer bag filled with brilliant red berries. "Cool, it looks like blood!"

"Who sent that?" she asked.

"Beats me." He handed her a card and opened the container of whip.

It was Danny Shoals's card with contact info. On the back, scrawled in red—"A little sweetening for a dull night."

"Honey, don't eat that before dinner!" she pleaded. "And wash your hands before you go pilfering my food."

"Aww," he said, shoving the bowl of cream aside. "What's pilfering?"

"It's stealing," Sandy replied.

"I'm not stealing!" the boy protested. "It's mine too."

She had forgotten about the dessert discussion from their "date," but obviously Danny had not. Perhaps he was more perceptive and shrewd than he let on.

"I don't want any of this stuff for dinner," Jacob said, dismissing the entire goodwill of acquaintances and neighbors. "Can I have a hot dog?"

"Yes, just give me a minute."

The strawberries went straight into the freezer. She drew a finger through the whip and tasted it, unwrapped a fraction of the foil and sniffed the cake. She'd save it for later. They had a ritual of watching competitive reality shows or the cooking network until Jacob fell asleep, usually around nine. Most nights she'd sit up and grade papers and make lesson plans until midnight. No doubt she'd get the hankering around ten.

She threw a couple of cold wieners in a pot, set it on the stovetop to boil, and then stared out the kitchen window into the lot of the city park. A young black kid in enormous denim shorts, a wife-beater tee, and a nylon head rag gestured wildly to a scruffy white kid in the cab of a patchwork truck. They were so loud she could even make out a few of their angry slurs. She worried Jacob would hear their curses and repeat them on the playground, so she turned on the radio and engaged him by making him sound out words on the cereal box. She explained how food cooks in boiling water and then asked about the details of his day.

The white kid squealed out of the lot in his truck, and Jacob perked up and asked if it was Danny. "No, it's not him," she said. If she ever saw the deputy again, and she certainly wouldn't go a millimeter out of her way to try, she would mention these unsavory negotiations behind her house. She had mentioned it casually during their first date, really just a simple meal together. But what if she called to thank him for the cake and berries and told him again about the troublemakers hanging around, let him know they really bothered her? Just to see if anything would come of it. Maybe all she had to do was say the word.

Then again, she didn't want to encourage him. When she'd first met him she was charmed. It was nice to be noticed by someone, especially the dreamboat deputy. Their first encounter at the football game hadn't gone unnoticed by some of the other younger teachers, who embarrassed her and pushed for details that next Monday in the teachers' lounge. "It was nothing, he was just saying hello," she'd told them, but they still brought it up from time to time. They'd all heard about him stopping by her classroom to give a private pep talk to her students. She didn't dare mention their dinner date. It made her anxious now just to think of it.

Sandy fixed Jacob a plate—hot dog with mustard, potato stix, and a small cluster of grapes. "What food group are we missing?" she quizzed him.

Jacob stared wide-eyed at the plate. "Dairy?"

"That's correct," she said, passing him a tumbler of milk.

She looked out the window. The black kid was pacing the lot, talking on his cell phone. Was he laughing or yelling? He was a few years older but could have easily been one of her students. She wondered what was involved in getting transferred to the elementary school. Perhaps she could catch and divert their criminal tendencies young.

Jacob let out a rebellious burp and laughed. She scowled a soft reprimand and reapplied Danny's card to the plastic container, placed it in the fridge, and then served herself a pile of roast and carrots. The easy soul groove on the radio clashed with the aggressive booming bass from the parking lot and created a crosshatch of dissonance that pushed back her appetite.

"We didn't say the blessing," Jacob said with a mouthful of hot dog.

"You're right," she said and reached over to take his hand and bowed her head. Somehow they still weren't used to saying it.

- 26 -

He knew how to dispose of a man, how to break down a body to its basest elements and remove it from scrutiny. But how might one kill a man and disguise it as an apparent accident? Jay needed to know.

Scenarios cycled through his mind all morning. There was no shortage of opportunities for serious injury around the farm. It was preferable to be impaled or crushed, anything certain and instant. But it was imperative that it look like an accident.

Otherwise the insurance money wouldn't kick in.

Since returning from town, he'd spent his time figuring contingencies for the inevitable appearance of Shoals and his posse. Undoubtedly they were building their case, weaving their nets, plotting their raid, and justifying it all through legal chicanery. Surrender seemed despicable to him, but you started at your last resort and worked backward.

Trudging through mud in the bottom field, he came upon one of the more lethal implements he'd used in his garden—the section of old wrought-iron fence he'd staked as a trellis for climbing cucumbers. The top edge brandished spear-point finials that would pierce a man clean through if he were so unfortunate as to fall on top of it. But how to stage such a fall onto a six-foot-high fence in the middle of an open field?

Jay sat and studied the configuration. He could not get Tovis Boyers out of his mind. He kept seeing the photo from the newspaper and recalling the man's bio. He'd been thinking about Boyers and his family, especially the consolation of an insurance settlement from his death. Surely a foundry foreman would have a decent insurance package. But a body would have to be produced in order to collect a settlement. What if by destroying Boyers's body—if indeed the body had been Boyers's—he had deprived the man's family of compensation they were rightly due? Had his gesture of mercy backfired? And if he were being honest with himself, wasn't his act committed more out of fear and self-preservation than mercy?

The guilt was nearly too much to bear. He belonged here, pierced on a pike. But only if he could leave the family a nice bequest to ease their sorrow, something to remember him by.

His best idea involved a ladder from the house and a couple dozen old CDs and fishing line. He unfolded the ladder and set it up on the soft ground. Every time he stepped on the first rung, the ladder toppled in one of four directions as the legs plunged into mud. He slogged up the hill and brought a sheet of plywood from the shed and laid it under the ladder to displace the weight. It would appear to investigators later that he was taking precautions, trying to be safe.

He pressed his chest against one of the finials, in the little hollow there below his sternum. He judged how much pressure it would require to puncture the skin, how much guidance and effort it would take to stab through the old flubbing muscle. He didn't want to mess it up and dangle there half-alive all day and overnight until some hapless Samaritan found him and called the ambulance in time for a miracle recovery.

As he considered this drastic plan, Jay watched Chipper running the field, darting from scent to scent. The dog's hyperactivity would be a likely cause of the knocked-over ladder while Jay was high up over the fence, stringing CDs through fishing line. His death might create headlines worldwide, if only in news of the bizarre and idiotic. He began to consider the legacy that would haunt Jacob. At least the kid would be financially comfortable . . . wouldn't he?

Jay had taken out a half-million-dollar policy on his life years ago, but now that he thought about it, he hadn't paid bills in several months. He'd set up payments to draft automatically from his bank account, but he wasn't even sure the account was still open. There was certainly no money in it. It was possible that Sandy had started her own account when she moved to town and let the old one go. This was all pointless if his wife and son weren't active beneficiaries.

Even if the policy was intact and Jacob stood to inherit a modest sum of money and the acreage, would it be worth the lifelong shame? Jay's own father had left nothing, aside from the limping Bronco, but would it matter if he had? A few thousand dollars at this point would be nice. There might be forgiveness in that. At this point, a couple hundred dollars would change his life.

A honking car in the driveway jarred him out of his daydream and nearly startled him off the ladder. He looked up to find the maroon hatchback with the revolving yellow light.

Jay climbed down from the ladder and waddled through the mud to see what Purnell had for him. It was another certified letter, again from Sandy.

"Looks like a project you got there," said Purnell, passing him the letter and a pen to sign for it. "What are them shiny things?"

"CDs," Jay said. "You string them up, and when they twirl in the light, it scares the birds away."

Purnell didn't seem to buy it, but it didn't matter as long as he believed that Jay had been engaged in a genuine project and not intent on leaping to his death.

"Hey, you know where this guy Weaver . . . Eugene Weaver lives?"

Purnell stopped and squinted, rubbed his eye. "Ton of Weavers all together, like five houses on a dead-end county road," he said. "Four eighty, I believe. Come off Turpentine Road bout a half mile past that Wooten woman got a hair salon in her house, know where I mean?"

Jay nodded. "Yeah," he lied.

"It's eat up with Weavers back in there. I can't remember all their damn names, but I bet your Weaver is there. That's where the Ohio boy was staying, the one that went missing."

"Is that right?" said Jay. It was stupid of him to mention anything related to the Ohio man, but his curiosity was insatiable. "Did they ever find him?"

"Aint no telling," Purnell said, pessimistic. "They's some straight-up thugs back in there. He might've gone native, or else crossed the wrong somebody and just got lost, if you know what I mean."

Jay looked back at the letter, signed for it reluctantly, and Purnell sped away.

Jay sat down in the gravel and unsealed the envelope. There was no letter, just a hundred-dollar gift card from World-Mart. So she didn't trust him not to blow through cash. Now he'd have to scavenge through that hell of overstock and trinketry to root out the few essentials he'd need for a weekend with his son.

His mind tipped back to Boyers. He could've gotten "lost," as Purnell suggested. Maybe it was a different person altogether who'd washed up in the field.

In the newspaper, Boyers's wife said he'd been suffering stress at work and home. Maybe he wanted to be lost. What if he gave his relatives a false lead, drove out of town, burned his own car, and walked away forever? The case would eventually be closed. Everyone would assume he was dead. His family would hold out that nagging hope, but in time even they would give up.

There was something attractive to Jay about the freedom of such a decision. Just disappear off the face of the earth, and yet the world could still be yours. Start fresh, try and learn from past mistakes, make a conscious effort to be a better person without all the old reminders that you were a failure, that you were no use to anyone, just a burden or a bad memory, a mark or a suspect.

It didn't matter. Even if he decided to run—and he believed he was smart enough to get away, to go underground and remain incognito indefinitely—there would be no forgetting that he'd left his family holding the bag. His own father knew it.

The only way to truly forget is to stay gone.

– 27 –

It was just past midnight and Sandy was still awake. Too exhausted to read and her mind still reeling, she'd been flipping channels for two hours. Jacob lay next to her in the bed, sprawled out in profound slumber, his mouth gaping open. If not for his little-boy snore keeping steady rhythm, he would have looked disturbingly like a corpse.

Running through hundreds of hopeless options, she stopped on a program about competitive eating. The contestants were lapping up birthday cake in disgusting fistfuls. She wondered what made a person sign up for such a competition. Surely not for the love of food. They weren't eating it so much as seeing how much they could shove down their throats. How could you taste or enjoy it like that? Was it all for money? She could see herself competing at leisure consumption, some last-man-standing event. She wouldn't care if she grew to a quarter ton if there was no pressure, just limitless birthday cake. She could never have watched a show like this with Jay. Without saying a word, he would make her feel inferior for enjoying it.

Watching them eat with such gluttonous intensity, Sandy found it difficult to breathe. And then she became hungry. She crawled out of bed and went into the kitchen for her third postdinner snack. In the fridge, she plucked off a few more strips of pot roast, and then went in for another sliver of trifle.

There was a thump below her. She stopped and listened, heard it again, more pronounced this time. It was coming from the basement. She walked over and put her ear to the door in the little alcove between the kitchen and den. There was a definite commotion down there. She heard voices. More than one? Were they downstairs or on the TV? Next a distinct clatter, some piece of metal ricocheting off the concrete.

Here they are was her first thought. She'd been expecting them sooner or later. One of the lowlifes from the playground or the ball field or parking lot. They'd climbed into the basement from the windows at ground level. Rooting around down there in all the useless junk that belonged to the landlord.

It would be just a matter of time before they realized there was nothing down there and they would climb the stairs and try the door and see that a good swift kick or shoulder butt would release the flimsy lock. Whatever they had in store for her, she could handle it. But she couldn't abide what they might do to Jacob, or even that he might see them doing to his mother whatever they had planned or that he be frightened even for a moment.

Who to call? Of course not her father, alone in his hospital room, or Jay without a phone and half an hour away. 911? Waste of time. There on the counter, the answer to all her prayers, sat the empty Tupperware bowl with Shoals's card attached. She scurried to the bedroom on tiptoes, careful not to draw attention by squeaking the floorboards. She dialed his number on the cell. He answered right away, said he was still in town and would be there in two seconds.

She didn't own a gun, not even a baseball bat. Her best weapon was a shower rod, which she plucked down and clutched to her chest. She closed and locked herself in the bedroom until she saw the silent blue light spinning from the dash of his car in the driveway.

She crept back into the hallway and put her ear to the door. She heard him down there, through gritted teeth demanding, "C'mere, you son of a bitch." A scuffle, more cursing, something heavy falling over. More grunting, cussing, and rustling feet. Then came the gunshot. Everything shuddered to a halt, the gun's report capable of altering reality. She imagined someone dying beneath her.

There came slow and careful footsteps up the stairs, then a knock. Who was the victor?

"Sandy, it's me."

Jacob walked in, sleepy terror in his eyes and his hair in shock. She unlatched the door and opened it. Shoals was there, glistening and huffing in a half-open, oatmeal-colored leather shirt, wearing a Mississippi-shaped belt buckle, holding up by the tail a very large, dead, and leaky armadillo.

"It's a good thing you called," he said. "This is almost as bad as an intruder, really. These things carry leprosy. If he'd got up here and took a bite out of you, we'd be peeling you off the floor from now to kingdom come."

Jacob stared up at her, bewildered, verging on tears. He wasn't sure if this was a dream or simply the new reality of their nights alone together. She pulled him close and buried his head in her nightclothes, which Shoals was carefully admiring.

She invited him to dispose of the animal, and he carried it through the kitchen and out the back door. She ushered Jacob to the bedroom, coaxed him back to bed. On the television, cakes begat pies. She stared for a moment, lost in the corpulent smiles smeared red and blue.

He appeared at the doorway, brazen in superfluous leather, a cocky, expectant look on his face. It felt strange and a little dangerous to have him here. She gave him a gesture to wait, pushed the door closed, and put on a sweater. She caressed Jacob for a moment, and he went back to sleep, seeming to believe it was all a dream.

Part of her wanted to lock the door and call Shoals to thank him and ask him to let himself out, but she'd left the phone in the kitchen. The whole affair had a weird staged quality, as if he'd set the armadillo loose in the basement himself, knowing she'd have no one else to call.

Another, far sadder part of herself wondered what it would feel like to let him have the reward he so obviously and clumsily sought, just lead him down in the basement and let him ravish her there atop a pile of old magazines, speckled with armadillo blood, then send him away forever. It might help her sleep. It might numb her emotions. But she knew it wouldn't end there. He'd be back tomorrow with a lump in his blue jeans, hoping to save her again.

He'd made himself comfortable on the couch in the living room. He leaned over, inspecting some family photos on a bookshelf, the weapon sticking out of the back of his pants. When she entered, he turned and smiled. "Sorry about the gunshot," he said in a loud whisper. "He wouldn't go quietly."

Her eyes were drawn down to his hand. She thought she'd caught him stroking himself through his jeans and gasped, looked away.

"Oh, here," he said and reached into his pocket to pull out a black cylinder. "I got this for you."

He reached out, his gesture suggestive, or maybe it was her mind driven to this carnal regard. He offered her the tube. "This might make you feel a little safer. If God forbid anybody got in here, a dose of this in the face and they'll be holed up in your shower for the next half hour spraying their head off, guaranteed."

She accepted the can of pepper spray, feeling a bit shameful. "Thank you," she said. "I feel silly calling you over for that."

"Hey, it's nothing," he said. "It's what I do."

"I swear, it sounded like someone down there."

"I bet it did," he said, a breathy intensity about him, the soft taint of alcohol. She withered, just knowing he was going to make his move.

"I heard voices."

"Oh, it was just a Hotdog and T-Bone marathon," said Shoals. "Somehow the rascal turned on a transistor radio down there."

She shook her head in disbelief. What kind of hoax was this?

"You look shook up," he said. "I bet you could use a drink. I didn't see anything in the cabinet."

He put a hand on her shoulder and bent his head down, trying to force eye contact like a hypnotist who could make her drop her night pants with just a look. "I've got a little stash in the glove box."

She looked into his eyes and saw an ocean of stupidity there. "I'm really exhausted, Danny. Maybe another time."

He held his mesmerist's gaze. It was never over for a guy like him.

"I cannot thank you enough for your gallant effort here tonight," she said, giving him her best smile of finality. The last thing she wanted was to pepper-spray him. "Another ne'er-do-well has been silenced in Bayard County."

He smiled. "Well, I find it hard to sleep if I don't shoot a varmint out from under at least one pretty woman's house every night before bed."

She opened the front door. "Then you should sleep just fine tonight."

On his way out, he stopped to give her one last chance. "I had to break one of your windows out, I'm afraid. I'll take care of that tomorrow."

"You don't have to do that, really," she said. "I'll have my landlord tend to it."

"Trust me," he said, leaning in. "I don't mind crawling under there and fixing you up."

She hung her head. What shameless bargaining, what priceless insurance he could provide. If it was more than pepper spray she needed, and if it was tonight that she needed it, then here he was.

"Okay," she said, closing the door quietly. "Let's go down and take a look. See just how big a mess we're talking about."

A hint of a sly smile crossed his face and he knew better than to speak. She led him into the kitchen, stopped and gave a listen down the hall. She opened the cellar door and descended daintily ahead of him, her nerves pulsing, a slight blush in her abdomen. He placed the gun on the kitchen counter and followed, eager to go down with her to this secret place where strange bodies could be fed what they so ravenously deserved.

− 28 −

Two nights later, Shoals tried and failed to raise Sandy on the phone. She was busy, playing hard to get, whatever it was women did when they were suppressing their true desires. He began to ponder Baby George's offer. He wasn't interested in hunting ducks with the boys, especially while Dun Spiller was away. Dun was one of the city cops going on the trip, which created an opportunity that Shoals had been waiting a year or more to exploit. He'd done a little research and learned that Dun was taking both sons, the dogs, and the neighbor too. The circumstances were too perfect to ignore, his urges too dark to suppress.

Dun's wife was the beautician Rochelle, whose famous curves had all the boys wondering if the goods were genuine. He'd cased the house already, found a three-inch sliver of open bedroom curtain, but had never been able to set foot in the yard for the rambunctious dogs. Dun himself was no one to cross, a chiseled-out, six-foot-six musclehead, who lacked any sense of humor or mercy or even the capacity to appreciate and satisfy such beauty as lived under his own roof. With all obstacles removed, it was Shoals's scene to investigate.

He followed her Friday after work. She stopped for a drink with the girls and made it home by 7:30. Shoals was already there, hunkered down in a lawn chair out back in the shrubs right beside the window. She went straight to the shower. He couldn't ask for a better scenario.

She came out of the bathroom wearing only a towel turban. He watched her air-dry and decided she was all natural by the way her breasts wobbled when she pranced and bent over. She stood and admired herself in the full-length mirror, the sheen down her butterscotch body, not a tan line in sight. She squirted up a palmful of lotion and began lathering her legs, reaching deep between her thighs. She kept things proudly mammalian down there, which surprised and delighted him, she being the professional groomer, always so polished and smooth in her exposed features. These were the details that excited him, the things only the most intimate loved ones or medical professionals knew about her. Holding this information granted him membership to an elite club, and it was being in the know, as much as the obvious sexuality, that excited him.

But Shoals got greedy and brought out the video camera, perched it on the windowsill and captured her lubricated hands as they moved over her stomach and ribs, kneading her breasts, those splendid orbs slipping and twirling through her fingers with the ease and pliability that only natural flesh can achieve.

Rochelle must have seen the pinprick of red light from the camera. She stopped cold as a wary doe in a scouted field, calmly wrapped up in her robe, and disappeared into another room. He thought nothing of it until she appeared around the corner with a high-beam flashlight and a baseball bat. He managed to scramble over the fence, but not before she recognized him and called him out by name.

Five minutes later he was doing ninety in the Boss, his heart racing the back roads toward Silage Town. If he could reach the mud races in time, he'd have an alibi. But then his uncle called and told him to get his ass back straightaway.

In his office, the sheriff was fuming. "Her husband is a friend of mine," he said with characteristic stern calmness. "I practically had to beg her not to call the city to investigate this. She wants to press charges."

"What has she got?"

"Invasion of privacy for sure. Did you expose yourself to her?"

"Hell no."

"She said you were taping her, Danny. Is it true?"

"What, do you want to confiscate the evidence?"

"This is serious, son!"

After a dressing-down by his uncle, Shoals sought immediate counsel from another high school buddy, Jim Tom Fussell, the notorious local attorney, a few shades paler even than Shoals in his scruples. The deputy confessed his trespass while his old pal listened intently. "Okay, first off," said Fussell, "are they real?"

"I believe them to be."

"You lucky son of a bitch. And you couldn't convince her to let you stick around and finish the rubdown?"

"She didn't appreciate the interruption."

Fussell took notes and asked pertinent follow-up questions. "This is a simple one," the attorney assured his client. He telephoned the woman right then and there.

"Hi, Rochelle? This is Jim Tom Fussell. Sorry to bother you at this hour, but I heard you had an unpleasant run-in earlier this evening. . . . Well, I assure you I take this matter in the strictest confidence. Were you able to identify the prowler? . . . He's sitting right here in my office and swears to me he was not even in town at the time you described. . . . I see. Okay then, listen, Rochelle, I'll have to insist that you not pursue this any further, okay? . . . Because my client is a respected servant of the people with a clean record, and he did you no harm. . . . Well, then, Rochelle, this could get ugly very fast. . . . Because, dear, by law your curtains were open enough that my client was able to view, without obstruction, your nakedness and lewd behavior. . . . You exposed yourself to him and committed an indecent act in full exposure to the public. By law you have committed the crime, Rochelle, and I am not afraid to bring this to trial. . . . I assure you it could easily be construed as indecent. We have some pretty damning evidence. Pretty damn impressive at that. . . . What would you say if I told you there'd been complaints in the neighborhood that he was investigating? . . . Well, the scenario that concerns me is the eleven-year-old boy on the second floor of the Baptist recreation center behind you, innocently looking out the window and catching a view through your open curtains of what you've been doing in your bedroom. He's too young to be exposed to that."

Shoals squirmed in his chair. He'd been in a pickle a time or two stemming from his virile nature, but he had never felt like he was taking advantage of people he'd sworn to protect, even though this was technically outside of his jurisdiction. Bringing in his profession was a bad move. He knew Jim Tom was just trying to get control of the situation, but this seemed out of bounds. He tried to wave his attorney off, but Jim Tom gave him a thumbs-up and a nasty grin.

"Fondling one's genitalia in front of an open curtain within view of a church has always and ever will be considered indecent, at least in any community where I intend to live," the lawyer said as he ran his hand over his own chest in lewd exaggeration, flicking his tongue out spastically over his prim goatee.

Shoals shook his head. Dun was going to murder him. Word would spread all over town by Monday afternoon.

"My client is willing to drop this completely and let it always remain an awkward incident between the two of you. No one else has to know. But if this gets out and his reputation is jeopardized, we're going all the way. I'd hate for this video to go live on the internet. Don't put your kids through that shame."

There were several more painful minutes, during which Shoals could hear Rochelle screaming through the phone. Fussell mocked her anger with a chattering hand gesture. He was having a blast.

The negotiation ended in a stalemate as near as Shoals could tell, but Jim Tom assured him it was over. "She won't breathe a word, believe me. She'll cool off and realize she's got nothing to gain and everything to lose by starting a fight."

"You know, I should be on top of the world right now," said Shoals, "so why do I feel like everything is going south?"

"Forget about it, man," Jim Tom insisted. "It's not *your* fault she's got the most bodacious tatas in town. Believe me, you're not the first man to try and sneak a peek. Hell, I might consider getting an injunction and rigging a camera up in the tanning beds."

Shoals thanked his counsel, shook his hand, and told him good night.

"Ho, ho, ho. Wait a minute, pal. Let's see this videotape. That's your retainer, fella."

"There is no tape," Shoals lied.

He took the long way through the country, barely driving sixty, and he didn't have any particular place to go. He didn't want to go home. He'd be too tempted to watch the video. He certainly couldn't bear visiting his mother.

He wondered how this would affect his run for sheriff. The only proof was under his seat, a small unmarked cassette. It was tempting to stop on a bridge and throw it in the river, but that would be like dumping the *Mona Lisa*. He tried to convince himself that everything was fine, that it would all blow over. He could twist it any way he wanted. Neighborhood watch. He was checking on a fellow officer's family, all of it just a misunderstanding. But this sort of sensitive information, if it found its way into the wrong hands, could be devastating to him.

As he rounded one of the darkest curves on Silage Town Road, his headlights honed in on the ass end of a rusty Pontiac Bonneville splayed out in the lane. He swerved to the left to keep from hitting the car. A handful of black kids went wide-eyed in his beams. He ripped the wheel back to the right and just missed hitting a dog in the oncoming lane. The Boss spun around and nearly flew off into a kudzu gulley, but Shoals managed to glide it to a backward stop on the shoulder. He shuddered and inhaled as his heart swallowed a gush of adrenaline. The slalom stripes on the road painted a story of near disaster. He saw the motorists hooting and jumping.

A biblical rage flared inside him. He erupted from the car and gave them all a rawhide cussing. A wail of depravity and damnation that found everything about them to insult.

One of them with large bleary eyes and wild wiry hair charged back, "Who da fuck you think you is?"

Shoals ran over and got right in his face, threw back his vest with the shield. "I'm the goddamn sheriff, you spook motherfucker!" he cried, the

Colt on his leg offering silent validation. "And who're you? Was this your bright idea, to leave this piece of shit out in a blind curve?"

There came no response, neither from the tall bold one, nor from a string-bean teenager with nervous eyes pacing behind the car, nor from the cool woman with tight lips and a bandanna tied around her head, standing in the weeds. They were all young but wised up quick. They'd probably heard the stories of furious white men who should never be crossed alone on a country night.

"Don't you know what the shoulder of the road is for?" Shoals hollered. He put his finger in the big one's face. "Now get this goddamn wreck out of the road before I stomp a mudhole in your ass and walk it dry, boy!"

The kid off to the side ran into the woods. The big one turned to look and then shrugged. "Who gonna help push?"

The three of them tried to heave the car forward, but it wouldn't budge. "Put it in neutral, dipshit!" Shoals barked.

The woman hopped inside and put it in gear. At this point Shoals was so dosed he could have flipped the car into the ditch by himself. He helped push the whale out of the road and asked if they needed a tow. No one answered.

"Are you deaf *and* dumb?"

"Can't pay for no tow," the man said, a bit too snippy for the deputy's taste.

"What's the matter, your welfare check hasn't come in?"

The man simmered.

"You could afford to put this stupid-ass spoiler on a goddamn Bonneville. That's a waste of good cash if you ask me."

Everyone panted in the nervous dusk. A truck driving in the opposite direction barely slowed down.

"You live close?"

"Close enough."

"Close enough to walk?"

No one dared give away the address.

"Wait here."

Shoals stormed off, his arms churning, his scowl cutting deep into his face. "Your inspection sticker's out of date too!" he yelled, smacking the car hood. "And whose fucking dog is this?" Even the mutt, standing anonymously across the road, ducked his head in deference to the crazed deputy.

Shoals jumped in the Boss and threw a shower of gravel over the stranded motorists.

When he was back in range, he called a tow truck driver he knew out near the highway. The sheriff's department would be charged, but it was better than somebody getting killed. These country dopes didn't have the sense to operate precious machinery. The fact that they were ever granted licenses in the first place was proof of a broken bureaucracy.

Danny sped with sick urgency over the empty back road. He started to despair ever so slightly, having never spoken to citizens that way. Any other day he would have seen an opportunity to help, a lesson to impart instead of a fool to insult. He'd need several stiff drinks and some primo tail to come down from this angry high.

He turned onto the Tockawah Bottom road and let the engine unwind. Down near Mize's place he wondered if word of his indiscretion would ever reach Sandy. He could write her off if that happened. The night before she'd only offered him a taste, and now he wanted the whole pie. But she wouldn't come tumbling into bed with a back-alley perv. She was too smart and good. He needed her to reform him, if only just a little.

Across the river, a crowd had assembled off to the right in one of several acres of fields spread out and segmented by thin stands of river birch. He pulled over to the shoulder and got out, leaned against the warm car, and watched the scene in the bottoms below.

Two rented light towers, fed by a sputtering generator, stood at either end of the field, streaming down their halide glare on the track, which was a single muddy lane running the width of the field. Trucks were parked in semiorder along the turnrow, all the way to the road, and a ragtag rock band hacked out dubious classics while guys in jeans and tight white T-shirts clomped around in the mud, their faces obscured by low caps. Some of them were draped with girls in snug jeans or hot pants, their wrists laden with bracelets and sloshing cups of amber desire.

Two large mud trucks were parked at one end of the track, waiting for sport. Men in coveralls fussed underneath, running from one end to the other, perched on step stools and peering under the hoods.

When the time arrived, the crowd was called to order by a barker with a bullhorn. Distant cheers followed, and the band collapsed their tune in reverence. Motors revved, cups were raised, hoots and hollers sounded in the moonglow. A pistol cracked and the trucks erupted in a shower of black rain. They scrambled and fishtailed down the rutted lane, the crowds cheering them on. Some of the women turned away from the spray while the men held out their arms to embrace it. It couldn't have lasted more than eight seconds, a close finish. The bullhorn proclaimed one of them the winner.

Shoals decided it was best to watch from the road. If he went down to join the fun, he would drink way too fast and he might get sloppy, hustle one or two of these lovelies into the Boss and drive them to his place. He'd take things a little too fast, maybe get a little too rough, and they'd be stranded together until morning. They might get their feelings hurt, start calling daddies and boyfriends. It was not the way to go, but he wanted it terribly after such a shameful night.

A hooting truckful blew past him, some perky blondes in the back waving their arms, shaking their tails and their plastic cups. He could feel the sap rising inside him. He'd already picked out the one he would take home, could see their humpback frolic like a flash from the future.

Just then a scream arose from the mud pits. A woman's shriek. Hard to tell if it was a playful drunken girlish scream or one of true horror. He observed them bunching together. The crowd's murmur became excitable and uniform in recognition of a common danger. He jumped in the Boss and sped down the gummed-up lane toward the melee, his official blue beacon twirling on the dash.

He parked in the row and went straight for the knot of rubberneckers.

"What's all the fuss?" he called, and the crowd parted for him. Girls braced each other, and underage kids dumped their cups.

Hutch Littlejohn stepped forward and proud. "Get a look at this, Danny," he said, pointing a flashlight beam on the ground.

Shoals took the light and squatted to the earth. "I'll be a son of a bitch." He took a pen from his inner vest pocket and poked at the lump in the mud, turned it over.

"What is it?" asked a tipsy blonde.

Danny picked it up by the pinkie. "We've got us a crime scene, boys and girls."

Racing fans disbanded as though he'd offered to take them all to the station. There came a frenzy of kids crawling into trucks and a long trail of taillights and mud tracks tearing toward Silage Town, rambling fast and innocent back into the night.

Friday night Jay talked himself into driving to town to pick up Jacob. He thought they might go to World-Mart and spend the gift card on supplies for the following weekend. He figured the cops would be too busy with weekend mischief to give him a passing thought. He'd get in and out, maybe judge Sandy's response, her sense of surprise, to determine if she was in cahoots with the law.

While preparing to leave, he heard a pistol shot across the river. He shushed the dog and listened to the sound of whining engines and raucous cheers in the distance. He stopped and felt their strange vibrations and knew it must be the mudders.

Jay followed the din down the driveway to the road and along the shoulder toward the washed-out bridge. He saw the faint corona of light over the tree line and felt the buzz of humanity across the river.

As he crossed the Tockawah, an ominous train of vehicles appeared in the distance, bearing down on him. He turned and ran, dove into a stand of rotten cane by the roadside and cowered there, watching them come, off-road by custom by sport utility by Jeep. Their faces through the glazed windshields were a drunken hodgepodge of antic fear, excitement and uncertainty, and they came a hundred strong.

This had the makings of an exodus. He wanted to press on, to witness what brand of upheaval had conquered their sacred mud sport, but something told him to go home. Whatever had made them abandon their revelry was moving this way.

He stayed up the entire night waiting until first light fell gray. A thick coating of fog was pulled over the world. He took the dog and stood at the bottom of the driveway in the empty expanse. They walked the middle of the road, across the bridge to Bobby Waterman's place, from where it appeared the riders had emerged. Their double-stripe mud tracks painted the road and left a trail of clods, which led down a gravel turnrow into Waterman's field, splaying out in a hundred directions with the attending footprints, all leading to a series of large ruts like jagged ditches cut across the rows of spoiled beans. Jay knew the farmer Waterman, had worked with him through the agency, and was surprised he had agreed to mud races on his land. He was a sober businessman and a disciple of the industrial model. He didn't have a house here, which may be one reason he'd accepted the mudders' deal. He must have opted to get any money he could from this wasted crop.

Jay and Chipper walked through the tillage and inspected the portable light towers and then heard a rumbling engine and the slow crunch of tires. Jay turned to see a faint pair of headlights coming off the foggy ridge into the bottom. It was the deputy's Mustang. He took off in a wide-legged scramble, as far as he could manage through the dense mud, whistling for the dog to follow. They ran for cover in a field of gray cornstalks spilling over with mildewed ears. They stopped and Jay strained to see through the wisps of fog. He could just make out the headlights and heard a voice calling out, "Hello!"

Chipper barked a reply.

"Shut up!" Jay hissed. Chipper barked again.

He snatched the dog and ran deep into the hinter field, making clumsy tracks through virgin mire, flushing out morning quail feasting in the quiet furrows. They scuttled through the woods and plunged into the Tockawah, swam back across to his side of the river. Between the fog and the trees, the deputy would not have recognized them, but it wouldn't require many guesses as to who would be wandering the bottoms on foot. Jay fully expected Shoals to show up at his place next.

At the house he scrubbed the mud from his legs and boots and the dog's fur. They tumbled inside and dried off. Chipper ran from window to window, growling and whimpering. If the deputy came, he would be looking for a dog. Jay fetched the duct tape, told Chipper, "I'm sorry, pal," and wrapped several layers around the dog's snout, leaving his nostrils free to breathe. He put the dog in the cellar and covered his ears from the whimpers and feet scratching against the door.

There was nothing to do but wait. He convinced himself they were establishing a perimeter, biding their time to ambush. He fully expected the SWAT teams and television vans at the foot of the drive, shooters in the woods, teams rappelling out of helicopters. Of course, if it was just the county involved, it would be a more modest affair, maybe an old-fashioned stand-off. They'd sit out front for days and finally smoke him out, some old bow hunter flinging a fiery arrow into his attic. He prepared his weapons, stashed them around the house in a handy configuration.

What probable cause did they have? He'd scoured the property foot by foot. He'd shoveled every square inch of tainted ground, even burned the hillside to eliminate all traces. They had nothing on him but speculation.

It was midmorning before the deputy showed up. Jay walked out wearing only sweatpants like he'd just woken up.

"Morning," Shoals said.

"Good morning, Deputy, what can I do for you?"

The deputy scrutinized the scorched hillside. He looked a touch hungover. "What happened to your yard?"

"I was burning leaves and it got away from me."

The deputy queered his eyes in a skeptical glare, looked him up and down in half-dress. Jay noticed a blond Lab panting in the backseat. He wondered if the animal would sense that Chipper was locked up and muzzled inside.

"We found a hand over on the other side of the river last night. It may belong to our missing Ohio boy," said Shoals. "We're gonna check your land this morning, me and some searchers. See if we can't turn up anything else."

Jay hadn't anticipated this staggering news but managed not to flinch.

"That good with you?" the deputy asked.

They wouldn't find anything. Jay knew because he'd walked every inch himself, the field riddled with his footprints, like a battlefield on which an army of size elevens had skirmished. But what if he'd missed something? Besides, didn't this kind of search require a warrant? To refuse, he thought, would be the worst sort of incrimination.

"I dropped a pocketknife and walked the whole property just last week," Jay said. "Didn't see a thing. If that helps . . ."

"Not really," Shoals said. "I have to satisfy my own curiosity."

Jay shrugged. He felt confident that he'd covered all his bases, but the idea of them canvassing his property unnerved him deeply. Better to give them a cursory inspection, maybe even let them contaminate the site than have them come back with metal detectors and crime scene specialists.

"Then do your job," Jay replied. He'd said it by way of invitation, but the deputy bristled, hearing a challenge in his remark.

"That's what I intend to do," he said curtly.

"It's cool. I'll lend you a hand."

"Is that supposed to be funny?" Shoals said. "Lend me a hand? This is a human being we're talking about."

Jay winced. "Of course. There was no pun intended."

"Well . . . pun taken," the deputy said.

"Sorry, just let me get dressed and I'll join you."

"That won't be necessary," Shoals said. "This aint skip-to-my-lou. There's a trained method to it."

"I understand," said Jay, his voice mellowing, seeking favor. "I can follow directions. I'd just be interested to see y'all work."

His ego tickled, the deputy reluctantly agreed and told him to meet them down in the front field.

Jay walked inside feeling like he'd run a mile, his heart thumping, sweat streaming. *They know,* he thought. *They know that I know.*

He put on a flannel shirt that covered the .38 Special tucked into his waistband. If they trumped up some evidence and tried to take him in, he'd have at least six chances to get away. The yellow Lab made him nervous. He'd taken precautions against animal searches, hence the burned yard, but he wasn't certain he could match wits with a properly trained animal. What if the dog zeroed in on the spot where the dead man had lain? How far was he willing to play this gambit?

He walked down the driveway and was surprised to see nearly a dozen people gathered in his field near the road. Cars were lined up along the roadside and in the driveway as if it were a party. There was at least one deputy squad car, but mostly unmarked vehicles, including a familiar mud-streaked racing truck. Who were these people? Possibly a few wives and girlfriends. A couple of nonpolice types who could have been friends, relatives, or groupies drawn to the thrill of the hunt but unhirable for any of various reasons. Jay recognized the hotheaded mudder Hutch, who had paid him a visit last week, along with a couple of his buddies. Clearly they were in league with Shoals, just as Jay had suspected. So far he'd been right about everything. He still knew more than they did. If he could keep his cool, he might pass this inspection.

Shoals took charge. He passed out wooden stakes and metal pins with orange flags attached. The Lab was his hunting dog, Suzie-Q, and Jay guessed right away she probably couldn't even fetch ducks, much less scout cadavers.

Shoals retrieved a black plastic bag, unsealed it, and held it to Suzie-Q's nose. She squirmed and snapped, no doubt hoping for a retrieving game. Shoals sealed the bag, which must have contained the hand, and patted her flank.

"Is that it?" Jay called to the deputy. He wanted to get a look, to try and match it with the body, maybe see the half-finger, but Shoals ignored him, tucking the goods away and calling his search party to order.

"Okay, everybody line up side to side!" the deputy yelled. He handed Jay three stakes and flags and pointed to the others.

"Newton and Bissell, y'all are gonna be the anchors. I wanna take this nice and slow. Everybody spread out to an arm's length. We're gonna march forward. You've got your sticks if you need to move anything, but don't touch with your bare hands. Keep your eyes down and in front. You see anything suspicious, tag it and holler. Anything at all out of the ordinary, I wanna know.

Once we make it to the end of the field, we'll shift down and go the other direction. Everybody clear?"

It was a leisurely hunt. Jokes were traded, insults cast. One or two carried beers in their jackets. Shoals let the dog run free, sniffing and peeing all across the field and along the edges, a curious nuisance with no sense of mission. Jay kept one eye on her and one on the ground. A silly woman at the end wearing expensive sunglasses and a ski vest flagged a bloated gray hand-shaped object, and Shoals hurried over to proclaim it a dead toad.

There seemed to be more interest among search party members in the state of Jay's field, the motivations and efficacy of his unconventional farming tactics, than in actually finding any clues to the missing person. Their ignorant comments about his beds and implements rankled him, and he grew testy.

"What the hell is this?" asked one zit-faced young deputy, swatting the eight-foot-high mud stack with his stake.

"Well, it *was* a ziggurat," Jay said.

"A zigger what?"

"You know, a ziggurat. Modeled on the ancient Sumerian temples? Precursor to the pyramid?"

An awkward silence descended.

"It was an experiment for small-space gardening, like a cramped backyard or indoor terrarium. It's plumbed and everything. Had a rain catch on top, but I don't know where that went."

"Rain must've caught it," another searcher said, and the others snickered.

They complained about having to climb over the slippery railroad ties that divided his raised beds and made tasteless jokes after his watermelon trees. They poked fun at his gunked-up tractor and his piecemeal greenhouse. He considered asking them all to leave. "Come back when you have a warrant and half a clue," he wanted to say. He was playing nice, letting them all tramp back and forth across his field, searching for something they'd never find. Shoals was way out of line. If Jay insisted on a warrant, the deputy would probably roust a judge out of his duck blind and bring one for spite. Anything beyond total acquiescence at this point just raised suspicion.

"Hey, Danny, I didn't know your dog knew yoga!" cracked one searcher.

Everyone turned to see Suzie-Q in the middle of the field, bowed up in a mystical hunch, her legs achieving a wide and perfect parabola. A cigar-shaped turd emerged beneath her erect tail.

"Hey, is that a finger?" cried another.

"Real funny," Shoals replied. "Suzie, back on point!"

The dog finished by rocking on her haunches, her tail bobbing up and down with a graceful wave like an eagle's wing. One smart-ass broke ranks and staked a pin in the droppings.

The charade went on for an hour or so, and Jay grew more impatient by the minute. He sighed and straightened a collapsed beanpole tepee one of the searchers had knocked askew. When at last he turned to Shoals to complain, the deputy drew a .44 from his vest.

"Step aside," he told Jay, raising the weapon, staring straight through him.

Jay took a leap back as Shoals let sail a thunderous volley into the field. He turned to follow the deputy's aim, and his heart nearly leapt from his chest.

There, in the precise spot where he'd recovered the body, sat the turkey buzzard pecking at the ground. Suzie-Q made a beeline for the bird.

Shoals sighted the buzzard, a good eighty yards away, its expanded wings giving him a wide target, and fired a second shot. He might have nicked it, but it was hard to tell. The bird shrieked and climbed into the air with lazy loft. The deputy sent another round into the sky but hit nothing.

The crowd of searchers gave Shoals hell for his aim. "I was trying to scare it off," he said.

"At least you didn't hit the dog!" someone said.

The deputy frowned. He looked at Jay and seemed to channel his anger at the farmer. "I wonder what that bastard was hunting," Shoals said.

Jay shrugged.

"When we're done in this field, what do you reckon we'd find back in that pasture or along the river there?"

"I have no idea," Jay replied. "The water didn't get into the pasture."

"Who said this is contained to the waterline?" asked Shoals. "What makes you think some dog didn't carry it off into the pasture?"

"Carry what off?"

The deputy stopped. Did he even know what he was looking for? "You seen any strange dogs around here?"

"Yeah," said Jay. "They're running loose all over the county."

"You shot any?"

"Hell no!" he cried.

"Where's your dog?"

"I don't have a dog."

"You don't have a dog?"

"No."

"There's never been a dog out here?"

"What are you getting at, Deputy?"

"I'm just asking if you ever had a dog. There's a lot of tracks out here that aint all Suzie's."

"My son had a dog. But he doesn't live here anymore."

"Your son or your son's dog?"

"Neither!"

"Where's your son's dog then?"

"I thought we were looking for a hand, Deputy. Do I need my lawyer present?"

"That depends. Who's your lawyer?"

This is it, Jay thought. He felt the cold steel against his lower back. Or he could just make them all leave, buy some time to get packed up and hightail it out of there.

"Hey, Danny!" the younger deputy called.

A commotion arose from the back of the field. Everyone turned to see what had been found. One of the searchers was running after Suzie-Q, who had her nose in the black plastic bag. She snatched the hand and ran off with it before collapsing in a mudhole and gnawing it like a ham bone. Shoals ran over to scold her, and the dog took it for a game of chase. After a lap around the field, they finally wrestled her onto her leash, and the deputy deposited the chewed hand back in its plastic home.

"Game over!" Shoals cried. "We're done here."

He sent Jay a long suspicious stare, tiny white flags in his eyes. Jay felt a certain flush of confidence. He'd overestimated this hick deputy, and now he had the upper hand. More than ever, he believed he could get away with this.

PART

V

PART

V

Leavenger pumped a shell into the breech and held one in the chamber and then slung the shotgun over his shoulder. He smeared on face paint with jittery fingers, slipped into his bowling gloves, and grabbed the crutches from the truck bed. "It's on," he told the photo of his girl Virginia, dangling from the rearview mirror.

Dressed every inch in camouflage, the woodsman left the truck parked in the highest grass he could find. It couldn't be seen from twenty yards away. The light had gone to putty, and the wind passed through the oak and cypress.

He was fast on the crutches now. A bit of his former upper-body strength had come back with the hindered mobility and his ravenous appetite for protein. He was bronze and shallower. The hunter in him had been called out of retirement. He moved like a limping puma down into the thicket. The clay and silt had firmed considerably since his last pass, and he was able to maneuver easily through the toppled saplings and rotten timber. The floor was riddled with the footprints of scavengers, some intimidating. Were there still bear lurking around this old bottom?

He came to a swamp just as the last blur of sun left the trees. He feared being eaten alive in the night and wanted to pass through quickly and camp on the high bank. He traversed dry sandbars until his crutches began to sink, and then he flung himself into a tree. He let the crutches hang on his shoulders and tried to monkey across, but he gave out midway. He would have to make a bed in the branches and hope the mosquitoes didn't devour him by morning.

He had watched an Aussie special-ops guy on TV and knew how to make a bed in awkward quarters. But even as a seasoned woodsman, he clutched the branches and held on for dear life at the noises of the midnight swamp. Was it a beaver, a gator, a possum, snakes, the swamp witch? He flinched and dropped his flask in the murk, didn't sleep a dash, and when the night finally expired, the daylight rose to shame him. He was in a dip about the size of a little league baseball field. He dropped gingerly into the black water and searched beneath the water for his flask. When he found it, the contents had swirled with swamp juice, but he was in desperate need of spirits and dared a sip. He waded out cupping his nuts, so prone was he to leeches.

Half an hour later he came to the place in the river where he'd hidden from the dog killer. The picnic table was still lodged there. He recognized the little snare of limbs where he'd cowered, now nesting fifteen feet inland, marking the river's retreat. The old shotgun he'd abandoned lay there on its side, the barrel rusty and clogged. He walked across the shelf where the murder had occurred. Grass had grown up to erase all evidence. With the tip of his crutch, he mashed the head of a sunning lizard in commemoration.

This need for vengeance bore into him like parasites under the skin. He'd been crippled by injustice and would commit anything to give some back. And so the woodsman heaved himself along the riverbank in vague search, dragging his swollen legs. He craved a beverage but dared not drink from the oily pools or risk climbing down the jagged clay banks to sip the shit-brown river. He'd come too far to go over the brink and wash up in some factory cesspit the next county over.

Finally he approached what looked like a dry cove. It was a cradle of mud scooped out of the bank, streaked up with tracks from something slithering and rooting around. Wild hogs? He clutched the shotgun. Two birds called out across the trees. One seemed to say, *Hey, watch this.*

Limbs rustled in the blind ahead. He saw nothing coming until it was there, out of the brush. He drew his weapon, stupefied. It was the last person in the world he expected to see coming through the trees.

"The nigger lives!" he hissed. The woodsman cocked the weapon and took dead aim. "How come you was dead?" he cried.

There came no answer from the specter, just a livid ghost-eyed stare.

- 30 -

Shoals arrived at the sheriff's office midmorning on Monday. He stopped at Desdimona's desk to ask about her weekend. She wouldn't even look up at him, just shook her head. "You in some shit today, Sugar."

He walked back to face the music from his uncle. Bynum was already there in midtirade. "There he is," the chief deputy said.

"Morning, y'all," Shoals said with casual cheer.

Bynum couldn't wait. "Imagine this—the state investigators arrive first thing this morning from Jackson. There's a new lead in a national missing person case. For the first time, we have evidence suggesting possible foul play. A major interstate crime, likely perpetrated right here in Bayard County. They've come for this vital piece of evidence, which was discovered, unbeknownst to the lead investigator, by one of our very own deputies. Our department turns it over. They open the bag and what do they find?"

Shoals pinched the bridge of his nose.

"A goddamn chew toy, Danny!"

"I'm sorry, Robbie."

"Why didn't you notify me or the sheriff that you'd found a severed hand?" Bynum demanded. "Did it not occur to you that maybe that was worthy of mention?"

"I didn't want to interrupt y'all's weekend," Shoals replied. "And besides, I could handle it."

"You didn't, though. You didn't handle it correctly. You fucked up my whole investigation, Danny." He threw the file against the wall for effect, papers spilling everywhere.

Shoals looked to his uncle, stern and dispassionate as ever.

"Look, Robbie, it's not a total loss, okay?" Shoals said. "Suzie-Q played with it a little, but it don't change the simple fact of what we found and where we found it."

Bynum threw his hands in the air and spun around, some dramatic act of exasperation. "You didn't even mark off the scene. You didn't follow procedure at all. Assembled your own civilian team to search the woods nearby? You don't have a clue, do you? You truly have no idea what you're doing or what your job requires. You are as unqualified for this job as any jackass off the street."

"Tell you what," said Shoals, bowing up in defense, "we can take a walk out back and I'll demonstrate how *not* to conduct an interrogation."

The sheriff stood and ushered Bynum out of the office, closed the door, and invited his nephew to sit. "This isn't good, Danny," his uncle said. "I have to agree with Robbie on this one."

Shoals leaned forward, elbows on his knees and pleading. "I know, Sheriff. I stepped in a big pile on this one. I was just trying to show you I could take the lead on something, okay? But I need your help to show me the right way to do this stuff. I want to lead."

The sheriff sat back and crossed his legs, stared long and thoughtful at his nephew, probably wondering how much horseshit he was shoveling.

"Dun was here this morning," the sheriff said. "I think it might be wise for you to lay low this week."

Shoals bowed his head. What else could go wrong for the good-luck kid? All of this for showing some initiative?

He looked up at his uncle. "I've been laying low for too long, Uncle Bud. I'm ready to play ball. Don't cast me aside. I want you to know I've got it in me to be great like my dad."

The sheriff considered this, hands clasped, fingers to his lips. He opened his desk drawer and pulled out a small black leather Bible. He had a verse ribboned, which he studied, and then closed the book. "Paul wrote the Philippians from prison, and do you know what he told them?"

It might be said that his uncle, an abider of peace, had spared the rod a merciful time or two when Danny was young, but never the Scripture. It was a book he knew intimately, the only one, and he used it like a man who believed words could change the wicked.

Shoals told him no sir. He had no idea what Paul would have said about any of this.

"'I have often told you, as I do now with tears, that there are many who walk through life unaware that they make their way as enemies of Christ,'" the sheriff said, taking the words for his own. "'They are headed for destruction, my friend. Their bodies are their god, and they take pride in what should bring shame. Their minds are set on earthly things. And for them, there will be no escape from this earth.' *No escape from this earth.* Doesn't that sound horrible?"

Shoals pursed his lips and nodded thoughtfully.

"I don't mean to preach to you, Danny, because I aint a preacher," his uncle said, flicking the official seal of office displayed on his desk. "I'm just giving you a heads-up, okay? Your fly's open. Like that."

Shoals checked his pants and smirked. "I hear you, Uncle Bud. I appreciate it."

"You don't have to be a hero," the sheriff added. "Just be a good man."

Shoals stood to leave, shook his uncle's hand.

"May not seem like it, but I look to you more than all the rest," the sheriff said.

Shoals nodded and left. He took slow, thoughtful strides down the hall and out into the reception room.

"Hey, Sugar," Desdimona called him back.

He stood soberly over her desk. She passed him the horseshoe. "You might need this back," she said.

He took it in his hand, studied its curves and ridges. Earthly stuff.

"Nah," he said and passed it back. "I'm good just by myself."

He shot her a wholesome grin and turned to leave but stopped before he hit the door. He turned and came back, put his arm against the doorway to the station room, and leaned in, called out loud and clear enough so that the deputies at their desks could hear and heed him—"Listen up, fellas. If he shows up again, you can tell that bald-headed son of a bitch Dun Spiller I'm looking for him too."

– 31 –

He sprang into World-Mart with the smiling confidence of a successful young professional. Clean-shaven and closely cropped, he moved through the aisles with a sharp stride, his buffed dress shoes snapping purposefully over the linoleum. He kept his sunglasses on, a sign of healthy ego, and his crisp shirt and pressed pants—dug out of the closet, still wrapped in plastic from the cleaners—painted him above reproach. He pushed a lazy-wheeled cart through the maze of products, referring slyly now and then to the palm of his hand, where he'd composed a shopping list. As he made his brisk way around the giant complex, he observed the positions of other customers and security cameras mounted in the ceiling under shaded bubbles. In the packaged meat aisle he crouched behind a display of ready-made school lunch kits and choked down half a sleeve of raw hot dogs with tasteless dispassion. If he believed anyone in the control room was watching the security cameras, he might have waited until he'd unloaded his purchases in the parking lot. But today he felt a brief and blessed freedom from fear of scrutiny.

He shopped thriftily for two. They wouldn't need much, only each other's company and a bit of comfort. In the sporting goods section he spied an affordable junior dome tent and sleeping bag set and added it to his stash. Who needed to sit indoors and mull over the lack of lights or television when you could sleep outside for only thirty dollars?

It was all going fine until he tried to pay for his goods. There were forty or more checkout lanes installed, only two in operation. He stepped into the far shorter line and was confronted by a lady in an official World-Mart jumper, who inspected his basket. "Sir, you'll have to wait in this line," she insisted, directing him to the longer queue.

"I'm sorry?" he asked.

"Ten items or less here, you'll have to move to the next," she said, reprimanding him dispassionately. His cart contained maybe twenty-five items. The other lane was backed up ten deep.

Jay opened his mouth to complain, to state the obvious, but then he remembered that he was in a temple of consumerism where the normal rules of logic did not apply and where every corner which might guarantee customer well-being had been cut, a necessary sacrifice that made possible the base cost of goods and exploited the weakness in those who craved the thousands of useless objects on display, objects that would, for just a moment, numb the pain they felt in their daily lives, being squeezed by every other segment of society from trifling employers to providers of utilities and goods and services, health care and insurance to credit scams and substandard education to mindless soul-sucking culture and intractable political discourse, not to mention demanders of taxes, fees, penalties, and . . . He shuddered and then smiled simply and nodded, steered his cart to the other lane.

He struggled to maintain equanimity for twenty minutes as he waited to pay, and in the homestretch, after he'd calculated his purchases several times in his head, Jay realized he would have about twenty bucks left over, locked forever inside his World-Mart gift card. It was assured by now that he would never return here under any circumstances, unless it be looting in the wake of whatever cataclysm society was meant to suffer for such as this, so he transferred the balance to a credit gift card that he could use anywhere else.

He stowed his purchases in the back of the Bronco and checked the time. He had an hour until pickup, so he swung by the public library to scope out recent newspapers for any updates, especially concerning the weekend's gruesome discovery. No mention of severed hands or search parties. Either the sheriff's office was keeping a tight lid on things or the whole operation in Jay's field had been staged, some sort of setup or subterfuge. Having watched the deputy at work, Jay found it hard to believe that he might be capable of conducting anything that required subtlety or careful forethought.

He gave himself plenty of time to arrive at the school, but nothing could have prepared him for the car pool line—a many-tentacled beast, churning and pulsating in prerehearsed merges and loops and switchbacks. To an idle father it was unforgiving, a closed system designed to expose and defeat his questionable humanity.

Jay's first mistake was trying to enter from the wrong direction. He came up Saddler Avenue from the south and attempted to make a left-hand turn onto the campus, but he could tell from the stone-faced response of the giant SUV-driving dad in fierce shades that he wasn't cutting line today. He drove up farther, following the snaking line of vehicles several blocks, and performed a three-point turnabout, frustrating drivers who came at him from every side. Nor did his rookie shame subside upon entering the campus, for he was clueless about which lane to take. Though the procession moved at a snail's pace, something in its ruthless efficiency suggested that children must be collected quickly or else they'd be sent back to the gymnasium or study hall while their real parents were called.

There was also Jacob. How would he react to seeing his dad after all this time? Two months must seem to him like two years. Would they even recognize each other? What if, upon seeing his father, he refused to get in the Bronco? What if he ran crying into the arms of a teacher and they radioed to the policeman on duty, for surely there must be one here, scoping out potential crazed parents or disgruntled students with lumpy duffel bags and black trench coats.

God, he had the pistol in the glove box. If they searched the vehicle, he would be taken straight to jail, no questions asked, his mug on the nightly news. A cursory inspection of his home might not turn up anything, but some second-sight detective could make a pass, tug the right string, and unravel the whole sordid mess.

He looked in the rearview mirror. He'd already entered the campus and there was no way to turn back now. He was hemmed in on all sides. He felt the thousand judging eyes of parents and teachers. Who was this, some administrator staring at him, her mouth against a walkie-talkie? All of his paperwork was in order, the screaming orange placard attached to the passenger-side windshield, printed with MIZE and a number-letter code, which he'd picked up, along with Jacob's things, hidden in the carport at the Waller Street rental, a negotiation that required twenty minutes of creeping around the neighborhood's outskirts, making his cautious way to assure that he wasn't being followed or that the hot-rod deputy wasn't waiting in the alley or the gas mart next door or the abandoned factory parking lot down the way.

When he merged right toward the elementary building, the line split into a three-pronged formation. He stuck to the outside lane, where he felt most comfortable. If all else failed, he'd be able to make a getaway across the immaculately landscaped campus.

Finally it was his turn at the head of the line. The clutch of vehicles was given the signal. They all eased forward into their respective slots. A tall staffer in an orange vest conducted them with a stop sign, his whistle at the ready. On the far right side, a throng of eager kids fidgeted in anticipation. When everyone was in place, they were released like hounds at a foxhunt. Jay scanned the crowd for his son but could not find him among the kids, all dressed alike in their maroon and khaki uniforms, scampering through the maze of sport-utility wagons.

A strange woman appeared at the passenger door, tried the locked handle, and tapped on the window. He reached over to unlock the door, and then it opened and his precious son was there, wide-eyed and tentative. Jay could say nothing, only hoist a grimace onto his face as the high-pitched lady cried, "Jacob, is this your ride?"

The boy nodded and climbed in, a bit unsure. He looked the same, his hair a little shaggier.

"Okay, then, y'all have a good break," squealed the teacher and closed the door.

They stared at each other for a cruel suspicious second and then fell into each other's arms. They both cried. Clutching Jacob was like a charge that set Jay's metronome right. All the horror and guilt and paranoia melted away in an instant. This child held a life-giving force which was saving him. He inhaled the boy's scent, a combination of schoolroom antiseptic and musty playground sweat, an odor sweeter to him than a field of wildflowers, and for once his olfactories were cleansed of the putrid phantoms.

A horn honked behind them. They'd been given clearance and their reunion was holding up the line. Jay sat up, wiped his eyes, and threw the Bronco in motion. "Oh, buddy, I've missed you like crazy," he said, unable to let go of his boy, and the child scooted over and clutched his father's arm as if it were a log floating down a runaway river.

Finding it cumbersome to drive with the boy so fixed to him, Jay pulled over at the tennis courts up the street and they embraced awhile longer.

"Look at you," Jay said, holding his little man at arm's length, his swollen eyes full of pride. "I must be insane to be away from you for so long, you beautiful boy." Jacob, a red-faced mess himself, crimped his little mouth in an embarrassed grin but could say nothing.

"How old are you now, like eleven?" Jay asked.

The boy giggled. "No, Dad."

"Twenty?"

"No!" he cried.

"A hundred!"

"Dad!" Jacob bellowed. "I'm six, silly!"

"Hey, I know something . . ."

"What?"

"Are you hungry?"

The boy's eyes shot up to the left in quirky contemplation. "Yes," he replied, almost as a question.

"Me too," Jay said. "I haven't eaten in six weeks. How does a pancake feast sound to you?"

"Yes," the boy hissed, cocking his arm in triumph. It was a foreign gesture, something he'd picked up along his fatherless way.

On the outskirts of town they stopped at the Tour Chef, a defunct truck stop that remained simply a diner, famous for its all-day breakfast. It was legendary in these parts, singular greasy highway fare in a world of bland knockoffs. They grabbed a window booth and ordered a tall stack to split. Jay took coffee and let Jacob have soda. "How about some sausage and bacon too," Jay added. The diner aromas were stoking his old beastly hunger.

While they waited Jay studied his son and admired his wavy brown hair, the smattering of freckles that had appeared along his nose and cheeks. He was a good-looking boy, calm, curiosity in his eyes. "I've been looking forward to you coming back to the country," he told Jacob.

"Me too," said the boy.

"I've been cleaning up the place and planning all sorts of things for us to do."

"Like what?"

"Well, I thought we could go fishing and camping, cook out. Maybe we could clean up some more and see if we can't get Mom to agree to move back. What do you think?"

Jacob smiled absently, his mind whirling. He was trying to make sense of everything.

"I hope you don't think it's your mom's fault that you had to move to town. I know the apartment's not the greatest place in the world to live."

"It's not too bad," Jacob said. "But I like the country house better."

"I'm glad."

"But we do have TV in town," Jacob said.

Jay frowned. "Your mom got you TV, huh?"

"Yeah."

"You like watching that, I bet."

"Yeah."

"Well, I hate to disappoint you, but I still don't have TV."

"That's okay, Dad," the boy said. "I've watched enough anyway."

Jay thought he was already so considerate and kind, trying to comfort his old man, who was too cheap to pay the hookup fee, too crazy to believe it was anything but a box spewing poison into the home.

"Hey, there's plenty of cool stuff for us to watch. You ever heard of caveman TV?"

"Caveman TV?" the boy asked in comic exaggeration. "I've never seen that show."

Jay laughed. "It's not a show. You'll see."

The pancakes and bacon and sausage arrived, and they dove in. "You can do whatever you want this weekend," Jay said, hefting the syrup dispenser and pouring the brown sweetness right over his tongue. He got an astonished look and a great laugh out of Jacob.

As they ate, Jay became distracted by a man sitting alone a few tables away. He wore a skullcap and a cumbersome jacket and mumbled to himself, his voice rising occasionally to complain or accuse. Something in the man's face and complexion resembled Tovis Boyers. Jay watched and listened for a while. The guy would lap up his meal and smack his lips and cluck his tongue as food tumbled out along with inscrutable curse-laden admissions.

"Man, this bacon is hitting the spot," said Jay, trying to focus on enjoying his food. It had been so long since he sat to eat a meal at a normal pace, not just scarfing it down like an animal.

"Hey, Dad," Jacob said.

"Yeah, bud?"

"Why did Mom leave the country and take us to town?"

Jay finished his coffee and wiped his mouth. "Well," he said and nodded for a refill. The waitress brought the pot over and poured. "I guess your mom and I just didn't see eye to eye on some things regarding the farm and the house and what I was doing and what she wanted to be doing."

He shook his head, frustrated with his own grasping excuse. "I know it's hard to understand, but mostly it's no fun to be a grown-up. Except being a dad. That's definitely the best part."

He thought he might be pouring it on too thick. This kid was no pushover.

"I mean, we both want you to be comfortable and happy, but sometimes we have different ideas about how to make that work. And so . . . well, we just had to take a break and be apart for a little while. So that we wouldn't get so mad at each other that we couldn't be friends anymore."

"But you're not friends," Jacob said. "Mom's your wife."

Jay smiled. "You're absolutely right. And sometimes when you're a grown-up, you forget those very simple things that you knew so easily when you were a kid, like yourself."

"You mean you get dumber?"

The man in the nearby booth cackled, antagonizing in his volume. What was he carrying under that bulky coat in this mild season?

"In some ways you do, Jacob," Jay said, trying to keep their conversation in line. "You can get to be so smart that you find you've come back around to being dumb again. It's funny how things work. But you don't need to worry about all that stuff, okay? You just need to have fun. There is plenty of time for trouble and worry later in life."

"I don't want trouble and worry," Jacob replied.

"No one does. It just sort of comes with it, you know. The better you learn how to handle it, the happier you'll be."

Jay groaned inwardly at himself. He sounded like one of those TV dads whose every remark was trying to impart some wisdom and advice.

The waitress came with the check, and Jay handed her the gift card. She didn't seem concerned about the man cursing profusely to himself. Maybe he was a harmless regular. Should Jay mention something, or would it just unnerve Jacob? Anyway, the boy didn't seem to notice. He just babbled on in excited detail about school and his teachers and friends.

Soon Jay had become distracted again, this time by a balding, red-haired cop who walked in and leaned over the counter, chatting up one of the other waitresses. He wore a county uniform, a tan shirt and dark green pants that ballooned out across his wide duff. Had Shoals put a tail on him? The cop didn't seem particularly observant, just oblivious, crowding a poor guy on the corner stool trying to eat grits.

The waitress returned with the card and told Jay it was declined.

"Declined? I just bought it today."

"You activated it?"

"Activated?"

The waitress flipped the card around, studied it tight, and pointed to the fine print. "Call this here number and tell them you ready to pay some folks."

"I don't even have a phone!" He almost shouted it. The deputy noticed, turned and took stock of Jay.

"Hold up and I'll fetch mine," said the waitress. She tottered off again. The deputy took an open seat at the counter and twirled around on his stool to openly observe the diners. The man in the booth laughed to himself, the sound of a wet hacking belch.

The waitress returned and handed Jay her cell phone. He spent the next several minutes trying to figure out the phone and the automated dial-in activation. He should have known these credit swaps and checkout lane bargains were never as simple as advertised. If somebody was going to get screwed here, it shouldn't be the waitress. She reminded Jay of his mom. God forbid this was her ten years down the road, killing herself to make the rent while her husband rested peacefully in the ground, his problems solved by checking out early. What's the use in living to a ripe old age if you spend your days serving waffles to slack-jawed deadbeats?

After navigating the credit card's call center, Jay handed the waitress back her phone and the newly endowed card. She took it away to confirm. He noticed the deputy paying attention, but he didn't let on that he'd noticed. He smiled a lot and kept asking Jacob if he'd enjoyed his meal and tried to ignore the man and his mouth, which was open and stating loudly and definitively, "Shit, I'm fixing to eat me some goddamn eggs, motherfucker!" The man cocked his head to the side and only then did Jay notice the hands-free phone stuck in his ear. So he was simply a boor and not insane. That should have made Jay feel better, but it didn't.

Jay crunched ice from his water glass and mashed the empty plastic butter cups flat with his thumb as he waited for the waitress. He made daring eye contact with the police officer for several fraught seconds, until the walkie-talkie on his belt squawked and the cop turned his attention away.

The waitress returned the card, which had processed successfully, and Jay left her the balance as a tip, smiled and waved to her as they stood to leave, and clutched Jacob close as they walked out of the Tour Chef and into the parking lot.

They climbed into the Bronco, and Jay sat for a moment to catch his breath.

"What's wrong?" Jacob asked.

"What do you mean, bud?"

"You seemed really mad in there."

"Was I mad?" Jay replied. His discomfort was so obvious that it made children anxious. He wondered what hope there was for him, really, when he couldn't even fake his way through a simple negotiation like dining in public with his son. "I'm sorry, Jake. Your dad's no good in town."

The diners went on inside as before. He could see them through the window. There was no change but the tension was gone.

"In the end, that's probably why your mom wanted to move out. She couldn't understand why I was mad all the time."

"Who made you mad?"

Jay thought about it for a moment. How to simplify such a broad aspersion? "The people who gave me that credit card. Never get a credit card, okay? Cash only."

Jacob nodded and said, "Okay."

"You see, there are people out there who make life more complicated than it needs to be." Jay turned to look at his son. "If everyone just minded their own business and were more considerate to one another, there would be much less trouble in the world."

The boy acknowledged his father and pretended to understand.

Jay cranked the Bronco and backed out of the lot, and they rode toward home in silence with the windows down, the Bronco moving at a good clip along the stolen roads, trying to make up for lost time.

– 32 –

Sandy's staff meeting let out after lunch on Friday, giving her a rare and unexpected free afternoon. She stopped by the hospital, where the situation was unchanged. Her father was stable and resting. The doctor was encouraged by this, insisting that his body needed to fight the infection and would require every ounce of reserves. They were monitoring the situation closely and would call her if anything changed.

She considered sitting by his side, maybe reading a book. She also felt a strong compulsion to ride out and check on Jacob, but she didn't want to interrupt whatever metamorphosis might be taking place between father and son. Jacob was most likely having a wonderful time. What she really wanted, after so long, was a moment to herself.

In line for a soda and candy bar at the hospital gift shop, Sandy was drawn to a magazine cover showcasing a famous actress's new pixie haircut. She was struck all at once by the urge to enact some drastic fashion shift of her own. Wouldn't it be so wonderful, in all of her running to and fro, to just swipe a wet comb through her hair and be done? She purchased the magazine, and on her way home, she made a swing by the beauty salon with the slim hope of a walk-in appointment. The wide-eyed receptionist seemed thrilled to see her. Her usual stylist had just started a dye job, but there was a vacancy with one of the other associates and she could take a chair immediately. For once, things seemed to be going Sandy's way.

She sat down and flipped through the magazine, tapped her foot to the jaunty country pop playing at a tasteful volume through the salon's stereo. A petite young stylist bounced over and introduced herself as Tink. *Can Tink handle a pixie?* Sandy wondered. Why care? Tink was welcome to shave her down to the scalp as long as she could sit quietly without having to talk or listen for an hour. Sandy showed her the magazine, and the hairdresser seemed eager to attempt Hollywood coiffure.

Sandy closed her eyes and surrendered to Tink, who bundled her up in a nylon cape and reclined her seat. There was a luxurious session at the shampoo sink. It was so peaceful there, the requiem of water eclipsing all other sounds as Tink's young fingers pulsed against her scalp, the fruity essence of mangosteen overtaking the soggy cardboard smell of wet hair. She could have slept right there for the rest of the afternoon.

As the whisk of scissors went by her ear and she felt the soft tug and release of strands being snipped from her head, each lock a leaden weight fallen away, Sandy let her mind unspool without a care for the world around her. There in the salon chair she fell deep within herself, to the white dream space beyond the bluster of her daily tempests, and there the true cast of herself was revealed in a lovely prismatic scatter. Life was not so bad in here. Her husband was simply lost, not deranged or dangerous, and her father's spirit was waiting loyally nearby, still intact and earthbound. Even her downstairs dalliance last week, though the particulars were unsavory, had revealed a new side of herself, nothing ugly or promiscuous but bold and adventuresome, open to the possibility of life beyond Jay. The words of her father's Buddhist text came hurtling back to her—*Be mindful even of the ground beneath your feet, where all the waste of nature is remade as nutrient in the earth. So does our pain and suffering compose the soil where tomorrow's peace will grow.*

The hardship of recent months, and whatever else was due, had created a weight that she would learn to carry, that would make her stronger. She must pivot, she must exact changes as she was doing now. She must look at the world through new eyes and seek opportunity where before she had never dared. For instance—what if she went platinum blond as well? She would be forced to see herself differently, as would everyone else. And as she pictured herself with a tight and bright new life-refining burst of hair, she was jerked to the surface by a reluctant impression . . . *Danny Shoals.*

Her eyes shot open and she expected to see him right there, leering down at her. But he wasn't. It was only someone talking about him.

Tink swung her chair around for a fresh angle and Sandy met the glare of her usual stylist, Rochelle Spiller, working another head across the salon. Rochelle, so funny and pleasant all these years, was sneering at her. She snapped her gum and practically hissed as she applied paint and tinfoil to her customer's hair. Everyone nearby was held rapt by Rochelle's story, which Sandy strained to hear.

"I was completely naked!" Rochelle described. "And then I looked in the mirror and noticed a little red light outside. I thought it was a car or something, and then I looked closer and thought, *Oh my God, that's somebody outside taping me!*"

The women gasped and shook their heads. Rochelle shot her a look that said, *Are you getting this, bitch?*

"So I put my robe on and got a flashlight and a baseball bat and I walked around back. *Oh my God, y'all,* I thought, *what if this person tries to rape me?* But I go out back and shine the light and it's *him!* It's Danny Shoals from the sheriff's department! And he's sitting there with . . ." The conversation faded to a whisper, followed by a sharp intake of ladies gasping, hands to mouths, more shaking heads.

"Is that not *disgusting?*" cried Rochelle. "Protect and serve, my ass!"

Sandy shouted out involuntarily across the salon, "Danny Shoals videotaped you naked?"

Rochelle turned and cocked her head. "He's got a video of my coochie!" she shouted back. "He threatened to post it on the internet if I told anybody!"

The room stiffened from the hairdresser's scorn—or maybe they were all imagining the violation of their respective coochies being filmed and broadcast globally. "At this point, I'm like, Go right ahead. I'm not ashamed of this thing. You can't turn my own body against me and hold me hostage that way!"

The ladies agreed and cheered her on.

"Shoot, maybe I'll get famous! It's about time!" She could have run for mayor, so charged was the crowd by her righteous indignation and refusal to be victimized.

Sandy was livid, dumbfounded. She couldn't believe she'd let this person in her house, much less into her basement. Had he set up a camera in the basement while he was murdering the armadillo? Did he have video of her as well? Would he post it online? What if Jacob found it, or her father, or the girls from church?

She cried out again, "What was he doing outside *your* window?"

She'd meant to put the stress on "doing," but it came out all wrong, and the shop went silent. Rochelle put down her brush and walked halfway over, hands in plastic gloves on hips. "I don't know. I guess someone isn't giving it to him right so he has to come sneaking around other women's houses while their husbands are away."

Sandy shook her head. Was it public knowledge, then, that she'd repaid him for his protection? Just a nominal compensation, a gratuity really. But a transaction intimate enough to require a whole new set of obligations.

"I'm so sorry that happened, Rochelle," said Sandy. "He sounds like a horrible person."

"Uh-huh," replied Rochelle with cool disbelief.

In the midst of the standoff, a customer on the far side of the salon, a middle-aged beauty, ripped off her cape and made long dignified strides across the room, leaving a trail of curlers shaken from her hair, paying no one a bit of mind as she barged out to a clatter of door chimes.

Rochelle bent over in laughter. The other stylists cringed and laughed through bared teeth.

"What is it?" Sandy asked.

"That's his mother," replied Tink, spinning the chair back around toward the mirror.

That poor woman, Sandy thought, and then she caught a glimpse of herself, her red puffy face and spiky hair. She looked like a tired British pop singer, some cherub on the wane. A bratty child with glue in his hair.

Who was this person? Who had she become?

She tried not to burst into tears, as if holding back a dam with bare hands. If she had any strength, any resilience at all, she would hold her head high and walk out of there with that atrocious hairdo and her humiliating ties to a peeping pervert. If his own mother could do it . . .

"What do you think?" Tink said with a wince.

Sandy held up the magazine. "Not what I pictured," she replied. "I'm sure you did your best. Can I pay you now?"

The charges were obscene. She could have achieved the same thing herself with a pair of child's safety scissors. But she handed over her credit card proudly while the girls whispered and giggled on the other side of the salon. She signed the receipt and left a large tip.

On her way out, Rochelle called, "Um, excuse me, Mrs. Mize!"

Mrs. Mize? Sandy thought. She turned back.

"Rochelle?"

"Mrs. Mize," the stylist said with high-pitched faux cheer, "if you see your friend Danny Shoals, please let him know that my husband is going to kick his ass when he finds him."

"I'm sure I won't see him," Sandy replied. "I barely know him. I don't know what you've heard, but he's certainly no friend of mine."

She stamped out into the harsh white light of an afternoon in ruins and climbed into the Maxima, keeping herself poised all the way to the shitbox on Waller, where she locked the door, closed the blinds, and shut herself away for the weekend.

— 33 —

Chipper sensed them a mile away. No dog had ever been so glad to find its boy. He was howling when they came up the drive, scratching at the door when they came in from the carport. They released him from the laundry room and he tackled Jacob, licking him thoroughly. Watching the boy and dog tumble on the linoleum, the late sun streaming through the windows, the house alive again for the first time in ages, Jay wondered how he could have wished a cruel fate for this animal.

They pitched the tent in the pasture where the ghosts had left. Jay taught his son how to build a proper campfire, how to light it with straw and a flint. They roasted hot dogs, and after dinner they skewered marshmallows on straight-bent clothes hangers and let the flames brown them and mashed them between graham crackers and divvied-up chocolate. It was a particular joy for Jay to watch his son's marshmallow-strewn grin and believe everything was going to be all right. *These are the only concerns we need*, he believed. *Neither yesterday nor tomorrow, just a belief in the moment.*

He caught Jacob transfixed by the flames. "I see you're enjoying caveman TV," Jay said.

"Why do you call it that?" the boy asked.

"Because a long long time ago, before people lived in houses and drove cars and had jobs and went to school, they lived in caves and this is what they did for entertainment at night. They stared into the fire. It was like their television."

The boy grimaced. "They must have been bored," he said.

"Not necessarily. Watch it for a while. You may start to see pictures and stories as good as anything else on TV."

The kid smirked and his eyes bulged in disbelief.

As night took hold and the fire nestled into the logs, they doused the tent in mosquito dope, zipped the mesh door closed, and spread the sleeping bags flat, making a wide pallet. They lay side by side under a quilt and talked for a while of inconsequential things, like what makes someone burp and why the leaves turn colors in autumn, and then they spoke of more serious things, like what it felt like for Jacob to see his grandfather unconscious in a hospital bed, and why he wasn't allowed to attend the funeral of his other grandfather, Jay's dad, all the while skirting around larger issues, which they were somehow addressing without speaking to them directly.

The boy rolled over toward Jay and clutched him suddenly, as if seized by an idea. "Dad, I don't know what I would do if you died." He broke into convulsive sobs, and Jay gripped him in an assured embrace. He felt a flare of pride stitched with shame for taking comfort in the boy's fear and sorrow. He tried to console his son without lying to him, without insisting that he wouldn't die any time soon.

"Odds are," he said, "you'll be older than I am right now when I finally die. I'll be an old, cranky man, and you'll probably be relieved."

"Were you relieved when your dad died?"

"No."

They lay awake in the dark, the conversation growing thinner until each of them drifted off. It wasn't a comfortable night's sleep. The junior dome tent was thirty-dollars big, and Jay had to sleep in an arc around the perimeter with Jacob curled up in the middle. Another quilt would have been nice, but it was too cold and dark to run inside and search for one. They got by on catnaps most of the night, and just when it seemed that the sun might forsake them, the birds began their early forage and daybreak found its way into the hollow. Jay crawled into the morning coolness to rebuild the fire, made coffee and fried eggs, which they ate with cold bread and jelly.

When the sun was up they walked down to the front field, and Jay told his son about the flood and showed him how high the water had risen. He told him how he'd floated around on the field as if it were a pond. Jacob asked if they could take a boat ride, and Jay told him the boat was gone. It sprung a leak, he said. The boy wanted to find another boat, and Jay told him they would go fishing later and not to worry about it.

They walked along the edge of the field near the compost bins and Jacob got it in his head that they would need worms. The boy remembered all the worms wriggling through the compost, and so he ran to the bins and plunged his fists into the prime curing batch where Jay had spread the char and ashes.

Jay could see the black fibers collecting in the tiny hairs of his son's arm. "Let's not take those worms," Jay said. "There'll be more down by the river."

"Aw, why can't we have these?" the boy whined.

"Because these worms have a job to do."

Jay explained how the worms chewed through the dirt and distributed the nutrients and kept the soil nice and loose so the plant roots would spread. The boy lost interest and went poking behind the bins, where he turned up a football-size watermelon in the weeds. "How do you like that?" Jay said. "There must have been a seed in the compost. Sometimes they grow on their own and don't even need us except to spit seeds."

Jacob wanted to eat it, and Jay said it would be sweeter if they let it ripen a bit. He explained how composting was just making new dirt, which was built out of dead plants and grasses, rotten fruits and vegetables, ash and manure.

The boy maintained slight interest. "Manure is like dookie, right?" he asked.

"That's right."

He considered this a moment. "Those hot dogs we ate, were those grown in manure?"

"That's tricky," said Jay. "Hot dogs aren't grown in the ground and hence don't come into contact with any animal wastes. On the other hand, hot dogs themselves are most likely just the ground-up guts and buttholes of cows and pigs and chickens."

"Gross!" Jacob cried and spat. "You didn't tell me I was eating butts!"

"I didn't know you had a problem with it," Jay said, laughing. Ideally, he explained, they would one day be able to raise their own animals and produce their own food. That way they would know exactly what they were putting in their mouths. No butts, he promised his boy.

They ambled back to the house and messed around under the carport, sifting through boxes containing random, unsorted possessions, most of which would be put on the curb for trash pickup.

Jacob was excited by a plastic bag containing old coins and asked if he could buy something. Jay remembered the few coins, mostly buttons and trinket medallions, which he'd found in the bottom field when he first tilled it. He said these coins wouldn't spend, that they were most likely from the Civil War and maybe of use only to a collector or historian.

Jacob wanted to know about the Civil War, and Jay told him about how the country divided a long time ago and fought each other over their differences.

"Like you and Mom?"

"Kind of, but worse. When a lot of people disagree, sometimes they fight to the death over it. That's what happened. A lot of people died."

Jacob's eyes glazed over in contemplation. "Dad," he said, "did someone die down in the field?"

Jay considered the boy's tone and wondered if he'd overheard someone mention something. "What do you mean?" he asked finally.

"Is that why the money was there? Did someone die, or did it just fall out of their pocket?"

Jay studied the coins as if trying to discern the real answer. "I'm not sure. It happened so long ago, there would be no one alive to tell us."

Jacob wanted to keep everything, and there was much negotiation over what was trash and what could be kept. The boy dug out a carton of copper BBs and asked if they were candy. Jay went inside, found the air rifle in the hall closet, and took Jacob into the backyard. He collected an armful of faded aluminum cans from a ripped garbage bag, waiting interminably to be dropped off at the recycler. He propped them on a pile of old tractor tires, stepped back twenty yards or so and demonstrated how to load and pump the rifle, then levered and flicked off the safety. He gave his son a quick lesson on sighting and squeezing the trigger, then took the first shot. A satisfying ping resounded off the fallen soda can. The boy's eyes grew wide and he took to the sport instinctively, refusing to quit until they'd used up the whole carton of shot and left a massacre of cans.

"I love shooting," Jacob said.

"It's a good skill to nurture," said his dad. "Maybe we'll get you a .22 for Christmas."

"Can I ask Santa?"

"You bet."

Jacob asked his dad if he ever hunted. He'd seen a lot of shows on television about killing animals.

"My dad took me hunting when I was about your age," Jay recalled. "It was a very important thing in my dad's life. I've hunted some recently. I think it's fine as long as you're hunting to feed yourself and not simply to kill."

Jacob thought about this. "It's bad to kill animals," he said. "If you kill an animal, you're killing God because God made all the animals and He is part of all living things."

"I never thought of it that way." Jay was surprised and intrigued. Had Sandy been taking their son to church?

"It's still fun to shoot em," Jacob said.

Jay laughed. "Well, even though I don't hunt with a gun, I do love to catch fish. What do you say we go catch some fish?"

"Yeah!" Jacob shouted.

"Wouldn't that be a great dinner tonight? Instead of stinky old butt dogs?"

Jacob laughed, and they agreed it would be a fine meal, so Jay gathered tackle and fishing poles and a few bottles of water, and they stopped in the woods to root around under leaf piles and collected some earthworms in a short bucket, and with Chipper tagging along they hiked to the river.

In preparation for this outing, Jay found a slough along the river's edge where a fallen tree had made an inlet, the perfect bed for crappie and bream, maybe even a catfish. He'd already set the poles with fresh lines, bobbers, and sinkers, both his cane pole and the junior fly rod he'd cleaned and rewound just for Jacob. He demonstrated the cast and let the boy practice a few times before he tied on the hook. Then he showed his son how to fix a worm to the hook, a nasty business but secretly the best part, next to catching a fish.

"Ooo," Jacob wailed when the little poof of worm guts exploded from the hook puncture. "Let me do yours!" the boy begged.

With the sun behind them in the trees and the fall breeze off the river, it was really the most idyllic setting. They found their sweet spot and had already yanked out one nice crappie. Enjoying the easy rhythm of life, Jay finally felt like a legitimate dad as they engaged in one of the most natural pursuits a father and son could share.

With shorter patience, Jacob reeled and baited and recast frequently, so it was inevitable that he'd get hung up in the branches of the fallen tree. He tried to jerk the line free, but it wouldn't come. He turned the pole over to Jay, who could neither dislodge it nor break the line. He searched his pocket and the tackle bag for a knife or cutters but came up empty.

"Oh, wait," Jacob said and dug into his shorts pocket. He pulled out a handsome Swiss Army knife.

"Whoa, this is nice," said Jay, inspecting all the flip-out features. "Did your granddad give you that?"

"No. Danny gave it to me."

"Who's Danny?"

"The policeman."

Jay stopped. Shoals? *That* son of a bitch?

"How do you know him?" Jay asked. He tried to keep a calm voice but felt a waver.

"Oh, he comes to see Mom sometimes."

So it was true. They were watching him. He felt like a dupe all over again.

"What does he do when he comes over?"

"Well, sometimes he plays with me. He gave me a Wiffle ball and bat and showed me how to hit. That was fun."

Jay heard his own heart and tried to slow his breathing, drawing deep to keep from losing his cool. "What about him and Mom, what do they do?"

"Nothing, they just talk."

"Do they talk about me?"

Jacob shrugged. "I don't know what they talk about. He just brings stuff like this knife and the Wiffle ball bat. He did bring flowers and a balloon once. And strawberries and whip cream, that was good."

Sandy's favorite dessert. What the hell was going on? Jay's heart broke loose at a gallop. Were they here? He glanced around cautiously, watching and listening for clues, a glare off sunglasses or an errant walkie-talkie. He fought to keep a handle on his temper. He had a thousand questions. The boy would start to worry, maybe start lying, if he appeared too upset over this.

"Does he visit Mom a lot?"

"Not too much. He came to the hospital to visit Granddad."

Were they seeing each other, for chrissakes? Or could it be that Shoals was trying to ingratiate himself with Sandy just to get clues about Jay? She was too smart for him. She would see right through his bullshit.

"I like his car," Jacob added. "It's supercool."

"Yeah?"

Goddamn it! Was she angry enough to cooperate?

"He said he's gonna take me for a ride in it," Jacob said.

"I know that guy," Jay said, clipping the snagged line with the flip-out scissors. "I don't think he's so nice."

Jacob was quiet for a moment. "He seems nice to me," he replied.

"Yeah, well, he's nice to kids. But he's a trickster. You know what that is?"

"No."

"He tells you what you want to hear and gives you good stuff like this knife and your Wiffle ball bat. And then just when you think he's your friend, he does something bad."

"Like what?"

"You can never tell with a guy like him," Jay said. "Maybe you say something you shouldn't have, or do something your mom told you not to do. He'll be the one to run and tattle on you. Or maybe he comes to you and says, 'Remember that knife I gave you? I want it back.' And he takes your knife and he just . . ." Jay folded up the blades and tossed the knife far out into the river.

"Dad!" Jacob shouted. He stood up as if to dive in after it. Tears welled in his eyes and his face crinkled in pain. "Why did you do that?"

"I'm sorry, man." He put an arm around Jacob. "I'll get you another one. A better one."

"But I loved that knife," the boy blubbered, shoving out of his dad's embrace. "I never had one before."

"Look, he's a bad guy, okay? It's not good to keep things that belong to bad guys."

The lost knife cast a pall over the rest of the afternoon. Jay let Jacob fish off his cane pole, but their conversation was sunk. The boy pouted awhile and regained his enthusiasm only after landing his first fish, another crappie, and later a nice striped bass to end the excursion.

As a treat, and to make up for the lost knife, Jay took Jacob to the muddy wallow where he'd been making regular visits to scrub down. He encouraged the boy to take off his clothes and flop around in the mud, but Jacob was hesitant, as if it were a trick. Jay doffed his shorts and boots, pulled off his shirt, and launched himself into the pit with boyish glee. Jacob followed with caution, and soon they were wrestling and leaping, yelling and laughing, until the sun began to dive behind the trees and take its precious light. They emerged from the hole encrusted in mud, only their eyeballs and teeth shining white.

They walked home caked in river mud and enjoyed the sensation of it drying and hardening on them like a second layer of skin. Jay showed Jacob how to make white cracks appear by flexing his muscles.

"You look like you're made of chocolate, kid," Jay said. "I'm getting kind of hungry!" He chased the giggling boy up to the house, where he'd repaired the cistern and rigged a gravity-fed shower with a tank of rainwater attached to it. They stood under it and braced themselves and let the bitter cold water run the mud off.

They wrapped in towels and returned to the campsite, where Jay built a fire. They sat on logs and warmed up in the gray dusk, listening to the tranquil rhythm of insects in the trees. Jay demonstrated how to clean the fish by flaking off the scales and cutting out the guts with a kitchen knife. "See, you can carve out the butt when you catch it yourself," said Jay, making a V-shaped incision in one of the fish bellies and slicing off the offending orifice.

When the fire died down, he set the grilling grate low over the coals, greased a small cast-iron pan with shortening and fried the fish one by one. He showed the boy how to eat around the bone and how to get the tiny morsel of meat out of the head and how to eat the crunchy skin like a potato chip, not wasting a bit. They made up stories by the fire and built s'mores with the last of the chocolate, and as they had the night before, they crawled into the tent and under the blankets.

They both lay there awake for a while, their minds tumbling through the events of the day. Jay could tell the boy was awake, probably thinking about the knife. He couldn't bring himself to mention it or to justify his behavior. He wanted to tell Jacob everything, but a young and innocent boy didn't deserve to know such horrible secrets. Still, if things unraveled and the law came down on him, he would want his son to know the truth, that he'd done nothing wrong, that he was not a murderer.

"Jacob," Jay whispered. He repeated it louder. His son was already asleep. Jay rubbed the boy's head, his hand following the contours of bone. He felt the tiny jaw and traced its juncture, remembered how the mandible is hinged around by the ear, and how the spine fits into the base of the skull. He knew these things intimately now. He even knew what force is required to wrench them apart.

Jay fell asleep to the mourning of doves in the grass and slept solidly most of the night. He woke first, in the steely hue of an undeclared dawn, to the sound of footsteps around the campfire. He opened his eyes and lay still, trying to rationalize the noise. Maybe a bird hopping in the grass, a squirrel, at worst a fox. But the steps moved with heft and slinking certainty, and he knew it was someone who'd stumbled upon them and lacked the sense to leave. His heart tripped into a quick rhythm, and he reached into his pack for the pistol. He collected himself, then sat up with calm assurance, unzipped the flap, and slipped out to confront the visitor.

The buzzard stood over the pile of fish bones. They acknowledged each other gravely. Jay couldn't shoot it now. The noise would terrify Jacob. He stepped toward the bird, but it didn't flinch. He took another step, then another, and only then did the buzzard hop back a foot. They played this game, one step forward, one step back, until they'd moved away from the camp. Finally the bird stopped, and Jay stamped to chase it off.

It hissed.

"Fuck you," he hissed back.

The bird shuddered and gagged and hacked up a wretched-smelling gray clod that splattered against Jay's bare feet. He rubbed his toes in the grass and drew his arm over his face to cover the devastating smell. The buzzard seemed to cackle at him, its mouth propped open in a gruesome taunt. He'd never hated an animal this much. He lunged for it, and the bird hopped backward, flapping its wings to take flight, but it was too slow. Jay had it in his grip and wrestled it to the ground, surprised to find the filthy thing in his grasp. It jerked and moaned. Jay bashed its head repeatedly with the butt of the pistol, punched it flat until the bird flopped over limp in the grass.

He might have kept on killing it had he not been afraid of waking Jacob. He looked back and could just make out the inanimate mound inside the tent. He knelt down and studied the bird. The beak was cracked, and its eyes were missing, bashed inside its skull, which leaked red and creamy white. The mushy head didn't look much different than it had alive, a disgusting fleshy red wad. He pulled it by its tail feathers over a ridge and hurled it into some brush. One more living witness gone.

– 34 –

Shoals had a sixth sense for when wives were home alone. No husbands, no children, no encumbrances. It was as if he were mystically attuned to the quiet longing that pulsed from their eager dwellings.

He felt it as he made the park loop near Sandy's house late Friday afternoon. He kept a block out of sight to remain inconspicuous. If there was a drawback to the Boss, and he would never admit to such a thing, it was that it made a lousy undercover car. There would be no hanging out in the parking lot behind the baseball field watching for shadows in the window. Not today, not ever again. And certainly there would be no peeping, even though he detected, through the small opaque square at the back of the house, the softest dancing orange light that generally heralded a candlelit bubble bath. No, if he was going to see her in all of her bare glory, it would be earned.

Surely he had earned it. His performance in the basement had to have piqued her interest. She'd been shy, waiting for the hanging bulb to go out before dropping her pj's below her knees, letting him explore, but only down there, with his hands and face. He was anxious to show her what other, larger-bore apparatus he had in his tool kit. He had bided his time, been a patient gentleman, had fucked up and done penance. Now it was time to prove that he was a good and trustworthy man. No more prowling around, no more hitting every little kitten that raised her tail for him. He'd found the right one, and she was worth playing by the rules.

As for her husband, it was obvious that Sandy was done with him. After all, who did she call when she needed a man to rush over in the night?

He found the courage to pull right up in front of the apartment. He walked to the front door with a confident swagger, rang the bell, knocked on the door. He waited. Her Maxima was there, she had to be home. He regretted not swinging by his mother's house and plucking a bouquet of flowers, something rare and exotic, aphrodisiacal.

He sat on the front stoop and considered what he might say. How would he explain this visit? He'd always just happened by or had a delivery to make or been invited to exterminate some leathery rapscallion. He could be sexy forward, tell her he'd come to finish the basement job. Or perhaps it was time to come clean, to let her know how he really felt about her. She made him feel like becoming a new man.

He waited five minutes or so before Sandy opened the door, her robe pulled tight. He was shocked by her appearance. What had happened to the knockout MILF he used to know? She looked like a battered housewife with her puffy eyes and wrecked hair.

"Hey, girl," Shoals said, standing up and brushing off his jeans. "Wow, you cut all your hair off."

She said nothing, just stared at him through the storm door.

"I knocked and didn't get an answer. Figured you were taking a bath or something so I thought I'd wait here."

"Were you peeping in the window, is that how you decided I was in the bath?"

Shoals hung his head.

"Did you get a good look? Did you videotape me? Are you going to post it online?"

"I guess you heard the ugly rumors about me," Shoals said. "You can't imagine what I've been going through this week."

"What *you've* been going through?" She was astounded, her mouth agape. "What about Rochelle? You threatened to post a video of that innocent woman—naked!—online. She has children! She's done nothing to you!"

Oh, she did something, he wanted to say. *She did something every day when she dressed that way and shook her ass just so.* He didn't lay a hand on her, just met her halfway. Why put it out there if she wasn't trying to lure?

"And do you have a tape of me too?" She looked around for eavesdroppers. "In the basement?"

"No!" he said. "It was so dark I barely saw anything myself."

"So you would have, then, if the conditions had been suitable?"

"No, Sandy! I'm not that kinda guy."

"You're no kind of guy, you're a child! Worse than that, because a child doesn't know any better. You are an emotionally stunted bully. What happened to you? Did something happen when you were fifteen that kept you from developing like a normally mature human being?"

"Come on, now . . ."

"It's like you're stuck in high school with your ridiculous car and haircut and clothes." She was really having a time tearing into him like this. Her face twisted into painful contortions with every aspersion. "Your whole persona is an embarrassment. I wonder if you have one genuine bone in your body."

His eyebrows raised and he inhaled to respond but thought wiser and swallowed his remark. There was nothing to say. He was indefensible.

"What a letch! The way you treat women is abhorrent, it's criminal! All to convince yourself that you're not a loser, but it's an illusion! You *are* a loser, Danny, you're a sad cliché. You are the saddest thing I know. There is no way in hell I would spend another moment alone with you. In fact, if you don't leave right now, I'm calling the police."

The door slammed. He looked around to make sure there were no observers, and then he slunk back to the Boss, climbed in, and howled away. It wasn't far to the country. He wanted to get as far away as possible.

Weeks and weeks of careful work had blown up in his face. It was doubtful there was anything left to salvage. He thought of a wise old maxim—there's a thin line between love and hate. And then he thought how he'd like to drink an entire bottle of whiskey, so he whipped the car around in a treacherous about-face and proceeded back to a little country bar hugging the city outskirts, an anonymous place to get shitfaced.

At the bar he demanded a tall glass of Dickel and sloshed it down. The room was too small, the women a little too bovine with their inbred beaus. The back porch was noisy with boisterous floozies and knuckleheads out for an early happy hour.

"Why don't you wrap that bottle up and let me take it to go," Shoals told the bartender.

"That aint strictly legal, friend," he replied, to which Shoals threw his badge down on the bar.

Two minutes later he was back in the Boss, rocketing ninety and sucking back a hot swig, managing the curves with one hand. The flesh-colored horizon vied for his attention, split in half by a mound of purple clouds. The sun was tucked underneath, and he just wanted to make it home in time to watch the lake swallow it up.

He lived out by the reservoir, a little A-frame cabin with a loft bedroom and a screened-in back deck. It was the most perfect place in the world to him, out on the far edge of the county, a place where he could hide out and where company felt they could be entertained discreetly.

He made it home as the sun was bidding the day farewell. He had half a bottle and plenty of heartache to unload. As he stopped to unlock the front door, he noticed a freshly pounded fist hole through the screen door. His neighbor, a flagrantly queer teenager, was sneaking a smoke out in the bushes and stuck his face through the hedge.

"Hey, Danny," he called.

"What is it, Kelvin?" Shoals asked, perturbed.

"There was a cop here looking for you earlier."

"Who was it?"

"Lieutenant Spitzer?"

"Spiller?"

"That's it!"

"Shit."

Shoals went inside and locked the door. Suzie-Q was all smiles, tail wagging and legs galloping. At least someone was happy to see him. He turned the lights on and checked the messages. His mother had called, sounding foggy and distant. They'd been playing phone tag for a day or so. He didn't bother making a drink, just took it down in sober gulps from the bottle. It bothered him that Spiller had been here. The guy must be a real maniac.

He went out back to sit on the porch and watch the sun. He had a perfect view of the horizon and liked to prop his feet up on the coffee table, watch the sun fall between his legs like a starburst blonde. But it was gone already, somebody else's tonight.

He went into the yard for a whiz and watched the lavender sky glaze down over the treetops. "Screw this!" he said and took his bottle and got in the car and sped back to town.

He walked into the city police office and yelled, "I'm here to see Dun Spiller! I understand he's looking for me! Well, here I am—it's Danny fucking Shoals!"

Baby George appeared from one of the offices and came over to intercept Shoals. "Dude, what are you doing?" he said, clasping his old friend by the shoulder. "You been drinking a bit, buddy?"

"Naw," said Shoals.

"Whatever's going on between y'all is a personal matter. Don't bring that shit up in here, please."

"What's a matter with you, Baby?" cried Shoals. He was getting slurry. "You on Dun's side now, I guess. City boy solid, is that it?"

"Take it easy, bro," said George. "You want some coffee?"

"Hell no, I just want to talk to Dun. He's griping my ass, leaving messages all over creation. I'd like to fix this one way or another."

"Well, I'd watch my step if I were you," said George. "He's a big ole boy."

"What're you saying?"

"I'm saying if I was you, I'd get myself sober before I tangled with him."

Shoals stopped and looked around. Heads were peering out of offices, cops pretending to be on phones watching it unfold. What a disgrace. He would never work the city force. They were all a bunch of pencil pushers and citation writers. There was nothing he could say they didn't already hate themselves for, so he turned to stagger back out to his car when George called out, "Danny."

Shoals turned back and George stepped to him, leaned in close like he was giving advice. He looked around to make sure none of the others were listening. He whispered. "Are they real?"

"Shit yeah they're real!" Shoals cried. "And you can tell the rest of the boys she's wild down below. Looked like she was riding a mink!"

He regretted giving that last bit away. Not one among them deserved to know it. He was just trying to hurt Dun. He felt like he needed to hurt Rochelle, and Sandy too. He wanted to hurt his mother and Uncle Bud, anyone who ever doubted him. He wanted to show Big Jack he had a swinging prick on him too, that he could do anything he damn well dared.

He shot off into the night like a loose bottle rocket, content to crash wherever his powder ran out.

− 35 −

Jay felt carved out and hollow all of Sunday, anxious for her to show. Would she be alone? Well, of course, he knew that. And then what would he say to her? Was there a simple answer for all of this or would he have to fight to get it out of her?

The only sure way to know whether or not she was with the deputy would be to look her in the eyes, to study every gesture. Even without trust, they knew each other too well. You're with someone long enough and you graft into one another. Sometimes you have to run in horror when you see the other side of yourself.

Sunday hadn't been as easy with Jacob, whether he was simply tired or still sore over the knife. He'd spent a good portion of the day whining about the empty BB gun, pleading for more ammunition. He just wouldn't let it go. Later he cried when he discovered his mom hadn't packed his handheld video game. He wanted desperately to play it, and when Jay asked him the point of the game, he reverted from a bright and curious boy to a mumbling automaton who couldn't even convey the details, just kept saying, "You're this little thing and you move things around and get things."

So this was what it meant to live in town, Jay decided. The blessed artifice, the instant cure for want. Everyone was digging themselves deeper, surrendering the key to their being. No one saw the need to redress these things. No one saw how terribly it would all end. How could he send Jacob back there? What kind of father would he be?

He was wondering this alone when he heard tires on gravel. His heart took cover. He crouched at the window and traced her slow, nervous ascent from the road. He moved to the kitchen window and watched her sitting in the car, waiting for her boys. She finally got out and looked around. He made her wait, let her realize that this was no longer her home. He did this even as it pained him to see her this way.

Before she could knock, he popped into view, startling her a little. She'd cut all her hair off. She looked bloated and drained of life. Something was happening to her too, he realized, and he was seized by a kind of empathy that was still borne from deep love.

Jay opened the door and slipped out in socks as Chipper darted ahead of him. He closed the door carefully behind him.

"You scared me," she said with a bit of a smile.

He smiled back. "Hey."

"Wow, you're looking a lot better," she said.

Clean-shaven, tight hair, and bronze skin, a bit of food filling in his sunken features. "Thanks." He wished he could say the same about her, even just to be nice. Nevertheless, she had a rosy wounded aura about her, and he wanted to grab her up and carry her inside, tend to her and take from her and never let her leave. If it had just been the two of them living here, would they still be together?

"How was the weekend?" she asked.

"It was perfect. We did a few chores, we camped and fished. We played with Chipper."

Chipper was standing before her, his neck craned up with a goofy smile and his whole back end wagging.

"It was just what we both needed, I think. I'm glad you made the offer."

They stood facing, each sizing up the other. They could have come together and embraced and cured everything in that moment but for the oppressive doubt crowding between them.

"How's your dad?" he asked.

"He's still in a coma. Stable but . . ."

"God, I hated to hear it. But I know he'll come out. Right?"

"I don't know, Jay. I think. Maybe."

He let the coarse silence linger between them, gave her room to confess. He tried to penetrate her thoughts, to convey his knowledge of her disloyalty through the air like a clairvoyant.

"So where is he?" she finally asked.

"Who?"

She gave him a queer stare. There was an innocent confusion there, possibly fear or even a well-played conceit. She was unwilling to confirm anything. "Jacob. Who do you think?"

"He's in there."

"Well, is he ready? We probably need to get back and start preparing for the week."

"He's just taking a nap."

She checked her watch. "It's kind of late to be napping. I don't want him to be up all night."

"Sandy," said Jay. "I think he needs to stay here with me awhile longer."

"No." She said it as if she'd heard something mildly outrageous. "What makes you say that?"

"It's good for him to be with his father."

"Yeah, but he has school. How will you get him to and from?"

"I can teach him all he needs."

"No, Jay. That's ridiculous."

"Why? What will they teach him in town that I can't teach him well enough or better out here, Sandy? Say? Teach him how to be a stoolie?"

"A what?"

"Rat out his old man?"

"What are you talking about?"

"You think I don't know about this deputy?"

She paused too long, snared in some baited half-truth.

"What are you telling him about me?" Jay asked.

"Who? Jacob?"

"No, the deputy. He's been out here. He keeps coming out to harass me. Did you know that? Did you put him up to it?"

"Jay, I barely even know this man."

"Oh, of course. Such strangers that he gives Jacob nice gifts and visits you and your dad at the hospital."

"No, Jay. You've got it wrong. I never asked for his help or invited him anywhere. He just insinuated himself into our lives, and finally, this weekend in fact . . ." She started to weaken, to choke up. "He showed up at the house and I told him to leave us alone. It scared me, if you want to know the truth."

"So you called him off, just like that? After he's already brought half the sheriff's force out here to search my land, like I'm a common suspect. There's a murder case, Sandy. And I'm forced to entertain his scrutiny and his humiliating implications any time he feels like dropping by. Did you give him a hot tip or something?"

"What?"

"Did you tell him about my grandfather? He seems to think I'm cut from the same cloth."

"I have told this man nothing. He knew about your grandfather already. He must have been using me to get more information about you, but I gave him nothing, I swear to you."

Hysteria was finding her.

"Using you? What, did he get more than just information?"

"That's disgusting," she said. "This is too much to think about right now, Jay. Just bring Jacob out here and let me leave."

"I said he's staying with me. You won't use our son as leverage against me."

"This is insane, Jay!" she cried. "You bring him to me right now!"

"Why don't you call your deputy and report me?"

"Jay!"

She was crying now, terrified. It seemed at this moment that all hope for their family was lost. All that was left was a bitter fight that would leave every-one permanently injured.

"Look what you've done, Sandy. And you thought it was me all along. I only wanted a private life for all of us, but you didn't trust me. It wasn't comfortable enough. Now you've brought strangers in to arbitrate our life. Idiot strangers with their own axes to grind."

"What *I* have done? You don't even know what you're talking about! It's your usual paranoia!"

"You're damn right I'm paranoid. When a man tries to come between me and my son."

"Let me see him, Jay! Let me see him at least."

"Why, so you can bawl and grovel and make him feel guilty for staying here with me? It's what *he* wants, Sandy. It's his own idea."

"He's a child. He needs to be in school."

"I said I'd take care of that."

"Real school, Jay! Not your indoctrination!"

The boy appeared at the door, rubbing his eyes, a sleepy confusion on his face. Jay opened the door and let him out. Chipper licked him savagely, and the boy nudged the dog away. "Mom?"

Sandy fell to her knees and scooped up her boy.

"What's wrong, Mom?"

"I didn't know where you were."

"I was sleeping. What happened to your hair?"

She clenched him with no intention of ever letting go.

"I told your mom you wanted to stick around a few days longer," Jay said.

"Can I, Mom?"

She didn't answer for a while, not until she could control her emotions. "Oh, honey, but school starts back tomorrow. Don't you want to come home?"

"No, Mom. *This* is home. *You* should come back."

Jay looked at her and shrugged. She cocked her eyes at him oddly, tears forming a prism of vacant glare, her mouth tight and quaking. He'd won on a technicality, but now he felt that he'd boxed her out. There was no way she could stay, no way she could leave with her son.

He crouched down beside her. He didn't feel comfortable with her in this supplicating pose. "We're fine here," he assured her. "Go and be with your father. He needs you. Let me help. It's what a family does in hardship."

"Oh, this?" She couldn't help but laugh, ironically, her eyes swollen as sponges.

He was only trying to give her a graceful exit but could tell by the horror on her face that he'd revealed his own worst nature. He'd become someone who didn't stand as a good husband, a person he would never have tolerated or believed himself.

She held the boy in front of her, kissed him on the forehead. She told him she loved him more than anything, more than everything together, and then she stood up and staggered red-eyed and rejected back to the car. She got in and drove out of sight, into the harrowing distance. Father and son stood there in shamed silence, incapable of words, each discovering, either for the first time or all over again, how a woman's tearful surrender can shatter all you ever thought you wanted.

– 36 –

Sandy drove home in moving violation, weaving and speeding and slowing, guided by memory or luck through her bleary-eyed view and the spider-web cracks of her marriage, which was totaled now. Nothing could save them. Not even Jacob, who didn't deserve to watch their disintegration. He would learn that all love ends in spectacular cruelty and that you just limp away toward the next fling, always craving more passion and anger.

She awoke from her stupor when she walked into the total darkness of the shitbox. The nights came quicker each day, and she was unprepared to meet it alone. There was a creak at the far end of the house. She fumbled through her bag for the pepper spray and stood in the hallway with her arm outstretched, the canister poised and waiting for someone to appear. But there was no one.

She walked through the house to embolden herself, to beat back the darkness. She had nothing to fill it except noise and light, so she turned on every lamp, fired up the television, and vacuumed the one rug over and over. The more she created this impression of life, the lonelier she felt. It had been this way all weekend, but even more now that the prospect of Jacob had been erased. It was all she could think, that she had forfeited him.

She opted to visit the hospital. Maybe a miracle awaited her there. Instead, the situation was unchanged. Her dad was hooked to the same machines, lying there with the same pursing lips and soft napping eyes. He looked so peaceful that she stopped feeling nervous about him. She even thought it would be nice to switch places and sleep for a month herself.

She took the elevator downstairs and walked the anonymous corridors, past a family huddled in grim teary-eyed vigil, to the cafeteria, where she sat alone in a corner and ate a plate of cold chicken strips and a salad, a baked potato, two ice cream bars, a bag of salty chips. She went back up to the room and kicked out the vinyl sleep chair to its chaise setting, put her feet up and held her father's hand. She turned on a reality show about couples racing across the world, arguing and screaming at each other in airports and rental cars. She fell asleep and was shaken awake by a nurse at 9:30, past visiting hours. She kissed her dad on the forehead, walked briskly through the ominous heat-lamp glow of the parking lot, and arrived back at the well-lit rental house by ten. She made herself a second dinner and sat down on the twin bed where Jacob's scent was trapped in the covers, a balled-up pair of dirty socks under the pillow and a half-empty cup of juice on the nightstand. She watched a movie on the television that starred the actress from the magazine cover, wearing her old pre-pixie haircut, and it looked so much better. She fell asleep in twenty minutes with all the lights on.

On Monday she could barely summon the will to teach. The kids were geared up for homecoming week and couldn't sit still long enough to do their work, so she checked out a video from the library, a documentary about bears. The kids wouldn't even sit still through the film. They insisted on rewinding one scene over and over again, a national park grizzly charging and head-butting a parked car. They cheered the violent impact and laughed mercilessly at the terror-stricken man trapped within.

She went directly to the hospital after work, dined on the same thawed-out fare, caught up on all the local crime and national celebrity scandals. When she couldn't bear to watch any more, she switched off the television and sat on the edge of her father's bed. She confessed to him that she'd lied so long ago when he asked if she approved of his marriage to Miss Sue.

"I was thirteen and selfish," she said. "I was embarrassed that you were marrying again so soon. I just needed you to be sad with me for a while longer. She didn't deserve to be with us."

He lay tranquil. His static features betrayed nothing. Her painful admission hadn't made a dent, but she had it off her chest.

The next morning she called in sick, covered the windows, and switched on the horrid daytime television lineup. She raided the cabinets, turned out all the snacks. First she decimated a bag of candy she'd been saving for Halloween, and then the breakfast tarts, the granola bars, the cheese sticks and popsicles. With everything else gone, she found a wax harmonica and was filled with a reprehensible desire to taste it. She had to throw it behind Jacob's bed, into that gulley of dust bunnies and toy cars and old raisins, to keep from devouring it.

In the bedroom she raised the window shade, took off her nightgown, and studied her body in the mirror behind the closet door. She was turning dumpy, just shy of whale. Her haircut was slow to recover. Her cheeks were round and red, her upper arms and thighs had doubled, maybe even tripled in size since she stopped working on the farm. Her breasts were fuller but in an oozing way, and her lap was a woolly nest.

Who was this person? Why would anyone find her attractive? Who would waste their time outside her window with a video camera or beneath her like a dog with his nose in her backside?

She changed into her robe and lay on the couch in flu-like misery, though she hadn't a fever or a sniffle. She had always dismissed depression as a kind of lazy, willful sadness, but she was starting to understand how it got its tentacles around you, pulled you under, bound your muscles with no recourse, dimmed your mind by lack of oxygen. She started to find it physically difficult to breathe and had the phone in her hand at one point, taunting herself to call the ambulance. The only thing that kept her from dialing was the fact that she couldn't abide going back to the hospital. She was consumed with guilt for not being there now with him, but she couldn't imagine walking through those automatic sliding doors again, making that long dreaded trek to her father's room. The smell of the place was permanent in her clothing, she could smell it when she lay down at night. Sometimes when a car passed by her window, she jerked awake thinking the nurse had come in to check vitals.

She drifted off to sleep and was woken some time later by thumping car stereo bass, shuffling feet, and a man cursing outside. Was it Jay? Danny? He was aggravated, possibly unstable, standing right by the door and probably peeping at her through the rectangle of window. She lay motionless, as if the tormented guest were some wild animal blind to anything without movement. There followed a rustle of paper in the mailbox and a wretched scuffling retreat. She got up and peered out the window, trying to catch a glimpse of her disenchanted caller. Only the mailman. She watched his tragic silhouette in the mail truck, head in hand, hopelessly sorting through the next block's batch of deliveries. Who wasn't completely ruined by life?

She cracked the door and reached out for the wad of letters in the box. Catalogs and advertisements, bills and notices. She unfolded the weekly circular, a page of news and the rest of it ads. On the cover was the photo of a smiling young boy who had drowned fishing at the reservoir. His body had not been recovered. She began to weep for the boy's mother, and it made her miss her own son terribly until she couldn't catch her breath. The world was spinning cruel and her Jacob was out in it. She trembled, or maybe it was only the whump-whump from the parking lot, vibrating over the earth and up through the legs of her chair. Out the back window was the ridiculous tricked-out gold car, the young thuggish driver on his phone. She imagined charging out and ramming her head into the passenger door.

She resigned herself to calling the cops finally. She dug the phone out of her purse and scrolled through the numbers. There, where she'd called him two weeks ago to catch her basement prowler, was Shoals's number. She highlighted the digits and willed herself not to punch it. He would do whatever she asked. She could have this loitering fool put in jail, possibly murdered. At this point, he'd probably even drive out and bring Jacob back if she wanted. Could it be done, she wondered, without involving the whole department or making a record of it? Just have him go out and fetch the son she'd given away. She hadn't given him up, only protected him from seeing his parents at each other's throats.

She wondered how her father would handle the guy in the parking lot and realized it was none of Shoals's business. It had nothing to do with Jay and his terrified delusions or possible insanity. It wasn't even about dear Jacob. It was about Sandy Messler Mize. *Who are you going to be? Who will you be, alone in the dark?*

She gripped her pepper spray and charged out the back door onto the rickety deck and through the strip of backyard. The car sat ten paces from her door, rattling with bass, and she wondered how anyone could find this sound musical. It made no rhythmical sense, was just noise generated by some amateur in a studio playing with the knobs. She leaned down and yelled through the open passenger window, "Move along, or turn that shit off! People are trying to live here!"

The dude turned, startled, and gave a half-nod and a passive wave, rolled up the automatic window and eased forward, right on through the lot and up Waller, simple as that. The renewed silence made way for songbirds and the noise of children down the street. She sat on the deck and listened to the newfound peace.

She could always just drive out and take Jacob herself. Or she could use this time to start packing. They could move into her dad's place, get ready for his return. He'd need help with the recovery. No more of this halfway house, no more quaking bass, no more school. She had to be a mama grizzly.

And then the phone strummed in her hand, a strange number.

"Hello?"

"Sandy—" It was Jay, breathless and far away. "Something's happened. We need to meet."

It was a summer-lit fall afternoon, a rare cloudless day. The water was turning cold, the trees were tinting down to a slow yellow. Father and son were beside the river, soaking in the muddy wallow. They'd enjoyed intermittent sparks of deep camaraderie over the past couple of days, but they'd also begun to understand how they needed Sandy's overarching sense of purpose. Theirs was a kinship of universal inevitability, and they were starving some essential part of themselves by not having her here.

Jay began to suspect it might take only a drive into town, kidnapping her and bringing her back here to their lair. They'd both been wrong, and maybe there was only the joint fessing up to make things right with the Mizes once again. A muddy cleansing would reset their lives, wash away all the obsessions and regrets and mistrust, and bury them back in that simple love where they all first knew each other.

When Jay stood up to execute his plan, the ground beneath him gave way. He fell flat on his chest and began sliding toward the cliff. Jacob, splatting the earth with a firm stick, responded quickly by launching the stick out toward his dad, who grabbed it and steadied himself. He slowly wriggled and clawed his way inland, fearing that he and Jacob might both fall off into the river and be churned up under a ton of mud. It was a steep drop, guaranteed to cause serious injury. He reassured Jacob, instructing him to inch his way back toward dry land where Chipper stood, wagging his tail, a wrinkle of concern across his furry brow. The boy did as he was told, serious and enthralled, with no sense of fear or surrender.

Their hearts were racing by the time they'd pulled free of the pit. They stood shivering in their underwear, encased head to toe in a slick brown fudgy coating. "It's telling us to stay out now," Jay said.

He knew it was vital to heed the wild cues. The whole world seemed to be telling him the same thing. The pasture and the front field, town and country both. So where did a man take his family to remain sane?

They walked a short ways upriver to get a better vantage on the wallow and noted the trench that had washed out underneath it, a scar running from the mud bowl all the way down to the water. One good storm and the whole thing would collapse in a mass wasting.

"Let's go," he told Jacob, who needed to first stop and pee. Jay walked out ahead of him through the scrub and toward the clearing, yearning for a taste of sunny warmth to cure the chill that had taken up inside him, and that's when he heard Chipper growling, followed by a cry in the woods ahead. He thought at first that someone was in trouble. He walked out of the brush and looked around but didn't see anyone. It came again—"Hold it there! Show your hands!"

Jay turned to see a man in camouflage with a shotgun trained on him. Somehow he didn't flinch. His first thought was Jacob. He'd have to dive in front of the blast when the kid came tromping out of the woods and startled the man. He put his hands up and tried to whistle Chipper back from his sudden fit of insane yapping.

"What the shit!" the man called. "By my own eyes, you was dead. Right there in that river. What happened to your hand?"

Jay wiggled his digits. He dared not look back for Jacob, just silently willed the boy to hide, to stay in the woods or go back to the river. The madman came closer on crutches, disbelief or rage fueling his wild glare. He used one of the crutches to swat the furious pup away. His head cocked suspiciously, the gunman got right up close and his eyes widened. "Oh," he said, showing his yellow niblet smile and paint-greased face. "It's you. Mize. The son of a bitch who shot my dog."

Jay likewise recognized the man as the nosy passerby from the road, the camo truck, and Hilltop Grocery. Meeting him out here in the woods at gunpoint was more than a coincidence.

"Just the man I was looking for," the stranger said. He seemed relieved, even overjoyed. "The sheriff's deputy knows all about you. I told him what you done. He's onto you, buddy. He's stringing you along, just waiting for you to fuck up. But I aint so patient."

"Who? Which deputy?"

"Shoals," the man said. "Let's go see him together. You can tell him what you did."

"What on earth are you talking about?" Jay demanded, frustrated. He didn't make the connection and could barely hear over the dog's piercing bay. He needed to keep up the distraction in case the boy appeared. "You'll have to explain what you think I've done."

"My dog, you asshole!" The stranger spat at the ground.

"What did I do to your dog?" Jay yelled over the barking.

The stranger turned the gun on Chipper and let rip a thunderous round. The dog yelped, tumbled backward into the leaves, and lay still.

"That!" the woodsman cried in the new silence. "That's what you done. We're even now!"

An incendiary rage flared up inside Jay. He yelled at the man—"Why did you do that?"—and he hoped that it would be enough to stay the boy while he attempted to overcome and subdue this clearly deranged person who had limped into their midst and was too distraught and confused to not harm Jacob. No doubt he had heard the shot and the shouting and was hiding in the brush like a good boy.

"It hurts, don't it?" the man said, nudging Jay with the smoking gun barrel. "Now shut up and get moving."

A cool head came over Jay, and he obeyed the gunman, marching forward, peeking back over his shoulder. He didn't see Jacob.

As they walked through the woods along the riverbank, he believed he could handle this. The guy was on crutches and obviously unsound. At the right distance he could kick the crutches out and stomp the man's injured legs, wrestle the gun away. After that he could take it as far as he liked.

But the wiser thing would be to stall, let this play out and find out what the guy had seen, how much he knew or suspected. They walked on in silence, Jay having to slow his pace for the gimped kidnapper. Soon they came to a familiar bend, and the stranger leaned on the old picnic table, still upturned and wedged into the earth, to catch his breath.

Jay looked back for any signs that Jacob was following them.

"This is where it happened," the stranger said. "This is where you murdered Virginia. You didn't know I was here, did you? Hiding right down there under the water in that clump of limbs. Of course, the river was higher then. But I seen you and what you did. Putting those fish back. Shooting my dog for no good reason. What the hell are you about, Mize?"

Jay couldn't imagine how it was possible that the man had been there. What was the likelihood of him stopping at this random spot on the river? But it explained the dog being there, and if he'd only been calmer and had stopped to look around, to take careful stock of the situation, he would have noticed the man in the river, spared his dog and Jacob's in turn. Maybe all of this could have been avoided.

"I apologize about your dog," Jay said. "If you'd just showed yourself, I would have let it go. It aint wise to let wild dogs roam your property."

"Yeah, but she wasn't wild," the stranger said. "And this aint your property nohow."

"It was a misunderstanding, that's all," Jay said. "A dumb accident."

"Well, your dumb accident is gonna cost you plenty," the stranger replied. "Now shut the hell up and keep walking."

They moved at a hobbled pace, out from the river and up into the woods until they came to a clearing, a field of high grass. They wandered around in a zigzag fashion, the gunman occasionally raising his keys and pressing the panic button.

Jay seized on this distraction and said, "Why do you have to take me in to the deputy? Can't we just settle this here between ourselves?"

"I was trying to show some mercy, fella. You don't want me to handle this my way."

"Does he know what you did to that guy from Ohio?"

The woodsman got right up in Jay's face, jamming the gun barrel under his jaw. He smelled like swamp and wintergreen chew. "Just what in hell do you mean by that?"

"I mean you know about that missing guy from Ohio the deputy's been looking for, and he's going to be far more interested in knowing those details than in any dog of yours that I may or may not have killed."

The woodsman tensed, his face working out the miscalculations of justice. He screwed the gun barrel tighter to Jay's neck. "Maybe then we don't make it into town."

"Don't look like we will. You can't find your damn truck."

"Look here, Mize. You better keep your mouth shut. It's already taken my soberest will to keep from blowing your head clean off."

"Did you kill that guy?"

The woodsman stalled. Maybe he was trying to decide whether to spill his guts, or just trying to remember. He seemed lost in his own cruelty.

"He was already dead!" the woodsman barked, now prodding Jay in the ribs with the gun barrel. "Dumb-ass got caught in his own fishing line. It was wrapped around his wrist, tangled up in some limbs. He was trailing along behind it, hell, I thought it was a catfish caught on a trotline. Then I seen his hand there." His eyes went dazed recalling it. Any minute now, Jay thought, he might be able to give the old guy the slip. "River was too high or the son of a bitch couldn't swim, one. Too stupid to untether hisself. All I did was lop off his hand with my machete. Set him free."

"They found the hand in Bobby Waterman's field," Jay said.

"And they won't never find the rest of him."

"Why's that?" If the woodsman let on that he knew, Jay decided, he would leap at him and take the gun away. He could make it look like a suicide. Or just drag him to the river, do him like his dog.

"Hell, he's probably out in the Gulf of Mexico, that was weeks ago. He's shark bait by now."

In a momentary lapse, the stranger removed the gun barrel from Jay's ribs and tipped it up. Jay took advantage and grabbed the stock, pulling it toward him. The woodsman jerked the weapon back with his trigger hand, and the sudden explosion startled both men. The blast took off the woodsman's hat, along with the front cap of his skull. He stumbled backward, not falling, but his eyes became engorged and his mouth fell open, taking in great heaving gasps. It all happened in a fantastic instant. Jay was sure he hadn't touched the trigger, only the stock, but the man abandoned the weapon and it slid into Jay's arms, and then he was cradling it, clutching the fore end. With the other hand he reached out to help the man, who swatted him away. He leaned in to see if it was just a flesh wound, but there was a terrible hole and the man's frontal lobe was oozing out like cheesy baked cauliflower. He stumbled on a log and fell onto his back, arms outstretched as if he were clutching an invisible assailant by the lapels, and he reared up several times like he wanted to stand, his mouth wrenched open in dumb rictus, issuing a sad primal moan.

The man was done for, and whether out of mercy or fear, Jay clutched the weapon and went to finish the job. He ejected the shell and came up empty for another round. He bent down and patted the man's pockets and vest. The stranger's eyes went wild, his moan louder and wild with terror. Some untouched part of his brain must have realized what was going on and he thrashed out for the gun, as if he might turn it on Jay and take him along. Jay surrendered the gun, but there was no retribution for this. The man had done it to himself.

On his knees there, without his clothes or any weapon of his own, Jay was powerless to help, so he plowed his hands into the leaves and scraped up a handful of dirt, then rammed it into the old fool's mouth. He packed in another load and then another until the woodsman's eyes threatened to burst out of his skull. The round, soil-crammed gob gave the woodsman an almost comical look, like a howling cartoon madman. He flailed and shook, his arms stretched out in a zombie reach, and he seemed about to explode until he lunged up in one final measure of defense and finally slumped over motionless in the grass.

– 38 –

Word had gotten back to the sheriff about Shoals's drunken high jinks at the Madrid precinct. His uncle insisted on a leave of absence, just a week or so to get himself sobered up and sorted out. The next afternoon he took Suzie-Q for a few days in the Delta, called in a favor with a guy he knew who had a duck camp close to Money. He didn't hunt, just lay up in one of the bunks and snoozed. Watched some TV, fished idly. There were four or five crazy hunters who stayed over that Saturday, and he drank with them, stayed up late telling stories.

They hunted Sunday morning and then the hunters returned to their lives and Shoals had the place pretty much to himself, except for an old black man who lived in a cabin nearby and kept the place up. He tried speaking to the man, who just waved and shuffled off. These Delta folks had a different code. Still a whiff of the feudal about the place.

"Making hamburgers tonight if you want one," Shoals said after he cornered the man hosing off the mud porch.

"You liked to scared me, boss," the man said. He was small and withered, hunching around in a pair of overalls and mud boots. He had a face chiseled by years and experience, a lot of it bad probably, but he kept a wise, childlike grin.

"You live around here?" Shoals asked.

"Down the road."

"You like working here?"

"Don't know whether do or not," the man said. "Hadn't studied on it too much. It's a job, glad to have it."

"You wanna go for a ride in my car?" Shoals said.

"Who-wee, sure is pretty," the man replied. "Bet you fetch some ladies in that there."

"More than you know."

"Feels good to have one or two fine things."

The man had an honest laugh, aged and crackling, and an all-around admirable ease. "What's your name?" Shoals asked.

"Granger."

"I'm Danny, good to know you."

"Yessir, yessir."

"I bet you seen em come and go."

The man gave him a smile and a weighted look that said, *Oh, yessir, more than you know.*

He asked the man again if he wanted to hang out or go do something, but Granger slyly evaded him, changed the subject. He was probably set in his old negro ways and didn't want the trouble of making conversation with a white man.

Shoals couldn't stand to be alone so he drove to Greendale and sat in a bar, struck up a conversation with the bar back, a shy and wiry black girl who moved with fetching grace. He admired her tiny body and full chest. He waited until she got off and they went and sat on the levee and tussled like naked wrestlers in the high dewy grass.

"Why you here?" she asked him.

"On vacation," he replied. "I think I'm gonna have to whip a cop's ass when I get back."

"How come?"

"Honor," he said. "Men's stuff."

He stayed until Tuesday. A new batch of hunters from up north were due in that afternoon, so he left after lunch. He'd hoped to say good-bye to Granger, but there was no sign of the old black man. He cruised the back roads nearby, angling for a view of the man out in front of his tar-paper house, maybe feeding dogs or hoeing a little patch of greens.

He stopped a woman walking on the side of the road and asked if she knew where Granger lived. She shot him a wary sidelong glance and shook her head.

Home was an hour and a half away. He couldn't say he felt rejuvenated, but a few days in the wild had taken the edge off. He went back to work with renewed enthusiasm. He was still committed to flying right and moving up in the department.

He went in to the office that afternoon and sat at his desk for the first time in a long while. He checked his phone and found a peculiar message from Leavenger—"I'm out here in Tockawah Bottom, bout to get straight with Mize. Just wanted you to be aware in case things go sour, it's on your conscience. A pitiful shame the citizens of this county have to resort to vigilante justice, but so be it. Hasta la vista, motherfucker!"

Shoals called him back but got no answer.

"Do my eyes deceive me?" asked Bynum, who moseyed in with a self-satisfied air. "I thought you were on sabbatical, Danny." He must have thought he had the sheriff gig all sewn up.

"I want no beef with you, Robbie," Shoals replied. "We're on the same team." He stood and offered his hand.

Bynum crimped his face and returned the shake.

"I'm gonna make up for my mistake," said Shoals. "Just let me know if there's some legwork I can do for you."

"Uh-huh, I know what kind of legwork you have in mind."

"I'm serious, Robbie, now dammit!"

Bynum stopped and reconsidered him. "Okay, okay. We'll sit down tomorrow and figure out where we stand. You'll be here in the morning?"

"I can be here anytime you want," Shoals assured him.

"Okay, then. Let's do nine thirty."

"You got it," said Shoals, clapping Bynum on the shoulder, burying the hatchet.

He called Leavenger again but got no answer and drove off toward east Bayard on a county road about five miles outside the city limits. He wheeled into the gravel drive of Leavenger's ramshackle bungalow. His car was gone. Shoals rang the number again and it went straight to voice mail. He replayed the message Leavenger had left earlier. Had things gone sour? Maybe he'd pay Mize a visit too, just to be safe. Two missing persons in as many months, all in that neck of the woods—it painted a curious coincidence. The afternoon was waning. If he wanted to get out there before dark, he'd have to shag ass, maybe slip by the cabin and call some backup from the gun cabinet.

He hit the road again, thinking of cool old Granger and how nice it would have been to take the guy for a ride, maybe to spend a few days with this man, follow him out in the fields, hunt with him, learn his ancient ways. He thought maybe the old guy would take a modest salary to become his spiritual guide. Teach him to be that even-keeled, to harbor it all right there in your eyes. Everyone around here seemed to have a stick up their ass. He thought the islands might be a good sanctuary for him, someplace where your favor rose when your shirt came off. Someplace where wet, pretty, and naked were the norm, not the shame, not hidden away in dark basements. *So what if I saw your tits, don't let it ruin your life.* Maybe Granger would come along. He'd probably never set foot on an airplane or even seen a jet on the ground. The gift of a lifetime before he moved on to the old shotgun shack in the sky.

Got to scrape that shit right off your shoe.

The first thing he heard when the buzzing subsided in his eardrum was the Rolling Stones playing deep inside the dead man's clothing. Jay rustled around and retrieved a lighter and keys before he found the phone, lit up from the caller "BayCo Sheriff Dep." He let the song play until it chirped off.

Shoals was checking his trap. This guy had been telling the truth. The deputy could be on his way, or he might already be sitting up at the house. One thing was certain, they wouldn't buy this as a suicide.

He heard the faintest hint of a scream coming from the forest. It might have been the shotgun still ringing, but he thought it could be Jacob too. He fled the scene and doubled back along the river, frantic to locate his son before anyone else did. The phone sang again in his hand, "BayCo" checking in. He switched it off and stopped beside the river, hurled it into the current, and stood for a moment to listen.

"Dad!" came a panicked cry far in the distance.

He made difficult, barefooted progress through the woods. It took nearly five minutes to make it back to the mudhole, hollering out for his son the entire way, stopping now and again to listen for his reply. He overtraced their tracks from the wallow through the brush and finally saw him there, sitting in the leaves beside his lifeless pup.

"Jacob!"

"Dad?" the boy shrieked, unsure if it was his father or the riverside dog slayer.

Jay ran to the boy and scooped him up. Jacob tensed and looked up through red horrified eyes. It took a beat to confirm it was his dad, and then he burst into a sobbing wail. His little fingernails grasped and scratched like the claws of a scrambling, mewing cat. Jay locked his arms around the boy, convulsing with shock, and they both took tortured comfort from each other. "I'm so sorry." Jay repeated it over and over. There was no explanation for any of it, and the boy sought none, just quietly shuddered.

When Jay went to kiss his head he saw blood on the boy's ear and jerked him out at arm's length to inspect for injury. "Are you hurt?"

The boy's eyes fluttered up. "It's you," he spoke.

Jay touched his forehead, and his fingers came away red. Blowback from the dead man. He wiped his hands in the leaves.

They watched poor Chipper for a moment before Jacob began whimpering questions about the man. Who was he? Why had he shot his dog?

"I don't know," said Jay. "He thought I was someone else."

"Where did he go?" Jacob looked around as if the man might still be out there, waiting to unload on them.

Jay considered it a moment. This was a preview of the interrogation that awaited him back in town once the law followed up on the stranger. The pieces would start to click into place, and even if they couldn't recover any evidence of the Ohio man on Jay's place, they could take him in and put the screws to him, spook him and beat him until he confessed.

"He's gone," Jay said.

"What if he comes back?" asked Jacob.

"He won't. But we should probably get home."

"What about Chipper?"

Jay looked at the dog, keeled over, flies already finding his raw wounds. It wouldn't take long for him to stiffen and stink. "Tell you what, let's go up and get clean," said Jay. "Then we can come back and bury him by the mudhole. He loved it there."

Jay carried the boy in his arms. They came a roundabout way through the woods, a light touch on the leafy floor so they could crouch and get a line on the house before they entered the yard. They watched and waited, and Jay shushed the boy when he began to ask what they were doing.

If he left the body where it lay, maybe it could still be an accident. He'd have to dig the dirt out of the dead man's mouth, wash it clean, try and remove any clues that would lead investigators to the ultimate cause of death, suffocation. Any good forensics team would see right through the charade. But the department would spare the expense of calling in experts if they could close the case neatly. It had to look like a convincing suicide.

If he threw the body in the river, it became murder, clear and simple. The corpse would wash up somewhere downstream and declare itself a homicide. Or maybe it would flush clear to the Gulf of Mexico, shark bait, as the man had said himself not thirty minutes earlier. Jay considered filling the skull with rocks and sinking the body. Would they bother to drag the river for such trash?

Jay knew he didn't have the grit to butcher and cook and grind and compost the man. He was no longer that guy. Maybe it just ended here. He could tell the truth and let come what may.

Convinced that no one was lying in wait, Jay made a beeline for the outdoor shower. The tank was empty, so he transferred several stagnant bucketsful from the open blue barrels. He let Jacob stand under the spray first. Instead of their old jovial water play, Jay scrubbed the mud off the boy, anxious and hurriedly, until his tender skin was red, and before he stepped in to rinse himself he heard a patter and detected movement in his periphery.

"What the hell?" a voice called.

Jay spun around with a bucket in his hands, the only weapon within reach. Hatcher loomed over them. The neighbor sized them up, taking the measure of their fear and guilt.

"Is that blood in your hair?" Hatcher asked.

Jay buried his face in the water and scoured it away. He searched himself for more, and saw there were several ruddy stains on his briefs that wouldn't wash out.

"Somebody shot Chipper!" Jacob cried.

"Do what?" said Hatcher.

"Some old guy with a gun down by the river," Jacob confirmed.

"I heard the barking and gunfire. Where is he now?"

"He ran away."

Hatcher looked to Jay for confirmation. Choked with confusion, Jay didn't know how to respond.

"I heard a second shot back yonder," Hatcher said, gesturing toward the west and the high grass where the woodsman lay. "What happened, Jay?"

Jay told Jacob to go inside and dry off and put some clothes on, but the boy was too afraid to go in alone. "I'll be right there," he said and walked his son to the mudroom entrance, pushed him inside, and shut the door.

Jay turned to Hatcher, who'd followed him into the carport. All he could think was that he'd been caught finally. Not by the cops, but by someone perhaps equally suspicious of him, someone who hadn't bothered to conceal his doubt. He wanted to tell Hatcher everything.

"Come on, son," the old neighbor said. "Let me help you."

There was really no choice but to trust him. Jay looked at the storm door and saw Jacob pressed against it. He turned his back to the boy and faced Hatcher and spoke in a low aside. "I ran into somebody down by the river, old dude with a shotgun. He said I killed his dog and wanted to take me in to see the sheriff. I tried to take his gun away, but when he snatched it back, it went off, blew out his forehead."

Hatcher didn't flinch.

"It was an accident, man, I swear."

"He's dead?"

Jay nodded.

"Did *he* see it?" asked Hatcher, gesturing toward the house.

"He didn't see the man, only the dog."

"You know him?"

"Crippled guy on crutches. Bad hair and teeth. Camo truck. I've seen him on the road down here."

Hatcher nodded. He walked into the yard and lit a cigarette, took a few thoughtful drags, and turned back to Jay.

"Where does the sheriff stand in all of this?" Hatcher asked.

Jay shrugged. "The sheriff, I don't know. But there's a deputy gunning for me."

Hatcher crossed his arms and quietly puffed. He was probably trying to decide whether or not to turn him in, Jay thought.

"Clean up and get dressed," the neighbor said. "I gotta show you something."

Jay stood under his rain shower and rubbed the mud off his skin. He went inside and left his bloodstained briefs in the mudroom utility sink, something else to destroy later. He went to the back and put on a shirt and pants and an old pair of tennis shoes and helped Jacob get dressed. When they came back outside together, Hatcher was sitting in the Bronco. They climbed in and Jay cranked it, checked the fuel gauge.

"Is it far?" he asked Hatcher.

"Nope. You packing?"

Jay nodded.

"Let's go then."

First they drove up to Hatcher's house, and the neighbor turned to Jacob. "Can you wait here a few minutes while your daddy and I run up the road?" Hatcher asked. "Just don't say nothing to the missus about that man shooting your dog, you hear, son? She gets scared easy."

"Dad, what about Chipper?"

"It's okay, Jacob. We'll be right back, I promise. Then we'll go down and bury Chipper."

Jacob nodded, and the neighbor took him inside to see Mrs. Hatcher, who set the boy up with a plate of cookies in front of the television.

They drove down to the Tockawah bridge, and Jay pulled off on the smooth shoulder, a bare groove worn down by bridge fishers. They got out and walked down the little foot trail that wound under the bridge and doubled back underneath the structure, walking up near the abutment around the high water and then a short ways downriver along a trail beset with black-berry stickers and discarded beer cans and trashed minnow buckets.

Hatcher stopped and crouched, pointed to the far shore. Jay bent down to look but saw nothing.

"On the far bank there, right at the water's edge," Hatcher said.

Jay squinted and finally discerned its girth, half-submerged, half-buried in mud. It seemed a reasonable part of nature until he noticed its pissed-off stare floating on the water's surface and the hind claws gripping the bank.

"Holy shit!" said Jay.

"Goddamn bull gator," Hatcher said. "Saw it this morning, liked to shit myself."

"I've never seen one around here."

"That's cause there aint none. This one probably rode in on the flood. They're coming north more and more. State's got a season for em now. Folks got cause to breed em."

"That's big, isn't it?"

"Looks plenty big to me. Ten, twelve feet, I'd reckon."

It was still as stone. What kept it from swimming across and having them for lunch?

"They feed at night," said Hatcher. He checked his watch. "Plus, it's late in the year for him. Probably not too swift once the sun goes down. Still, I wouldn't want to be defenseless around here come dark."

It occurred to Jay only then why Hatcher had brought him to see this. He looked at his friend in silent collusion.

"Do you think . . . ?"

"I don't think shit," Hatcher shot back. "I got no damn idea about noth-ing. And don't want to. I leave well enough alone and expect the same cour-tesy in reply, you dig?"

Jay nodded.

"I just thought that being a man of science and all, you might want to see such a specimen of nature," Hatcher said.

They wandered back toward the truck. Jay tried to imagine how he'd finish this business once and for all, if it could ever be complete and not at infinite loose ends. He'd need a boat but knew better than to ask Hatcher. Also, what could he do with Jacob? He couldn't leave him with the Hatchers. The neighborliness stopped here. There was only one place to go. Anywhere was safer than with him.

"Hatch," Jay called. "Just one favor?"

His neighbor turned, looking grim and doubtful.

"Can I borrow your phone to call my wife?"

– 40 –

Here she was again, rocketing over country roads, running back to Jay. But this was the last time, Sandy decided. Once she had Jacob safe in her possession, she'd proceed with the divorce, make it binding and cutthroat, whatever it took to win full custody. They'd have no more of Jay and his aura of misfortune. She wouldn't sacrifice Jacob's innocence for one more paranoid notion.

Already this was too outrageous—a poacher accosting them in the woods, shooting the dog point-blank in front of them? Was he joking? Was this a ploy to lure her back and further humiliate her, in front of her son no less? She was no longer nervous, or hopeful, or apprehensive. She was simply fucking pissed.

He insisted she drive three-quarters of the way out to meet them, all the way to Grinder's Switch. It was the junction between Silage Town and Flintlock, where the railroad spur used to split the county. The train hadn't run this way in ages, and only the wrecked shell of an old general store remained there now. It was an ideal site for rural divorcées to swap their charges, someplace to argue in relative privacy.

She pulled into the empty gravel lot and found the Bronco parked far back off the road, obscured under the littered canopy of a withered mimosa. She approached and parked, left the engine running. She vowed not to fight in front of Jacob. If Jay started it, they'd just drive away.

Jay sat on the Bronco's rear bumper under the liftgate, and Jacob spidered in and out of the vehicle through the open windows. She busied herself cleaning fast-food wrappers out of the passenger seat to make room for Jacob.

Jay walked over frowning and rapped lightly on the window. She lowered it an inch.

"Come join us," he said. "Family picnic."

"What? You call and tell me to rush right out, Jacob just witnessed his dog being murdered. Now you want to sit and have a picnic?" She gripped the steering wheel, her eyes furious behind sunglasses.

"He was never in harm's way," Jay insisted. "Just get out."

She called past him, "Jacob! Let's go!"

The boy tumbled out of the Bronco and onto the gravel, kicking up a gloomy dust cloud. He shuffled over and met her with a wounded stare. "C'mon, Mom, it's okay now," he said, affecting his father's condescension.

Jay bent down and spoke softly into the slip of window. "Let me make a peace offering."

She switched off the engine and pried the door open. Jacob ran over and buried himself in her breast before she could get out. "Chipper's dead," he whimpered.

"I know," she said and clasped him to her. "I'm so sorry."

Jay was anxious but let them have their moment. Soon they walked over to join him at the Bronco. The trees were nodding in a new-sprung wind, and mimosa trash floated down like ticker tape on their homecoming. They sat on the truck bumper, and Jay rolled a watermelon from the backseat.

Jacob tugged at her skirts. "I found that," he said softly.

She smiled and Jay cracked the melon like a giant egg against the bumper. "Hmm, yellow meat," he said. "Don't remember having those."

He passed around the crude wedges and they all sampled the pale flesh. "Not quite sweet enough," Jay observed. "Late bloomer. Too much rain. It missed the good heat this year."

She sighed quietly. Always a critique, nothing ever living up to its full potential.

"Oh," he said and went around to the front seat and brought back jelly jars and a bottle of tequila. He poured two drinks neat and passed one to her.

"Really?" she said.

"I've been saving this for our reunion," he said. "This is a celebration I'd live to regret missing if it ever came to that, so I arranged it here. Maybe a bit premature, but oh well . . ."

For Jacob he'd brought along white grape juice, which he poured in a similar jar and served. Jay doffed his sunglasses in respect, raised his jar, and delivered a rehearsed toast: "To us. May the smoke of men blow way yonder, and let us once more see what is written in the stars."

She rolled her eyes, finding it hard to follow his constant wayward gaze. She raised her glass. "To a good dog and a good friend," she added.

Jay nodded and smiled. "Hear, hear."

They all drank. She felt it trickle down into her pit, a sudden burst of warmth spreading out to her extremities. Jacob took his down by the gulp. She noticed Jay's foot bobbing nervously, his finger silently tapping against his glass, the mania barely contained.

"Before the unpleasantness, we had a good visit, didn't we, Jacob?" Jacob acknowledged by tipping his eyebrows.

"You should have been there with us, Sandy. We ate pancakes in the afternoon, we camped out, we shot the BB gun, we played in the mud. What else did we do, Jacob? We dug for worms, went fishing. We made s'mores! You would've loved it."

"Jay."

"I told Jacob how we used to sleep outside on Nutt Street sometimes, even built campfires there in the yard. Remember when we ran an extension cord and brought our TV outside? Remember we breathed in helium balloons and told ghost stories in those ridiculous pip-squeak voices?"

"Why are you telling us all of this, Jay? What happened today?"

His smile melted away. "I told you on the phone what happened. We don't really need to discuss it further." He cut his eyes toward Jacob. *Not in front of the kid.*

She turned to her son. "What happened, Jacob?"

The boy described hearing Chipper bark and the man yelling at Dad, the gunshot and the puppy yelp, the voices disappearing for a long time, and then going to Chipper, who was like a limp toy animal covered in blood.

Finally, hearing the six-year-old's account, she could believe the story without taking it for gross exaggeration. "My God, Jay, who was this person?"

Jay propped his elbows on his dangling legs and shook his head. "I don't know, just some country troll out poaching. Maybe Chipper scared him, or maybe he was weak and needed to feel strong by murdering a defenseless animal. I don't really know. We didn't press him."

She turned to Jacob and gave him a skeptical look. The boy tucked his head.

"You start to see things different at the other end of that gun barrel," Jay added.

He knocked back the rest of his drink, poured himself a few more splashes of reunion spirits, and offered her another taste. She covered her jar and shook her head and then gave in. He poured hers and they both tilted back, held it in their mouths awhile, felt the tingle that flared up through the nostrils and into the brain.

"Do you remember being up at the lake house, renting that canoe and finding that abandoned island, the bird refuge?" he said. "We were the only two people in the world."

He cut his eyes up at her, a playful, cheating look. They'd made love on the beach, let themselves run free and gone thrashing into each other like the moon and tides had taken over their bodies. They'd always imagined this occasion as the boy's conception.

"I wish we could take Jacob up there and let him swim in that cold lake and roam those empty beaches," Jay said.

Jacob was daydreaming, dead-eyed, his arms wrapped one each around his parents' legs.

"What if we dumped it all for cheap and left with the clothes on our backs, just went somewhere else?" said Jay.

She thought about it. She could leave the job without notice but not her father.

"Jacob, will you go and put your bag in the car, hon?" It took some haggling to get him to go alone, but finally he carried his things away, out of earshot, while she worked up the courage to confess something to her husband. She didn't know if he might flip out hearing it.

"I'm a little scared of you," she said finally.

He gazed at her, incredulous. "Why?"

"I worry you've lost your mind."

His face, all the angry lines and angles, clenched and shifted.

"Maybe I have a little too," she admitted, trying to balance the accusation. "But when I look at our life, living in this shitty rental house and dodging every lowlife in town, I can't help but blame you. I trusted you. I did, and then you went off the reservation, worrying about things that haven't even happened and that we can't control anyway. And then you humiliated me in front of our child. You're no longer the person I know. Haven't been for a while."

"Okay," he said. "And is that why you turned your back on me for the goddamn common world?"

They sat in the fallout silence. Neither of them had the will to fight, for they both held valid grievances. They couldn't bridge, not even believe, the chasm that had come between them. It seemed undeserved and unnavigable, and it possessed the mystical finality of death. As in death there was still love, but there was no occasion for it outside of their imaginations or the boy.

"And there's still the deputy," Jay said.

"I told you, he's nothing. I threatened to call the police if he came around again."

He snorted a laugh and shook his head in disbelief. "Calling cops on cops doesn't work. Anyway, he's coming for *me* now."

"Jay, he's not coming for you, he's—" How could she tell him that it was about her, that it had always been about her? If she told him the truth, there was no telling how enraged he might become. "What is it you think he wants from you? Does he simply want to destroy you? Him and all the rest of the world and the earth itself and God too, they're all coming for you? Don't you see how crazy it is to think that way? I mean certifiably crazy. Jay, I've tried to speak reason to you until I'm blue in the face, and I can't do it anymore. I have a son to raise, bills to pay, a father dying in the hospital. It kills me to cut you loose, but you're dragging us down with you."

He stared at her with nervous, tick-tocking eyes, with calculations and confessions, justifications and regrets. He stood up from the truck and looked at Jacob, who was in the backseat of the Maxima.

"Jay, you need help," she said. "You have—"

"I killed a man," he said. "That man back there, the one who shot Chipper."

She must have shown him an expression of disbelief.

"I did, Sandy. I took his gun away and murdered him in cold blood."

She stood.

"It was him or me," he said. "Him or us."

She looked at Jacob.

"Don't worry, he didn't see anything. The guy took me into the woods at gunpoint, and I waited until we were far away and I could get the drop on him. It was self-defense, yes, but mostly for Jacob. And for you. I was defending all of us. That's all I've ever done."

"Oh, Jay . . ." She wished she weren't hearing this. Was there some way to make him take it back?

"The deputy knows. That's why he's coming for me. I have to go back and take my lashes."

He appeared calmer, more focused, as if confessing this had cured him.

"Jay, you're not planning to—"

"The thing is, Sandy, I don't know if I can get out of this. I'm going to do my damndest to try, but the odds of this coming out in my favor . . ."

She couldn't reconcile what he was telling her. It seemed like a dream, even her response. "Come back right now, we can all go together. We'll leave, just like you said." She was willing to accept culpability for him in this moment.

"Dad!" Jacob cried, running toward them. "I think someone is in the woods back there!"

Jay got up and walked slowly across the lot. The thought occurred to her to scoop up Jacob and run, get in the car and speed away. She clutched her son and they watched Jay approach the thicket. He stood before it a moment, clenching and unclenching his fist. He bent down and drew a handful of gravel. "Who's in there?" he shouted and flung the rocks. A couple of quail launched out.

He turned around with a smile on his face. It was the man they both knew. "You see," he said, walking casually back to them. "It's okay, it was nothing."

Jay touched his son on the shoulder and knelt down and fixed him in a gaze. "This is going to be hard, buddy, but you need to take one thing away from this today—don't be afraid. Not of that man back there. Not of me. What that man did back there, that was because of me, okay? Not you, not Chipper."

"What do you mean, Dad?" asked Jacob, a little tremulous.

"He was getting back at me for something I did."

"What did you do?" the boy asked.

"Listen. I hurt his dog. In a moment of weakness. It's because I was scared, and I made a bad decision. Now, your mom and I have taught you what's right and what's wrong, and when it comes time for you to make that decision, you can make the right one. Don't ever be scared to do what's right."

The boy listened to his father intently.

"It's not easy. Usually doing what's right is the harder decision, so it's natural to be scared. But you need to swallow that fear. Just do it like that, okay, like you're chewing it up and swallowing it. You got me?"

He put a piece of watermelon in his mouth, chewed and swallowed. "Just a piece of food you grew yourself."

"But what if he comes back?"

"He won't, Jacob. I promise. He'll never come back."

The boy nodded, tears brimming. Jay kissed him and walked him over to the Maxima and put him in the front seat. He bent down and whispered to him softly, then fastened the seat belt and kissed him again and closed the door.

He walked back to Sandy and took the jar from her hand. She was crying. "I'm sorry," he said. "You're right."

"You can't come with us," she replied, somewhere between a question and a statement.

"Did you keep my insurance going?" he asked.

"What?"

"The life insurance. It was drafting every month."

"Why, Jay?"

"Did you?" he demanded.

She considered her finances. "Yes, I believe so. Everything switched to my account."

"Okay," he said. "Listen, if something happens and I disappear . . ." He held her at arm's length and studied her.

"What?"

"The lake house."

She nodded without understanding. He kissed her long on the mouth, and she relented, and then he shut the Bronco's rear gate and climbed behind the wheel and cranked it and left her in a cloud of dust.

She and Jacob drove home in silence. She was too consumed with thoughts to interrogate Jacob or to comfort him. She thought about calling Shoals and telling him to leave Jay alone. This was retribution, she knew, or outright insanity. She could tell him that she loved her husband but he wasn't well. Or she could swear her own revenge, maybe threaten to call the sheriff, file a harassment suit. She had the phone out, her thoughts racing, but it wasn't something to negotiate with Jacob sitting right there.

She looked in the rearview mirror and thought she saw the Bronco barreling down on her, but it was just some impatient 4Runner that shot around her and disappeared over the lolling hills.

Jacob was red-eyed and silent beside her. She asked him, "What happened to the man in the woods? Did he just leave?"

He looked at her with sad eyes that pleaded not to make him tell, but she coerced him softly and finally he said he didn't see them leave together, but they were both gone for a long time. It seemed like forever. And later he heard a gunshot far off in the distance and after a while his dad came back with blood on his face.

She checked the rearview mirror, tried to show no emotion. She couldn't comprehend it all, and in the place of that understanding came panic. She thought of all the news dramas about husbands who crack, come home and murder their children and spouses before turning the gun on themselves. What if he came back and bound them, doused the shitbox in gasoline and sent them all up in flames to make a statement? Was he capable of it? Or what if Shoals returned, his pride wounded to the point of sadomasochism or some other violent perversion? What about the parking lot thugs, the rabid basement creatures? Ever since reading *In Cold Blood* in high school, she was terrified of random evil, the world flipping inside out to reveal a glimpse of hell. There were pockets everywhere waiting to be reversed.

Just then her guts began to hiss and twist. The fruit had soured in her belly and been lit afire by the tequila. She was growing weary, short of breath, close to sudden unmanageable grief. Her eyes misted, and she held it all back until she could no longer even see the road for being underwater. The curves came quicker and darker. The wheels caught the shoulder and the car shuddered. Jacob squealed and so did the brakes.

They fishtailed to the side and stopped dead in a dust cloud, and she poured out of the car and ran for the thick waist-high ditch weeds, where she barfed unmercifully, followed by a jag of sobbing. It lasted only a moment. The tickle of puffy grains in her ear reminded her of Jacob. She wiped her mouth and turned back to the car. He was staring stonily out at her, his face melting into a violent sunset through the half-reflected car door glass. It was Jay the boy, who hadn't a clue what to do with so much love.

− 41 −

By the time Shoals reached the reservoir, the sky was bruised from a storm head clobbering the west. He should have gone straight to Tockawah Bottom but wanted to swing by the cabin and pick up his old friend Luther, a short-barrel twelve-gauge with a pistol grip and a nasty spread. When he pulled into the driveway, he was surprised to find the sheriff's squad car already there. This was out of place. The sheriff wasn't one to pay social calls.

The front door was open a sliver. He walked in cautiously, looked around for anything out of place. Nothing was disturbed. From the living room he could see out the sliding glass door to the back porch, where his uncle watched the lake from a rocking chair, stroking Suzie-Q beside him. Something wasn't right. His uncle cast a soft glance backward when he stepped through the sliding door. Suzie jumped up to be petted.

"Hey there, Uncle Bud," said Shoals. "What's up?"

"Hope you don't mind me waiting here, but we need to talk," the sheriff said.

"Everything all right." He said it certain, willing it to be so.

"Have a seat."

Shoals sat down on a stump he used for a footrest. He didn't like the feel of this. Hadn't he imagined this scenario before? He braced for the worst, some sudden tragedy. *God, I'll do anything if you let it not be Mama*, he bargained.

"Danny, we've got a problem," his uncle said.

"Tell me what's going on."

"It's that Spiller girl and all of that mess with the video camera. It aint going away, Danny."

Shoals huffed in relief. "Uncle Bud, I told you, all that's been taken care of. Jim Tom said I'm not liable. It's not going to court. She's gonna keep her mouth shut."

"Danny, you know as well as I that she aint keeping her mouth shut. And it's just a matter of time before that big old husband of hers finds you out alone somewhere."

"If it comes to that, I can take care of myself."

"Well, that aint what I'm so worried about. It's the fallout from this. We're spending more time than we ought to trying to keep a lid on it. It's not the first time we've had to cover up some of your hanky-panky."

"Well what do you want me to do?"

The sheriff pulled a brochure from his coat pocket and passed it to Danny. A glossy trifold with photos of flowers and patios, lakes and trees.

"Garden Walk? What is this?"

His uncle sat there a moment, his mouth tight. "It's a treatment facility outside Tuscaloosa. I think you need to check yourself in, Danny. It's time to face facts. You've got a serious problem."

He didn't drink that much. Just for a good time and not that often in public.

"Walk in my kitchen right now and tell me how many liquor bottles I have," he demanded.

"It's not for that."

"You want me to go to Alabama for sex rehab?"

"Compulsive behavior therapy. I think you should, yes."

"All due respect, Uncle Bud, but that's the stupidest damn shit I've ever heard. I'm not a sex addict! So I like a little nooky now and again. Since when is that a cause for treatment? Me and half the world are on a damn near constant hunt for it."

"Danny, it's affecting your work. It's affecting my work. It's affecting the way we conduct business in our office. It's affecting the citizens of Bayard

County. How does it look when people catch wind there's a deputy on my squad trying to peep on their wife or sister getting out of the shower? And not only that, videotaping it for who knows what purpose. How safe do you think that makes them feel?"

Shoals was wide-eyed and indefensible.

"You sure got a lot of videotapes in there around your TV. What would I find if I went in and stuck one in that tape player?"

"Hunting shows! Movies and stuff. Go look for yourself."

"All right," said the sheriff and stood up.

Shoals jumped up and nearly threw a block. "Hold on now, Uncle Bud. Let me just get this straight. Do you think I'm some kind of pervert or something?"

"That's not for me to judge. But I think you need help. I think this is affecting your work and your life in a bad way, and I want to help you get straight. You do me no good like this."

"So what happens if I don't agree?"

"Then you don't come back to work."

"So that's it then? I'm fired?"

"I'll hold your position, Danny. You go down to Garden Walk, you run your therapy, it's a six-week deal. You perform your follow-up treatments, take whatever medication they prescribe, and show me you're better, and bam, you're back on the job."

"Medication? What do they give you, saltpeter or something?"

"I have no living idea. I'm no medical professional. I do know they're supposed to be one of the best programs in the Southeast. They say you can even study tai chi as part of your therapy."

"Tai chi? What does that have to do with sex?"

"Hell, Danny, I don't know. Something to do with focus, I reckon."

Shoals turned his back to his uncle and stared out at the water. This couldn't have come at a worse time, here on the cusp of proving himself a valiant law officer. Does Mize get off scot-free while Shoals is penned up, simply for scratching an itch?

He recalled stories from one boy who'd been in sex rehab. They made him dip his hands in blue dye every night before bed and checked his dick in the morning to make sure he hadn't been massaging it all night. This guy said the treatment did nothing but taught him how to climax without touch, just his own dirty thoughts.

More than anything, it was humiliating. This wasn't what Danny Shoals was about. He would become a joke, a laughingstock. He would lose his edge as a law officer, not to speak of his persuasion as a man. You don't clip an eagle's wings. This was madness, a death sentence.

"Does Mama know about this?"

The sheriff winced. "She does."

"You told Mama? When?"

"I haven't spoken a word about it to her, but she heard it somewhere. That's what I'm telling you, Danny. The word is out."

This was the most crushing guilt of all. No wonder she wouldn't take his calls. She must think she raised a degenerate sex fiend. "Who else knows? You didn't come up with this on your own."

"I discussed it with your aunt."

"And?"

"And Jenny." His cousin was the same age as him. They were close growing up, sometimes too close. "She helped us find the facility. It was her idea in a way."

She *would* be the architect. She lived in Atlanta now and was invested in all sorts of new-age crackerjack. Expressing her feelings and therapy were all part of her way, and now she'd decided everyone needed to confess. He imagined she was getting back at him for their teenage dalliance. Nothing major, just a little peekaboo, a little rubbing and tugging. They were such beautiful children.

"She helped me understand that it's an illness, and that it can be cured," said the sheriff.

"An illness? It's a primal instinct!"

Shoals couldn't believe what was happening to him. Everyone would despise him now. Everyone would mistrust him. You couldn't just fuck up quietly anymore in this world. Too many stood to gain from a public takedown. Mistakes were rebuilt twice as high in hindsight so they could all stand around and congratulate themselves when the whole mess came clattering down.

The only way he could see through this was getting Mize. Time was wasting. He needed to get a quick grip on this situation, to win his uncle's pity and then earn his respect. If he could make an arrest, things might cool down for him. Then he could take some time off, maybe go out West to the mountains and fish, clear his head a bit. That little Delta respite had definitely rubbed out a few kinks.

"Okay," he said, taking his seat on the stump, burying his head in his hands. "Okay, Uncle Bud. You've got me. I understand what I need to do."

The sheriff nodded. He preferred it this way. Quiet, simple duty rather than a lot of bluster and emotion.

"I'm on my way to something. I feel like I've got a grip on this Boyers disappearance. A little piece that won't flush. Let me go see about this, and then I'll turn my stuff over and go wherever I need to."

"What do you have?"

"This Mize fella out in Tockawah Bottom. He's hiding something."

"Does Bynum know about this?"

Shoals nodded. "I was just with Bynum. He gave me the green light."

The sheriff looked skeptical. "Need any help?"

"No sir. I'll be in to see you first thing in the morning."

"All right, Danny. Just keep your head up and your you-know-what in your britches, you hear me?"

"I sure do, Uncle. Thanks for believing in me."

"We love you, Danny. I know this is embarrassing, but in six months it'll all be water under the bridge."

Shoals felt a sob deep down trying to shimmy free. He threw his arms around his uncle for old times' sake, but the sheriff flinched at physical love. He went cold and stiff, like maybe he thought his nephew was trying to throw a hunch on him.

After his uncle left, Shoals pulled out a garbage bag and scooped up all his videos, locked them in the gun cabinet, and grabbed Luther and a box of shells. He drove toward Silage Town, and when he got within service range he called his mother. She didn't pick up, but he left her a message, told her she didn't need to be afraid to answer, that there was nothing wrong with him, that he'd been caught in a moment of weakness was all. He was only sorry that she had to imagine it or feel responsible in any way, and that at his uncle's insistence he would be getting help. He was still her son after all, he said, and he still loved her more than any other woman.

– 42 –

Why had he confessed to a crime when it was only an accident? Well, maybe it was because he felt that everything he'd done—from burning the body and using the ashes for fertilizer to shooting the dog and tripping up the man who then blew his own head off, not to mention bringing his family out here and starving their needs—maybe it all added up to something like murder. There was no jury to decide this, only something he supposed. It was an equation without logic, or else the logic of nature, which he hardly understood.

He'd spent the afternoon studying what he'd done and what there was still to do, whether to report it as an accident and take his chances with the law, or to ignore it, take the family and go, and hope no one came upon the scene until spring at the earliest, when the mowers found the stripped skeleton in the pasture. The repeated phone calls from the deputy cast doubt over these alternatives. Shoals would have another search party trampling the woods if his calls continued to go unanswered, and when they discovered the body, the inconsistencies would mount up quick—the missing cell phone, the deceased's dirt-filled mouth, Jay's bare footprints all over the scene.

No, he had to get rid of this body too, if he ever hoped to make it back to town and earn his family's forgiveness. He had to bury everything out here, the worst of himself and his deeds, both purposeful and accidental, and so he resolved to turn it all under, give it back to the land and let her take her muddy justice.

He brought a couple of contractor-grade plastic trash bags, along with various other supplies, flapped one open and rolled the woodsman's corpse inside, fastened it with a knot, and stuffed the bag inside one of the blue plastic drums from the house. Lying there beneath the man, indented in the earth, were the missing shells. Jay pocketed them and inspected the ground around the body, which was saturated with black blood. He used a spade to scoop up a few wedges of incriminating earth, tossed them in the barrel, placed the woodsman's crutches and shotgun inside, along with the spent casing he found in the leaves, and sealed the lid. He gave the barrel a shove and rolled it over the jagged terrain, the body thumping around inside like a mound of heavy towels in a clothes dryer.

When he got to the river, Jay stopped to catch his breath. The afternoon sky had become choked with clouds, and the air was thick in anticipation of rain. He was too far upriver from where he needed to be, but he'd made preparations for this. There was no time left for mistakes and improvisation.

He removed the barrel lid and pulled out the body bag and the gun and the crutches and then rolled the drum down to the river to dump the dirt clods and wash out the blood. He dragged the plastic bag and the woodsman's things down to the bank and covered them with brush and tied the victim's bandanna to the branch of a fallen tree so he would see it from the river.

He sealed the empty drum and rolled it back through the woods to the staging area, the same riverside spot where he'd murdered the stranger's dog nearly a month ago and where he'd also stashed three more of these fifty-five-gallon blue barrels. He'd brought along as well an eight-foot bamboo pole from the pile of salvage wood he'd been collecting for frames and supports. The piece was sturdy and possessed a nice ridged grip. He used it to pry the old washed-up picnic table from the sand and dry mud near the bank.

He dragged the table legs up from the shore to firm, level terrain and lashed together the four plastic drums, which all fit squarely beneath the picnic table and would act like pontoons for his fledgling rivercraft. He shoved the raft down to the shore, flipped it over into the water, and scrambled aboard with the help of the bamboo pole, stepping first onto the bench seat and finally atop the table itself. It made a hilarious and improbable craft, its decking two feet off the water. It required strict balance to steady the constant wobble, and he felt like a drunkard dancing on a tabletop. The threat of toppling over was ever present, but with a little practice he found his equilibrium and gave the picnic raft a gentle shove into the current with the pole.

Due to the vessel's height, Jay lost a good two feet of pole, but if he didn't drift too far into the middle of the river, he should have enough length to nudge the floor. He spent several anxious moments getting a feel for the raft. He started out at an awkward side-to-side crawl but quickly learned it was better to push from the back, careful not to thrust too deep into the river bottom lest the mud snatch the pole away from him. Soon he let the pole glide in the river, using it like a rudder, and found the bamboo and water would perform the work.

The current was mild, and before long he was nudging himself along as if it were just a pleasant outing. For a moment he felt positively free and adventuresome, like old Huck Finn, whistling his way downriver to recover the dead man he'd stashed in a trash bag along the shore. When he came within sight of the bandanna tied to the fallen branch, he briefly considered shoving on, just bypassing the whole gruesome task, let the river take him where it may. But unlike Huck, he wouldn't be able to hide for long. He doubted the world still held so many wide-open spaces or even nooks and crannies where one might disappear.

He guided the table to shore, moored it to a stump, and jumped into the brush. He uncovered the body bag and got plenty wet wrestling it onto the raft. He tossed the crutches on board and fished a couple of shells from his pocket and loaded the shotgun and slung it over his shoulder. He climbed aboard precariously and moved his new cargo toward the front and middle as a counterweight. When everything was settled and it seemed like the table wouldn't flip, he set himself and turned the skiff around and began to punt his way upstream.

The return trip was not nearly so idyllic, pushing against the flow with twice the weight aboard while racing the thunderhead that advanced from the north. If that storm let its entire payload go, they would be washed away—gun, barrels, picnic table, corpse, and all.

By the time he climbed back upriver to the wallow, Jay was exhausted. He poled over to the bank and tied on to a drooping birch branch, shimmied across a limb and climbed to shore. He found his clothes where he'd left them, but that was not what he'd come for. He passed through the thicket and explored the clearing until he found Chipper's mangled body. He collected the dog and scoured the ground until he found the shell casing.

Back on the raft, he took a reverent moment to commit the pup to the river. It reminded him of what was at stake. No matter how cracked the plan seemed, it had to be executed.

A light steady rain was falling now. The current had picked up. Soon he saw the bridge in the distance and redoubled his efforts, pushing himself along as color drained from the sky. Just when he'd grown confident maneuvering the raft, it was nearly time to cross the river. As he ventured near the middle, his pole was dipping lower and lower, threatening to crawl right out of his grip. There was no guarantee there would be a bottom to touch if he drifted too deep. Without control, he'd be no better than riding a piece of driftwood.

He poled his way past the little sandy washout where Hatcher had introduced Jay to his coconspirator. No sign of the brute now. He pushed onward, scoping the shore. Maybe the beast had found dinner already. What then? There was no backup plan. He'd bet the farm on this roll.

He passed into view from the road and was relieved to find no bridge fishers overhead. The rain was a mild deterrent and the rest was luck. Under the bridge the light disappeared, giving him a preview of the darkness he would soon encounter as the day slipped completely away. Water sluicing off the bridge made an echoing cascade. Even his heavy breathing reverberated off the concrete. The air filled with a deep groan, like a crypt opening. He wasn't sure if it was the raft straining or the bridge shifting or the gator lurking around the piers.

Jay punted a short way past the bridge, scoping out the banks of the river before he decided to head back the way he came. To turn the raft around he ventured a crossing into deeper water. He lost the bottom and clutched his pole tight while the rig drifted free. He leaned left and right, throwing his weight, searching for control of the vessel. The raft behaved at first, catching the accelerating current and moving him toward the opposite shore, but as he passed back under the bridge, an eddy near the piers snagged the craft and whipped it around. He repositioned himself, stumbling over the bagged corpse, which switched places with him at the stern. He caught traction with his pole off the port side and tried to slow the raft while pulling it to shore. It was working until he lost his footing and slid backward, causing the bow to rise. The raft nearly flipped backward. Jay scrambled forward on his knees, alternately guiding and braking with the pole. He heaved the trash bag forward to reassume his place at the rear while maintaining control and balance as the rain lashed down in cold, razor-edged drops.

That's when he felt the nudge. Something brushed against his pole. He mistook it for a log before it came again from the opposite direction, whacking the barrels. The craft shuddered and spun. He saw the ripple of stony black skin crest the surface of the water, which was churning with the weight of rain, and he watched it pass in front of the raft. He swatted it with the pole to confirm, and the creature doubled back and snapped the pole to splinters in its spring-trap jaws.

Without his pole, the picnic-table raft picked up speed and asserted its own trajectory. He lost the beast in the rain, and then came a wallop from behind. It was pushing him ashore to beach and feast. They careened straight toward a tangle of limbs and brush on the bank. He knelt down and untwisted the knot of plastic and dumped the woodsman's corpse onto the deck. He wrapped the shotgun in the garbage plastic to keep it dry for his last stand.

When they capsized, everything went black. Jay felt himself in the river and the slap of the heavy wood as the table landed on top of him. He cradled the plastic-wrapped gun and offered the corpse out ahead of him. Water passed over him and then released him, and he held his breath until he felt a violent tug and his hands were empty. He took up the weapon and stood. Froth flew in his eyes and it was impossible to discern from the splashing whether it was mud or flesh. He heard grunting and thrashing but saw nothing. He flailed backward onto a slick tongue of land and into the claws of vegetation at the river's edge, scrambling away deep into the belly of night.

– 43 –

The first drops of rain pecked the windshield of the Boss as Shoals eased up the driveway toward Mize's. Reception on his phone flickered in and out. Maybe that's why he couldn't raise Leavenger after repeated attempts. The house was black, not a wick of light in the place. He sat in the driveway waiting for someone to come slinking out. Finally he killed the engine and got out, sat against the car listening to the loose pellets of rain brush the trees and gravel. It began to stream before long and he ducked under the carport, pulled out his pocket flashlight, and nosed around. No one answered his repeated knocks, so he tried the knob and let himself in.

He called out for Mize and flipped the light switch, all to no avail. He waved the light around the mudroom and found what he thought to be a pair of men's shit-stained underwear draped over the washtub. Upon closer inspection he determined the rusty stain to be blood. Shoals lifted the sopping wet skivvies with a screwdriver and dumped them in a plastic grocery bag for evidence, then made his way into the kitchen. Just looking for clues, he'd convinced himself. A fifth of good tequila called to him from the counter. He uncapped it and took a glass from the neat row in the cabinet and poured several healthy swigs. He meant to add a splash of water at the sink tap but nothing came. The place must be abandoned, Shoals decided. He walked room to room, swinging his beam, expecting at any moment to stumble upon slaughter. But each room was spare and orderly, no signs of struggle or wrongdoing. Just a mild rotten scent like dead mouse or leftover garbage.

After a complete sweep of the house, Shoals came back to the living room and explored the bookshelves while the tingle of liquor made its own course through him. The book titles meant nothing to him, just represented ages of wasted time. He was interested to find a little wooden box containing marijuana dust and some paraphernalia. And then he discovered a child's shoe box filled with photographs.

He found a votive candle stuck to an empty CD case and lit it, sorted through the images by candlelight. They were mostly of the baby—sleeping, eating, standing, crawling, sitting up in the wading pool, sniffing a beer bottle, gobbling a mango. The baby, stupefied, propped up on his mother, looking over Sandy's shoulder, a nice view of cleavage.

There was Mize standing awkwardly beside another man, had to be his father, similar build and facial expression. He appeared sheepish next to the old man, more out of shame than out of reverence. There were friendly shots of the couple in their fairer days, always cuddled up and smiling. He collected the photos of Sandy and set them aside—her laughing, holding a football in the yard in a big jersey with a bandanna tied around her head. Intent, slicing birthday cake. Frustrated in glasses.

He was mystified as to how a loser like Mize had won her heart, how he'd managed to lure her into the sack enough times to make a child, an admittedly cute little sucker. And he was curious about how he ultimately lost her. Had he taken his life for granted? Why? To Shoals it was unforgivable. He was never one to covet another man's possessions, but he was touched by the rare desire to trade places with Mize, to go back to the start if only to look over his shoulder and imagine how he would do things differently. To solve the case at least.

He helped himself to another glass of tequila and went back to the photo box. "Lord have mercy," he proclaimed, his attention snared by a well-handled photo, the wife in a flimsy bathing suit, which must have been taken years ago. He sat down in an easy chair and studied every millimeter. It deserved to hang in a museum, he believed. A candid classic of cheesecake photography. She was young and hopeful, very playful, suggestive. The look on her face said, *This suit won't last long past the shutter.*

He felt a stirring in his loins and might have been moments from intimacy had he not heard that most pleasing and dreaded of sounds, the chuck-chuck of a pump shotgun being readied. At the edge of candlelight, a barrel emerged from the shadows, followed by Mize, drenched and bedeviled, a look of queer menace all about him. A jolt of adrenaline raced up the deputy's bones. He'd left the flashlight facedown on the shelf, and his gun was tucked under his leg. "Well, well, well," he said with boozy cheer and peaceful intentions. "Look what the storm blew in."

"Where's your warrant?" Mize asked.

"No, just came for a friendly visit," the deputy replied.

"I don't find it so friendly."

"But you just got here," said Shoals. He remained pasted to his seat, trying to squirrel away the bathing suit photo into his pocket. "Hope you don't mind I let myself in. Didn't want to stand out in the rain."

Mize looked around, trying to piece together the scene. He noticed the box of photos on the floor, the glass of tequila on the armrest.

"Look, I'm not trying to hide anything," said Shoals. "Put the gun down and have a seat."

"You're trespassing," Mize replied. "You think you got special rights over and above me?"

"Well, I kinda do. Don't want to abuse them, but maybe it appears to you that I am."

Mize held quiet, his weapon still trained. For him, the explanation would never be good enough.

"Okay, I guess you could say I'm here on official business," Shoals said with sternness, speaking to reason, trying like hell to talk the gun to rest position. "It's not all good cheer and conversation."

"Unless you got a warrant or a goddamn good explanation, you better get your ass out of my house or we're gonna have some real trouble."

Shoals moved his leg millimeter by millimeter, trying to maneuver the holster free, to put the weapon within clean reach. "What have you been doing out in this weather?" he asked, trying to stall, to draw something out of Mize. He seemed crazed and unreliable. "You look a wreck, friend."

"Once more," Mize said. "Tell me what you want, or get the fuck gone."

Shoals came to the bottom of his drink and set it aside. "A friend of mine has gone missing, called me yesterday evening and told me he was coming to see you. A fella named Leavenger. You know him?"

"How come every time somebody comes up missing, you start nosing around here?"

"Well," said Shoals, "I started asking myself that same question. It intrigued me."

"It doesn't have anything to do with my wife, does it?"

So he knew. They'd obviously been in contact.

"What would your wife have to do with this?"

"You think I don't know what's going on?" cried Mize with a quake in his voice. "You got something on me I suggest you bring it or leave me alone. I got no time for this cat-and-mouse shit."

"I don't have a damn thing," Shoals replied. "My friend Leavenger, on the other hand, has made some interesting accusations. Interesting enough that I would be well within my rights taking you in for questioning. I didn't want to play it that way, but your peculiar brand of hospitality gives me cause to reconsider."

Mize lowered the gun ever so slightly. "I don't know any Leavenger. No one has been here in a week."

"You might remember Leavenger. Strange older guy, limping around, trying to get revenge for you killing his dog?" said Shoals. "It's doubtful you'd forget him. Actually, I was hoping to get to you before he did. He aint altogether right, and I was aiming to protect you from whatever crazy idea he had rattling around in that hollow skull of his. But now I'm starting to wonder if I was trying to protect the wrong fella."

He caught Mize withering a bit. Shoals wasn't sure if he could take him in peacefully. If Mize was guilty, he might be prepared to go all the way. They had that, among other things, in common.

"And as for that pretty wife of yours," said Shoals, licking two fingers and rubbing them together with his thumb, "I'd hate for her to get drug into this as an accomplice."

He reached over and plucked out the candle and rolled to the floor. The shotgun erupted with thunder and flash and a shatter of glass. Stray shot nipped Shoals in the side, the tender meat just above the hips. He yowled, whipped out his Colt, and returned fire, a couple of wild rounds that scarred up the walls if nothing else. He heard screeching feet in the kitchen and crawled out in blind pursuit.

Shoals followed the sound of the storm door slam and burst through it. He just made out Mize in the glow of the half-clouded moon, hauling ass over the hill into the pasture, and cried after him, "You're gonna rot like your granddaddy, Mize!"

His instinct for pursuit was not on foot but astride his Mustang. He had complete faith in this beast and spun it through the backyard, up the hill at an angle, and whipped it back into the pasture, bucking over the terrain like a hell-bent steed or some spastic, tricked-out barrio lowrider. The bouncing headlights spotted the man in flight on the next ridge. Shoals found the path of least resistance and eased up, careful not to bottom out or rip the fender off. He made it over the next hill and found a level stretch, caught some speed and shrunk the distance. Mize was barreling for the tree line. The Boss hit a soft patch at the soggy bottom and fishtailed. Shoals let off before it bogged down. No sense fighting the mud. The vehicle wouldn't make it into the woods anyway, but it put him back within fair reach. Shoals snatched a big flashlight from under the seat and yanked Luther up by the strap, fed it a few shells, and slung it over his back. He inspected his side, which had begun to itch and throb, and raced into the trees, trying to land his man before he hit the river.

– 44 –

His first night back, Jacob insisted that his dad would be home and they would take his new sleeping bag into the park and camp under the jungle gym. But Jay never showed. Sandy made a concession and let Jacob set up his pup tent in the living room. She spent half the night packing their clothes and personal things, stacking everything in the foyer, ready to load the trunk and backseat of the car in the morning. The other half of the night she spent at the window, watching for her husband or whomever else might show up and further disrupt their lives. At 4:00 A.M. she turned off the lights and sat on the couch and listened to Jacob snoring inside the tent, holding the canister of pepper spray in one hand and her cell phone in the other.

The phone rang a little before eight. It was Shoals. She rejected the call and blocked his number. She knew it was time to go.

She crawled in the tent and tickled Jacob awake. "Wake up, little camper. We're going on an adventure!"

"Where?"

"Don't *you* wanna know," she teased him.

She was convinced Jay wouldn't show and loaded the car with their clothes and essentials. They would leave most of it behind, she decided, in order to make a clean start. Anyway, there was no one left to help her move the heavy furniture.

She handed Jacob an empty cardboard box and told him to fill it with any personal effects he wanted to keep. He bargained with her to take all of his toys, but she said they were sticking to the one-box plan. He filled it easily with video games and toy cars and robots and stuffed animals, along with a plastic bag containing a few buttons and rusty coins. "Dad gave them to me," he told her. "He found them in the dirt down in his field. We can't spend the money though."

She opened the bag and dumped the coins into her hand. They were just small ancient currency with an engraving of a Native American in head-dress. A few faded fancy buttons with vaguely militaristic insignias. One of the smaller pieces looked like a scorched lump of copper or rusted metal, filigreed with some design she had to scrub clean with her fingernails to read. Levi Strauss & Co.

"I found that in Dad's compost," Jacob said.

"It looks like a button off a pair of blue jeans."

"I know, I want it."

"Why would you want a filthy button?"

"To remember Dad."

Useless ornaments and unspendable money. She couldn't begrudge her son this pitiful tribute. She put the objects back in the bag and sealed it and tossed it in with the rest of his junk, which she agreed to load into a larger box.

At the bottom of his things she found a sheaf of papers, more of Jay's stuff. Here were all his farm diagrams and notes, including the map of his proposed underground complex.

"Dad asked me to keep that for him," Jacob said.

Disconcerted, she tossed the packet back into the box. Was he getting rid of it for good or just passing it along to their son like some congenital obsession?

"Mom," Jacob said. "Where are we going?"

"We're moving."

"Is Dad coming with us?"

"I don't know," she said. "He still has a lot of work to do at the farm."

"Don't tell Dad," Jacob said, "but I don't think I want to be a farmer when I grow up. It's too much work."

They'd left by lunch, carrying their things in one giant load. There was barely enough room to ride in the Maxima, and they looked comical, all crushed and contorted against boxes and bags and bins of their possessions, but it was only a ten-minute drive across town to her father's house.

Sandy filled her old room with their things. She didn't want to impose on her father when he returned. It was a spacious house, but it could fill up quickly, especially if they had to make room for a day nurse to come in and help with his recovery.

Sandy spent the afternoon tidying, and by early evening she and Jacob were set up comfortably. They ordered delivery pizza for dinner, which they ate in her father's bed, snickering, sometimes laughing outright at a bloopers-and-pranks show on television. It was their first easy moment since Jacob had returned from the farm.

After the show, she left Jacob in bed while she took a shower. She returned fifteen minutes later in pajamas, her spritely hairdo already dried, and Jacob said the hospital had called. "It sounded like an emergency," he said.

She called the number back but the line was busy. She called the front desk and got lost in reroute. Her heart sagged and seemed to pull free of its tether, just hanging miserable down there in her chest. She pulled on sweats and then decided on something less casual. She put Jacob in a pullover and jeans, deaf to his childish inquiries. She couldn't breathe or find the words to explain where they were going.

She didn't remember the drive to the hospital. It was someone else driving, some transition between the real Sandy and the person who had briefly mistaken her life for something tolerable.

At the hospital they walked the same sterile, fluorescent-lit maze of halls they'd walked a hundred times already, the passages mostly empty at this hour, only a grim, hopeless few left in waiting rooms they seemed unlikely to leave anytime soon, and down the oldest, most haunted corridors of the hospital with its outdated fixtures and depressing signage that hinted at worse possibilities ("Radioactive Medicine"), and they endured the same overly long wait for the aged elevator to groan and hoist them up to the third floor, where the same haggard faces at the nurses' station and the same sharp whiff of antiseptic would greet them. No matter what was happening, why ever they had been called, she believed this would be the last time they'd walk this route.

The halls were narrow here, the rooms on every side dark, until it seemed she was walking a whip-thin line of white. The linoleum, recently mopped, shone crystalline, and every clip-clopping step she took across it shouted back in amplified echo. She kicked off her shoes, left them in the hall, and glided over the floor as if over thin ice. She kept a hand on Jacob behind her, their march a quiet escape, as if they were trying to achieve an end without notice, trying to keep from wandering off into the darkness.

The door to her father's room was closed. She put her hand to the brushed metal handle, paused, reached for a squirt of sanitizing foam from the pump on the wall. One for Jacob too. The patient's chart was missing from the clear acrylic sleeve on the door. Maybe the doctor had it inside. Was he recording the patient's miraculous improvement or fulfilling the do-not-resuscitate request?

Crossing the threshold meant a new life for them. Nothing would ever be the same. She bowed her head, said a quick word of prayer. She knocked once, perfunctorily, then pushed open the door. There were people within, their backs turned, and she eased out, closing the door.

She looked down at Jacob. "Maybe you should stay here for just a minute. Just let me find out what's going on."

He took her hand. "It's okay, Mom," said her little man. "I'm not afraid."

− 45 −

The rain passed and moisture fell from the trees, pelting the underbrush like a search party in the woods. Jay burrowed under an old wet stump and raked damp leaves and branches over himself for added cover. Chances were good he could wait out Shoals until morning, but if the deputy's searchlight found him tucked under here, it was over. Straight to jail, with good reason.

Life would never be the same. He'd fired at an officer of the law with the weapon of another man, a man whose disappearance the deputy had come to investigate, the same man he'd fed, just an hour ago, to an alligator upriver. Surrender was not an option, but how far would he go to ensure his escape?

He'd lost the gun somewhere, probably dropped it back at the house for fear of using it again. If he wanted to take Shoals, it would have to be by bare-handed challenge, against whatever arsenal the deputy carried on his person. A suicide mission.

If he could just get to the river, he might jump in and ride it down, all the way to the Gulf. What did he have to lose? His body was prepared for any deprivation. He felt the river close by and worked up the courage to rise and peek around. He saw a beam of light swinging to the south, the deputy off on a dead trail. This was his chance. He stood quietly and took swift rolling steps over rain-muffled leaves. The searchlight moon shone down on him in the clearing, and it was hardly a surprise when the first shot came like cannon fire over his shoulder. He sprinted ahead, feeling his way through the maze of gulleys and fallen limbs, his body exerting a foreign will and effort.

He came to the riverside, where the brush was thick and concealing, and down the bank he found the familiar cleft torn out by the river. He kicked off his boots but didn't bother removing his clothes, just slithered down into the mud, flat on his back until he was submerged. In the dark, he would be impossible to find unless Shoals climbed down and stepped on him, but by now he was so adept at maneuvering this formidable terrain he believed he could wrestle the athletic deputy to advantage if necessary.

Shoals came along not far behind and stalked around the edge of the gulley, catching his breath. "Where'd you get off to, Mize?" he cried, puffs of vapor billowing from his exhalation.

The flashlight beam played over the pit floor, down the bank, and all along the water's edge. Jay could hear him gently cursing above.

"I got those bloody drawers from your washroom, Mize," he yelled, unaware his perp was just below, not twenty feet away. "Now you want to tell me just what in the hell is going on?"

The wallow was soft from the rain, and Jay wriggled deeper until his entire body lay buried up to his lips, just a ripple in the mud, sucking air with the quiet, patient gasps of a beached fish.

"What happened to Leavenger? I bet you know a thing or two about this Boyers fella too. Best to start talking, it'll go that much easier for you."

Jay knew the deputy was telling the truth about the bloodstained underwear. He could admit that mistake, but it also confirmed every suspicion he'd ever had about the local law. It didn't matter what had happened in the woods or in the field, they would invent their own story. Even as he lay there lamenting the farm and that his family would worry about him in the coming days, he felt a peculiar satisfaction that he'd been right all along. He wasn't crazy or paranoid. It was the world, with all its lazy presumptions and cockeyed conclusions, that had gone insane. Was there a place in this world anymore for a reasonable man and his family?

"Come out, you little chickenshit!" the deputy hollered toward the river. "You can't get away so easy, Mize. You owe it to me to put up a fight."

Jay guessed the deputy wouldn't come down to the wallow for fear of getting his jeans dirty. At some point he would lose interest and venture off, and that's when Jay would make his getaway.

"Okay, then, let me confess something to you," the deputy called. "It's over for me, all right? They're done with me. You happy? They're shipping my ass off in the morning. This is my last chance to be a hero."

Jay waited to learn if this might be his way out. Was Shoals suggesting a truce? A collaboration? Or was this one of his tricks?

"Hell, I'll *let* you shoot me," Shoals said. "Just make it count. I can't go out like a chump. It's gotta be a fireball, Mize, you got me?"

Either Shoals was coming apart or he was a good actor. It was hard to tell without looking the man in his eyes.

Jay heard a scratch of leaves and a cough in the distance and thought Shoals had wandered off. He waited a few minutes and was preparing to stand up when he heard whimpering above him. It sounded like the deputy sitting in the leaves, mumbling to himself quietly.

Finally he called out to Jay, "I'm not gonna lie to you, Mize, I'm scared to die. But hell, I'm almost scared to go on living at this point. How do you like that? I guess you feel pretty superior now."

The deputy sounded sincere, as if he might be speaking aloud to himself. "Come on, man. You already gut-shot me. Just finish the job."

"I don't have a gun!" Jay cried out, inexplicably. The walls of the pit distorted his cry. His voice bent and echoed, and Shoals jerked his head from side to side, trying to pinpoint the source.

"Where the hell are you?"

Jay said nothing, just clinched his body, waiting for the cheap shot.

"Here! Take mine!"

The light beam tracked across the mud without finding Jay. He heard the clank and splat of the .44 Magnum as it landed an arm's length away.

"That's my daddy's gun," Shoals said. "No one will believe I gave it freely. And if you ever get caught, you better tell them I put up a hell of a fight."

There was a long quiet spell, several minutes before Shoals spoke again.

"Not gonna do it, huh?" He had a bit of the swagger back in his voice. "I didn't think you had the stuff. I guess you'd rather spend the rest of your life in your grandpappy's old cell. That's fine. Well let me tell you a little story you can think about while you're jerking your chain down there on Parchman farm."

He was up and scuffing through the leaves again and then he stopped. His voice came at Jay direct, as though he'd pinpointed his buried figure there in the slough.

"The other night I get a phone call around midnight. A pretty little thing who lives down by the ballpark, says she has a prowler in her basement. Her husband is too much of a sad sack to deal with it so she asks can I come see to it. I show up, she lets me in, takes me down to the cellar. Well, of course, there's nobody down there, and she turns to me and says, 'How bout you investigate this, Danny,' and wouldn't you know it, she whips off her pajama pants."

He's just trying to flush me out, Jay kept reminding himself. *Trying to bring me to light and put a bullet between my eyes.*

"It was a trap, see? The best kind of trap. The kind you don't mind falling into again and again."

The deputy circled and waited for a sign that he was making inroads.

"I'm generally the one laying the trap, but now she's laid one for me. And, buddy, lemme tell ya, it was one hell of a lay."

It sounded like the deputy was down there with him, his stale tequila pant and sweaty aftershave just inches away.

"I don't guess I need to give you all the fine details. We've been to the same place, done similar things. She said I was better at it, but that's neither here nor there. All to say, we're a lot alike, you and me."

Jay slowed his breathing and tried to achieve equanimity, to purge the anger. These were only tricks.

"You ever slurp fresh oysters, Mize?" Shoals said. "You gotta work to get that shell open. Buddy, when you do, it's like wetting your tongue in the ocean after you done walked across the desert. Man, I can still taste her on my lips."

The deputy inhaled deeply, dramatic and satisfied. "Mmm, I can smell her too. Like a ripe muskmelon still warm from the field. You know what that's like, don't you, Mize? Well, maybe not."

It was difficult to keep from shooting him, but Jay rationalized it. Does a man deserve to die for wanting to love a good woman? If so, then the whole world deserved its apocalypse.

"*Sweet Sandy loves the candy.* That was our little saying."

And yet there was a spark of vulgar truth in this confession that lit Jay's fuse.

"Oh, and don't worry about Jacob. I'll take him under my wing while you're gone, teach him all the things you were too busy to teach him. Like baseball and hunting, all the things boys love to do. And when it comes time, I'll show him how to be a man."

Jay bolted up and reached for the Magnum, his muddy fingers fumbling the hammer. Shoals gave a startled yelp and dropped his flashlight, and before Jay could get off a shot, there came a thunder and flare off the ridge. His hand lit up with hot metal, and he felt the sensation of angry yellow jackets swarming his arms and neck, the earth's sucking gasp beneath him. The ground splayed open like whiplashed skin, and he fell through the cut, sliding backward and upside down into shallow water. Mud cascaded over him, driving him into the black river, and as much as he wanted to resist it, to fight and to save himself, he knew to just let it take him, that the river and the earth would decide.

The young farmer found himself at last in the middle of the river. The water was so cold it clenched him to the bone, and when he gasped he sucked in the whole world. His senses tuned to everything around him—the sound of hurtling water, the wet taste of a wild fermented land, the white splatter of a million stars above him, and the heavens in splendid turmoil. He'd never seen it from here, spreading out in all directions, never-ending, capable of pushing him all the way to the Gulf and from there wherever after. The flood had not strangled this river but expanded it, pushed against the shores, tearing into the land to make a wider path, and now it ran with new purpose.

A dark figure came up alongside him in the water, rolling long and solid. He flinched to get away, but it already had him snagged in its limbs. A tree stripped from the bank. It still had its leaves and enough sturdy branches to pull him from the current like a paddle wheel arm.

He clung to it in slothful repose and decided he would ride it all the way to the mouth. Maybe when he arrived, he'd camp and lie low, take an odd job, save up for the train ride north and go find that little cabin on the lake, a retreat from the hell of living this civilized way. He would wait a month or two, earn back his strength and his wits, and then he would send them a post-card, an image she'd remember with a scribble on the back, some code she might recognize. She would've put the land up for sale by then and maybe made a sale, paid off the loans and still have enough left over to bring the boy north to start a new life.

It seemed reasonable that the deputy would let him go. He'd armed and shot a suspect just to prove him guilty and then sentenced him to the river. *There's no way he survived*, Shoals would swear to the boys at the station. No body, no crime.

And this is how it will end. Not without a little penance, for what in this world is worth doing that doesn't require a portion of one's body and soul? And it would still be a long meandering course back to himself and to his people and to his dream of achieving.

He began to tremble from the cold and his injured arm, which had gone numb in shock. He reached up for a top limb to pull himself higher on the log when he noticed that he was missing half his palm. Only a dead thumb dangled there and blood coated his entire forearm. He never felt a thing, just the hot blast and then the river. And he'd been dragging it through all the bacteria and microbes for the last several minutes? Hours? He had to get it bandaged, but what hospital would welcome him off the street in this condition without first calling the police? A hamburger claw and buckshot all up his arm. Where could he slip into port and score some gauze and peroxide, maybe a plastic bag to wrap it for swimming? There were no convenience stores or emergency stops along this way. His heart began to race, shunting the blood upward as a geyser. He held his hand over his head as he slipped off the branch and back into the cold river.

He reached out and grabbed one of the tree limbs and was towed for a while. The current sucked the socks off his feet and then his pants. He raised his head now and then to catch a breath and kept his injury above the waterline. *Just hold on till the current slows*, he told himself. He would find the strength to climb back on the log. He could make it. He'd made it this far, hadn't he? It was that or wash up in someone's field.

But the current didn't slow before his good arm gave out and he lost his grip. He trailed along behind the tree, mud in his shirt pockets weighing him down. He looked again at the missing hand and wiggled his missing fingers, and he felt them but they weren't there, and he threw back his head and laughed.

He scooted his feet and felt for rock bottom. He heard the laughter of fish and the whimper of a wasted dog and watched his son crawl around the wading pool like water going down the drain, bloodstains scumming the bare Jacuzzi bowl, a bowlful of cooked organs and the hungry hordes standing in his field, praising him and his farm tower with their thankful faces. And finally, at the bottom, where the mud was soft and warm, where the moon and tide held their furthest reach, he and his wife found love again, planting a new seed in their precious fledgling ground.

Floodwater swept into his smile and made a lake inside him. His eyes twitched awake to a darkness greater than sleep. The terrible meaning became clear. He thrashed and reached for the surface, and in the last blue breath his chest swelled and his mind bargained and pleaded and repented to his new God, *No, I'm not done, help me please it can't be over, I haven't done anything and my wife and son need me, I'm sorry, I'll do it right this time, let me do it again I want to do it again I want to do it all over I can make it right I can if I*—and his heart ruptured with an explosion of love for them, for all of them.

Everything vanished in that span. He became one with the disaster of his life, as if he and the memory of his family and the scraps of their mistakes and failures were mashed together in the hands of some greater power, pressed down, rolled into a ball, stacked, watered, tumbled, and spread out to grow taller and stronger, ready to flourish at last in practiced earth.

Acknowledgments

The author wishes to acknowledge those whose wisdom, interest, and/or generosity inspired and improved this book:

R&D—Bill Beckwith, Peter Hirst, Dudley Pleasants, and BB's Meat Processing for help with the biochar experiment. Dr. Dickson Despommier for his influential book *The Vertical Farm*. George Williford for solid police work. Carol Puckett for sanctuary. The Mississippi Arts Commission. The reliable staff of Turnrow Book Co.

Publishing folks—Federico Andornino, Elizabeth Breeden, Dwight Curtis, Loretta Denner, James Gill, Emily Graff, Lisa Highton, Amanda Lang, Grace Stearns—and especially Marysue Rucci and Jim Rutman.

Friends and readers who nudged this along and otherwise aided in essential ways—Ben Arnold, Corinna Barsan, Richard Flanagan, Peter Jenkins, Alane Mason, George Saunders, Daniel Wallace, and Brad Watson.

In memory, for their priceless guidance—William Gay, Barry Hannah, John Tidwell.

My parents, Gary and Andrea Kornegay, for a lifetime of encouragement and high standards. Nancy Bridges, for nurturing. Sophie, Bay, and Ruby, who helped me find a story. And to my best friend and most astute reader, my love, Kelly.

Simon & Schuster Paperbacks
Reading Group Guide

JAMIE KORNEGAY

When Jay Mize moves his family from their comfortable small-town life to a beat-up farm in the Mississippi flood basin, he's not just looking to get away from it all; he's looking to change the world. But when nature interferes with Jay's plans to revolutionize farming, and his paranoia about modern life starts to get the best of him, things unravel. Separated from his wife and son, left alone to stew in fear and anxiety on a flooded, ruined farm, Jay is convinced he's hit rock bottom. And then he finds the corpse. In a better state of mind he might have reported the body, but with his paranoia mounting and the local hot-rod deputy poking around his property, Jay convinces himself to dispose of it on the farm. With the pressure mounting, Jay is caught in his own personal apocalypse—his only remaining hope lying with attempts by his estranged family and his hippie neighbor to reel him back in from the brink.

TOPICS FOR DISCUSSION

1. *Soil* opens with a description of a weather pattern alternating between drought and flood. How do these contrasts influence the course of the story and its characters?

2. Early in the novel, the narrator offers an interpretation of Jay's future actions: "A young man, especially one so clever, will grow restless and sometimes throw away everything when he turns elsewhere to affirm his life's purpose." What do you make of this sentiment—what do you think the author means?

3. "Somehow the smallest things can break a man," the narrator muses. How do the smallest actions sometimes take on outsize proportion in our own lives? Why do little things come to serve as symbols or as catalysts for action?

4. Throughout the novel the author plays with the timeline of events—the book opens with a description of something we see much later from a totally different angle. What effect does it give to the experience of reading the book?

5. The tone of the writing also contributes much to the narrative and storytelling. Discuss how the style and tone change according to the character or action being described. How does the author bring out humor, drama, and horror?

6. Throughout the novel, a central theme is the influence of family history on individuals. It is most strikingly illustrated in the Mize men, from Jay's grandfather to his son, Jacob. How do history and heredity influence the actions of characters, and their thinking? What do you think is the author's point of view on heredity?

7. Aside from the Mize family, the character we learn the most about is Deputy Shoals. How does your perspective on Shoals evolve throughout the story? How is his character revealed and made increasingly complex? How does he serve as a foil and antagonist for Jay?

8. Aside from Shoals and the Mize family, *Soil* is populated by a plethora of minor characters. Whom did you find most surprising? Whom did you most enjoy reading about?

9. Discuss the scene in which Jay sights two mating deer and subsequently envelops himself ecstatically in the nearby mud. Is this episode a turning point for him?

10. Sandy sees Jay's paranoia and its consequences as a self-fulfilling tragedy: "I think that you believe your life will only have purpose if the world is falling down around you." Do you agree with her perception of Jay? Do you think there are people in the world for whom this characterization is true?

11. Even for all of its darkness, *Soil* is frequently very funny. What effect did humor have on your reading experience?

12. Like Jay, Sandy endures her own, minor disintegration. She asks herself, "Who are you going to be? Who will you be, alone in the dark?" What does she mean?

13. Throughout the novel Jay maintains that it's the world—not Jay himself—that's insane. What do you make of his condemnation of modern life? Do you sympathize with it, even a little?

14. One of the central themes of the novel is the conflict between nature as a reserve from the pressure of contemporary life and, at the same time, nature's indifference to human need. How would you characterize the author's view of nature? Is it anything like your own?

15. Images of soil, dirt, earth, and mud permeate the novel. How does the author explore the various meanings of soil?

16. Discuss the ending of the novel. How do you interpret Jay's death, his final thoughts, and the images the author uses in the last few paragraphs? Did it affect your view of the story as a whole?

Enhance your book club

1. The history of the Mize family, and to some extent of the Shoals family, forms a crucial part of *Soil*. Reflect on some aspect of your own family history—your parents' or grandparents' lives, or even further back. Has it influenced you?

2. *Soil* explores Mississippi hill country in depth—with all its quirks, weirdness, dark places and bright spots. If you were to set a novel in your own town or in another place that you know well, what would you want to bring out of it? What kinds of characters would live there? How would the land and climate influence people's lives?

3. From John Grisham to William Faulkner, Mississippi is the source and inspiration of a wide body of fiction, film, and TV. What do you think makes this region such a rich source for fiction?

A CONVERSATION WITH JAMIE KORNEGAY

This is your first published novel, after years of working as a bookseller. Were you always a writer, or did you come to it gradually? How long have you been working on *Soil*?

I think I've been a writer since I could read. I wrote my first novel around the age of eight, by longhand, in an *E.T.* spiral-bound notebook, and mailed it to the publisher of my favorite Judy Blume books. Sadly, it was sent back with a form rejection letter. Many years and a few failed novels later, I began *Soil*. I came up with the concept and then developed it in my mind for years while I started my business, Turnrow Books. When I sat down to write it, it took about three years or so, but the book has been in my head for ten or more.

Where did this story come from? One can only hope it isn't drawn too much from real life—but were there elements from your own history, or from stories you had heard?

Taking the back roads to work one day, I drove by flooded farmland and noticed a rotten stump sticking up from the mud. My imagination got the better of me, and for a moment I thought it was a corpse. I began to imagine things through a Dostoevskian lens. Soon I had conceived a story in which the protagonist would find a dead body and cover it up, through some twisted, misapplied guilt, which led to more questions and justifications and scenarios, all things used to build characters and stories from scratch. This led me to the gestation years I mentioned, in which I procrastinated by conducting a lot of research, including studies of planting and agriculture, and trying to develop a method by which Jay could dispose of a dead body—a method that hadn't already been done a hundred times in movies and novels—and done in a way that would erase all the evidence and wouldn't draw the attention of those who might or might not be watching. The chapter where Jay is wandering around the pasture thinking about this, coming up with various scenarios and contingencies, is a condensed form of the conversation I had with myself and with other thoughtful conspiracists, including my father-in-law, a private detective. I arrived at the solution pretty much the same way Jay did: imagining charcoal as a way to filter the inevitable smell of a burning body. I discovered how charcoal was made in the past and how it was used as fertilizer. It fit perfectly into the novel's theme. I consulted a New England biochar company and figured out how to design the barrel retort, sought the help of a local metal worker to build it, and secured a deer carcass from a local processor for my "organic material." I conducted the experiment in my backyard in town, the model for the Nutt Street house, just as Jay does it with the bones in one batch and the organs on the propane burner. I had everything ready, and then it rained for three days straight, so by the time I got to the bones, they were rank and disgusting. It was a hideous project. All the revulsion and anxiety and insanity that Jay feels come from genuine emotions and experience.

The culture of Mississippi is its own character in the book—one that is treated acerbically, but not unsympathetically. Did you feel as though there were prejudices or stereotypes about the South you were engaging with, or trying to alter?

If I was toying with stereotypes, it was because I was trying to present things as I see them here—which may clash with some readers' expectations and which will hopefully create a nice, screechy feedback. Some of the prejudices about the South are well-earned, but what I find most interesting is the bedrock on which all those assumptions and prejudices are laid. It's not as simple as you see on television and in movies. In some ways, the novel is about how our misperceptions can cause unnecessary and irrevocable damage. I actually saw this even more as a story about rural America in contrast to the urban world. Mississippi sets the tone and obviously inspired me, but you can place these characters in any rural community in America and find people dealing with the same issues—interactions with the land and wildlife, issues of privacy and territory, anonymity and community, age-old family disputes and prejudices. I'm very interested also in how the old ways, more preserved in the rural setting, where life turns at a slower pace, interact with the new ways.

The treatment of Jay's paranoiac mania is one of the most fascinating elements in the novel—how did you get so deeply into that kind of mental space?

Well, clearly I've already outed myself as somewhat obsessive. You take an experimental garden in the backyard, heaps of compost, a deer carcass, and an oil drum crematorium, and extrapolate from there. But I think this is what writers and artists do. They take their interests, obsessions, and fears and reel them out like taffy. I'm not normally so paranoid, but it only takes delving into the threats of the world to make you push them toward the edge. I pushed them, went to a place well past comfort, and hopefully mined some believable paranoia and madness. I actually scaled a lot of it back in the editing process. It got fairly grim there for a while, and I think that's when the deputy Danny Shoals came on the scene to balance things out.

The struggle between indifferent nature and a frightening or threatening modern world is one of the central conflicts in *Soil*, one that you exploit wonderfully without picking a side. How do you strike a balance in your own life? Do you ever feel yourself longing to pull a Jay and go back to the land? Or do you see that as a naïve fantasy?

I certainly feel that compulsion to go back to the land. I grew up in the country and spent a lot of time as a child playing in the woods. I live in town now, but when I get the chance, I still enjoy retreating into deep nature. It's a tranquil, holy place but not without its difficulties. The conflicts you find in nature seem more honest to me than those you find in town with people. So yes,

I daydream about moving off the grid, setting up a self-sufficient system, and living with my family. The only thing naïve about committing to that lifestyle, at least for me, would be to think that one could easily leave all the trappings of civilization behind. And definitely, as Jay learns, you can't shut out other people. Escaping to the wilderness would simply be a means to greater privacy, easier access to nature, possibly even a solution of thrift. But in the end, we're herd animals and need to interact with other humans to feel complete.

Soil is a unique blend of intense and graphic violence, dark humor, and thoughtful, almost elegiac prose—what kinds of scenes or bits were the most difficult to write? Which were the easiest? Is comedy or drama more interesting for you to write?

Without a doubt, the hardest scene to write was Jay dismantling the dead man. As the book exists, the reader is not invited into the tent with Jay, but in earlier drafts, we got right up beside him. I wanted to create revulsion in the reader so that perhaps they would understand what kicks Jay's madness into overdrive. It was too much. I'm thankful to early readers who advised that less would be more in that instance. As I said, when things got too grim with Jay, I always enjoyed turning to Shoals for comic relief. Not that he was easy. His instincts are base and I had to plumb to hit bottom, but I enjoyed watching him swagger around the story. I think my favorite chapter to write was the one where he turns up at Sandy's house after she calls him to investigate a prowler in her basement. Based on a true story.

Some of the most moving and natural passages in the book come in the interactions between Jay and Jacob—indeed, one of Soil's central themes is the father-son relationship. What do you see as the difficulties and rewards of this bond? What did you learn about these relationships while working on the book?

On the acknowledgments page, I thank my kids for giving me a story, and that's the truth. In that break between conceiving the story and writing it, I became a father and raised children. Suddenly, this book was about more than a dead body in a field. This became a story of redemption and purpose through growing another life. One thing they don't tell you before you become a parent—especially a father, who lacks that immediate, biological imperative that takes over so naturally in the mother—is how difficult it can be to sacrifice all or even some of your driven pursuits in the sudden, diverted interest of raising a child. Men are bound to falter trying to make this adjustment. (And women like Sandy, whose bodies are hijacked and rewired by this other life, so often get short shrift as they quietly endure it all.) This is what happens to Jay, who is so hell-bent on his plan to save the world from hunger that he neglects to save his own family. Tragically, this realization hits him too late. I like to think he would have turned his life around but for that fateful walk back from the river when he meets a stranger who has come to seek revenge for a prior misdeed.

Science, with all its benefits and hazards, is a strong theme in *Soil*. Are you naturally interested in farming technology, compost, and—well—dirt? Or was this a product of lots and lots of research?

Like a lot of people, I really became obsessed with soil and farming and composting after reading Michael Pollan's *The Omnivore's Dilemma*. It arrived at the perfect time in my life. I'd already started experimenting with a garden, but the civic possibilities intensified after I read that book. And that spiritual aspect of nature became very keen to me the more I got my hands dirty. I could understand why someone would see this benevolent manipulation of earth as redemptive and holy. With science, as with anything, I think humans are instinctively trying to do good. What interests me as a writer, though, is that point at which they cross over from positive to destructive.

***Soil* has roots in many different literary traditions, and a lot of its power comes from its ability to blend those elements into a coherent whole. Who (or what) do you identify as your primary influences? How do you write your way out from under those influences, to create something new of your own?**

I had a teacher in junior high who challenged me by assigning *Crime and Punishment*. Even though I didn't comprehend it fully at the time, that book changed my thinking about literature profoundly. It was the first book that haunted me. I've studied writers like Faulkner for his ambition and structure, and Hemingway for his tone and characters. From Patricia Highsmith, I learned about creating tension, and from Charles Portis, the value of comedy in observation. Another major influence for me was Barry Hannah, my teacher at Ole Miss. This is someone who embodied colorful language and daring thought. He was an enemy of dullness. If I ever feel bland and can't shake anything pertinent loose onto the page, I dip into his work. No other writer's sentences set my mind ablaze like his. He also taught me the value of listening to music as a means of training rhythm into your prose. Tom Waits, whose lyric sets the scene at this book's opening, is a tremendous influence. I'm astounded by his ability to match vivid, artful lyricism with evocative music. Working with all these influences, taking their examples and setting all of it to the tempo of life here in Mississippi, that's how I've made a coherent whole.

Do you have plans for another book, or are you working on something now? Are you interested in remaining in the South, or are you looking further afield?

I'm definitely looking further afield. I'm dabbling in several different ideas, some of which take place in the wider world. But the South, Mississippi especially, is such a rich and complex place. I could write forever about this place and never exhaust the material. I only scratched the surface in *Soil*, which is set in the northeast Mississippi hills. It's a different geography and culture from the Delta, where I live now. The book I'm currently working on is set in the modern-day Delta, on a farm, though much larger in scale—180 degrees from Jay. The Delta is Mississippi in its most concentrated, potent form, and I'm taking everything—those themes of nature, society, history, family, violence, comedy—up a notch or two. It's going to be fun. Conceptually, think of a hybrid of *Moby-Dick*, *Jaws*, and *Duck Dynasty*.